CRIMINAL ENTERPRISE

OWEN LAUKKANEN

CORVUS

First published in the United States in 2013 by G. P. Putnam's Sons, a division of the Penguin group.

Published in e-book in 2013 and paperback in 2014 in Great Britain by Corvus, an imprint of Atlantic Books Ltd.

Copyright © Owen Laukkanen, 2013

The moral right of Owen Laukkanen to be identified as the author of this work has been asserted by him in accordance with the Copyright, Designs and Patents Act of 1988.

All rights reserved. No part of this publication may be reproduced, stored in a retrieval system, or transmitted in any form or by any means, electronic, mechanical, photocopying, recording, or otherwise, without the prior permission of both the copyright owner and the above publisher of this book.

This novel is entirely a work of fiction. The names, characters and incidents portrayed in it are the work of the author's imagination. Any resemblance to actual persons, living or dead, events or localities, is entirely coincidental.

Book design by Katy Riegel

10 9 8 7 6 5 4 3 2 1

A CIP catalogue record for this book is available from the British Library.

Paperback ISBN: 978 1 78239 368 9
E-book ISBN: 978 1 78239 369 6

Printed in Great Britain by CPI Group (UK) Ltd, Croydon, CR0 4YY

Corvus
An imprint of Atlantic Books Ltd
Ormond House
26–27 Boswell Street
London
WC1N 3JZ

www.corvus-books.co.uk

For Line D'Onofiro,
in loving memory

LONDON BOROUGH OF HACKNEY LIBRARIES	
HK12001819	
Bertrams	16/10/2014
THR	£7.99
	04/09/2014

1

THEY CAME INTO the bank around one-thirty, a man and a woman. Both of them wore ski masks, and both carried guns. The teller was busy with a customer, the last of the lunchtime rush. She didn't see them come in. She helped her customer cash his paycheck, and when she looked up, they were there.

Two of them. The man about six feet tall, the woman almost a full foot shorter. The woman carried a shotgun, sawed off and menacing, the man an assault rifle. Bank robbers. Just like in the movies.

They swept in to the middle of the bank before Larry, the big guard, could react from the door. The man fired a burst with his machine gun through the ceiling, and customers screamed and scattered. Larry half stood at the door, his hand on his radio. The woman pointed the shotgun at him. "On the ground." Her voice was hard. "Don't be a hero."

The man with the rifle carried a duffel bag. He tossed it to his partner, who held her shotgun on Larry, waiting as he sunk, sheepish, to the floor. "Everybody on the ground," the man said. "Whatever you're thinking you'll try, it's not worth it."

The customers hit the floor, all of them, ducking for cover in their suits and heels and nylons, hiding where they could behind countertops and in doorways. The teller snuck a glance at Cindy beside her. Cindy was shaking, staring hard at the man and his big machine gun, her hand on the silent alarm.

The man caught her gaze and walked over. "I said get down." Cindy shook harder, tears in her eyes. The man hit her, hard, with the butt end of his rifle, and Cindy made a little grunt and went down. Sprawled out on the floor behind her station, her nose bloody, her breathing fast and panicked. She stared up at the teller, but she didn't move.

Down the line of tellers, the woman was emptying the tills, filling her duffel bag with cash. The man with the machine gun turned, and the teller started to duck away. "Wait," the man said. The teller flinched, stuck halfway between standing and kneeling. The gunman came closer. "Stand up."

The teller obeyed. "Please don't hurt me."

The man studied her as his partner worked her way down the long row of tellers. He had blue eyes behind the mask, icy blue. Unnatural. He looked like he might be smiling, but there was no warmth in his eyes.

"I could kill you," he said. He leveled the big gun at her chest, and she watched it, surreal. Felt her legs start to give, and reached for the counter to steady herself. "I could just pull the trigger," he said. "It would be easy, wouldn't it?"

She nodded.

He stared at her for another moment. His partner had reached Cindy's station. The man gestured to Cindy's till with the gun. "Open it."

The teller obeyed.

The woman with the shotgun put the duffel bag on the counter, and the teller reached inside Cindy's till and took out a stack of twenty-dollar bills. Mechanically, she started to count them. A reflex. "Don't count the money," the man told her. "Just put it in the bag."

She cursed herself. *Of course you don't have to count it.* She put the stack in the duffel bag and reached back into the till. Took out the last of the money.

"Good," the man told her. "Now yours." The teller crossed to her own till and started to empty it. The man walked to the middle of the lobby as she worked, swinging his machine gun on his hip, watching the customers on the floor. In the distance, the first sirens started to sound.

The woman with the shotgun watched the teller. "Hurry up." There was nothing kind in her voice, nothing human. The teller kept her head down until she'd removed the last of the money from her till. Then she dared to look up.

"There's no more," she said.

The woman glanced in the till. Zipped the bag closed and turned back to the man. "Let's go." The man picked up the bag as the woman started for the door. The teller waited for the man to follow. He didn't. He stared at the teller until she met his gaze. Then he leveled his gun at her chest again. He winked at her.

"*Pow*," he said. Then he turned and walked out the door. The teller watched him until he disappeared into the sunlight. Then she sunk down beside Cindy, shaking and sobbing, her knees to her chest. She didn't look up until the police arrived.

2

CARTER TOMLIN IGNORED the sirens in the distance as he walked, slow as he dared, to the Camry parked at the curb. Ahead of him, Tricia had the backseat door open and was sliding inside. Tomlin closed the last few feet of sidewalk and dropped the money bag in behind her, then slammed the door closed and climbed in the passenger seat as Dragan pulled away from the bank.

"Go slow," Tomlin told him, twisting in his seat to watch the first police cars slam to a stop behind them. "We need to blend in."

Tomlin sank low in his seat, sweating through his clothes. He pulled off his ski mask and rolled down the window, savoring the cool air as Dragan made for the highway.

Tricia peeled off her own ski mask. "Holy shit," she said, her face flushed. "That was awesome."

Outside, two more police cars sped past, their cherry bomb blinkers clearing a path down the wide street. Dragan pulled over with the rest of the traffic. Neither cop glanced in their direction.

When the police cars were gone, Dragan pulled out toward the highway. Made the Interstate on-ramp and did the speed limit up the west side of downtown Minneapolis, everything calm, just three everyday rubes in a midsize sedan.

In the backseat, Tricia unzipped the duffel bag. "Jackpot." She looked up at Tomlin. Smiled at him, big. "Must be thirty grand, boss. And no dye packs."

"Thirty grand," Tomlin said. He was shaking.

DRAGAN TOOK the Washington Avenue exit and headed south into downtown Minneapolis. Drove into a pay parking garage a few blocks from the downtown core, and parked on the fourth level, between a black Jaguar sedan and a silver street-racer Civic. Tomlin climbed out of the Camry, and Tricia followed, dragging the duffel bag with her. "It's heavy," she said. "Thirty grand, easy."

Tomlin took the bag from Tricia and opened it on the hood of the Camry. Peered in at the money and felt an electric thrill. *Thirty grand*, he thought. *Easy money*. He took out a stack of bills and handed them to Dragan. "Here's a down payment," he said. "Tricia will settle up when we get a count."

Dragan thumbed through the bills. "Tomorrow," he said.

Tricia kissed him. "Tomorrow, babe. Promise."

Dragan glanced at the money again. "Thirty grand," he said. "Rock and roll." He kissed Tricia and climbed in the Civic. Backed out of the stall and drove off.

Tomlin unlocked the Jaguar. Stowed the money in the backseat while Tricia hid the guns in the trunk. Then he slid behind the wheel and fired up the engine and drove out of the garage with Tricia.

They took the Interstate east to downtown Saint Paul, Lowertown. Tomlin parked on the street in front of a squat office building and exhaled, long and smooth. He closed his eyes and inhaled. Exhaled again. Then he opened his eyes and tied his tie in the rearview mirror, fixed his hair. Reached in the backseat for his briefcase and glanced at Tricia. "You ready?"

She grinned. "Just waiting on you."

They walked into the building, carrying the duffel bag with them. Took three flights of stairs and a featureless hallway and stopped in front of a frosted-glass door. Tomlin fumbled with the key, pushed the door open, and ushered Tricia inside.

Tricia waited until he'd locked the door behind them. Then she squealed, and her arms were around him. "We did it," she said, squeezing him tight. "Didn't I fucking tell you we would?"

Tomlin let her hug him. He could smell her shampoo, feel her warmth. "You told me," he said. He nudged her away and walked to his inner office, where he unzipped the duffel bag and dumped the money onto his desk.

Tricia squealed again. "Look at that cash."

Piles of bills—twenties, tens, some bigger, some smaller. Rumpled, well used, untraceable. And lots of it. Tricia hugged him again. Kissed his cheek. "Let's count it."

They counted. Tricia was close: thirty-two thousand and change. Fifteen each for Tomlin and Tricia. The rest a bonus for Dragan tomorrow. Tomlin shoved his share into the bottom drawer of his desk, locked the drawer closed. Tricia gathered her money and disappeared with it.

Tomlin sat down and turned on his computer. *Fifteen grand,* he thought, as the machine booted up. *Not bad for a few hours' work.*

Tricia poked her head back into his office. She'd calmed her pixie pink hair and looked presentable again. Professional, even. "Don't forget, you have a three o'clock with Mr. Cook."

Tomlin frowned. "Cook."

"The hypochondriac with estate-planning problems, remember?" She winked at him. "And your wife called. Wants you to pick up your Madeleine from dance."

Tomlin inhaled deeply, then exhaled again, a regular guy now, the money and the guns forgotten. "Cook," he said. "Dance class. I'm on it."

3

TWO HOURS AFTER Carter Tomlin and his gang walked out of the First Minnesota branch in Stevens Square, Carla Windermere stood in the middle of the bank's tiny lobby, surveying the now-chaotic crime scene. The thirty-two-year-old FBI Special Agent cut an unusual figure amid the confusion: tall and slender, dressed smartly in a white blouse and razor-crisp pantsuit, Windermere looked more like a TV news anchor than a successful investigator.

Her eyes, however, were a cop's eyes. They were drawn tight and narrowed, calculating as she looked over the bank lobby.

The place was a mess. The whole building was packed full of law enforcement—mostly Minneapolis city cops, first responders—standing in corners and doorways, drinking coffee and bumming cigarettes, shooting the shit and getting in her way. Here and there, a plainclothes cop poked his nose into something—the fingerprints on the tellers' counter, the bank manager's office—steadfastly ignoring Windermere and the rest of the FBI investigators who'd taken over the scene.

Windermere looked around the bank, then out into the street. "Eat Street," they called this place. A couple of miles of trendy res-

taurants a few minutes south of downtown Minneapolis and conve-
niently located near Interstates 94 and 35, two quick getaways for
bank robbers with wheels.

Windermere caught the eye of a technician kneeling on the floor
over a bunch of shell casings nearby.

"What's up, Laurie?" she said, her voice still betraying the last
vestiges of a southern accent. The accent had accompanied her from
Mississippi to her first FBI posting in Miami; despite her best efforts,
it had followed her north to Minnesota five years later. Along with
her cool demeanor, and, she sometimes suspected, the color of her
skin, it served only to reinforce her position as an outsider within
the Bureau.

The tech didn't look up. "Two-twenty-three Remingtons," she
said. "Probably an assault rifle. His partner had a sawed-off shotgun."

Windermere ran her hand through her hair. "An assault rifle," she
said. "Shit."

"Probably an AR-15." Laurie looked up at Windermere, caught
her blank expression. "It's like an army M-16, but for personal use.
Hunting, home defense."

"Bank robberies."

Laurie shrugged. "Hubby keeps one around. Says it's for deer season. I figure he just likes to play army with the boys. Men and their
guns, right?"

Windermere studied the shells and didn't like what they told her.
Most bank robbers were amateurs, impulsive degenerates, for the
most part unarmed. The Bureau tended to catch up with their lot
pretty quickly. Kept a high clearance rate. Today's contestants,
though, didn't look quite so primitive. Assault rifles and sawed-off
shotguns hardly ever meant amateur hour.

Windermere straightened again, and looked across the lobby to
where the bank tellers stood huddled in the corner. She locked eyes
with the youngest of the bunch, a pretty little twentysomething

who kept looking at Windermere like she wanted to talk. *Your witness*, Windermere thought, and she started over.

The teller shrank like a scared kitten as Windermere approached. Not uncommon. Witnesses, suspects, cops, hardened criminals, male and female alike: They all tended to take a step backward when Windermere turned her gaze on them. Most of the time, she didn't mind it. Most of the time, she let someone else coddle the wallflower witnesses. Focused her efforts on breaking down suspects.

No such luck today, though. Windermere forced a sympathetic smile and tried to look warm and fuzzy. "What's your name, hon?"

The teller looked away. "Nicole."

"Nicole," said Windermere. "Okay. So what happened, Nicole?"

Nicole took a deep breath and wiped her eyes. "I don't know," she said. "They came in, the two of them. You probably know this stuff already."

Windermere shook her head. "Tell me."

"It was a man and a woman," Nicole told her. "They came in with guns. He told everyone get down on the floor and Cindy and I didn't, so he hit Cindy with his gun."

Windermere glanced around the group of tellers and found Cindy, a middle-aged redhead with a black eye and an ice pack pressed to her forehead. Cindy gave her a weak smile.

"I thought he would hit me, but I couldn't move," said Nicole. "But he didn't hit me. He just looked at me with these intense blue eyes. He said he could kill me and it would be easy."

The teller exhaled. "I told him don't hurt me," she said. "Then he made me empty the tills into a big duffel bag. When I was done, he made like to shoot me."

Windermere frowned. "What do you mean?"

"Aimed his gun at me and smiled, really creepy. '*Pow*,' he said." "*Pow*."

"*Pow.*" Nicole nodded. "Like he wanted me to know he could do it."

"Probably just keeping you in line." Windermere glanced at the front door, the street outside. "You see where they went when they walked out of here?"

The teller shook her head. "I was scared. I didn't want to know."

Windermere studied her. *Okay*, she thought. *Good enough.* Some creep with blue eyes and an AR-15 assault rifle. A woman with a sawed-off shotgun. A duffel bag full of money, and a power fetish. Windermere thanked the teller and turned back into the chaos. *Someone*, she thought, *must have seen these guys leave.*

4

I N CARTER TOMLIN'S WORLD, a man provided for his family.

He'd never considered himself a violent person. He wasn't a drug addict or a gambler, didn't cheat on his wife or his taxes. Until the layoff, he was a respectable man. A husband and a father and a decision-maker at the firm, a corner-office man on the executive track.

In Tomlin's mind, real men dealt with adversity. They didn't complain or talk about fairness. They didn't take handouts; they solved their own problems. They provided.

He'd robbed his first bank a few months after the layoff. A Bank of America branch in Midway. He'd been waiting to talk to a loan officer. Hating himself, but needing something to help him keep up with the mortgage, the car payments. The groceries and the phone.

He left the bank without ever meeting the loan officer. Hurried into the Walmart next door and bought a clumsy disguise, then came back and shoved a hastily scribbled note into the teller's hands, wondering what the hell he was doing as she emptied the till. Bugged out like a scared rabbit and walked with an envelope full of cash.

IT WAS HIS OWN FAULT, most of it. The mortgage, for sure. Tomlin had known deep inside that they couldn't afford half of what the
broker promised to lend him. The accountant in him had screamed
when he'd signed the papers.

But how could he say no? The way Becca smiled when she talked
about a Summit Avenue address, a beautiful Victorian dream home
surrounded by trees and green space, away from the crush of the city.
The way Heather and Maddy laughed as they chased each other
around the picture-perfect front lawn. Bill Carver and Chuck Lawson had both taken the plunge, purchased homes for their families
nearby. Now they came to work talking about riding lawn mowers
and neighborhood cookouts, family trips out to the lakes.

This was what a man was supposed to do for his family. This was
how life was supposed to turn out. A big house on a tree-lined street,
happy kids and good neighbors, and hell, even a puppy. So what if it
meant taking on a little debt? A mortgage was a fact of life. Home
ownership was the American Dream. Of course, this was before the
whole economy imploded. Before housing prices collapsed. Before
the firm decided to downsize.

"I've given this company twenty good years," he told Carver and
Lawson on the day the guillotine dropped its blade. "Now you're just
going to kick me to the curb?"

"We've got a great package for you, Carter," Lawson told him.
"Very generous. A golden-parachute deal."

"And we're happy to provide a reference," said Carver. "You've
been a great employee here. This wasn't an easy decision."

He'd called the recruiter the next day. Met her in a swanky suburban office. She was about twenty-five, he figured. Her haircut
looked like it cost more than his watch. She'd looked over his CV
and then studied his face. "No offense," she said, frowning. "My clients are paying me to cherry-pick the best."

"Twenty years at one of the best firms in the state," Tomlin said. "You don't think I can cut it?"

The recruiter shrugged. "My clients make the rules. And they're not looking to hire from the unemployment lines."

"You think I'm not worth your time," he said. "Because I'm laid off. So what the hell am I supposed to do?"

She shrugged again, and handed back his CV. "Maybe take a class?"

He'd forced himself to thank her and drove home, where he sat in his car in the driveway so long that Becca came out to see what was the matter. She sat in the passenger seat and held his hand. "We'll sell the house," she said. "The cars. Whatever it takes. We'll get through this."

He stared through the front windshield up at the house. It stared back as though mocking him. He counted six rooms with lights on, probably more in the back. All that wasted electricity. Money frittered away. "We're underwater," he told her. "We can't sell."

"The cars, anyway."

"Resale on these things is criminal," he said, shaking his head. "We'd be lucky to get pennies on the dollar."

Becca squeezed his hand. "What about bankruptcy?"

She might as well have said suicide. "We're not declaring bankruptcy," Tomlin told her. "I'm solving this thing on my own."

BECCA TOOK a maternity-leave position at the local middle school. "Just until you find work," she told Tomlin. "Let me do my part."

Tomlin fought her as long as he could. He'd sworn when they'd married she would never work again. But the firm's severance money dwindled. Every month another chunk disappeared, to the mortgage and car payments and the rest. They switched to basic cable and canceled their cell phones. Didn't eat out anymore, or go to the movies. Becca started to shop at the discount grocery store.

Finally, Tomlin gave in. "Just for the short term," he told her. "Not forever."

She came home after the first week exhausted. "Those kids are a handful," she told him, her jaw set. "I forgot how awful they could be."

The next weeks were worse. Tomlin felt like he was watching her age in front of his eyes. Her beautiful blond hair now hung unkempt and stringy; her blue eyes were perennially shadowed and dark.

Then they stopped making love. Becca swore nothing was wrong, but she stiffened when he touched her, turned away in the night. Sometimes she relented, but even then Tomlin was distracted, unable to focus. He lay awake while Becca slept fitfully beside him, and in the morning he would try not to notice the rings under her eyes. They spent long hours in silence, and when they did talk, they fought. Even the kids could sense something was wrong.

Finally, Becca sat him down. "We should think about bankruptcy," she said.

He felt choked, suffocated. He didn't say anything.

"We're dying here," she said. "We need a lifeline."

"It's not bankruptcy," he told her. "I'll find another way."

"There's no other way, Carter." Her face was stony, and her eyes hard. "We can't live like this anymore."

TOMLIN WENT TO the bank the next day. He wasn't sure what he was doing, but he knew he needed help. Christmas was coming. The car loans. The mortgage. A mountain of unpaid bills and unrealistic demands.

He looked around the bank as he waited to talk to the loan officer. The tellers, the customers, all of them living their lives while he watched from the margins, an invalid. An impotent man, a failure.

He could already predict the loan officer's response.

He glanced at the bank tellers again, at the customers cashing their paychecks. The robbery idea seemed to worm its way into his brain. *You could do it,* he thought, searching almost reflexively for the security cameras. Four of them, no, five. The bank didn't even have a security guard.

You could rob this bank, he thought. *Easy.*

Tomlin thought about Carver and Lawson, both of them buying up Xboxes and diamond earrings for Christmas. He saw Becca's face on Christmas morning, Heather's and Madeleine's. He saw the house up for sale, the cars repossessed. He thought about walking into that loan officer's little room and begging for more money he couldn't afford.

Forget that, he thought.

He looked in once more at the loan officer in his office—a skinny, balding man with thin glasses and an ill-fitting shirt. Then he turned and walked out to the parking lot. Twenty-five minutes later, he walked back through the bank doors, wearing a clumsy Walmart disguise and clutching his note.

This time, he walked out with cash.

5

WINDERMERE INTERVIEWED the bank manager, a middle-aged mouse who'd been out on his lunch break when the robbers came in. He was sweating, kept pushing his glasses up his nose, and, for a moment, Windermere thought maybe he was involved. Then she chased the thought from her mind. The guy was about five-five. Had a half-eaten Subway sandwich on his desk. Besides, he looked almost as terrified as Nicole, the poor teller.

Windermere threw a couple curveball questions at the guy, just to keep him honest. Then she thanked him and walked from his office, locking eyes with a plainclothes cop skulking toward the coffee machine. "You city?" she asked him.

The guy looked longingly toward the coffee. "Yeah," he said, sighing. "Fifth Precinct."

"FBI's got this place covered," she told him. "You want to help out, get some patrol cars and some uniforms knocking on doors. Maybe we get lucky and this crew is local."

The cop made one last play for the coffee. "Go," Windermere told him. "I'll buy you all Frappuccinos when you bring me a suspect."

The cop glared at her and slunk off toward a bunch of uniforms at the exit. He said something and they all looked her way, then turned like a troop of sullen tenth-graders and made for the sidewalk. Windermere held her gaze on them until they'd all disappeared.

"Carla." Bob Doughty, her latest partner, coming her way. A plastic smile and a size-forty-eight suit. "You figure this thing out yet?"

Windermere shrugged. "Some goofs get a bright idea they're going to rob the neighborhood bank, easy money. Sooner or later, someone rats them out for two hundred dollars in a Crime Stoppers payoff. The end."

Doughty frowned and pretended to think about it. "That's how it plays, huh?"

"In general, yeah."

"Well, fingers crossed," Doughty said. "Want to watch some tape while we wait for that call? I just hooked up the security footage."

Windermere looked around the bank. No city cops to chase out, no more tellers to scare. Even Laurie looked about ready to go. "Why not?" she said. "Let's see how these guys operate."

She followed Doughty into the bank's small back room. There was a desk and a chair and a monitor showing split-screen security cam footage. Doughty gestured to the chair. "Have a seat."

Windermere sat and leaned toward the monitor. The footage showed four camera angles: three from the lobby and one from the vault. The time stamp read a quarter past one.

Doughty dragged another chair into the room and sat down, pressed close to Windermere in the cramped little room. Windermere felt the big man shift beside her, and for a second, she felt déjà vu, remembering another bank of security monitors and another tiny back room, a grocery store in Seattle and an unlikely partner.

Stevens. She felt something twinge inside her, nostalgia or something, and then she felt Doughty shift and she realized he was looking at her. "You okay?"

Windermere shook her head and the grocery store vanished. "I'm cool," she said. "Roll the tape."

Doughty fiddled with the mouse, and the screens came to life. A series of customers filed through the front doors, past the big security guard, and lined up, bored, before the bank teller's window. A couple minutes passed. More customers walked in. More walked out. Business was steady for a Tuesday afternoon. The bank manager emerged from his office and walked out to lunch. Then Doughty pointed. "There."

Moments after the manager disappeared, the stickup crew came through the front doors. Windermere watched as they walked past the guard, the big rent-a-cop barely registering their presence. *Come on, Larry,* she thought. *Hone those crime-fighter instincts.*

The man on the screen held an assault rifle, just like Laurie said. The gun looked big enough to mow down a platoon, forget the deer. Windermere watched as the man fired a burst into the ceiling, sparking chaos.

The hit played like the tellers described it. The female robber filled the duffel bag while the man focused on Cindy first, then Nicole. *Typical,* Windermere thought. *Guy's flirting with the bank tellers, making his woman do the work.* She watched as the man leveled his gun at Nicole. Watched her stiffen as she stared down the barrel. Then she emptied her till, and her partner's beside her, and the man pointed the gun at her once more and was gone. Windermere stopped the tape.

"You talked to the teller," Doughty said. "What was that guy doing?"

"Creep stuff," she told him. "Some power game. Who knows?"

Someone knocked on the door behind them, and Windermere turned around. Laurie. She smiled at Windermere and then spoke to Doughty. "Got someone outside wants to speak to you guys."

"Who?" Windermere said.

"Some kind of witness," she said, shrugging. "Said he saw the getaway car drive off. Should I bring him back here?"

Doughty shook his head. "We'll come out."

Laurie had the kid waiting in the lobby. He wore a fitted Twins cap and saggy jeans. Looked about twenty. He glanced at Doughty as they approached and then fixed his eyes on Windermere. "Damn, sister," he said. "You're a cop, huh? Maybe you want to put the cuffs on me?"

Windermere shook her head. "I think I'd rather use a Taser," she said. "You see something out there or what?"

"Yeah, I saw something." The kid let his eyes roam her body. "Saw the getaway car. Didn't that other girl tell you?"

"Agent Tremain told us, yeah. Describe the car."

The kid grinned at Doughty. "She always this pissy?"

Doughty played along. Shrugged and smiled. *Shit*, Windermere thought. "The car, man. Come on."

"All right, chill," he said. "It was a Toyota Camry. Gold. I saw those armed motherfuckers run out the bank and jump in the backseat."

A gold Camry. Had to be thousands of those cars in the Twin Cities. Blending right into the background. "Where were you?" she said.

"Down the block, waiting on a delivery." The kid suddenly looked sheepish. "I'm a pizza guy."

"Good for you," she said. "So you watched them run out to this gold Camry. Then you saw them drive away."

"Like it was nothing. Real slow."

Windermere looked at Doughty. "Everyone and their sister has a Camry."

Doughty nodded. "Good cars."

"So how do we go about finding this particular vehicle?"

The kid shifted his weight again. "You guys want the plate number?" He dug in his pocket and handed over a notepad. Flipped it open to a couple drawings of muscle cars and half a naked woman. And at the bottom of the page, scrawled real quick, three digits, three letters.

Windermere looked at the notepad. Then she looked at the kid. The kid shrugged. "I was bored."

"Yeah, I guess so." Windermere tore the page from the notepad. "You can't draw for shit," she said. "You get sick of pizza, think law enforcement, not art." She turned back to Doughty. "Let's dig up that car."

6

TOMLIN'S FIRST SCORE wasn't exactly textbook.

He parked the Jaguar in the Walmart lot across from the bank and bought a cheap disguise inside, a pair of winter gloves and aviator sunglasses. Found a scrap of paper in his glove box and scrawled out a note. "I have a gun. Empty the till."

Keep it simple, he figured.

He stared at the note for a few long minutes. Almost tore it up. Then he thought about Becca again, about the way she looked at him lately. Weary, disappointed. Like he wasn't the man she'd once thought he was.

Just do it, he thought. *Your kids need to eat.*

He left the Jaguar in the Walmart lot and crossed back to the bank on foot, his whole body shaking. Every step seemed surreal, like a bad dream. He paused at the front doors and then urged himself inside. Walked straight to the short line of customers and looked around at the security cameras and back to the front door as he waited. He couldn't stop shaking. The line took forever.

Then he was next. A young brunette teller waved at him from the end of the row. She smiled as he approached. "Can I help you?"

Tomlin stared at her, unable to move. Steadied himself on the counter and reached into his jacket and fumbled out the note. Slammed it down on the counter, too hard. The teller picked up the note, read it. Her eyes went wide.

"Don't say a word," Tomlin told her. Even his voice sounded alien. "Don't say a word, or I'll hurt you."

The teller stared down at the note. She was a pretty girl. Big eyes and a kind face. Innocent. He felt like a monster. She swallowed and reached beneath the counter. "Wait," he said. "What the hell are you doing?"

"I'm opening the till." She couldn't hide the shake in her voice. "Isn't that what you wanted?"

"Yeah," he said. "Yes. Hurry up."

She opened the till and took out a stack of money and dropped it into an envelope. All twenties, and lots of them. "Hurry up," he said. "Faster."

She stuffed another stack of twenties in the envelope. Was that a siren outside? Tomlin spun and stared out at the street. Felt like the whole bank was watching. He turned back to the teller. "You pushed the alarm."

She shook her head. "No."

"I said, hurry up." Tomlin's pulse pounded. He snatched for the envelope. "Just give me the money." He turned for the door. Started to run and couldn't make himself stop. Burst out of the bank and into the parking lot, slipped in a slush pile but stayed up and kept going. Cut across the lot toward Walmart, dodging a minivan and a Lexus as horns blared. He didn't hear any sirens, not yet.

He reached the Jag. Unlocked the doors and pulled off his jacket and shades. Stuffed the cash in the glove box and climbed behind the wheel. The bank was a red-and-blue light show behind him, two Saint Paul city cruisers angled outside the front doors. Tomlin forced himself to drive away slow. *You're in a ninety-thousand-dollar car. Bank robbers don't drive Jaguars.*

He did the speed limit for three or four miles. Then he pulled into a Burger King lot and parked. Opened his door and puked onto the pavement.

7

THAT FIRST FUMBLED score netted eighteen hundred dollars. A pittance. Tomlin drove home and didn't sleep and searched for his face in the newspaper the next morning. The *Star Tribune* did a story, four paragraphs. A blurry security camera shot. Tomlin stared at it a long time and could barely tell the subject was human, let alone a white male.

The heist money didn't go far. Didn't even cover the mortgage. Tomlin saw Christmas coming like a shark in the water. He waited a few weeks, and then he robbed again. Had to do it. No choice.

He was calmer this time. Walked into the bank and showed the teller the note. Walked out with three grand and drove away in the Jaguar. Stashed the money in the basement and still didn't get caught. Even three grand, though, just wasn't enough.

Tomlin did some research. The FBI's clearance rate on bank robberies hovered around sixty percent, mostly from dumb-schmuck, single-shot impulse robberies. The guys with the machine guns, the action-movie crews, those guys could skate with a hundred grand in one pull, a million or more if they hit an armored car. And if the stats were any indication, they hardly ever got caught.

Two scores, he'd pulled. Scared the shit out of himself and hadn't even made five grand. The risks just weren't worth the rewards, not at these stakes. He kept looking for work. Called old friends, shared his story. Whatever you have, he told them. Pay me what you can. I need something right now, anything.

His friends shook their heads. Couldn't meet his eyes. Picked up the lunch tab and disappeared to their offices. Finally, someone took him aside. Dan Rydin, at North Star Investors. They'd played hockey together in college. "Carter," Rydin said. "You're just—you look desperate, man."

"I am desperate," Tomlin told him. "I have a family to feed."

Rydin looked him up and down. "I mean your suit, your shoes. Your whole personality. You look like you're a bounced check away from giving hand jobs for cab fare."

"Fuck you," said Tomlin. "You think this is funny?"

Rydin held up his hands. "No offense, man. I really wish I could help."

Rydin promised to try and send some freelance work Tomlin's way. No guarantees, though. In the meantime, Becca's teaching gig was about to expire. The kids wanted Santa Claus to bring them a Wii.

Short of packing up his balls and declaring bankruptcy, Tomlin only had one real choice if he wanted his family to survive.

Bank robbery, and no more petty shit this time. It was time to get his hands on a gun.

8

THE PIZZA BOY'S license number was a dead end, literally.

Doughty and Windermere traced the plates through the DMV system to an address in Merriam Park. They trekked out with a tactical team in tow, swept down a quiet residential street to a little bungalow a couple blocks from the river, where they scared the shit out of a middle-aged woman shoveling snow off her front steps.

"The Toyota," the woman said, when the tactical guys had backed off and everyone had calmed down. "My mother's."

She was a tired-looking woman with tangled gray hair bursting out of the bandanna she wore. She leaned on the porch railing and squinted at Windermere and Doughty. "This was her house," she told them. "My mother's. Died a couple months back and left it to me and my sister. Course, we can't afford it, but with the housing market how it is . . ." She sighed. "I don't know."

Windermere looked around the neighborhood. It was a pretty place, quiet. Not exactly bank robber territory. "The Toyota," she said, turning back to the woman. "You said it was also your mother's."

"Was, yeah. That's the operative word."

"Because she died."

"Because she sold it. A couple months before she died."

Windermere frowned. "She didn't file any papers. Neither did the purchaser."

The woman sighed again. "This is an eighty-year-old woman we're talking about. She could barely remember whether she'd eaten breakfast, much less figure out how to process a used-car sale."

"Still," Doughty said. "There's no record of a sale."

"You see a Toyota?" The woman gestured around the yard. "There's your record of sale."

Doughty glanced at Windermere. Windermere shrugged. "No," the woman continued, "she sold it. We told her she could have given it to us, something useful, but she said she needed the money." A rueful laugh. "Not that it was much of a payday. Guy gave her a thousand bucks, cash."

"Guy ripped her off."

"Bet your ass he did. My dad bought the thing for twenty-five grand. Barely drove it."

"The buyer," said Windermere. "You know him? He a neighbor or something?"

"No," the woman replied. "She put an ad in the paper. Kind of wish I did know him, though. It's practically robbery."

"Robbery." Windermere smiled, small. "That's our guy."

"Well, he's a lowlife, whoever he is." The woman stood up and leaned on her shovel. "Is that it?"

Windermere gave her a business card. "Call us," she said, "if you remember anything else."

THE BULL PEN was chaos when Windermere returned to the Criminal Investigative Division (CID), all clamoring phones and rattling keyboards, a couple of junior agents playing catch with a Nerf football. Windermere waded through the mess to her tiny cubicle, sat and stared at her computer, wondering where to look next.

These Eat Street guys were pros, she figured. People didn't just walk into a bank with assault rifles and shotguns and that kind of poise. From the bank tellers' statements, the guy with the rifle was dead calm, almost playful. He'd taken the time to play his cruel prank on Nicole, scared the wits out of her. He was comfortable with what he was doing. Meant he'd probably done it before.

Statewide, Minnesota averaged between fifty and seventy-five bank robberies every year. Most of the heists took place in Minneapolis or Saint Paul; in the last eighteen months, there had been sixty-six robberies in the Twin Cities region. Twenty had been solved, and eighteen people arrested. Somewhere in those unsolved forty-six, Windermere figured, the Eat Street crew had pulled another job. The trick would be finding the thing.

But if they had, in fact, pulled jobs in the past—and if they weren't, say, a traveling road show like the Pender gang last year— they hadn't been so ambitious the first time around. Windermere's first glance through the unsolved case files bore no similar jobs, no male/female assault-rifle/shotgun combinations, no really professional hits. Didn't mean they weren't in there, just meant Windermere would have to do some real looking.

The football whizzed by her ear and landed a few feet away. Windermere straightened and looked around, frowning. "Sorry, Supercop." Derek Mathers jogged past and retrieved the football. "The balls are bigger in college."

Windermere rolled her eyes. "Cute," she said. "Screw off with that Supercop crap, would you?"

Mathers flashed her a goofy grin and ran a post route through the maze of cubicles. Windermere watched him, resisting the urge to nail him with an open-field tackle. Maybe shut him up about Supercop once and for all.

It had started a year ago, after she'd closed down Arthur Pender's gang of professional kidnappers in Detroit. Someone saw her picture in the paper, taped it to her cubicle with *Supercop* scrawled across, highlighted in pink. Soon every G-man and -woman in the Minneapolis office had picked up the nickname. Whether it was meant to be praise or an insult, Windermere wasn't sure, and after two years in Minnesota she still didn't know anyone well enough to find out.

She turned back to her computer, paged through more open-case files. *This would be easier*, she thought, *if I'd worked any of these cases before.* She hadn't. Rachel Hill, the Minneapolis office's bank robbery whiz, was off on some vacation cruise on the Mayan Riviera, and Drew Harris, Special Agent in Charge of Criminal Investigations, had dumped Windermere in bank robberies until Hill returned. "Or," Harris had said, winking, "another Supercop case emerges."

Windermere sighed and looked up from her computer again. For all of the Supercop bullshit, the Pender case remained her proudest achievement as an FBI agent. For weeks straight, almost a month, she'd tracked Arthur Pender and his roving group of kidnappers, teaming up with a Minnesota state cop named Kirk Stevens as she followed Pender and his gang from Minneapolis through Seattle and Florida toward a bloody shoot-out in Detroit. It had been a blockbuster case, a career-maker, and working thirty-five-thousand-dollar bank scores seemed a tedious anticlimax, even with assault rifles and ski masks thrown into the mix.

And she still missed Kirk Stevens. The security office in the Bank of America had triggered a memory that Windermere had since been unable to shake. She'd grown fond of her colleague, though he was more than a decade her senior and happily married, and kind of corny besides. He was a hell of a cop when it mattered, insightful and decisive and brave, the rare kind of partner Windermere could trust. They had promised to keep in touch after the Pender case ended, but they'd broken that promise quickly; apart from a quick, awkward cup of coffee a month or so later, they'd fallen out of contact.

Of course they had. Stevens was married and had his family to take care of. And Windermere, face it, had dedicated her life to the Bureau in the year since Mark, her last boyfriend, had finally walked out the door. She'd kept herself busy, took on as many cases as possible, and worked hard to keep the past from her mind. Now, though, holed up in her tiny cubicle and enduring Mathers's FBI Super Bowl while she paged through a seemingly endless string of wanted-bank-robber pictures, Windermere let her mind wander to Stevens again and wondered if he ever longed for another shot at the glamorous life.

9

KIRK STEVENS SAT at his desk in the Bureau of Criminal Apprehension headquarters in Saint Paul, staring at the stack of cold homicide files on his desk and trying to dredge up some enthusiasm.

It wasn't that he didn't like working cold cases. In his fifteen years as a BCA agent, Stevens had learned to enjoy the challenges they presented. They were puzzles, all of them, old and dusty, invariably missing a couple key pieces. If you had the time and a little bit of luck, you could sometimes put something together that looked right. And when you did manage to solve a cold homicide, well, the feeling of accomplishment almost matched the satisfaction of taking down an Arthur Pender. Almost.

These files, though, these ones on his desk, were the oldest, dustiest cases on the shelf, the puzzles missing half of their pieces. The unidentified, buckshot-filled bodies pulled from some godforsaken northern lake. The severed hand in a mailbox in Monticello. These were the puzzles nobody could solve.

Stevens paged through another cold file, a fifteen-year-old homicide. A drifter with his throat cut behind a liquor store outside Detroit Lakes. No witnesses. No murder weapon. No suspects. Stevens flipped through the slim file. Then he closed it and threw it on his desk with the others.

So you're a little bored, he thought. *It's your own damn fault.*

The Arthur Pender case, with its sensational premise and its bloody, made-for-TV finale, had made Kirk Stevens something of a minor celebrity. His face—alongside Carla Windermere's—had appeared on news broadcasts across the country. His name was in newspapers for weeks as the full scope of Pender's audacious scheme gradually was revealed, and then again as the ringleader's accomplices stood trial. There were interviews, and award ceremonies.

And there were job offers.

There were job offers from police departments all over the map, many of them quite generous. A few of them really tempting. The BCA, anxious to protect its star agent, had offered Stevens a plum position at the head of a newly founded Major Crimes task force. It was a compelling offer, a career-making promotion, and Stevens turned it down. He turned them all down.

That final Detroit shoot-out with Pender had been an incredible thrill. It had also been incredibly stupid. He'd risked his life like a cowboy, and Carla Windermere's, too. Put his life in the hands of a madman when he could have stepped back and let the FBI's hostage team do their job.

"If you died," his wife had told him. "If you died, Agent Stevens, this whole family would be ruined."

He'd shaken his head, played it tough. "I wasn't going to die, Nancy."

"That man had a machine gun pointed at your head," Nancy Stevens retorted. "You and your little friend Windermere both could have been shot. And where would that have left me?"

Newly minted hero he might have been, but Kirk Stevens's tough act played only so far where his wife was involved. And Nancy had a point. She'd struggled to manage the family alone while he chased

Arthur Pender—wrangling the children to doctors' appointments and volleyball games while keeping up with her own responsibilities at the Legal Aid office, all so her husband could get his rocks off playing action-movie hero.

"I married a cop," Nancy told him. "I knew what I was getting into. But this hero stuff doesn't work. Not for me, Kirk. I need you."

He'd thought about it for a long time. Had weighed the Pender-fueled adrenaline rush against the tedious, day-to-day work inside the BCA, and he'd known which lifestyle he preferred. A part of him longed for that excitement again.

In the end, though, he was a family man first, and his wife and kids needed him more than the BCA did. So he'd sighed and looked Nancy in the eye and told her he was sorry, had turned down the bureau's promotion, and let the phone ring unanswered when the job offers came through. Soon enough, the calls slowed, and then they stopped altogether, and Stevens had settled into a quiet existence working cold cases and coming home nights. It was a good life, and satisfying, most of the time.

Except now, one year after Arthur Pender, Stevens could feel that old restlessness returning. It was the same itch he'd felt as a Duluth city cop, looking for something more than convenience-store burglaries and domestic disputes. It was the same itch he'd felt after ten years with the bureau, the itch that the Pender case had satisfied—briefly.

Stevens leaned back in his chair and stared across the BCA office, letting his thoughts settle on Carla Windermere. He'd seen her picture in the *Star Tribune* a few days back; she was working some bank robbery in Minneapolis, glamorous stuff.

Windermere looked the same in the picture as she had the last time he'd seen her, a beautiful woman and a competent, kick-ass cop. Sent a little jolt through his body, seeing her like that, along with the same vague sense of guilt. The guilt didn't make any sense—

Stevens's relationship with his young colleague had never been anything but professional—but then again, neither did the thrill.

Stevens wondered what Windermere was up to right now, whether
that boyfriend of hers—Mark—had stuck around. Wondered about
her bank robbery case and if she ever got bored working the high-
octane stuff. If she ever longed for something slow-moving, low-
pressure. Knowing Windermere, the answer was no. The woman ate,
slept, and breathed in the fast lane.

Stevens picked up another cold case file and flipped it open.
Chased Windermere from his mind and started to read.

This one was a middle-aged couple out of Saint Cloud, the Danzers. Vanished around Christmas a couple years back. Stevens remembered the case from the newspapers. They'd been driving to
Duluth to visit relatives for the holidays. The man's body turned up
behind a rest stop in Moose Lake; he'd been stabbed. The papers
figured the wife did it, had murdered hubby and disappeared. But
officially, the investigation had produced nothing. A statewide man-
hunt hadn't found the missing wife or the beat-up Thunderbird she'd
been driving.

Stevens studied the pictures in the file, the dead husband and his
missing wife. Elliott Danzer had a mess of gray hair and a wide smile.
Sylvia Danzer was regal, an arched eyebrow and a twinkle in her eye.
They were in their mid-fifties, had been married thirty years.

Just a few years older than me and Nancy, Stevens thought. *Not
even a decade.* He looked at the pictures some more, flipped through
the file. Then he turned back to his computer and typed in the
case code.

Let Windermere have her fast lane, he thought, settling in. *I can
do slow and steady just fine.*

10

TOMLIN FOUND the gun he wanted a week before Christmas.

Finding the gun was easy; obtaining the gun was a pain in the ass. The state of Minnesota prided itself on honoring its citizens' Second Amendment rights, and Tomlin found truckloads of weapons for sale online, from pistols to all-out assault rifles. Every seller, however, wanted proof of a police-issued purchase permit, and the last thing Tomlin wanted was a record of sale.

Still, he scoured the classified listings and finally found a decent handgun in Hastings, about an hour southeast of town. The seller didn't mention any permits or ID, and Tomlin sent him an e-mail using an alias and a free Hotmail account. "Interested in your pistol," he wrote. "Can bring cash if we close today."

The guy replied an hour later. "See you tonight."

That afternoon, Tomlin borrowed Becca's Navigator and drove southeast, tracing the bank of the Mississippi down Route 10 into Hastings. It was dark when he arrived in the town, and he stopped at a gas station and dialed the guy's number. "It's Roger Brill," he said when the guy picked up. "I e-mailed you earlier about the gun."

The guy's name was Schultz. He gave Tomlin directions to a

farmhouse south of town. "Come whenever you like," he said. "I got nothing going on tonight."

"Twenty minutes." Tomlin hung up and drove out of town, picking his way along the empty back roads, the lights of farmhouses like ships in the distance. He missed the place once and doubled back and found it, drove up the long driveway, and parked beside an old Ford alongside the house.

The house was small, wooden, drafty-looking, a couple lonely lights on in the windows. Tomlin climbed out of the truck and heard a door open at the front of the house. "You Roger?"

Tomlin looked up at the porch, where a man stood silhouetted in the doorway. "Mr. Schultz?"

"Call me Tony," the guy said. "And come on inside. Too damn cold to be farting around out here."

Tomlin walked the front path to the house, climbed the creaky front steps to where Tony Schultz stood waiting. He was a big guy— not fat exactly, but big all around. The kind of guy used to getting his run of the jukebox at the neighborhood bar. "Glad you made it," he told Tomlin. "Come on in. Want a beer?"

"Beer's good." Tomlin followed the guy into the house.

Schultz disappeared into the kitchen. Came back with a couple of Budweisers, and handed one to Tomlin. He gestured into a spartan living room. "Said you came in from the city?"

"Minneapolis, yeah." Tomlin cracked his beer as he followed Schultz into the living room. "You live alone out here?"

"Alone, yeah. My ex lives in the city. Reason enough to avoid it, am I right?" Schultz took a long pull of his beer, set down the can, and stifled a belch. "Probably want to see what you came for."

Tomlin nodded. "If you don't mind."

"Course I don't mind."

Schultz stood and walked out of the living room toward the back of the house. Tomlin heard him fiddling with something, a lock, probably, and then he came back holding a small plastic box, like a tool kit or something. He set it down on the table in front of Tomlin, unsnapped the latches, and opened the lid. Tomlin peered inside.

It was a terrifying weapon. Sleek and solid and deadly. Tomlin stared at it and couldn't imagine ever wanting to use it. *This was a mistake*, he thought. *Put it away.*

"Go ahead and pick it up," Schultz told him. "It's not loaded."

Tomlin hesitated. Then he reached in and lifted the gun, testing the weight in his hand. He pictured himself aiming it at a bank teller, feeling sick at the thought. But he thought about Becca and the girls, about the money he'd make, and he forced himself to examine the gun closer.

"Sig Sauer P250," Schultz told him. "Hell of a gun."

"Looks brand-new."

"Couple months old. Birthday gift from my brother-in-law. I like a Ruger myself, but this here is a hell of a gun. Stop any intruder cold."

It's just a tool, Tomlin thought. *Like a hammer. It's a means to an end.* He held the gun up, aimed it across the room. Schultz grinned at him. "What do you think?"

Tomlin held the gun a moment longer. Then he laid it back down. "Five hundred, you said?"

Schultz nodded. "Retails for seven. Five hundred's a steal."

Tomlin pulled out his wallet and counted out five hundred-dollar bills. "Perfect," said Schultz. "Just need your driver's license and your permit."

Shit. Tomlin started to tell the big man to forget it. Then he stopped. *I need that gun,* he decided. He ad-libbed, made a show of checking his pockets. "Jesus," he said finally. "Must have left the damn thing at home."

Schultz frowned. "Shit."

"Left it on the dresser. Unbelievable." He looked at Schultz. "So what do we do?"

"Shit, brother. I guess you come back tomorrow."

Tomlin reached into his wallet again. "I got another two hundred here. Let me walk with the gun and it's yours. I'll come back with the permit tomorrow."

Schultz shook his head. "You know I get in shit if I do that," he said. He turned the gun in its box away from Tomlin and snapped the lid closed. "Save your money. Come back tomorrow, and I'll sell you the gun proper."

Tomlin stared at him, gauging his chances of snatching the gun and bolting with it. *Never happen*, he decided. *This guy's too damn big and too strong. He'd whip my ass for practice.*

Instead, he let Schultz walk him to the door. "Sorry for wasting your time," he told him, stepping out onto the porch.

"Not my time you wasted. Let me know if you still want the gun."

"I want it." Tomlin walked off the porch toward Becca's Navigator. *I need that gun*, he thought, trying to figure his next move. *The hell if I came all the way out here for nothing.*

Tomlin looked back at the house. *What does this guy know about me? Not my name. Not my address. Not my license plate number. Hell, it's so dark out here, he probably can't tell I'm driving a Lincoln.*

Tomlin walked to the truck. Unlocked the doors. Paused with his fingers on the driver's door handle. *I need that gun*, he thought. *For my family.*

He turned back toward the house and the outbuildings beyond. Something lay in the snow in the shadows, and he walked over to it. A piece of scrap wood, a two-by-four, heavy. Tomlin picked it up, tested it, swung the wood like a bat. He thought for a couple of minutes. Then he walked back around the front of the house, blood pounding in his ears. *This is for Becca*, he thought. *For Heather and Maddy. God forgive me.*

The snow crunched under his feet as he walked, every step an explosion. The porch steps creaked as he climbed them, and Tomlin imagined Schultz waiting inside, his gun drawn. But Schultz wasn't waiting at the door. Tomlin hesitated at the top of the porch. Then he knocked on the doorframe, twice, and stood to the side so the two-by-four wasn't obvious. Schultz opened the door, frowning. "What did you forget?"

Tomlin glanced down, made sure the man wasn't holding his gun. "I still want that pistol," he said, choking up on the lumber, his voice shaky.

Schultz blinked. "I don't get it."

Tomlin gritted his teeth. "You will," he said. Then he swung for the fences.

11

TONY SCHULTZ DIDN'T GO down easy.

Tomlin's first blow knocked the man backward but didn't topple him over. He staggered, his nose bloody, his eyes fire. "What the fuck?"

Tomlin stepped through the door and swung the two-by-four again, this time catching Schultz in the side of the head. Again the man stumbled, and Tomlin chased him backward and hit him until, finally, Schultz fell to the floor, bloody and unmoving.

Tomlin stood over him, breathing hard and suddenly nauseated. *He'll live,* he told himself. *He'll wake up and be fine.*

He looked down at Schultz until he was sure the homesteader wasn't going to stand up. Then he stepped over the man's body and into the living room, where the pistol still sat in its box on the table.

Tomlin opened the gun box and took out the pistol. Beneath the pistol were two magazines, and Tomlin loaded the first into the gun. He glanced back at Schultz, who still hadn't moved in the hallway.

The guy said he preferred his Ruger, Tomlin thought. *Maybe I can get a two-for-one going. Make sure he can't shoot me when I'm trying to leave, anyway.* He studied Schultz for a moment and then walked

through the living room to the back, where the big man had retrieved the pistol.

A back annex. An old washing machine and a locked cabinet.
Tomlin looked around for the key, couldn't find it. Didn't want to go
searching Schultz's pockets. He looked down at the pistol in his
hand, thinking, *Well, hell.* He aimed the gun at the lock and braced
himself and fired.

The sound was enormous. The lock disintegrated into shrapnel,
and Tomlin laughed despite himself, giddy, and wrenched the
cabinet open.

Payday.

A camouflage hunting jacket. A stack of *Penthouse* back issues.
Another small toolbox case that Tomlin figured must be the Ruger.
Beyond it two more cases, bigger. Tomlin laid the first case on the
old washing machine and unzipped it. Reached in and pulled out a
shotgun, sawed off. "Jesus Christ."

The bank tellers will shit bricks. They'll unload the vault for me.
Tomlin felt a sudden rush of power and he laughed again. Then he
caught himself. *Easy. That thing's dangerous.*

Tomlin stared at the shotgun, then set it back down. Unzipped the
second soft case and peered inside. His breath caught in his throat.
"My God."

It was some kind of assault rifle, an M-16 or an AK-47 or something. A crazy killing machine. Something you'd see in Iraq, or in
the hands of some militant anarchist out in the woods. The weapon
was obscene, its purpose singular. Tomlin stared at it, tempted and
terrified at the same time.

In the front hallway, Schultz groaned. Tomlin looked at the big
guns in their cases. *Leave them. You're running out of time, and besides, what good will those goddamn cannons do, anyway?*

They'll terrify the bank tellers. They'll know I don't screw around.
He stuffed the Sig Sauer into his waistband and picked up the shot-

gun. Ran it out to Becca's Navigator and returned for the Ruger and the rifle.

Schultz had rolled onto his side, awake now, when Tomlin returned. He made a grab for Tomlin's leg as Tomlin stepped past. "*Fucker.*" Tomlin struggled away. Pulled the pistol from his waistband and aimed down at Schultz, finger tensed on the trigger. Schultz stared back, his eyes dulled. *Do it*, Tomlin thought. *Nobody will know. Kill him.*

Schultz waited. Tomlin felt the blood pounding in his ears. Swayed a little, off balance, and stared down at the man. Almost pulled the trigger. Then he blinked. Lowered the gun and kicked Schultz instead. Watched him writhe, groaning, coughing up blood. Felt the gun in his hand and still ached to use it.

Easy, Tomlin thought. *Get a hold of yourself.* He straightened and walked to the back room again. Looked in the dark cabinet and wondered. He reached inside, past the porno mags and the moth-eaten jacket. Felt through to the back. Found dust rats and old socks, a big box of ammunition. And then, hidden against the wall, a couple of plastic-wrapped bricks. One held cash, hundred-dollar bills and lots of them. The other brick looked like cocaine.

The bastard's a drug dealer, Tomlin thought. *I'm doing the world a favor.* He picked up the cash and piled it on top of the box of ammunition. Shouldered the rifle in its case and turned toward the front door. Then he stopped and stared back at the cocaine again. *Don't do it*, he thought. *What do you want with cocaine?*

That cocaine equals money. That's a year's mortgage payments. Nobody will know.

"Shit." Tomlin stacked the cocaine on the cash and made for the front door. He piled the drugs and the cash and the guns in the rear of the truck, and then stepped back and surveyed his loot.

Christmas came early this year.

12

IT WAS JUST AFTER EIGHT in the evening when Windermere finally found something that fit. The CID office was mostly deserted; Mathers had packed up his football, and even Doughty had vanished, ducking out at a quarter after five with a shrug and a smile. "Family dinner," he told Windermere. "The wife gets mad when I'm late."

See ya, Windermere thought. Doughty was supposed to be riding herd on the city cops, overseeing a canvass of Eat Street and the neighborhoods nearby. He seemed to think the bank robbers were your everyday local underachievers, but so far Minneapolis PD had turned up only blank stares and silence since they'd started knocking on doors.

"Tomorrow," he told Windermere as he walked to the elevators. "We'll get them tomorrow. And if not tomorrow, the day after."

Maybe, Windermere thought, *but I want him today.* She kept her mouth shut. Grinding through the case backlog was a one-person job, anyway.

Still, by eight o'clock she was hungry and restless, getting nowhere, and she stood up from her chair, stretching, figuring to try out the new Thai joint down the block. But the face on her screen suddenly looked familiar, and she straightened and studied the picture.

The suspect had robbed a First Minnesota branch in Prospect Park in January. He'd come alone, with a pistol and a note, and had walked with just over six thousand dollars. A good score. In the still picture from the security camera, he looked to stand about six feet tall, wore a black Adidas track jacket, aviator sunglasses, and a black watch cap. A ready-made disguise. Not suspicious at all.

They should start treating banks like airports, Windermere thought. *Strip search at the door before you walk in. No guns and no shitty disguises.*

According to Rachel Hill's file, this guy was a serial robber who tended to hit banks the same way: a note, a pistol, a makeshift disguise. A long way from an assault rifle and a team takeover job; nothing like Eat Street at all.

According to Agent Hill, however, a witness had reported a gold Toyota Camry driving out of the neighborhood just after the robbery occurred. The witness hadn't gotten a good look at the driver, and Hill hadn't made any progress tracking down the car.

Windermere sat down again and kept reading, her pulse speeding up as the similarities started to pop. Same time of day, a Monday afternoon. Guy had blue eyes, too, according to the bank teller's statement. The bank teller's name was Darcy Passat. Lived off University Avenue, a few blocks from the bank.

Windermere checked her watch. Nearly eight-thirty. Her stomach growled. She ignored it. Reached for her notepad and copied down the woman's address. Then she stood again and reached for her coat. *Prospect Park,* she thought, walking to the elevator. *Let's see what this teller remembers.*

13

DARCY PASSAT LIVED in a little two-story company home just south of University Avenue. Windermere rang the doorbell and a dog barked twice, and then a man opened the door. Windermere showed him her badge. "Looking for Darcy Passat."

The man looked her up and down. He was a big guy, filled the doorframe. "You have a warrant?"

"Don't think I need one," she said. "I'm just here to talk to your girl."

"What about?"

"A bank robbery, chief. You the culprit?"

He shook his head slowly. "I didn't rob any banks."

"Didn't think so. Can I see her or what?"

The man stared at her. Then he shrugged and said something back into the house, and a moment later a woman appeared, a young brunette holding a struggling, wild-eyed beagle. "FBI," she said, wrestling with the dog. "I already talked to you guys."

"I just need a few minutes," said Windermere. "Got a couple more questions."

Passat dropped the dog to the floor and shoved it back, out of sight. "All right." She sighed and looked at Windermere again. "What do you want to know?"

TOMLIN FELT the weight of the gun in his waistband as he walked toward the First Minnesota branch. He glanced back at the Camry where he'd parked it down an alley, fixed his disguise, and kept walking.

Tomlin had found the Toyota for sale in the paper, made the owner a lowball offer. Paid for it out of Tony Schultz's fifty-grand brick and didn't bother to change the registration.

He left the car parked in a garage in downtown Minneapolis when he wasn't pulling scores. Paid cash for a year's lease on a parking spot in Roger Brill's name. Swapped cars before and after the job and drove home in his Jag, nobody the wiser.

He'd used Schultz's cash to pay off the Navigator, and put the rest toward the credit cards. Bought Becca diamond earrings for Christmas, told her he'd picked up some plum freelance work. But the bills kept mounting. The mortgage never ended. The kids needed school clothes, and the dog needed a checkup.

And now here he was, walking into another bank, the pistol tucked in his waistband. He'd left the shotgun at home, and Schultz's rifle; the big guns fascinated him, but they scared him, too. He couldn't imagine walking into a bank with either weapon. Not yet.

Tomlin joined the queue in front of the tellers. He stared straight ahead, almost relishing the way his heart seemed to beat faster as the line moved slowly forward. Then it was his turn. It still happened too soon.

The teller was an older woman, sixty or so, somebody's grandmother. She smiled at him, her head cocked to the side, and Tomlin forced a smile back and slid over the note.

He watched her eyes as she read it. Watched as she pursed her lips, shook her head. "Oh, honey," she said. "You don't want to do this."

Tomlin pulled the gun from his waistband. Held it up so the teller could see it. Behind him, someone stifled a scream. "Nothing crazy," he said, loud enough that the whole bank could hear. "Empty your tills, and I'll be on my way."

The teller looked at him. "Just think for a second."

Tomlin cocked back the hammer. "The till," he said. "Now." He turned the gun on the teller beside her, a young-looking brunette. The woman blushed red and opened her till. Tomlin spun around, saw the whole bank watching him. "I'll be out of here soon," he said. "Don't worry."

Behind him, the old woman had filled a plastic bag with cash. "You're throwing your life away," she said, as she handed it over. "You don't have to do this."

Tomlin snatched the bag. "I didn't come for a sermon." He turned back to the brunette, who was fumbling with her own bag. He studied her flushed face as he approached her counter. "Look at me," he said. The teller didn't look up. Kept filling the bag. Her whole body was shaking. Tomlin laid the gun on the counter. "*Look at me.*"

This time, the teller looked up. Her eyes were wide, terrified. Her lower lip trembled. "What are you afraid of?" Tomlin asked her. The woman shook her head. Didn't reply.

"Tell me," he said.

There was movement behind him, furtive. The young teller's till was empty by now, her bag full. The police would be here soon. It was time to get moving. Tomlin held his gaze on the woman. "You're afraid I'll kill you," he said.

The teller didn't react.

"Aren't you?"

Now she nodded, quickly, and looked away. She was crying. The thought didn't disgust him. "I could do it," he said. "I could kill you right here. *Pow.* Just like that."

She nodded again. Pushed the money bag at him. Tomlin smiled at her and leveled the gun, feeling a thrill as he watched her shrink back. *"Pow,"* he said again. Then he shouldered the money and walked out of the bank.

WINDERMERE STARED AT Darcy Passat. *"Pow."*

Passat nodded. *"Pow.* Just like that."

Windermere stared at the woman. *It's the same guy,* she thought, her heart starting to race. *Somewhere along the way he found himself some friends.*

Passat watched her. "So what?" she said. "You get what you came for?"

Windermere smiled and started back to her car. "I'll say I did," she said. *"Pow."*

14

WINDERMERE UNLOCKED THE DOOR and walked into the apartment. The whole place was dark, and the air was dead still; she barely lived here anymore.

She walked through to the kitchen and turned on the light, looked around at the spotless countertops and the empty sink. Mark hadn't been much for doing the dishes, but since he'd gone, she'd kept the whole place so clean it looked soulless, like a showroom suite or a spread in a high-end magazine.

Windermere set her keys on the kitchen counter. She took a beer from the fridge and walked into the living room and stood in the darkness, looking around at the gloomy silhouette furniture and beyond to the window and the Minneapolis skyline. She drank her beer, slowly, and she thought about Mark.

He'd practically had his bags packed when she finally came home from the Pender case. Had walked out a month or so after. He'd gone back to Miami, and was probably fishing every day, and dancing, eating ceviche on South Beach. He was working again, no doubt, and Windermere wondered if he was happier now, if he'd found someone new.

Not for the first time, Windermere wondered if it hadn't been a mistake to leave Miami. She'd had a good life in Florida, a happy relationship and good friends, a promising career and a '69 Chevelle she could drive every day. Now she was single, getting older alone, one of a handful of black cops on an otherwise whitewashed FBI force.

And as far as she could tell, there was no good goddamn ceviche anywhere in Minnesota.

Windermere finished her beer. *Right now, Mark's alone in Miami and wishing he could call you,* she thought. *You sure as hell don't need him to make your life better.* She chucked out the bottle and turned out the light. Walked to the front door and pulled on her coat. It was late, but she wasn't tired, and what the hell was she going to do in her apartment all night?

Twenty minutes later, she was in the FBI building, sipping bad coffee and staring at her computer screen. The office was empty and silent around her, but Windermere barely noticed. She sat forward in her chair and clicked through Rachel Hill's bank robbery reports, her mind working faster with each new page she read.

This guy, the Prospect Park guy with the Camry, he'd gone from pulling single-shot robberies with a handgun to taking over a bank with a driver and a sidekick. *So where did he come from?*

She worked through Agent Hill's robbery files again. Hill made the guy for another job in Robbinsdale, northwest of downtown Minneapolis, a few weeks after Prospect Park. Then another job, in Lowry Hill, southwest of downtown, a month or so later. A couple weeks before Eat Street.

Hill had come up with nothing before Prospect Park, though, and Windermere figured she'd double-check her colleague's work. She paged through the unsolved bank robberies for December, November, the fall. Found nothing that fit the Prospect Park MO, no gold Toyota Camrys, no men with guns and aviator sunglasses terrifying the tellers.

Maybe Hill's right, Windermere thought. *Maybe Prospect Park's his first score.* She broadened her search. Every bank job in the state. Just lonely men with notes, mostly; one sad-looking woman in a Bugs Bunny sweater. Windermere brought up the Prospect Park file and copied out the man's note: "I have a gun. Empty the till."

She searched through the files again. Got a couple of hits. A job out by the airport. Another in Midway, about halfway between Minneapolis and Saint Paul, a Bank of America heist last November.

According to the file, the Midway guy was a rank amateur. He'd panicked and bolted midway through the heist, made off with a shade under two grand. By the time the first police cars arrived, the man had vanished.

He'd scrawled his note on some kind of receipt, the file said. Wore woolen winter gloves. Aviator sunglasses.

Windermere stood and rode the elevator down to the evidence locker. A kid named Lucente sat guard at a desk, reading a paperback novel. He buzzed her in. "Welcome to the dungeon," he said. "What do you need?"

"Notes," said Windermere. "Bank robbery notes."

Lucente yawned. "Most recent stuff's that way," he said, pointing. "We keep it for a year before it goes to the warehouse."

Windermere thanked him and walked into the stacks. The shelves stretched to the ceiling, a jumble of bankers' boxes and dusty plastic bags. She found Hill's Prospect Park file quickly, glanced at the note. Blue ballpoint pen on white printer paper. The same unimaginative instructions.

Windermere walked farther and found the Midway evidence box. Not much inside besides the bag with the note. She picked up the bag and studied it in the light. The writing was shaky, in a hurry. Still, the wording matched the Prospect Park note, and the handwriting looked almost identical.

Windermere turned the bag over and examined the receipt. A parking receipt, she saw, squinting at the faded ink. Saint Paul E-Z Park. Dated last July. Whoever owned the receipt had parked in downtown Saint Paul on a Tuesday, from eight in the morning until almost six at night, and had paid twenty bucks for the privilege. Windermere walked out of the stacks and had Lucente make a photocopy of the receipt, both sides. Then she climbed back on the elevator and studied the receipt again as the elevator climbed back up to CID.

A worker bee would park in downtown Saint Paul all day on a Tuesday, she thought. *Someone with a job in an office somewhere. But what kind of worker bee robs a bank?*

Windermere looked at the address on the receipt. Memorized it. *Only one way to find out,* she decided.

15

THE INMATE CHEWED on the Snickers bar. "Sure, I seen a car like that. Wasn't nowhere near Duluth, though."

Stevens watched the man across the desk. A guard watched them both from the doorway. "An old Thunderbird," Stevens said. "Red."

The inmate finished the candy bar. Wiped his mouth, nodding. "I can see it in front of me," he said. "Could take you to it tomorrow, if you wanted."

Stevens leaned back in his chair and studied the man. Tried to gauge the odds he was telling the truth. The odds that this T-Bird was Sylvia Danzer's.

He'd been working the Danzer murder for nearly a week now. Had spent most of it retracing the Moose Lake sheriff's work, reviewing the BCA agent's notes, calling old contacts and reopening wounds. Hadn't come up with much but what was in the report: The Danzers weren't newlyweds, but by all appearances, they were happy together. Neither had had an affair. Stevens had even talked to their accountant. Neither Elliott nor Sylvia Danzer had any particularly eye-opening debts. They were comfortable financially; neither had any unusually large life insurance policies. As far as anyone could guess, there was no reason for Sylvia Danzer to have murdered her husband.

After a couple days of paper cuts and dial tones, Stevens had exhausted the high-percentage plays. Time to play the long shots. He had the Danzers' pictures printed up and sent around to every jail, drunk tank, and correctional facility in the state, along with a description of the Thunderbird and a rundown of the crime. Asked the guards and wardens to pass out the pictures, get the inmates talking, figuring maybe someone knew someone who knew something. The play netted about a hundred oddball claims in the first two or three hours, mostly desperate criminals looking for a reduced sentence. But then there was Ernie Saint Louis.

Saint Louis was a chocoholic serving a three-to-nine for marijuana possession with intent to traffic. He told Stevens he'd trade information for candy bars and a good word to the judge, so Stevens drove down to the federal lockup in Waseca with a bag full of chocolate bars and agreed to hear the guy's story.

Saint Louis rummaged in the bag and came out with a Milky Way bar. Opened the wrapper and took a bite. "Sure, I seen it," he said. "I seen that old T-Bird every week for about five or six months."

Stevens nodded. "Good," he said. "Where?"

"North." Saint Louis chewed. Looked across the table at Stevens. "I had a real good thing going," he said. "It was just pot, anyway, no big deal."

Stevens leaned forward again and looked through the man's file. He'd been picked up in Big Falls, maybe thirty miles from the Canadian border. Had nearly eight kilograms of marijuana stored in his Ski-Doo. "You ran drugs across the border," Stevens said.

Saint Louis shrugged. "Just pot, like I said. No big deal."

"And you saw this Thunderbird somewhere."

"In the bush, man." Saint Louis blinked, shook his head. "Just rusting away. Two years in a row. A damn shame."

"Sure," Stevens said. "You get a good look at it?"

Saint Louis shrugged again. "Wasn't really concentrating on seeing the sights." He winked at Stevens. "Kind of time-sensitive cargo."

"So what the hell was it doing out there in the bush?"

"Figured it was abandoned." Saint Louis shook his head. "Somebody got tired of it, drove it out on that old logging road and forgot about it. Was my guess, anyway."

"Abandoned it. An old T-Bird."

"Crazy, right? It was that same car, though. Same vintage, everything. Just rusting away in the bush."

Stevens stared at the ceiling, thinking. Saint Louis chewed, loudly. Finished his Milky Way bar and sat forward, his eyes hopeful. "Could take you there tomorrow, if you want."

Stevens pushed his notepad across the table. "How about you just draw me a map?"

16

TOMLIN SETTLED INTO a rhythm. A few days a week doing taxes for senior citizens, a couple contract jobs for friends at big firms. A robbery every few weeks, when the money got low.

Or, more and more, whenever the mood struck him.

It wasn't just about the money anymore. Not even close. It was about the excitement, the power, the quick jolt of electricity he felt when the pretty tellers wilted at the sight of his gun. It was the same thrill he'd once felt when he walked through his office, watching the worker bees stiffen at their cubicles, knowing the room's collective sphincter had tightened the moment he walked through the door. It was power. Control. Robbing banks filled the void while it paid off his mortgage. And nobody had figured him out.

Tomlin found a small office in Lowertown, east of downtown Saint Paul. It was an old, musty low-rise with patchy off-white walls and buzzing fluorescent lights, graffiti on the sooty façade. But Tomlin didn't much care for looks. An office would provide cover. An easy way to launder the robbery money.

He hired a receptionist, a punk-rock college dropout he found through a classified ad. A pixie named Tricia with neon-pink hair. She came in two or three days a week, did Sudoku at her desk and answered the occasional phone call. Lent an air of legitimacy to the place.

Rydin came to visit. "Freelance," he said, looking around. "You'll either get very rich or go broke. Probably the latter, from the looks of this building."

"Baby steps," Tomlin told him. "It's coming together."

Rydin promised to talk to people at his office, find some work to throw Tomlin's way. A couple other friends came through with leads, and Tomlin made up the difference hustling for contacts. Put an ad in the paper, another online. Craigslist. "Accounting Service. Your taxes done cheap." He spent long hours hammering out income tax forms for old ladies, a hundred dollars a pop. Bored him worse than bingo, but the work kept him busy.

He slept in some mornings, ate long breakfasts, read the paper. Came home early one or two nights a week, enjoyed the home and the life he was trying to maintain. He spent hours with Becca, reading novels together and walking the dog. They holed up in the bedroom for endless afternoons, feeling like two high school kids who'd skipped out of class, emerging fresh-scrubbed from the shower just as Heather and Madeleine returned from school.

Heather came home one day and announced that her school needed someone to help coach the basketball team, and Tomlin figured, *Why the hell not?* Now he spent Tuesday afternoons in a public school gym, teaching a gaggle of teenage girls how to shoot a jump shot. Thursdays were game days.

In the evenings, he watched movies with the girls in the rec room, or stayed up late puttering with his model train setup. He cleared out the spare room in the basement and built a tabletop empire, a miniature world of mountains and cities and tiny plastic people.

He stashed the guns in the train room—the Ruger in its case under boxes of spare train cars and supplies, the assault rifle in an alcove behind a hollowed-out mountain. The shotgun he left lodged in the bracing underneath the table, and he hid the spare shells inside a factory on a spur line in the model town he'd patterned after Saint Paul. It could be a munitions factory, he decided. Schultz's cocaine he hid at the office. Locked it away in his bottom desk drawer with the robbery money while he tried to figure out how to get rid of it.

Little by little, Tomlin rebuilt his life. Kept up with the mortgage payments, bought groceries, birthday presents, a new cell phone. Made love to his wife and went to bed happy almost every night.

And when the money started to dwindle, or he started to get bored, he dug out Schultz's pistol and hit another bank. It worked out well, in the short term. It would work, anyway, until the accounting business started to take off.

Life seemed perfect again, almost. Until one day in January, when it all changed again.

17

HE'D COME IN TO WORK early. It was about a month after he'd robbed Tony Schultz, four or five bank heists after that first Midway job. Heather had Spirit Club before school, and Tomlin dropped her off and drove straight to the office. Walked in and found Tricia with her nose in his bottom desk drawer.

She stood up, too fast, when he walked into the room. "What are you doing here?" she said. "You're early."

"I work here." Tomlin circled around to where she stood and examined the lock. She'd jimmied the thing with a nail file. "What are *you* doing?"

"It was unlocked," she said. "I was looking for staples."

"Bullshit."

She was silent for a minute or two. "I'm so sorry," she said finally, her lower lip trembling. "My boyfriend just dumped me. I don't know what I'm doing."

Tomlin glanced down at the open desk drawer. The cocaine and the cash. She had to have seen it. He studied her face, her pretty, scared eyes. "Get out," he said.

"No." She reached for his arm. "Mr. Tomlin, please. Please don't fire me."

He shook her away. "Get out of my office."

She stared at him, tears in her eyes. Tomlin held her gaze until she looked down again, at the nail file on the thin carpet, the desk drawer still partially open. Something hardened in her expression. "What are you waiting for?" Tomlin asked her. "I said get out."

She shrugged his hand off her shoulder. "That's a lot of cocaine."

"It's not cocaine." Tomlin slammed the drawer closed. "It's none of your business. Get out."

"Bullshit." She turned to look at him slowly, a new look in her eyes. She wasn't scared anymore, Tomlin realized. She was *smiling*. "So what are you, a drug dealer or something? Does your wife know about this?"

"For Christ's sake." Tricia's smile widened. Tomlin rubbed his forehead, looked at her again. Then he looked down at the drugs. "So what?" he said. "I'm supposed to just forget this?"

Tricia shrugged. "If you want," she said. She started for the door. Brushed by him, close. "We can pretend this never happened, if that's what you want. I won't say a damn thing if you don't try and fire me."

She could ruin everything, Tomlin thought. He suddenly felt light-headed. Then Tricia stopped in the doorway. "But pretend is so boring." She looked back at him again with that same funny smile. "Maybe we can have fun instead."

18

DOUGHTY WASN'T AROUND when Windermere arrived in CID the next morning. She wasn't surprised; it was early, not even eight, and the office was skeleton-crew barren. Besides, Doughty never showed up before nine.

Windermere kept her coat on as she booted up her computer. She printed off every security cam still she could of the Midway suspect, the Prospect Park suspect, Robbinsdale, and Lowry Hill, and then she turned off her computer again and rode the elevator back down to the garage.

The drive to Saint Paul took twenty minutes, downtown to downtown on I-94. Windermere passed the turnoff for Midway en route. She looked up and out of the Interstate trench and tried to figure out why the guy had chosen Midway, when every other job seemed to confirm Doughty's theory that the suspect was a Minneapolis local.

She picked up her phone and called Doughty's cell. Rang through to voice mail the first try, but he picked up the second. "Doughty, it's Windermere." She could hear a baby crying in the background, another kid yelling something. "Got a lead in Saint Paul. Check it out."

She explained her findings, Prospect Park leading to Midway and the E-Z Park receipt. "We're watching this guy evolve, Bob," she told him. "He's getting more and more dangerous as he builds up his confidence."

Doughty yelled something at the kid. Then he came back on the line. "So what are you saying?"

"I think we should broaden our search for this guy," she said. "Midway's his first score, from what I can tell. It's a rookie job. Could tell us more about him than anything later."

"Most of his scores are in southern Minneapolis," Doughty replied. "I'm making good headway with my local contacts."

"This first job, though, Bob, this is the big one. It's probably closer to his home base than those Minneapolis banks. Someone in Midway might know him."

Doughty gave it a beat. "You tell Harris?"

"No," she said. "I just thought of it now."

"And you're in the car already. Driving to Saint Paul." Doughty sucked his teeth. "You should have checked with me first."

"I'm telling you now, Bob."

Another pause. The baby wailed in the background. "That's not the point, Carla. Everything on this investigation's supposed to go through me."

Windermere rolled her eyes. "So all right. What do you want me to do?"

"Come back to the office. We'll talk this thing over."

"I'm halfway to Saint Paul."

"So you'll get to CID about the same time as me. See you there." Doughty hung up before she could reply. She stared at her phone for a second. *God damn it*, she thought. She let her foot off the accelerator. Then she pressed down again. *I can see Saint Paul up ahead. Damned if I'm turning back now.*

She found the E-Z Park entrance beneath a high-rise office complex. It was a garage underground, and she parked in a no-parking zone at the top of the ramp.

Before she was out of the car, there was an employee bearing down on her. "No parking," he said. "You have to keep moving."

Windermere flashed her badge. "Your boss around?"

The man stopped like he'd touched an electric fence. Then he turned and hurried toward an office, pausing to look back at her twice. He returned a minute later with another man, slightly older, in a wrinkled brown suit. "Can I help you?"

Windermere introduced herself. Showed the man the photocopied Midway note. "I'm looking for a man," she said. "He parked here once. In July."

The man examined the photocopy. Shrugged and turned back to the office. "Don't hold your breath."

"I have some pictures, too," she said. "Maybe they'll help."

The manager beckoned his employee over. "I spend my day in the office," he said. "Sanjay works in the booth."

Sanjay came over slowly, circling Windermere like a wary dog. Windermere held out the stack of security pictures, and the man paused before riffling through them. Then he shook his head and looked sideways at Windermere. "I don't know."

Windermere frowned. "Nothing?"

He shrugged. "I don't know."

She wanted to press him, but the manager had returned, holding the photocopy and another scrap of paper. "This account was paid for by a credit card," he told Windermere. "The credit card belongs to a man named Carter Tomlin."

"Carter Tomlin," said Windermere. "You know who he is?"

Both men shook their heads.

"He still park here?"

The manager shrugged. "Perhaps you could check with the credit card company." He shoved the photocopy back at Windermere, and the scrap of paper, too. He'd written Tomlin's name on it in block letters.

Windermere studied his face. Thought about telling him to go back and check for himself. Then she decided, why not go to the source? "Okay, boys," she said. "Thanks for your time."

The two men watched her climb into the car and drive out of the lot. They didn't move until she'd turned out onto the street and was pulling away. Windermere watched them in her rearview mirror. Hiding something, no doubt, but they didn't know squat about the bank robber.

Her phone rang. Doughty. She let it ring for a minute. Then she sighed and picked it up. "I got a name. Carter Tomlin, he's—"

"Where are you?" Doughty's tone was ice.

"Did you hear me, Bob? I have a lead."

"I asked you to meet me at the office, Agent Windermere."

She sighed again. "What's your point?"

"My point?" Doughty's voice lost its chill, replaced with barely throttled anger. "I'm senior agent on this investigation, Agent Windermere. That's my point. Come back to Minneapolis, *now*, and we'll talk about what happens next."

Windermere mouthed a curse. "I'm stuck in traffic," she said. "I'll be there when I can."

19

TRICIA SAID SHE had a friend, Javier, who could move the cocaine. "Good money," she said. "No risk. He's cool."

Tomlin stalled her as long as he could. "He's cool?" he said. "He's a goddamn drug dealer. That's cool to you?"

Tricia shrugged. "Why not?"

"How do you know this guy, anyway? I thought you were a student or something."

"I'm a lot of things," Tricia said. "What do you care? This guy, Javier, he's my ex-boyfriend's hookup. I used to see him three or four times a month, okay? We're cool." She cocked her head and smiled at him, confident. As though she brokered drug deals every other day. *Maybe she does*, Tomlin thought. *She could be the pink-haired Pablo Escobar, for all I know.*

"We doing this or what, boss?" she said. "Come on. Let's turn that brick into cash."

Finally, he gave in. *Pull the trigger*, he thought. *Someone else finds those drugs and you're looking at prison. Sell them to this guy Javier, and you're paying your bills.*

"Fine," he told her. "Set it up."

She smiled at him. "Great. Now, let's discuss my fee."

JAVIER LIVED IN an apartment by the university. He answered the door and smiled wide when he saw Tricia, kissed her on the cheek and ushered her inside. Then he looked at Tomlin.

Tomlin studied Javier as Javier studied him. The drug dealer was skinny, with a pockmarked face, probably in his mid-twenties. He had a scar above his upper lip, and though he smiled at Tomlin, his eyes were suspicious. "You're Tricia's friend."

"Yeah." Tomlin could feel the weight of the pistol in his coat, and he wondered how fast he could draw if he needed.

Javier squinted at him. "You a cop?"

"No. Hell, no."

"Not that you'd tell me if you were."

"He's okay, Javier," Tricia called from inside. "He's my boss. The accountant?"

Javier looked at Tomlin again. "The accountant." He laughed. "Fine. Come in."

The apartment was empty except for a beat-up couch and a huge flat-screen TV. There were two men on the couch, watching a talk show. Neither looked up when Tomlin walked in.

Javier led them into the kitchen and leaned against the counter. "Okay," he said, watching them. "Let's see what you got."

Tricia opened her purse and handed him the brick. Javier looked at Tomlin. "Where did you get this?"

Tomlin shrugged. "Found it in a dumpster."

"Whose dumpster?"

"What?"

Javier shook his head. "Save it. Just don't tell them you sold it to me, got it?"

"Fine, Javier," said Tricia. "Of course."

One of the men from the living room walked into the kitchen

holding a scale. Javier set the brick on the scale and waited a beat. Then he nodded. "One key," he said. "As advertised."

The other man produced a knife, and Javier split the package open. He dabbed a finger inside and tasted the powder. Then he looked at Tricia. "Ten thousand."

Tomlin blinked. "Ten thousand dollars? It's gotta be worth close to thirty."

Javier turned and stared at him with his hard little eyes. "You can get thirty for it, go ahead. I'm paying ten."

"Fifteen." Tricia put on her ingénue smile. "Then we all go home happy."

Javier studied her. Then he nodded. "For you only," he said. "Fifteen thousand."

His partner went back into the living room and returned with a bundle of money. Handed a thick stack to Tomlin. Tomlin flipped through it. "It's all here."

"Fifteen thousand dollars, my friend." Javier looked at Tomlin and laughed. "Don't forget to declare it on your taxes."

20

TOMLIN DROVE TRICIA to her apartment and parked at the curb. He shut off the engine and took out the thick stack of hundred-dollar bills. Then he sat back in his seat. "Jesus Christ. That just happened."

Tricia cocked her head. "It happened. You cool?"

"Cool?" He looked at her. "We just sold a kilo of coke to that guy. We just pulled off a drug deal. We're drug dealers. Are *you* cool?"

Tricia shrugged. "Yeah, I'm cool. We're fifteen grand up."

"And that's that."

She looked at him. "Yeah," she said. "That's that. We walked in there with product. We walked out with cash. It's not such a big deal, boss. Roll with it."

He laughed and shook his head. "Roll with it," he said. He counted out her take, seventy-five hundred, and handed it over. "To be honest, I thought we'd make more."

"Whatever," she said, slipping the money into her purse. "It's seven grand more than I had this morning. So what now?"

What now? Tomlin thought. "Now you go inside," he told her. "I go home to my wife and forget this ever happened."

Tricia shook her head. "I don't think so."

"What?"

"This is exciting," she said, a smile in her eyes. "Let's keep going. What other secrets are you hiding?"

He couldn't hold her gaze. "I don't have any secrets."

"The drugs," she said. "Where'd you get them? And don't try and bullshit me with that dumpster crap, because you know I'm not buying."

"It's found money," said Tomlin. "Who cares where it comes from?"

"It matters because I want to know what you're into," she said. "I saw the cash in that drawer of yours. You can't tell me that's all from doing taxes for grandmothers."

Tomlin started the car. "Nothing's going on. End of story."

Tricia leaned forward. The top of her blouse fell open, and if he'd wanted, he could have had a good look at the tops of her breasts. He had a funny feeling she knew just what she was doing. "All right." She smiled at him. "Let's play a game."

"I'd rather not," Tomlin said.

"Too bad," she said. "Let's say, hypothetically, that a man asked his secretary to help him unload some cocaine. A lot of cocaine. How about that?"

Tomlin stared at her. "What the hell are you getting at?"

Tricia held up her hand. "Let's say the secretary told the hypothetical man's wife all about what had happened. With the cocaine and everything. Maybe she even hinted about an affair. What do you think would happen?"

"Don't go there," Tomlin told her. "Don't even joke."

"Who's joking, boss?"

Tomlin pulled the pistol from his waistband. Held it to her face. "Don't talk to my family," he said. "Don't go there. Understand?"

Tricia didn't blink. "Just tell me what you're into. You want to do more drug deals with Javier?" She studied his face. "Or maybe you want to make even more money. I can help you."

Tomlin stared at her until Tricia pushed the pistol away. "Tell me where the drugs came from," she said. "Then we can talk about what we're going to do next."

Tomlin looked from her eyes to the pistol. Then he lowered the gun. "I robbed a guy," he said finally. "I needed a weapon, and he had one. The drugs were just extra."

"You couldn't just buy a gun?"

"Not for my purposes."

"Your purposes." She kept her eyes on him. "What do you mean?"

He wanted to impress her, he realized. He wanted her to see that he was more than some shitty accountant in some shitty office, that he was someone with power. He wanted to scare her a little. "Bank robbery," he said. "I needed a gun to rob banks."

Tricia sat straight up in her seat. "I fucking *knew* it," she said. "I fucking *knew* you had secrets. How many?"

"Banks?" Tomlin shrugged. "Five or six."

"Alone?"

He nodded. "I don't know many bank robbers."

"And you make decent money."

"The money's okay," he said. Then he caught himself. "It's pretty damn good, actually. Pays your wages, doesn't it?"

She smiled, wide. "Badass."

For a moment, neither of them said anything. Tomlin stared out at her ugly apartment complex, the rusted hulks in the parking lot. Then Tricia turned to him again. "You ever think of expanding?"

Tomlin frowned. "What do you mean?"

Her eyes were wide and excited. "You could do a lot better with a couple more people," she said. "If you had enough guns, I mean."

Expansion. She was talking about a crew. A professional gang, the kind the FBI couldn't catch. He realized he'd been waiting for this kind of chance. "I have enough guns," he told her.

She cocked her eye at him. "Big guns?"

"Big enough."

"So okay." She twisted in her seat to face him. "What if we made a little expansion?"

Tomlin frowned. "We?"

"You and me," she said. "If you're into it, I know a guy."

Tomlin sat back in his seat and said nothing. They'd make more money, enough to take care of Becca and the girls for a while. Enough to buy time to get his little business on its feet. Hell, he already had the firepower.

He pretended to think about it. The way Tricia was looking at him, though, he knew he couldn't say no.

21

WINDERMERE STOOD IN Agent Harris's office with Bob Doughty beside her, Doughty glaring at her like she'd just killed his dog. Harris leveled his gaze at her. "Agent Windermere," he said. "Agent Doughty came to me with a complaint about your behavior. What's the story?"

Windermere held the SAC's gaze. "Sir, all respect to Agent Doughty, but I have a lead on our Eat Street bank robbery. I'd like to check it out before it goes cold."

Harris studied her face. He was a few years older than Doughty but looked younger. Trim and well dressed, handsome in an aging college athlete kind of way. He was a fair boss, Windermere figured. She got along with him most of the time.

Now, though, he was looking at her like the principal looks at a problem student. "Agent Doughty is senior agent in this investigation," he said.

Windermere nodded. "Yes, sir."

"And he asked you to report to CID this morning for briefing. You drove to Saint Paul instead."

Windermere could feel Doughty's immense self-regard like a heat lamp. "I was halfway to Saint Paul already. As I communicated to Agent Doughty on the phone, I had a viable lead that I felt warranted investigation."

"So you disregarded his instructions."

"Yes, sir."

"You've been here two years now, Agent Windermere, but you still act like an outsider."

I could be at Carter Tomlin's house now, Windermere thought. She swallowed her frustration. "Yes, sir."

"You keep to yourself. You haven't made any friends. You charge into investigations without regard for protocol or your other team members. You solved one high-profile case, and that's great, but this is a team game, Agent Windermere. You're still flying solo."

God damn it. "Yes, sir."

Harris stared at her for a long time. "What did you find?" he said finally.

Windermere blinked. "Pardon?"

"In Saint Paul, Agent Windermere. What did you find?"

Windermere glanced at Doughty. "I'm pretty sure our Eat Street ringleader has pulled solo jobs in the past," she told Harris. "I have a bunch of bank jobs around Minneapolis that match his MO."

"An earlier MO," said Doughty. "There's nothing in any of those cases about a team storming a bank with assault rifles and shotguns."

"No." Windermere nodded. "This is the first. I think he's getting braver—"

"Or he's a whole different person and your robberies aren't related."

Windermere gritted her teeth and focused on Harris. "Sir, I have enough information to make a link between the Eat Street robbery and these earlier scores, including a heist in a Bank of America branch in Midway last November. My suspect wrote his demand note on a receipt from the Saint Paul E-Z Park, and I've traced that receipt back to a man named Carter Tomlin."

Harris glanced at Doughty. Doughty took the cue. "I have credible information of my own," he said. "My contacts through Minneapolis PD tell me these guys are Eat Street local."

Harris nodded. "You have names?"

"Working on it."

Harris looked at Windermere again. "Carter Tomlin. Who is he?"

I could be finding that out right now, Windermere thought. "I was going to check him out before Doughty called me in. The guy lives in Saint Paul, has a Summit Avenue address."

Doughty laughed. "Summit Avenue. So he's got a million-dollar home and he's out robbing banks."

"Could be a credit card issue," Windermere told Harris. "Or our suspect got his hands on the receipt somehow. I thought I should talk to Tomlin, see if he could tell us anything."

"Agent Hill already worked the Midway case," said Doughty. "She didn't find much. These guys are lowlifes from the south. We knock on enough doors and we'll find them."

"You keep knocking on doors," said Windermere. "See where it gets you. I have six previous robberies to dig through. And I have Tomlin."

"You have a tattered receipt, Carla. It's not exactly the smoking gun."

"*Enough.*" Harris waited until Windermere and Doughty turned to face him. "You guys are partners," he said, his features drawn tight. "I expect a certain degree of professionalism."

Doughty nodded. "Yes, sir."

Windermere said nothing.

"Agent Doughty, you're running this case," Harris continued. "If you're sold on the southern angle, you keep working it. Ride those city cops and keep knocking on doors. Agent Windermere, I expect you to work with Agent Doughty, not against him."

Windermere stared at him. "And Carter Tomlin?"

"Tomlin's your baby," said Harris. "If you think you've got something, you follow it up on your own. But you make damn sure you respect Agent Doughty's seniority. If he asks you for help, his request takes priority. Understood?"

Windermere could see the end in sight. "Yes, sir," she said.

Harris nodded. "Dismissed."

22

ONE DAY AFTER meeting with Ernie Saint Louis in the federal pen in Waseca, Kirk Stevens packed up his Cherokee, kissed his wife good-bye, and drove the three hundred miles north to International Falls on the Canadian border. He checked himself into an empty motel alongside Route 53, and then drove to the town courthouse, where he found a young sheriff's deputy waiting.

The deputy's name was Waters, and he shivered as he climbed out of his vehicle, a county Chevy Suburban with two snowmobiles strapped to the trailer behind. He pulled his coat tight around him and looked sideways at Stevens. "Would be a lot easier if you wanted to wait for the thaw."

Stevens surveyed the parking lot. It was cold, barely ten degrees, and the wind seemed to cut right through his heavy goose-down parka. The town was bleak, grim, and gray, and Stevens knew the woods would be worse. In a couple months, though, the weather would warm and the snow would melt away, making the Thunderbird a hell of a lot easier to find.

Still, Stevens thought, there would be black flies.

In his head, he pictured Sylvia Danzer's photograph. The wry smile. He knew he didn't want to wait a couple of months to see if Saint Louis's sugar-high lead panned out. He cinched his coat tighter and looked at Waters. "We do this quick enough, we get back before the Timberwolves tip off."

Waters looked at him for a beat. Then he shrugged and turned back to the Suburban. "Your call."

WATERS DROVE WEST out of town on Route 71, running parallel to the Rainy River and the Canadian border. Stevens rode shotgun and stared down at the crude map Saint Louis had drawn, then out into the desolate bush. He looked over at Waters. "You get many people trying to hop the border, this part of the world?"

Waters glanced at him and shrugged. "Who knows?" he said. "Not like we can stop them when the river freezes over."

Stevens nodded. "Sure."

"Don't know where you'd go if you did cross," Waters said. He looked at Stevens again. "It's as empty over there as it is over here."

Waters drove west a while longer, over the top of the Smokey Bear State Forest, the highway almost at the riverbank now. On the other side, Canada was a formless mass of trees, deep-green and black where the land wasn't covered in snow. Waters pulled the truck over at the head of a narrow snowbound road. "Guess this is as far as we get with the truck."

They unloaded the snowmobiles from the trailer. Waters gave Stevens a helmet and a quick tutorial, and then climbed on his own machine, revved the engine, and sped off down the trail. Stevens watched him disappear, the snow like a rooster tail behind the machine. Then he gunned his own engine and started in pursuit.

The cold was unreal. Stevens gripped the handlebars tight and bent low, the bitter wind buffeting him through his parka, his borrowed ski pants covered in ice and slush. Waters rode fast as the road wound through the bush, and Stevens pushed hard to keep up. After a half hour or so of hard riding, Stevens rounded a corner and found Waters pulled to a stop by the tree line.

The road had narrowed into more of a trail now, the ground beneath the snow rocky and uneven, the naked trees encroaching. Waters flipped up his helmet and gestured farther. "Used to be a logging road," he said. "Nobody uses it but hunters and four-wheelers anymore."

And fugitives, Stevens thought. He flipped up his own helmet and sucked in the cold air. He realized he was sweating.

Waters gave it a moment. Then he flipped his helmet down and was off again, his snowmobile revving high-pitched and hysterical as he took off down the slim path. Stevens caught his breath and then bent down to his machine again.

The bush had taken over the terrain here. The trees seemed to close in on him over the trail, their loose branches clawing at his helmet and his parka as he sped between them after Waters. There was no room for any vehicle larger than an ATV, certainly not enough space for a T-Bird.

Twenty minutes through the trees and the trail started to widen again. Gradual, imperceptible, until it was probably wide enough to slide a Jeep through. Waters slowed his snowmobile to a stop, and Stevens stopped behind. His legs ached when he stood; he was thirsty. The woods were silent around them.

Waters took off his helmet and ran his hand through his hair. Looked at Stevens, and then around the forest. "I'm guessing this is the general area," he said. "Going to take some searching, though."

Stevens pulled Saint Louis's map from his pocket. "A fork in the road," he said. "Just after the trail opens up again."

Waters pointed. "Just down there."

They walked down the trail about a hundred yards. Stevens peered in through the trees as they walked, searching for red paint.

The forest was dense, inscrutable. Anything beyond ten or fifteen feet would be invisible.

A hundred yards down, and the trail joined with another bearing from the northeast. Stevens walked to the fork and peered up the new trail. A wall of trees, impassable. Still, as he walked forward, his boots sinking deep in the snow, Stevens could see something half-lodged in the tree line, a snow-covered hulk hidden around a brief corner.

He walked closer. The hulk was buried in snow. It looked angular, though, geometric and unnatural. Stevens looked back to where Waters waited at the fork and then pressed forward, his heart starting to pound.

It was a car. He could see that from about ten feet away. It lay wedged between two young birch trees, as though the driver had tried to force her way through. Stevens covered the last distance quickly. He brushed the snow from the rear bumper and stared down at rust and red paint. A Ford logo.

He looked back at Waters again. Saint Louis wasn't lying. A red Thunderbird, lost in the woods. Now, where the hell was the driver?

23

TOMLIN STOOD IN his model train room, watching a long freight wind its way through the mountains. It was long past midnight by now; the house was silent above him. The little electric motors in the model locomotives sounded like diesel engines as the train rolled across the layout.

Tomlin's body was tired. His mind, though, couldn't slow down. Every time he closed his eyes, he saw the Eat Street robbery, a few days ago now but still fresh. He could feel the big assault rifle explode in his hands as he fired that burst into the ceiling. Could still see the pretty young teller trembling as she emptied her till, her eyes pleading with him not to shoot her.

The money's good, Tomlin thought. *The money buys the whole family a couple months, worry-free. The bank teller, though, and the gun?*

Tomlin shivered.

He parked the freight train in the Minneapolis yard and started up a passenger express for another loop. Thought about Tricia as the train picked up speed. For all of his misgivings, his spiky-haired punk-rock princess had come through as advertised. Brought him to her apartment a few days after the deal with Javier, introduced him to Dragan, a quiet Serbian kid with acne scars and a close-cropped haircut. *He looks like a basketball player,* Tomlin thought. *Or a rebel soldier in some woebegone Baltic state.*

"How do you know him?" Tomlin had asked her, when Dragan had ducked out, his mother on the phone.

Tricia shrugged. "I just know him," she said. "You ask so many questions."

"I'm hiring him to rob banks," Tomlin told her. "I'm allowed to ask questions."

Tricia glanced after Dragan. Then she sighed. "We went to the same high school," she said. "He used to drive for his big brother's crew. They took down a bunch of liquor stores in my neighborhood before they got caught. Dragan was young, so they let him out early. He's cool, boss. You can trust him."

"Are you two together?"

She gave him her funny smile. "Sometimes," she said.

He'd watched her eyes go wide when he'd brought out the guns. Frowned when she picked up the shotgun. "Careful with that," he told her.

Tricia scoffed. "You be careful," she said. "I'm no virgin."

"It's a big gun."

"My dad's a gun freak," she said. "Used to take me hunting. You ever want any pointers with this baby, let me know."

He let her keep the shotgun—or, rather, she claimed it, leaving Tomlin to get used to the rifle. The thing made his stomach churn, its purpose explicit and its menace undisguised. He'd stared at it for hours, almost afraid to hold it. Then he'd carried the gun into the First Minnesota branch and fired that first burst through the ceiling, and instantly his misgivings vanished. The building seemed to shake on its foundation. The bank tellers cowered, and he felt like a god. A god with a really big gun.

Tomlin watched the passenger train come speeding out of the mountains, toward the city. It passed the munitions factory, where he'd hidden the shotgun shells, and slowed for a stop at the big Saint Paul station.

Tomlin parked the train and turned off the engines. He shut off the lights and went upstairs and slipped into bed beside Becca, listening to his wife's breathing and forcing himself to wipe the robbery from his mind. Forcing himself to stop thinking about the money and Tricia and the terrified bank teller. He imagined he was on a train somewhere, in a sleeping car speeding through the night, and soon he was drifting off, picturing in his mind a late-night station stop, the clatter of the wheels on the tracks, a munitions factory dark in the distance.

24

STEVENS STARED AT the snow-covered hulk. Brushed more snow from the trunk, his gloves coming back rusty. The car had been here awhile.

He pulled off one glove and reached into his pocket and came out with a photocopy from the Danzers' case file. Glanced at their Thunderbird's registration and then knelt at the rear bumper and brushed the snow from the license plate. The plate was still there. He glanced at the photocopy again. The license plate matched.

Stevens stared at the car, his mind spinning with questions. Then he looked back to where Waters stood by the fork in the trail. "This is it," he called back. His voice seemed to echo for miles. "This is my car."

Waters stared at him a moment. Then he started toward the Thunderbird. Stevens turned back to the hulk and studied it again. Sylvia Danzer's car, marooned in the wilderness. *How in the hell did it get here?*

Waters arrived beside him. "Not the best road for a T-Bird."

"The plates match," Stevens said. "This is my fugitive's car."

Waters leaned forward and brushed snow from the bodywork. "So where's your fugitive?"

Stevens looked beyond the car and into the vast woods. "Could be anywhere."

"Probably long gone," said Waters. "Crashed the car here and set out on foot. Bummed a ride on the highway and disappeared again, right?"

"Maybe." Stevens studied the snow-covered windows again. "Or maybe not."

He stepped through the snow to the driver's-side door. Wiped the snow from the window and peered into the dark car. He squinted and looked closer. Waters watched him. "You see something?"

Stevens looked in through the window one more time. "We're going to want to call forensics," he told Waters. "It doesn't look like my fugitive got very far."

25

TOMLIN WOKE WITH the sun shining bright through the bedroom windows and the bed empty beside him. He sat up, rubbing his eyes, and glanced at the clock on the bedside table. Ten after eight. He'd be late for work, he knew, but he didn't care. He stared up at the ceiling and felt himself drifting off again.

Then Becca came into the bedroom, a strange look on her face. "Time to get up," she said. "Someone's at the door."

Tomlin opened his eyes. "Who?"

"A woman." Becca shrugged. "She's asking for you."

Tomlin rubbed his eyes again. *Tricia, probably.* "Tell her one minute." He sat up and pulled on his clothes from the day before. Brushed his teeth quickly, splashed cold water on his face, and examined himself in the mirror. Dark circles under his eyes. Maybe a couple new wrinkles. Otherwise, he looked normal. Likable. He buttoned his shirt and walked out to the hallway.

She was waiting in the front landing as he walked down the stairs. About halfway down, he knew it wasn't Tricia. Tricia was short and white and skinny and dressed like a punk rocker. This woman wore dressy low heels and slacks. She was taller than Tricia, and in her thirties, but just, with smooth coffee-brown skin and long black hair and piercing hazel eyes that watched him as though they already knew every one of his secrets. Tomlin felt a sudden chill as her eyes met his.

"Carter Tomlin," she said. "Carla Windermere. Got a couple questions to ask you."

She showed him a badge. FBI. Tomlin looked at the woman and then at her badge again, fighting the sudden, intense urge to start running.

26

TOMLIN STARED AT the young FBI agent in his doorway, his mouth suddenly very dry. *She knows*, he thought. *She knows everything.* He cleared his throat. "Questions," he said. "What's the problem?"

Windermere smiled, apologetic. "Sorry to bother you so early," she said. "Looks like you had a late night."

Tomlin forced a laugh. "Just busy," he said. "Tax season's coming. Everybody and their dog wants their refund tomorrow."

"You're an accountant."

"I try to be," he said. "Come on in."

He led her into the living room, and they sat as Becca came in from the kitchen. "Everything all right?"

Sure, honey. The nice FBI lady is just going to arrest me and take away all of your stuff. Tomlin pasted a smile on his face. "Everything's fine."

Becca looked at Windermere. "Would you like some coffee?"

"I'm fine," Windermere replied, her eyes still on Tomlin.

"Maybe I'll have a coffee." Tomlin stood. "Back in a second."

"Actually, Mr. Tomlin, this will only take a minute."

Tomlin stopped and looked back at the agent. She gave him the same apologetic smile. "I just need a few answers, and then you can get back to your business."

Tomlin looked at Becca, then back to the agent, wondering how fast he could cover the distance to the basement and his guns. Becca touched his shoulder, and he flinched. "I'll make you some coffee," she said.

Tomlin hesitated. Then he sat down again and looked at Windermere. "What did you say was the problem, exactly?"

"Bank robberies. Maybe you've heard about them. The one on Eat Street a couple of days ago. I'm trying to follow up on a lead."

"You're not going to tell me I'm a suspect."

Windermere smiled. "To be honest, Mr. Tomlin, we don't have any suspects. Not yet."

"Good." Tomlin held her gaze for a second or two before he had to look away. He laughed. "I mean, not good for you guys, but, you know. Good that I'm not a suspect."

Shut up. He turned away from those hypnotic eyes and stared out the front window instead, across the lawn to where Windermere's dark sedan sat parked by the curb. He tented his fingers. "So what does this all have to do with me?"

Windermere reached into her pocket and pulled out a folded piece of paper. She unfolded it and slid it across the coffee table toward Tomlin. "Take a look," she said. "Tell me what you think."

Tomlin picked up the paper. A photocopy of another piece of paper, smaller, both sides. A receipt; he recognized it. His shaky handwriting. Two sentences. He remembered scribbling out the words on the Jaguar's cherry dash in that Walmart parking lot in Midway. Tomlin steadied his breathing. "From the robbery?"

"Not Eat Street. A Bank of America in Midway. You see the flip side?"

Tomlin nodded, aware of how intently she studied his face. The parking receipt had been the only scrap of paper he could find.

"I talked to the attendants at that parking garage," said Windermere. "They pointed me here. Said you paid for that receipt with your credit card."

Tomlin nodded again. *Think carefully, now.* He glanced back toward the kitchen. *Where the hell was Becca with that coffee?*

"It's definitely my receipt," he told her, pretending to study the note. "I would have parked there that day."

"You work downtown?"

"Worked. I opened my own shop in the fall." He held up the paper. "Moved across to Lowertown. Park on the street."

"Uh-huh." She leaned forward again. "So, okay, listen. This is your receipt. How did it get into a Midway bank robbery?"

Tomlin shook his head. "No idea."

"Your car wasn't broken into at any point last summer?"

He started to tell her no. Then he stopped. Nodded slowly. "Yeah," he said. "Yeah, it was. That same parking garage, too. Funny thing."

Windermere gave it a beat. "Funny thing," she said finally. "You filed a police report?"

"They didn't take much," he said, thinking fast. "Just the change from my glove box. I figured they must have been addicts or something."

"And the receipt was in there, too."

"Must have been," he said. "The worst part was trying to fix that damn window. Cost nearly a grand at the end of the day."

Windermere nodded again. "You got it fixed where?"

Tomlin pretended to think. "One of those shops," he said, frowning. "Those auto glass shops. I don't remember which one."

"You keep a receipt or anything?"

He shrugged. "I can check."

"Do that." She smiled at him again. "It would really help me out."

"I'll be in touch," he said, standing. "Do you have a card?"

She stood quickly, digging in her wallet as they walked back out to the landing. She handed him a business card. "Call me anytime. We get that receipt, we cross you off our list of names."

"I thought you didn't have suspects."

She stopped on the front steps and smiled back at him. "We don't, Mr. Tomlin. Not yet."

Then she turned away, and Tomlin watched her walk down to her sedan and climb behind the wheel. She shot him a half wave from the driver's seat and then pulled away from the curb, and Tomlin exhaled as she disappeared down the street.

Becca was just coming into the living room with a tray full of coffee mugs when he walked in from the landing. "Where did she go?" she said, frowning.

Tomlin shrugged. "She left."

"Oh." Becca put down her tray. "Well, what did she want?"

He glanced out the window, toward the empty spot where Windermere had parked her sedan. "Something about a bank robbery," he said. "A misunderstanding." He turned away from the window and walked to the stairs.

"Don't you want your coffee?"

Tomlin didn't look back. "I'm going to be late for work," he told her, as he climbed the stairs. Stopped halfway up to lean against the wall and steady his thoughts, the FBI agent's piercing stare still burning into his eyes like a sunspot.

27

WINDERMERE PARKED the Crown Vic off Summit Avenue and sat back in the seat. She grinned at herself in the rearview mirror. *Carter Tomlin,* she thought. *You are so made.*

He was a rich man. Had a beautiful wife. Kids, too, and a cute yellow dog, judging from the pictures on the mantle. Your everyday American success story, pretty much. He even looked like an accountant, for God's sake: attractive, kind of boring. Harmless.

Still, the guy was so guilty he reeked. Same build as the bank robber from Midway and Prospect Park. Same icy blue eyes as the psycho from Eat Street. He'd squirmed and flushed as they talked, tried and failed to play innocent, fed her some bullshit story about his car getting robbed.

Didn't happen.

The way he'd latched on to that story, clung to it like a lifeline, she'd known he was her guy. Gave her some vague excuse, no details. Promised to get her a receipt they both knew he didn't have.

Windermere sat in the Crown Vic, staring out at the snowy street. *What a neighborhood.* Old mansions and vast lawns and European cars in the driveways. *What a neighborhood.*

Tomlin had changed jobs. Moved across to Lowertown. Cheaper

rents. Cheaper parking. Maybe money was tight. The mortgage on a house like his wouldn't come cheap. Maybe he had to rob banks to survive.

Harris and Doughty wouldn't buy it, she knew. Doughty, especially. And from the looks of things, Harris sided with the senior man—though whether the operative word was *senior* or *man* was still up for debate. Either way, they'd see the receipt as circumstantial, which it was. They wouldn't know Tomlin, wouldn't have seen him. If they saw him, they would know he was guilty.

Windermere watched as a big Mercedes-Benz cruised by, an unhappy woman at the wheel, a couple of angry kids in the back. *Good luck getting Doughty to agree to come out here,* she thought. *He's like a dog with a bone with that southern Minneapolis angle.*

Still, she had to try.

Windermere pulled out her cell phone and called her partner. "You just about done over there?" he said, when he came on the line. "Could use your help back at home base."

"Yeah," she said. "Listen, I have news."

"So do I. You're headed back?"

"Tomlin's an accountant," she said. "He's guilty as sin. Tried to feed me some line about his car being robbed, but he was sweating like an athlete the whole time. He's lying. I know it."

Doughty grunted. "How soon can you be here?"

"He's our guy, Bob," she said. "You don't believe me, but this guy bleeds guilty. Come out to his place and you'll see it."

"He's not our guy," Doughty said.

Windermere started to reply. Then she stopped.

"I have something better, Agent Windermere." She could hear the smile in his voice now, smug. "One of my Minneapolis PD contacts threw me a lead. Southern Minneapolis, just like I've been saying. Fits the profile to a T."

"Your profile," said Windermere.

"Our profile," said Doughty. "This guy's a career criminal. Some lowlife out in Phillips. Been throwing money around lately, bragging about a bank job. I looked him up in the database, found B and E's, assaults, grand theft auto. He's a pro. And he lives within driving range of every heist we've tracked."

Doughty paused, let it sink in. "This is our guy, Agent Windermere. Now come on back to base and we can take this guy down. I've already cleared it with Harris."

Windermere said nothing.

Doughty cleared his throat. "You there, Agent Windermere?"

Goddamn, how she wanted to wipe the smile from his face. "I'm here, Bob," she said, and sighed. She shifted into drive and pulled away from the curb, watching Tomlin's house disappear in the rearview mirror. "I'm headed back now. Give me a half hour or so."

28

TOMLIN LOCKED THE door to his office, turned out the lights, and retreated into his sanctum. He sat in the dark and stared out the pillbox window at the gray sky beyond.

He'd been stupid. Of course the FBI would trace the parking receipt back. Even a complete moron could have seen it.

He'd been so nervous on that first job. Hadn't been thinking clearly. He'd snatched up the first piece of paper he could find. He had scanned the receipt for his name and, not finding it, had assumed he was safe. He'd been stupid. And now the FBI was onto him.

Tomlin stood and walked to the dirty window and opened it, letting the cold winter air rush into the room. He stood at the window and stared down through the grime at the alley below. *It's only a receipt,* he told himself. *Purely circumstantial. You figure out a way to fake a record of that break-in and you're golden.*

Still, he thought, the fresh air sending a chill across his skin, *if they go back to the Midway job and start asking questions, you're screwed. What if someone remembers seeing a Jaguar drive off? What if the bank teller remembers your voice?* Tomlin realized he was shivering, the sweat on the back of his neck cold and clammy. He closed the window and sat down in his chair again.

He wanted to run. He had cash and ammunition and a super-charged car. He could bundle Becca and the girls up and drive north, right now, to the Canadian border. Get out of the States and try and disappear into the woods. Or simply ditch the Jag, sell it cheap for quick cash, buy everyone plane tickets somewhere warm. An impromptu vacation, forever. What would Becca say?

Tomlin booted up his computer and opened an Internet window. Typed Carla Windermere's name into the Google search window and got an FBI page with her picture on it, her stare almost as piercing in pixelated form, and then a bunch of news articles about a previous case.

It had been a big one. Tomlin clicked through to the first article, and then he remembered. Windermere was the cop who took down Terry Harper's kidnappers, those psycho kids in Detroit. Tomlin remembered reading about her, back when the case broke, almost wishing Harper had stayed kidnapped. Windermere had broken the case, killed the ringleader in a shoot-out, and sent his two partners to jail. And now here she was, working Tomlin's bank robbery spree.

Tomlin shivered again and read on with a sick fascination. Windermere had been paired with an agent at the Bureau of Criminal Apprehension, Kirk Stevens. It had been Stevens who'd made the big breakthrough, connecting Harper's kidnappers to a murder a week later in suburban Detroit.

Tomlin sat back in his chair. Kirk Stevens. In the article there was a picture of Windermere and the BCA agent, taken after the big shoot-out in Detroit. Windermere looked proud, almost defiant. Stevens looked tired and sheepish. Tomlin stared at Stevens's picture and wondered how he recognized the name.

Elliott and Sylvia Danzer, he thought. *That's the cop.*

The BCA agent had interviewed him a few weeks prior. Called him at home, scared the shit out of him. He was taking another look at the Danzer case, he'd said. Wanted to know if the Danzers had

had money trouble. If money could have been a motive for Elliott Danzer's murder, in Tomlin's professional opinion.

Tomlin had tried to help him, once he calmed down. Told Stevens he didn't think so, not from what he'd seen of their finances. The agent had thanked him, said good-bye. The whole call took maybe ten minutes.

Tomlin stared at the picture of Stevens some more. *Strange coincidence*, he decided. *I guess Saint Paul's not really so big.* He focused on Windermere again. He shivered. Even her picture made him nervous. He clicked the page closed. Then he opened a new search window and Googled Saint Paul auto glass shops, looking for the sketchiest, most cash-starved businesses he could find.

Get Windermere that proof and she'll back off your ass. Tomlin picked up his phone and started dialing numbers.

29

STEVENS SPENT THE night at the Silver Birch Motel in International Falls. The sheriff's office in town wasn't equipped for a detailed crime scene analysis, so Stevens and Waters had returned to town to wait out the arrival of the BCA's own forensics team in the morning. Stevens had a bowl of soup and a long, hot shower, and then he sat in the motel room and turned on the basketball game and thought about what he'd seen in the woods.

He'd avoided touching the Thunderbird any more than he needed to, not wanting to contaminate the crime scene. But he'd looked through the driver's-side window a couple more times, just enough to be sure that what he was seeing was a person. Or what was left of a person, anyway.

The body was blackened and bone, barely more than a skeleton and a few tatters of clothing. It sat curled up in the driver's seat in a kind of fetal position, its sex unknowable, its cause of death anything but certain.

Sylvia Danzer murders her husband, Stevens thought. *Leaves him to die in Moose Lake. Then she drives north and gets stuck on some lonely logging road in the middle of the forest. Doesn't try to keep going. Waits in her car to die.*

He watched the game without seeing it, thinking about Danzer and the abandoned T-Bird. Wondered what the forensics team would find when they examined the car in the morning. He thought about Sylvia Danzer and her husband, and wondered what had led them to murder.

The motel room was lonely, and Stevens's thoughts were bleak. He picked up the phone and called Nancy. "Hey, cowboy," she said, when she answered. "You miss me yet?"

"I'm in a sleazy motel room," he told her. "Just your kind of place."

Nancy laughed. "Maybe you'll take me there for our anniversary."

"Roger that. This place is a real winter wonderland. Nothing to do but hide out until thaw."

"Doesn't sound so bad." She paused. "Everything all right?"

"Sure," he said. "Why?"

"There's a hitch in your voice," she said. "You're not getting into any more hero stuff, are you?"

"Hero stuff." He smiled a little. "Not this time." He told her about the case. Elliott Danzer in Moose Lake. His wife in the woods. "These people weren't that much older than us, Nance."

"I remember when it happened," Nancy said. "You think the wife did it?"

"Don't know," he said. "I guess we find out tomorrow."

"Find out quick. We all miss you."

"Sure," Stevens said. "You probably won't murder me for a couple more years."

"If you're lucky," she said. "I'd get away with it, too. None of that getting stuck in the woods for this girl."

"That's a comfort. I guess I'll see you tomorrow."

"Your daughter has a basketball game at eight, if you think you can make it. Come and meet the new coach."

"Sure," Stevens said. "I'll show him the badge and the gun. Make sure he knows Andrea Stevens should be starting."

"You big bully. I knew there was a reason I married a cop."

"Thought it was my stunning physique." Stevens paused. "I'll try and make it. Been a while since I caught a game."

"Make it happen," said Nancy. "We'll see you tomorrow."

They told each other good night, and Stevens hung up the phone. He lay back on the bed and listened to the wind howl outside, and he thought about the Danzers some more.

30

THE FORENSICS TEAM showed up in the morning. Waters drove the Suburban south this time, took the county road west and met the trail at the southern end. There was a big snowplow waiting at the trailhead, and Waters pulled in to follow with the BCA van behind him, and they formed a slow convoy up into the bush.

They were still a mile or so out when the snowplow had to quit. The driver stopped the truck and leaned out of the cab. "Too narrow," he told Waters. "Good thing you brought those machines."

They readied the snowmobiles as the forensics team unloaded the van. There were two of them, a man and a woman, and they climbed on the back of the Ski-Doos with their kits as Waters and Stevens settled in to drive.

The technician gripped Stevens tight as he sped through the forest after Waters. Shouted something in his ear that Stevens didn't catch. And then they arrived at the fork in the trail and the abandoned Thunderbird, and Stevens helped the technician peel her hands from around his stomach and stood again on unsteady legs, looking in at the car.

He waited with Waters as the techs went to work. Hung back as they opened the driver's-side door and peered in. He still caught the scent drifting out of the car, noxious and permeating, two years of decay suddenly unsealed to the world. The techs set their jaws and started to work. Stevens watched them and paced to stay warm.

The female tech came back after a half hour or so. "Been there awhile," she said, grim. "You can forget the autopsies."

"Autopsies," Stevens said.

The tech nodded. "We'll have to ferry them back on the snow-mobiles, I guess. No other way to get back here."

Stevens stared at her. "Them."

"The front seat and the back." She cocked her head at him. "There's two of them in there, Agent. Is that news?"

31

WINDERMERE SAT IN the passenger seat of Doughty's Crown Vic, staring out at a patched-up stucco building on a street corner in Phillips. In the driver's seat, Doughty unwrapped a meatball sub. "Told you this guy was local," he said.

The building was a gray two-story cube, the paint old and uneven. It looked like it had been a garage once, or a storefront or something, before someone with more ambition than cash converted it into housing. Now it apparently housed Nolan Jackson, a thirty-five-year-old career criminal and alleged bank robber.

The location was good, she had to admit. Phillips was a high-crime neighborhood barely a mile east of Eat Street, and only a couple miles southwest of Prospect Park. Perfect positioning for most of the robberies. "How the hell would a Phillips guy get his hands on Tomlin's receipt, though?" she asked Doughty.

Doughty took a bite of his meatball sub. Sauce dribbled down his chin, and he wiped it away with the back of his hand. "Your guy said he was robbed, didn't he?"

"He was lying."

Doughty chewed. "Are you sure?"

Windermere said nothing. This morning, talking to Tomlin, she'd been sure. Now, after looking at Jackson's file, after stepping back and looking at Tomlin, a boring-ass accountant with a family and an expensive home, she could almost see Doughty's point. Almost.

"So, what," she said, "this guy Jackson just breaks into Tomlin's car for the parking receipt and a handful of quarters? He's a grand-theft-auto guy looking at a ninety-thousand-dollar Jag, and he's already inside. Doesn't he roll with it?"

"Maybe he found the receipt on the street. Picked it out of the trash or something," said Doughty. "It's not a case-breaker." He finished his sub. Checked himself in the rearview mirror. Wiped his chin again, and then turned to Windermere. "You ready?"

They strapped on Kevlar vests as they started toward the gray building. A car passed them, an Oldsmobile with a couple of rowdy kids inside. The driver honked the horn and the kids inside laughed, and Windermere shivered. She felt for her Glock in its holster and looked at Doughty. "We have tactical support here, right?"

Doughty nodded. "One block over. We say the word and they're with us." He stepped to the door, drew himself up, and knocked. Three times, and loud. No one answered.

Doughty knocked again. "Nolan Jackson," he said. "Federal agents. Open this door."

A door slammed somewhere around the back of the building. Doughty looked at Windermere. "Back door," he said. "Check it out."

Windermere nodded and hurried along the side of the house. Made the corner just in time to see someone hop a fence and start running. She gave chase. "*Stop! FBI!*"

The guy shouted something over his shoulder, kept running. She chased him fifteen or twenty yards. Then she slowed. *He's just a kid*, she realized. *Twelve or thirteen at most.* She let the kid go. Turned back to the house just in time for the shooting to start.

Two shots, from the front of the house. Then another. A window shattered. Windermere ran, swearing, drawing her Glock from its holster. She heard another shot, like a firecracker—*POP*—and then she reached the end of the alley and turned toward the front steps. Looked up at the front stoop and swore again, louder.

The front door was open. Doughty was gone.

32

WINDERMERE STARED AT the empty front stoop. "Doughty," she said. "*Damn it.*"

Two more shots from inside the house. Another window shattered. She heard Doughty shout something. Couldn't make it out.

Windermere pulled out her radio. Called in for tactical. Then she ducked her head and peered into the house, waiting for the shot that would put her on her ass. "Doughty," she called. "Where the hell are you?"

Another shot, like an exclamation mark. Then Doughty: "*Kitchen.*"

"How many are there?"

"Just one, I think." He sounded desperate. "He's got me pinned down, though."

Shit.

Windermere crept through the doorway. The house was dark. A TV played infomercials off to her right. Dead ahead was the hallway, and at the end of it, light. Windermere pressed her back to the wall and crept forward. Outside, the tactical van squealed to a stop. Sirens and doors slamming. The cavalry a couple seconds away.

"In here." Doughty's voice, from the back of the house. From the light.

Windermere moved slow, working her way down the hall. About halfway and she saw movement at the end, a gun. A moment later, Jackson opened fire.

Windermere ducked into a side room. Waited until the shooting stopped. Then she leaned out again and peered down the hallway. No sign of Jackson. No sign of the gun. "Nolan," she said. "Let's just calm down a second."

"Fuck you."

Three more shots. Windermere ducked back again. "You hear those sirens?" she called out. "Those are for you, Nolan. In a second this place will be crawling with SWAT."

Silence from the kitchen. Dust hung in the air.

"I kill you both, I can still make it out of here." Jackson's voice was ragged, on edge. All false bravado and fear masked as anger.

"I don't think so," she said. "You kill two FBI agents, the whole country comes after you. You give up right now and it gets a lot easier."

Another pause. She could hear him moving around the kitchen. "FBI," he said. "What the hell do you want?"

Windermere started to answer. Doughty beat her to it. "Bank robbery, Nolan. It's a federal crime."

Jackson swore. "Oh," he said. "Oh, shit."

"'Oh, shit' is right. You screwed up, buddy."

Windermere crept out of the side room, started down the hall to the kitchen again. *Something doesn't jibe here,* she thought. She heard movement behind her. Turned to see the tactical squad in the doorway, masks and machine guns. Made eye contact with the team leader, motioned to the kitchen. The team leader nodded, turned back to his men. Sent a squad of them around the back of the house.

Windermere watched them through those yawning front windows. Then she turned back toward the kitchen. "Doughty," she called. "Tactical's here. Stand down and we'll let them sort it out."

"*Motherfuck*," Jackson said.

Doughty laughed. "That's right, buddy. You're toast."

"*Doughty.*"

"One bank, you cocksucker. I never even—"

BOOM.

Windermere ran down the hallway. Burst into the kitchen, gun raised. Found Doughty standing upright by the fridge, breathing hard. Jackson on his back on dirty linoleum, a bloody hole in his chest. Windermere ran to the suspect, kicked his pistol away. Knelt beside him and looked up at Doughty. "I said tactical had it," she said. "What the hell, Bob?"

Sounds from the hallway. Jackboots on hardwood. The back door shattered open, and the tactical team burst into the kitchen, machine guns at the ready. Took in Doughty and Windermere and Jackson on the floor.

Windermere stared at Doughty. Doughty shrugged. "Had a shot," he said. "Had to take it."

Windermere shook her head. Looked at Jackson. He was a lanky guy, hard-edged and lean. He looked up at Windermere, his blue eyes open wide, his breathing ragged. "We're all right," Doughty told the tactical team. "Everything's under control."

Windermere watched as Jackson's breathing faltered. Watched those blue eyes go glassy. *Everything's fine, Bob*, she thought. *Just perfect. Except you just killed your big goddamn suspect.*

33

STEVENS STARED IN through the window at the backseat of
the Thunderbird, his sleeve over his face to mask the smell
from inside the car. "Two of them," the tech said beside him. "You
see her?"

Stevens nodded. "So who the hell's in the front seat?"

There were two skeletons in the Thunderbird. The first in the
driver's seat, the one Stevens had seen. The second lay across
the backseat. The techs figured the second was Sylvia Danzer. She
wore what remained of a synthetic North Face ski jacket, bright yellow. It was the same jacket listed in the missing person's description.
She looked small. The first skeleton looked bigger.

Stevens had been staring into the car for half an hour now, trying to get a feel for the scene as the techs worked around him. There
was a yellowed state map on the backseat beside the second body,
folded open to Koochiching County. There was an empty plastic
package of almonds, and what looked to Stevens like the remains of
a fire.

And then there was the knife lodged inside the first skeleton's
jacket.

The techs had noticed it as they'd photographed the scene. A hunting knife, plunged in to the hilt, chest level, slightly skewed to the left. Almost as though the passenger had leaned over and stabbed the driver.

She stabbed him, Stevens thought. *Then he crashed the car. No.* Rust aside, the front of the T-Bird was nearly pristine. It was the quarter panels that were scratched and dented. The driver had aimed between the two trees and then marooned the car. He would have had to drive slowly to get as far as he did.

He got stuck, Stevens thought. *Then she killed him. And then what?* She'd stayed in the car, eating packaged almonds and huddling around a small fire. Eventually, the food ran out, or the battery died and the night got too cold. She didn't set out for safety. She waited, and she died. *She killed this guy here almost definitely,* Stevens thought. *So what does that mean for her husband?*

This guy killed him. Or she killed him and ran away with this guy. Maybe. Or maybe we never find out for certain.

The tech cleared her throat. Stevens turned. "We're about ready to start moving them," she said. "I mean, if you're done with the scene."

Stevens took one last look inside. He shivered. "Sure," he said, stepping back from the door. "Let's get them out of here and go home."

34

TONY SCHULTZ STOOD in his kitchen, a pile of money on the Formica table, a smaller pile of rubber bands beside. He counted the bills into thousand-dollar stacks, wrapped the stacks in rubber bands, and set them aside. It was tedious work, a long fucking job, and even when he'd finished, Schultz knew he wouldn't have nearly enough to pay off the Mexicans.

Ricky had shown up the morning before. Schultz watched his big Cadillac truck bounce and jostle down the snowy dirt driveway to the house. He watched Ricky climb from the truck. Watched the driver climb out, too—a big fucker in a down jacket, probably a pistol or two underneath.

Schultz had toyed with the idea of shooting the spics, greeting them at the door with the TEC-9 he'd bought after the robbery, showing those brown fuckers who really was boss. He stayed put, though. Left the gun in the locker. Even if he killed Ricky, the Mexicans would send someone else. Better to try and talk things out.

Ricky didn't bother to knock. "Yo," he said, poking his head in the house. "Tony."

Schultz walked into the front landing as Ricky walked past him, into the living room. The fucker didn't bother to take off his boots, left a slushy track from the door to the couch. Schultz followed him back. Sat down opposite. The driver stood behind him and out of sight, the implication clear. "You know why I'm here," Ricky said.

Schultz shook his head. "I don't have it."

Ricky glanced at the driver. Schultz braced himself, but the hit never came. Ricky sat back on the couch. "You owe fifty thousand, straight up. Plus twenty for the brick. That makes seventy thousand."

"I told you," Schultz said. "I got robbed."

Ricky made a face. "Someone steals seventy grand in this little pissant town, you can't figure out who's the bad guy?"

"The guy came from Minneapolis," Schultz told him. "I'm working on it."

"Been fucking two months, Tony." Ricky looked at the driver again. This time, the blow came. When Schultz opened his eyes, he was on the floor of his living room, his face on fire in one of Ricky's slushy footprints. Ricky stood over him. "Try harder," he said.

NOW SCHULTZ STOOD in his kitchen, stacking money. He figured he had maybe eight or nine grand, the last payoffs from old drug deals and gambling debts. All of it wrinkled, five- and ten-dollar bills, a kitchen table's worth of dirty money and none of it worth spit to the spics.

Seventy grand. Bad enough that asshole Brill had taken his guns, knocked out his teeth. The money, though, and the drugs: that was a death sentence. There was no way he could come up with that kind of cash.

Unless he could find Roger Brill.

Schultz thought about it for a while. Had a bad idea, and pushed it aside. Thought about it some more, and couldn't come up with better. So he picked up the kitchen phone and dialed Hastings PD. Asked for his brother-in-law. "It's me," Schultz told him. "You busy?"

"Just about to head out on patrol. This important?"

"Life or death."

Scotty paused. "Gimme one second."

Schultz waited. Looked out the kitchen window at the snowy front field, the highway in the distance. Contemplated making a break for it. *If I can't find Roger Brill*, he thought, *I might just have to start running.*

Scotty came back. "Yeah," he said. "What's up?"

"I need help," Schultz told him. "That robbery of mine. I need to find the guy that did it. Roger Brill is his name."

Scotty sucked his teeth. "Probably not much anybody can do now. Not this long after the fact."

"It's assault," Schultz said. "Guy put me in the hospital."

"Chris Russell said you chased her off your property when she tried for a statement," Scotty said. "I can't imagine she'd be inclined to come back."

Tony stared out the window. "I need to find this guy, Scotty. I don't have time for fucking around."

Scotty said nothing.

"This is personal, man. This is more than just guns."

Another pause. Then Scotty grunted. "I'll talk to Russell," he said. "See if she's got any time. That's the best I can do."

Schultz mulled it over. "God damn it."

"You gotta talk to her this time. And clean yourself up. You get pinched cause of something she finds, they'll put you on *World's Dumbest Criminals.*"

Schultz spat in his sink. "Who're you talking to?"

"Some punk got robbed by a city boy, I guess."

"Fuck you." Schultz hung up the phone. He stared out the window a moment longer, then turned back to the pathetic pile of money on his kitchen table. *I need Roger Brill*, he thought. *That cop better find him, or I'm fucked.*

35

THE DEAD GUY in the Thunderbird was a real piece of work.

The techs told Stevens a DNA check would take at least a couple of days. Not much hope for a credible cause of death. Figured, off the record, the guy in the driver's seat died because of the knife in his chest, and the woman probably died of exposure. But nothing for certain, not yet and maybe not ever.

They found wallets, though; half-eaten leather and laminated IDs. The tech called Stevens back around lunchtime the next day, caught him pulling into a diner headed southbound on Route 53. "The woman in the backseat has Sylvia Danzer's ID," she told him. "So it's probably her, like you thought."

Stevens parked the Cherokee. "What about the driver?"

"The driver." The tech paused. "Yeah, that guy's the real story."

The driver's ID read David Allen Samson. The tech had run the name through the FBI's national database. Forty-three years old; spent ten years of his life in prison. Manslaughter and aggravated sexual assault, a litany of assault charges, battery and the like. He'd been out of the federal jail in Sandstone three weeks when the Danzers had disappeared.

"Sandstone's on I-35," Stevens said. "Pretty close to Moose Lake."

"Makes things a bit clearer, doesn't it?"

Stevens stared out at the diner. "Maybe."

"We'll work on the DNA, anyway. Get this thing closed. You sticking around?"

"Already gone," Stevens told her. "My girl's got a basketball game." He ended the call and sat in the Cherokee for a bit, staring out at the diner. *It was a place kind of like this one,* he thought, *where they found Elliott Danzer.*

He pushed the thought from his mind. Went inside and ate lunch and tried to forget about it. Later, though, on the long drive down 35 back toward Saint Paul, Stevens passed the diner at Moose Lake and, a while later, the turnoff to the jail at Sandstone, and he turned down the radio and thought things over again.

Simplest solution said David Samson murdered Elliott Danzer and took off with the wife. Headed north, possibly for the border, and got lost on a back road, got stuck. Maybe Sylvia Danzer saw a chance and she took it. When Samson was dead, she realized she was lost. Could do nothing but wait to be found.

The wind howled outside, rocking the Cherokee, blowing snow across the highway. It had been a hell of a winter, the year that the Danzers disappeared. If Sylvia Danzer got stuck in a blizzard with a dead battery, she was done.

Stevens tried to picture the woman huddled in her backseat, working on a little fire as the wind blew around her, Samson's body rotting behind the wheel. It would have been a bitter way to die, he thought. A miserable end. He shook the thought from his mind. Turned up the radio and drove onward, away from Moose Lake and Sandstone and south toward Saint Paul as the sun sank toward the horizon.

36

THURSDAY NIGHT. Another basketball game. Tomlin spent the day in his office, trying to track down a mechanic hungry enough to fake his receipt. He must have made fifty phone calls. No luck.

Between calls, Tomlin booted up his computer and Googled Carla Windermere again. Returned to last year's news story, the Arthur Pender case, and scoured it for details. Felt a perverse fascination, a kind of obsession. He hadn't been able to rid Windermere's knowing eyes from his mind.

She was a southerner, according to the slim profile in the *Star Tribune*. Mississippi born and raised. Had moved north from Florida. She hadn't had much to say to the newspapers. The reporters described her as private. Quiet. Intense.

Intense was a good word, Tomlin thought. She'd looked at him like she didn't plan to rest until she uncovered every last one of his secrets. Like she lived and breathed to solve cases like these.

She unnerved him. And every minute she stayed on the case was another minute she got closer to the truth. Tomlin knew he had to find a way to distract her.

The receipt would do the job. But so far the receipt wasn't happening.

TOMLIN LEFT THE OFFICE shortly after five. He drove home, walked the dog, and ate dinner with Becca and the girls. Then he bundled Heather into the Jaguar and together they drove the ten or twelve blocks to Kennedy High School. It was game night.

Tomlin waited outside the locker room while his team changed into their uniforms. He leaned against the wall and watched the stands fill with parents, and when his team was ready he gave them their pep talk. As far as pregame speeches went, it wasn't his best.

Tomlin was still thinking about Carla Windermere. He was thinking about all the parents in the stands, all the families, and what they would think if they knew the truth. If they knew he was a bank robber, a near-bankrupt deadbeat who could hardly provide for his family. He could hear the gossip already.

The girls were staring at him. Somebody coughed. Tomlin shook his head. "Sorry," he told them. "Let's win this, okay?"

THERE WAS A MAN standing courtside. He wore a heavy down parka, half unzipped, his hands in his pockets. He was talking to one of the Kennedy girls, a pretty blond point guard.

Andrea, Tomlin thought. *Andrea Stevens.*

The girl looked embarrassed. She kept looking back at her teammates. The man said something to her. Smiled and clapped her shoulder. The girl blushed bright red and ran back onto the court. The man stood courtside and watched as she joined a line of her teammates shooting layups. Then he turned and walked toward the stands.

The guy looked familiar. Uncannily so. Just the sight of him made Tomlin's skin crawl, but he couldn't place the man's face. Then he looked back at Andrea Stevens again, and he knew.

Kirk Stevens. The BCA agent. The man in the stands was Carla Windermere's former partner. He was the pretty blond point guard's father. And he was here for the basketball game.

37

TOMLIN STOOD COURTSIDE, scanning the stands as the buzzer counted down. On the court before him, the Kennedy girls trailed by one, but Tomlin hardly noticed the score. The cheers from the parents, the shrill piercing whistle, the squeak of shoes on the gym's hardwood floor, all of it seemed muted. He'd barely coached at all.

Instead of drawing up plays for his teenage charges, Tomlin had spent most of the game watching Kirk Stevens in the stands. The BCA agent sat holding hands with his pretty wife near the top of the bleachers, watching his daughter play point guard on the floor. His young son sat a few feet away, fiddling with his Game Boy.

Stevens was hardly an imposing figure. Probably he and Tomlin were the same age, though Tomlin was thinner and had better hair. Stevens looked like the kind of middle manager that Tomlin had terrorized at the firm, the dull kind of man who ate his lunch at his desk, who vacationed with the in-laws in Duluth, who never got the girl.

Except the BCA agent had found a girl, Tomlin thought, stealing a glance at Nancy Stevens again. And his daughter, God knew where she'd come from. He looked at Andrea now, on the court—a pretty, vibrant blond thing who one day, sometime soon, would be beautiful.

This girl came from Kirk Stevens's gene pool, Tomlin thought. *How the hell did that happen?*

Looking at Stevens, big and dumb, Tomlin would have figured him for a patrol cop, at best. Couldn't imagine the man cracking an interstate crime ring. But he had. He and Carla Windermere both. They were colleagues. Partners. Probably friends. Maybe they still kept in touch.

Maybe, Tomlin thought, *Kirk Stevens could provide a little cheap intelligence.* He turned away from the bleachers in time to watch Andrea Stevens pull up for a jump shot as the last seconds ticked off the clock. The ball rainbowed over the arms of a defender, arcing beautifully toward the basket as the buzzer sounded to end the game. The whole gym seemed to stop moving, stop breathing, waiting for the ball to land.

The ball hit the rim and bounced up again. It hung there, lingered for a few tantalizing seconds before falling again and ricocheting, harmless, to the floor. The whole gym exhaled in one dismayed breath, the other team swarming and cheering as Andrea stood at the top of the key, staring at the basket, alone for a moment. Then she turned and jogged back to her teammates, a sheepish half smile on her face.

Unflappable. Tomlin wondered if her dad was the same.

38

S TEVENS AND NANCY waited outside the locker room as the coach gave his postgame talk. JJ lingered nearby, his nose in his Game Boy. Nancy hugged Stevens's arm. "You made it," she said. "Solve the case?"

"Getting there," Stevens replied, wrapping his arms around her. "Doesn't look like the wife did it, anyway."

Nancy smiled. "Not this time."

"You ever want a ready-made excuse, just pick up an ex-con at a deserted truck stop. Let him take the fall."

She looked at him. Saw through his smile. "You okay?"

"I'll be fine," he said. Nancy shook her head, looked ready to say something else. Then the locker room door opened, and Andrea's coach came out. Stevens stepped forward and held out his hand. "Heck of a game, Coach. Tough loss."

Tomlin shook Stevens's hand. He had a firm grip, cool hands. "It's coming. We start getting the bounces and we'll start winning games." He studied Stevens's face. "Agent Stevens, right?"

Stevens frowned. Couldn't place the man, though something about him seemed familiar.

"Carter Tomlin," the coach said. "We talked on the phone a couple weeks back. The Danzer case. I used to manage their money."

"Tomlin," said Stevens. Suddenly, he remembered. "Sure, the accountant. Didn't recognize you, I'm sorry."

Tomlin laughed. "Tough to pick someone out from a phone call, Agent. You're Andrea's father."

Stevens studied the man's face. He was a handsome guy, younger by a few years, probably. He had icy blue eyes and a wide, easy smile that belied success and the confidence that came with it. Stevens nodded. "How's she doing?"

"Andrea? She's fine." Tomlin laughed again. "These girls, nothing fazes them. We've been working on that jump shot in practice. She'll get it."

"She's an athlete," said Stevens. "Just about beats me at H-O-R-S-E these days."

"You play ball?"

"High school. A little in college. Then I quit growing, and that was that. You?"

"Hockey," said Tomlin. "Never basketball. Kind of out of my element here."

The locker room door opened, and Tomlin and Stevens both turned to watch as Andrea emerged in the middle of a bubble of teenage girls, laughing and jostling. Tomlin smiled at Stevens. "See what I mean? Not a care in the world."

Stevens laughed. "The parents, on the other hand."

The girls broke ranks as they left the locker room, scattered to their waiting parents. Andrea saw Stevens and smiled at him, self-conscious. "Hey, kiddo," Stevens said. "Good game."

Andrea glanced at Tomlin and blushed. "Thanks."

"Tough break at the end there. You all right?"

"Yeah," she said. Then she shrugged. "It's only a game, Daddy." She smiled at Tomlin again and then walked away, joining her mother and her brother by the gymnasium doors.

Tomlin watched her go. Then he turned back to Stevens. He hesitated, then smiled. "Ever think about coaching?" he said. "I could use some help with these girls. I'm not exactly Phil Jackson over here."

Stevens laughed. "Who is, though?"

"Might be fun." Tomlin took a business card from his pocket. "Hell, drop by practice now and then if you get a spare moment. Could use someone with your expertise."

Stevens took the card. Carter Tomlin and Co. He studied it, then looked around the empty gym. *Coaching*, he thought. *Me?*

Tomlin was watching him, his head cocked. He was smiling. Stevens pocketed the man's business card. "I'm neck deep in this case right now," he said. "Once it breaks, though, I might have some time on my hands. Guess I could use a hobby."

"It's a hell of a lot of fun," Tomlin said. "Keeps me young."

"Can see that," said Stevens. He shook the coach's hand and told him good-bye, and then he walked to the gym doors where Nancy and Andrea and JJ waited, and he walked with them out to the frigid parking lot. He looked at each of them in turn and couldn't help smiling, feeling the stress of the Danzer case finally start to melt away.

39

TOMLIN BOUGHT the *Star Tribune* on the way into work the next morning. He didn't make a habit of reading the paper, but this morning, it was the headline that got him.

"FBI Shoot-out Leaves Bank Robber Dead" it screamed from the newspaper box on the corner outside his office. There was a blurry picture of Carla Windermere just below.

They got Tricia, Tomlin thought, fumbling in his pocket for change. He shoved quarters into the slot until the door unlocked, grabbed a copy of the paper, and skimmed the cover story. *Tricia,* he thought, *or Dragan. Somehow, Windermere got them, too.*

The picture of Windermere was a night shot, candid. Police cars and yellow tape in the background. She was standing with another agent, an older man, staring up at an ugly gray house. The caption read: "FBI agents Robert Doughty and Carla Windermere at the scene of a deadly shoot-out in Phillips last night."

Phillips. Southeastern Minneapolis. Tricia and Dragan both lived in Saint Paul. Tomlin scanned the story, found a name. Nolan Jackson. A degenerate and career criminal. The FBI liked him for the Eat Street bank robbery. Tomlin shoved the paper under his arm and ran

upstairs to his office. Swung open the door and showed the paper to
Tricia. "You read this?"

Tricia cocked her head at him. "Not yet."

He laid the front page out on her desk. Watched her big eyes go
wider as she read. "Is this—"

"Yeah," Tomlin said. "It's our guy. They think he's with us."

"And they killed him. Why?"

Tomlin shrugged. "No idea." He smiled at her. "I'm not exactly
going to call and demand a correction."

"Says they're still looking for accomplices," Tricia said, reading.

"Let them look," Tomlin said. "I don't know Nolan Jackson, and
I bet you don't, either. No way they connect him to us."

Tricia leaned back in her chair. "So what do we do?" she said.
"What happens next?"

Tomlin straightened and looked around the office. "What happens? I guess we go back to our everyday lives. Focus on our day jobs
and be thankful this guy Jackson died for our sins, right?"

Tricia frowned again. "You're saying we quit."

"For a while, sure."

"For a while or forever?"

Tomlin shook his head. "It's too risky," he said. "This is our second chance. We'd be stupid to keep going now."

"I have student loans," Tricia said. "I need cash."

You dropped out of college, he thought, but said nothing. Instead,
he crossed to his inner office and unlocked the door. Ducked inside
and took a handful of cash from his bottom desk drawer. "This
should do you," he told her, stacking the money on her desk.

She looked at the money. Then she sighed. "Great," she said,
scooping it into her purse. "Thanks."

"We can't do this anymore. It's not safe."

"Yeah, you said that already." She turned to her computer. "It's
fine. I have work to do, boss."

He watched her for a long moment, an ingénue everywhere but

her eyes. She started to type something, and he retreated to the doorway of his office, still watching her, wanting her to look at him again.

She wouldn't give him the satisfaction, he knew, and after another moment or two he surrendered, turned away and into his own office, where he sat in front of his computer and wondered why his big second chance felt so much like failure.

40

"Y OUR GIRLFRIEND'S IN the paper again," Nancy Stevens told her husband, pushing the morning's *Star Tribune* across the table.

Stevens took the newspaper from her, examined the headline over his coffee. A shoot-out in Phillips, he read. A wanted bank robber. A grainy picture of Windermere. She looked tired. Almost human.

"Guess she found a new boyfriend," Nancy said. "Kind of looks like you, doesn't he?"

Stevens studied the picture again. Windermere's new partner, Agent Robert Doughty, FBI. An older white man, pudgy and self-satisfied. *Do I really look that old?* he thought. He grinned across at Nancy. "Maybe we can double date."

Nancy rolled her eyes. "Yeah," she said, standing and gathering the dishes from the table. "That's just what I need."

Stevens waited as his wife rinsed out her coffee cup and walked out of the kitchen. Then he picked up the newspaper again and read the story in full. He'd heard about the Eat Street bank heist, a pretty ballsy affair for Minnesota. Two armed robbers in ski masks and heavy artillery, a getaway driver, and a five-figure score. Real action-movie stuff. Everyday work for an FBI agent.

The DNA checks on the Danzer case still hadn't come through.

Another couple of days, the tech said. Was a hell of a job, anyway; Sylvia Danzer wasn't even in the DNA database. They were tracking down next of kin now. There wasn't much he could do until the results came back, either. Could sit at his desk and bat theories around. Or open up another case and start digging again.

And meanwhile, Windermere had tracked down her man. Hadn't taken long. Another high-profile closure. Another climactic shootout. Stevens drained the last of his coffee. Made a face. Cold.

He studied the picture of Windermere and Doughty. *I'm not that fat. Or that full of myself. Nancy's just pulling my leg.*

"Oh, God." Nancy swept back into the room behind him. She'd changed, was fixing her makeup as she tried to slip her foot into a high-heeled shoe. "You're so in love it's sickening."

"Bull," Stevens said. "I'm just checking the weather."

"You're like a lovesick teenager." She uncapped a tube of lipstick and ran it over her lips.

"You gave me a complex," he said. "I don't look like him, do I?"

Nancy recapped the lipstick, dropped it in her purse. Walked to him and wrapped her arms around his neck. "You're much more handsome," she said. "Agent Windermere is a fool to choose him over you."

"I've got more hair than he does, anyway." Stevens pushed the paper away and walked his coffee cup to the sink. Nancy wrapped her arms around him.

"Tell me I look pretty and kiss me good-bye," she said. "Before you give *me* a complex."

"You look pretty." He kissed her, smeared her lipstick. Kissed her again. "You look more than pretty."

"I know." She squirmed out of his grasp. "It's for the judge, though, so lay off."

"Lucky judge."

She picked up her jacket and walked to the door. "You should be so lucky, Agent Stevens."

He followed her to the side door and watched her walk out into the snow. Blew her a kiss and closed the door behind her. Walked back into the kitchen, where the newspaper lay open on the table. He glanced through it aimlessly. Then he reached into his wallet and pulled out Carter Tomlin's business card. *Coaching,* Stevens thought again. *Well, why not?*

Stevens had always kind of figured he would enjoy coaching, the camaraderie with the kids, the opportunity to teach the same skills he'd worked hard to master. Andrea would be mortified, of course, but then when was she not?

I don't need Carla Windermere's life, Stevens thought, folding the newspaper and dropping it in the trash. *I'm a husband and a father and a BCA agent. That should be enough.* He walked out to the living room and picked up the phone. Dialed Tomlin's number and waited for the phone to ring.

41

"HEARD DOUGHTY BAILED your ass out on that shoot-out in Phillips," said Mathers. "That doesn't sound like the Supercop we all know and love."

Windermere looked up from her cubicle to find Mathers peering at her over the fuzzy gray wall. He wore a funny little smile like he knew he was hilarious, like he was waiting for the rest of the world to catch on. Windermere shook her head. "That's not how it went down."

"That's what the newspaper said." Mathers grinned wider. "They're not allowed to lie, are they?"

Windermere turned back to her computer. "Nope."

Mathers leaned closer. "I sense drama, Agent Windermere. Tell our viewers what really happened."

Windermere sighed. Then she pasted a smile on her face and looked up at her colleague. "Doughty wrote the report. Why don't you ask him?"

Mathers stared at her. Then he narrowed his eyes. "I see what's happening here," he said. He turned and walked away, pausing to flash her another sly smile.

Windermere watched him go. Then she turned back to her computer again. Checked her e-mail for the fifth time that day. Mathers was a little shit, but he was harmless. Kind of cute, even. If she hadn't been so preoccupied with Doughty and the Jackson ordeal, she might have played along. That Jackson ordeal, though, was sapping her will. She and Doughty had uncovered enough evidence in the suspect's home to make him for a desperado bank job at a Wells Fargo half a mile from Phillips. Guy walked in with a ski mask, a sawed-off, and a Timberwolves jacket, all of which they'd found in Jackson's bedroom closet.

So Jackson was a bank robber, as he'd admitted before Doughty shot him. If he was involved in Eat Street, though, he'd hidden it well. They'd found no gold Toyota Camry, no AR-15. No sign of any accomplices. As far as Windermere was concerned, Jackson was a red herring.

She glanced down the row toward Doughty's office. His door was open, and Windermere could hear him on the phone—laughing, loud. Not for the first time, she wondered if Doughty had known what he was doing, killing Jackson as she tried to convince him to surrender.

Shut up, she told herself. *Don't be ridiculous. Doughty's an FBI agent, just like you. He still plays by the rules. He's not killing a suspect just to spite you, you loon.*

Still, the whole thing seemed too clean. Or maybe she was still just too focused on Tomlin. She kept seeing the man's eyes when he'd looked at the receipt, defeat in his expression, like he'd been caught in a bad bluff. He was guilty of something.

Hell, he was probably guilty of bank robbery. He still hadn't provided any proof of that phantom car break-in he'd tried to sell. Probably figured now he didn't have to, now that Nolan Jackson was wearing the rap for every bank heist from Fargo to Duluth.

She glanced down at Doughty's open door again. As per the senior agent's orders, she was supposed to be chasing down Nolan Jackson's friends and family, looking for signposts in his criminal record that would point the way to his bank-robbing accomplices. She'd worked the damn case all day and found nothing.

So, she thought, picking up her phone, *nobody will mind if I take a little break, will they?* She dialed and waited for the call to go through, her eyes on Doughty's door. A woman picked up. "Carter Tomlin and Co."

"It's Agent Windermere calling," Windermere told her. "Be a pal and put your boss on the phone."

42

CHRIS RUSSELL PARKED her Hastings police cruiser behind a beat-up Ford pickup in Tony Schultz's driveway, turned off the car's engine, and surveyed Schultz's tiny farmhouse. *Hardly looks like a drug dealer's pad*, she thought, as she stepped out onto the snow. *Then again, this is Hastings. Everything's smaller out here.*

Truth be told, Russell didn't know why she was out here. She'd been working a little B and E action, a string of burglaries in the old storefronts downtown, when Schultz had called and demanded she come out and talk to him. "Sure, Tony," she'd said. "Scotty said you'd be calling. What's the problem?"

Schultz had sighed as if she should already know. "The robbery," he said. "Guy broke into my house, beat me with a piece of lumber, stole my guns. Don't you want to catch him?"

"Wanted to catch him," she said. "Three months ago, when it happened. Pretty sure the case has gone cold."

Schultz paused. "Don't you at least got to take my statement?"

Russell had looked at her computer screen, where she had the file open to the downtown break-ins. Someone smashing windows, emptying cash registers. "Historic downtown Hastings is a Minnesota landmark," Randy Telfair had told her. "Scares the tourists away when the crime rate goes up."

It's probably some kid, Russell wanted to tell him, *and anyway, what tourists?* Still, Randy was the mayor, and Russell had been planning to humor him, just to be polite. Until Tony Schultz called, just like Scotty Mo'd warned her he might. Didn't give up any details, just grinned at her like it was her problem now, the bastard. She'd more or less set it aside, but here Tony was, a day or two later, acting like he had something to say.

Funny he was calling about that old robbery now, months after the fact. Acting as if by rights Russell should have solved the case already, returned him his guns. In her fifteen years in Hastings, Russell figured the only times she'd seen Schultz talk to the police were at the tail ends of bar brawls and maybe an arrest for drunk driving. Sure, the rumors abounded: according to local lore, the big man fancied himself some kind of drug kingpin, had landed a supply of cocaine from the south and was trying to make a living slinging dope to the town's eighteen thousand residents. Either he wasn't much of a drug dealer, though, or he was better than anyone figured. So far, nobody on the force had been able to build a case against him.

Now Russell walked from her cruiser up toward Schultz's little house, aiming to change her department's woeful batting average. Schultz wasn't exactly the smartest guy in Hastings, and Russell figured she could convince him to implicate himself while she pretended to help him find his stolen guns.

It beat working those crummy B and E's, anyway.

SCHULTZ CAME OUT onto the porch as Russell walked to the house. He was just as big as she remembered, his muscle going to fat now, his hairline thinning. In his younger days, he'd been a force about town, a womanizer and an unpredictable drunk. Since he'd moved out to the homestead, he'd calmed down some, though who knew what he got up to when nobody was watching.

Schultz studied her as she approached, his eyes dark and suspicious. He still had a scar on his cheek from where the robber had hit him, she noticed, though it looked like he'd had his broken teeth fixed.

Russell let his eyes wander over her body as she climbed the porch. Then she fixed him with a look. "You going to stare at me all day, Tony, or you going to invite me inside?"

Seemed to take a moment to register. Then Schultz nodded and waved her through the front door. He followed her in, through the tiny front hall and into the plain living room, a couch and a chair and a rug and a table. Russell sat down on the couch, looked around the room. Nothing incriminating, not yet. Not out in the open, anyway. Russell took out her notepad and a pencil. "I'm going to take some notes while we're talking," she said. "That all right?"

Schultz hesitated. Fidgeted. Then he cleared his throat. "I don't like having you here," he said. "I want you to know that."

"Okay, so I'll go," she said, closing her notepad. "How about that?"

"You're not going anywhere." Schultz glared at her. "Not until we talk this thing through."

Russell held Schultz's gaze until the big man looked away. Then she nodded and opened her notepad again. "Okay, Tony," she said. "Why don't you tell me what happened?"

43

STEVENS PARKED his Cherokee behind a black Jaguar at the foot of Carter Tomlin's driveway. He got out of the Jeep and stared up at the house, admiring the fairy-tale architecture, the sprawling front lawn. *Imagine being the guy who lives here*, he thought.

He'd read somewhere that F. Scott Fitzgerald had lived in one of the mansions along Summit Avenue. The railroad baron James J. Hill had built a huge home for himself down the block; now more than a hundred years old, it was a tourist attraction. Every home on the street looked like a fantasy brought to life, a dream home for movie stars and celebrities. Stevens tried to picture his own family in one of these monsters; couldn't do it. He and Nancy lived in a perfectly serviceable little home in Lexington—about a mile and a half away by car but worlds apart in terms of lifestyle.

Stevens crossed the front lawn and climbed the stairs to the porch. Rang the doorbell and was met by a girl about the same age as JJ. "Is your dad home?" Stevens asked her, and she gave him a shy smile and ran off through the house.

Stevens waited at the door until the little girl returned, trailing a woman Stevens recognized as Becca Tomlin, Carter's wife. She was blond and blue-eyed and vibrant, five or six years younger than Tomlin, and almost breathtakingly beautiful.

"Mr. Stevens." She smiled at him, an all-American smile. "Please, come in."

Stevens followed her through the front hall to the living room. "Carter's just fiddling with his trains," Becca told him. "Can I get you something to drink?"

"I'll handle the drinks." Carter Tomlin walked into the living room behind his wife, as tall and confident and flawless as a presidential nominee, right down to the yellow Labrador retriever at his feet. He kissed his wife on the cheek and then held out his hand to Stevens.

The dog got to Stevens first, leaping up at Stevens's palm and immediately setting about coating it with his slobber. Tomlin met Stevens's eye and smiled. "Snickers has his own way of saying hello. I hope you don't mind."

Stevens shook his head. "Course not. Probably smells ours."

"A dog man."

"German shepherd. My son's Christmas present."

"So you understand, then." Tomlin gestured to the couch. "Have a seat."

Sounds like he's used to giving orders, Stevens thought. *Bet it serves him well as a coach. And in business.*

Tomlin disappeared into the kitchen. Came back a moment later with a couple of beers and sat opposite Stevens. "So," he said, leaning back in his chair. "Basketball. You decided to answer my cry for help."

Stevens smiled. "Wife wants me out of the house."

"The Danzer case break?"

"Waiting on some DNA," Stevens said. "There's not much I can do until I hear back from the lab."

"Must be kind of boring, isn't it?" Tomlin studied his face. "Going back to these stale murder cases after that big kidnapping thing."

Stevens laughed. "Pender and company. You heard about that."

"Read about it in the paper. An acquaintance of mine, Harper, was kidnapped across town." He smiled at Stevens. "Heard you were some kind of hero."

Stevens shook his head. "We got lucky."

"That sounds too much like modesty." Tomlin glanced out to the hallway. Then he leaned forward again, conspiratorial. "You still keep in touch with that FBI agent? The pretty one, I mean. Winter-green?"

"Windermere." Stevens looked out the window. "Carla Winder-mere. Guess we fell out of contact."

"Really?" Tomlin said. "She was a looker."

"Hell of a cop, too."

"Could tell from her picture she was a force," Tomlin said. "You guys must have made quite the team."

Stevens laughed again. "We got the job done."

"Yeah, I bet you guys were really something." Tomlin straight-ened. "Anyway, let's talk hoops. Basic strategy, right?"

Stevens almost wished they could talk more about Windermere, but he followed Tomlin's lead and the two men talked basketball for a while. Stevens outlined some strategy, and they made plans to meet again, before Tuesday's practice. Then Tomlin drained his beer and stood. "We'll have to have you and the wife over sometime," he said. "Bring Andrea around, too."

"Great idea." Stevens stood, too, and let Tomlin walk him to the door. "I'll rally the wife. And we'll be in touch about practice."

They shook hands at the door, and Stevens walked out to his Jeep, stopping at the car to turn back and wave to Tomlin, who stood watching from the window.

Good to get out of the house some, Stevens thought, backing the Cherokee onto Summit Avenue. *Maybe this basketball thing will be fun.* As he drove home, however, he thought about Windermere again, replaying Tomlin's conversation and feeling something a little like longing.

44

KIRK STEVENS TURNED out to be a big waste of time, as far as keeping tabs on Carla Windermere was concerned.

Even with Nolan Jackson in the ground, the FBI agent continued to call Tomlin a couple times a week. "Just trying to close out these last details, Mr. Tomlin," she told him. "Get me that receipt and I can quit harassing you."

He told her he was on it, was harassing the auto body shop himself. "They're playing hard to get," he told her. "But I'll get them."

"Maybe I can try," she said. "An FBI badge opens doors. What's the name of the shop?"

"Got it on my desk at home," he told her. "Call you back."

He hung up on her, didn't call back. Screened his calls, told Tricia to tell her he was out. But Windermere kept calling, and that alone made him nervous. Nolan Jackson was dead. The FBI claimed he was their bank robber. Shouldn't Windermere have moved on by now?

He worked his way down a list of auto glass repair shops in the Twin Cities. Worked quiet, discreet. Offered to pay cash for a doctored receipt. Got a lot of sideways looks, a lot of dial tones. Kept looking. And Windermere kept calling.

Tuesday afternoon, Tomlin met with Stevens before practice. Talked strategy for a while. Stevens knew basketball, anyway, that was for certain. The BCA cop more or less took over practice, got the girls running drills, trying out a new defense. Tomlin stood on the sidelines and watched. Filled water bottles. Fetched towels.

He tried broaching the subject of Windermere again. Told Stevens he'd seen the FBI agent's picture in the paper. A shoot-out in Phillips. The bank robbery case. Stevens looked at him funny, like he knew a little bit more than he should. Sent a chill through Tomlin's body, but then Stevens seemed to warm to the topic, seemed almost eager to talk about Windermere again.

For all that, though, Stevens knew less about Windermere than he did. The dumb cop hadn't talked to Windermere in months. How the hell could he know why she wasn't giving up?

Wednesday and Thursday, Tomlin hit the streets. Dropped by any auto repair shop he could find. Asked a couple of questions, drew mostly blank stares. Hit the jackpot with a shitty little back-alley joint just north of downtown.

"You're saying you want me to fake a receipt for a car window replacement." The guy behind the counter studied Tomlin, scratching his head. He was an older guy, grease under his fingernails. Torn overalls. "We don't even do windows."

Tomlin pulled three hundred-dollar bills from his wallet. "You do now."

The guy looked at the money, then at Tomlin again. "This some kind of insurance scam?"

"No," Tomlin said.

The guy looked at the money. Pursed his lips. "I gotta rework the inventory, too. Rejig the computer. In case somebody starts nosing around."

Tomlin took two more hundred-dollar bills from his wallet. Laid them on the table beside the first three. "Five hundred, even. Can you help me, or what?"

The guy looked at the money some more. Then he nodded. "I'm not going to go to jail, am I?"

"For a receipt?" Tomlin said.

The guy studied his face. Then he shrugged and scooped up the money. "Give me ten minutes."

45

TOMLIN COULDN'T HELP smiling as he climbed the stairs to his office. Pushed open the door, and Tricia looked up at him from her desk. "Afternoon," he said. "Keeping busy?"

She stared up at him, her eyes as bored and lifeless as a lion's in the zoo. Then she sighed and turned back to her computer. Didn't say a word. Tomlin walked to her desk and dropped the body shop receipt on her keyboard. "Fax that for me, would you?"

Tricia glanced at the receipt. Sighed again. "Where?"

"The FBI. Minneapolis. Agent Carla Windermere." He started into his office. "Make sure you fax it today."

"You have a visitor," she told him. "He's in there already."

Tomlin stopped walking. He looked back at Tricia. She stared at him, frowning. His heart pounded.

Who the hell is it now? He forced himself to straighten. Forced himself to walk into his office, slow as a prisoner walking to his own execution. His visitor turned in his chair and smiled. "There's the man."

Tomlin exhaled. "Rydin." He shook his friend's hand. "Thought you were the goddamn IRS."

Rydin's handshake was firm. "If you were cheating on your taxes,

I hope you'd get yourself a nicer place," he said. "How's tricks, anyway?"

"Same old," Tomlin told him. "Business is business."

Rydin sat down again. "Ready for a real job?"

"What, another contract?"

"Better." Rydin grinned at him. "North Star's hiring a new controller. Looking outside the firm. Thought you might want to throw your name into the ring."

Tomlin stared at him. "You're talking full-time."

"Full-time. Salary and good benefits. Get you back into the straight life." He leaned forward. "Best part of it is, I chair the hiring committee. I tell my bosses you're the guy and you're hired."

Tomlin shook his head. "Christ, Rydin."

"Good deal, huh? Should I tell them you're in?"

Tomlin stared at the man. Then he looked around at the dingy office, the gray window, the stained carpet. *Here's your reward*, he thought. *You kept your family afloat when things got desperate and now you're back in the straight life again. This is like a reset button on your life.*

Then he heard Tricia humming to herself in the lobby, and something made him pause. "Let me mull it over," he told Rydin. "Give me a couple of days."

46

"LET ME GET this straight," Harris said, glaring across his desk at Windermere. "You're saying this Jackson guy isn't your man."

"I'm not saying it," Doughty said from the window. "This is her story."

Windermere held Harris's gaze. "Sir, there's nothing in Jackson's house that ties him to Eat Street, or any of our suspect's previous robberies. We make him for one Wells Fargo job, and that's it."

Doughty sighed. "Let me say, *again*, that Agent Windermere's theories about our Eat Street bandit are her own. I don't believe this guy robbed a bunch of banks solo before he pulled this job, and I sure as hell don't believe he's some Summit Hill accountant."

"And let me say," said Windermere, "that Nolan Jackson copped to the Wells Fargo bank heist when we moved to apprehend him in Phillips. Unfortunately, Agent Doughty shot and killed Jackson before he could tell us anything else."

Doughty spun at the window. "You think I liked shooting him, Agent Windermere?"

Harris held up his hands. "Enough. Both of you."

Windermere turned to Doughty. "I don't know, Agent Doughty," she said. "I know we had tactical containment when you pulled the trigger. We could have backed off and let the negotiators bring him in peacefully. But you shot him instead."

"Fuck you," said Doughty. "You're so stuck on your own theories you can't see the facts."

"I see the facts," said Windermere. "The fact is, you're wrong."

"*Enough*," Harris said. "Shut the hell up, both of you."

Windermere turned from Doughty. Looked at Harris, his face bright red and mottled with rage. "Both of you," he said, breathing hard. "You're FBI agents. Act like it."

Windermere steadied her breathing. She felt foolish already, ashamed. *You have the facts on your side*, she thought. *Let Doughty do the shouting.* "I'm sorry, sir," she said. "That was way out of line."

"Damn right," said Harris. "Now, what the hell is your story?"

She told him again. Jackson's copping to the Wells Fargo bank job. Her inability to link him to Eat Street, or to anything else. No gold Camry. No accomplices. No evidence anywhere. Harris heard her out. Held up his hand at Doughty, who looked itching to rebut. He focused on Windermere. "Media thinks Jackson's our guy," he said. "We look like assholes if we tell them we were wrong."

Windermere shrugged. "So we're assholes."

"Agent Doughty." Harris turned to Doughty at the window. "You don't believe Agent Windermere's theory."

Doughty shook his head. "I think it's horseshit," he said. "Pardon my French, but I think Agent Windermere is so hung up on being right that she can't accept when she's wrong."

"Where's your proof?" said Windermere.

"We're having this conversation, aren't we?" said Doughty. "Our suspect is dead and his accomplices are at large, and instead of chasing them down, we're arguing your conspiracy theory."

Windermere held his gaze. "I'm talking about Jackson, Bob. Where's your proof he's our guy?"

Doughty glanced at Harris. Harris nodded. "Valid question, Agent Doughty."

Doughty looked from Harris to Windermere and back again, breathing hard. Then he shook his head. "Where's her proof, is my question."

"You first," said Windermere.

"No," said Doughty. "You first. You're so sure this accountant of yours is the guy, where's your evidence?"

"I talked to him," she said. "He played guilty, no question. Text-book."

"You talked to him," said Harris. "Anything concrete?"

"The receipt, sir," she said. "The note from the Midway bank job. He couldn't explain how his parking receipt turned up at the scene of the crime."

Doughty cocked his head. "Someone broke into his car, Agent Windermere."

She snorted. "So he said."

"And?"

Harris looked at her, one eyebrow raised. Windermere laughed. "And he was lying. Clear as day."

"Uh-huh." Doughty smiled wider. Brandished a piece of paper. "You should check your faxes," he said.

Windermere snatched the paper from him. Scanned it once, read it closer. "This is bullshit," she said. "Obviously fabricated."

Doughty shook his head. "It's not bullshit," he said. "I called and confirmed."

"So he paid them off. What does that prove?"

Doughty grabbed the paper back and handed it to Harris. "Sir, this is a receipt for repairs done on Carter Tomlin's Jaguar in July. Basically, it destroys Windermere's case."

"Bullshit," she said. "I can think of a hundred ways he could fake it."

"Conspiracy theories," said Doughty.

"*Facts.* This proves nothing."

Harris looked up from the paper. "Enough." His face was half pink again. "I've had enough of this mess. The two of you, squabbling like children without a shred of evidence between you." He looked at Doughty first, then Windermere. "You two are partners. I'm going to give you one shot to figure this out on your own. Then I'm reassigning you both."

He handed Doughty the fax. "Come back to me when you have a cohesive strategy."

Doughty nodded and turned to the door. After a moment, Windermere followed. She walked out into the hallway, closed Harris's door. Heard the lock catch and snatched the fax out of Doughty's hands. "You've got nothing," she said, "and you know it."

Doughty shook his head. "You can't let it go, can you?"

She stared at him. "What?"

"You think because you're the Supercop you're not allowed to be wrong, is that it? You'll ruin your reputation if you let someone else win?"

Windermere shook her head. "This has nothing to do with me, Agent Doughty," she said. "You killed the wrong man, and *you* can't let it go. It's your ego that's the problem, not mine."

She turned and walked away, down the aisle toward her cubicle. "Windermere," Doughty called. "Where the hell are you going?"

She reached her cubicle and pulled on her coat. Caught Mathers eye down the aisle. "I feel sick," she told him. "If Harris asks, tell him I'm puking." She caught the elevator downstairs to the parking garage and stepped out into a sea of dark, unmarked sedans. Surveyed them a moment, then turned and stepped back into the elevator.

Fuck it, she thought. She rode the elevator back up to street level and caught a cab to her apartment. Took the stairs to the garage, found her parking spot and her dusty Chevelle.

Fuck it, she thought again, sliding into the driver's seat and firing the car up. The engine growled like a murderous dog, seemed to shake the whole building itself as she backed away from her stall and idled out to the street.

Fuck it. Windermere brushed the hair from her eyes and floored the gas pedal. The tires squealed and caught, pasting her to her seat as the Chevelle roared, speeding fast and untamed toward Saint Paul.

47

BECCA SQUEALED and hugged Tomlin. Kissed him hard on the mouth. "I'm so happy for you, honey," she said. "This has been so tough."

Tomlin took a drink of wine. The girls had eaten early; Madeleine was at dance practice, and Heather was upstairs getting ready for another basketball game. The dining room was empty, save Becca, Tomlin, and Snickers, who nosed about beneath the table, waiting for scraps. Tomlin slipped the dog a crust of bread. "It's not like we're doing so bad right now," he said. "Things are pretty good in our lives."

Becca sat down opposite him at the table. She brushed a stray hair from her eyes. In the light, Tomlin couldn't tell if it was blond or gray. "You'd be making more money," she said.

"We're making good money right now."

She stared at him. "I thought you said it was stressful, your job. Finding contracts and clients. I thought you missed that steady paycheck."

Tomlin picked up his fork and wrapped it in pasta. Took a bite and chewed slowly. "I kind of like it," he said. "It's liberating."

Becca looked down at her plate. "Now I feel kind of stupid." She took a bite of pasta and chewed it in silence.

Tomlin watched her across the table. He knew he'd have to take Rydin's offer. No way he could pull bank robberies forever. Hell, the second he pulled another score, Windermere would know she'd been wrong about Jackson. And then she'd come calling again.

Anyway, wasn't this what he wanted? No more guns, no more getaway cars. No more laundering cash just to pay the damn mortgage. *You're looking at a second chance. A steady, secure paycheck and a good credit score and a healthy bonus at Christmas. Hell, maybe a new car.*

A salary and a mortgage and a family. A normal life. Simple. Boring. The thought, all at once, made Tomlin want to put Schultz's shotgun in his mouth now, and spare himself the slow death. He looked around the dining room instead. Didn't move. Drank a little more wine and forced himself to keep eating. He finished his dinner in silence.

48

"Y OU READY TO GO?"

Stevens leaned on the front door, watching, as Andrea searched the house for her jersey, her shoes, her iPod. She raced down the stairs and ran past him toward the laundry room, late and panicked, as usual. "Just one second, Daddy," she called back.

Stevens sighed and turned to the door. "I'll be in the car."

He walked out to the Cherokee, climbed in, and turned on the engine. Blasted the heater and pushed a Springsteen tape into the tape deck. *My coaching debut,* he thought, sitting back in his seat. *And if Andrea doesn't haul ass, we're going to be late.* He leaned on the horn. "Let's *go.*"

The side door opened, and Andrea came out of the house running, her coat half on and her headphones trailing behind her. She climbed in the passenger seat. "Mom said she'll meet us," she said, breathless. "After she's done with her case."

As Stevens backed out of the driveway, Andrea took advantage of his distraction to pop out the Springsteen tape and turn on the radio, filling the Cherokee with teenybopper pop music. Stevens reached for the volume. "What's wrong with Springsteen?"

"They're great, Daddy. I love them," Andrea said. "I just need something to pump me up, okay?"

The music, all synthesizers and pounding bass, set Stevens's teeth on edge, but he endured the teenybopper and four others just like him (her?) as he drove to the high school. He dropped Andrea outside the gym doors and then parked the car. He sat alone in the Jeep for a minute or two, relishing the silence, watching the steady stream of cars into the school parking lot. Then he shook his head clear.

You're a cop, he thought, reaching for the door. *This is just high school basketball. Man up.*

FOR ALL OF STEVENS'S pregame jitters, his coaching debut played out better than he might have expected. Not a win, but a moral victory, anyway. Stevens made a couple bonehead substitutions, nearly drew a technical foul when he lost track of his team's timeouts, but on the whole, a good start. Carter Tomlin, meanwhile, looked lost. Stevens took him aside after the final buzzer sounded. "You looked a bit distracted tonight," he said. "Everything okay?"

Tomlin blinked. Shook his head. "Work stuff," he said. "Tax season. Sorry." Then he gave Stevens a smile that looked forced. "Anyway, looked like you had things under control."

Stevens laughed. "Made some rookie mistakes, though. Could have used you."

"Next time," said Tomlin. "You'll get it."

He turned and sort of wandered away, took a couple steps along the sidelines, his hands in his pockets and his gaze unfocused and vague. Stevens watched him, frowning. He was about to follow the man when Andrea came out of the locker room. "Hey, kiddo," he said. "You played good tonight."

Andrea screwed her face up. "We got killed, Dad."

"It was that god-awful music," Stevens told her. "Should have listened to Springsteen."

"Not funny." She walked past him to where Nancy stood waiting by the gym doors. "Can we go?"

Stevens glanced back at Tomlin again. Then Nancy called his name from the gym doors. Stevens straightened and turned away from the coach. Caught up with Nancy and Andrea at the doors and followed them into the dark parking lot. Nancy had parked her Taurus way in the back, and Stevens walked out with them to the shadows. "You want to ride with me or your mom?" he asked Andrea.

Andrea cocked her head. "Can we get McDonald's?"

Nancy unlocked her door. "Not with me you can't."

"Then I'll ride with you, Dad. But no Springsteens."

Stevens was hardly listening. He was staring across the lot at a big old muscle car parked deep in the shadows. The light from the gym doors caught the front windshield at just the right angle that he could see the solitary occupant behind the wheel. *Can't be*, he thought. *You're seeing things now.* Andrea nudged his arm. "Nice car," she said. "What is it?"

That driver looks a hell of a lot like Windermere.

"Dad?"

Stevens glanced at his daughter. "Ride home with your mother," he told her. "I need to check something out."

"What about McDonald's?"

"Double cheeseburger and fries, right? I'll pick it up on the way."

"And a Diet Coke."

"And a Diet Coke," Stevens said. "I will deliver." He waited as Andrea climbed into the car, and he waved at Nancy as she pulled out of her spot. Then he turned back to the muscle car in the shadows. It was a big old Chevelle. A hell of a car. And the driver looked just like Carla Windermere. But what would Carla be doing parked outside a high school in Saint Paul?

It's dark, Stevens thought. *You're seeing things.* But he walked across the lot toward the Chevelle almost unconsciously. He crossed in front of her bumper, glanced in through the windshield. Stopped walking. It *was* Windermere. Stevens watched as she looked away from the gym door and fixed her eyes straight on him. Watched as those big eyes got wider.

"Stevens," she said. "Shit."

49

WINDERMERE WATCHED Stevens appear out of nowhere. Felt her heart start to pound, felt strangely guilty. As though he'd snuck up and caught her doing something she shouldn't.

Which, in truth, he had. She'd tailed Tomlin all afternoon, totally illegal, followed him as he drove his youngest daughter to dance class, then followed him here to the basketball game.

An everyday kind of guy. Totally boring.

She knew Tomlin was guilty. Knew his auto-body receipt was a fake. But knowing didn't mean anything. She had hoped he'd do something foolish while she watched him, slip up, give her a glimpse of his second life. Instead, she'd spent hours on his ass and he hadn't done so much as run a red light. And tomorrow she'd go back to the office and make nice with Doughty, try and work out a strategy before Harris fired her, if he wasn't planning to fire her already.

Stevens peered in the window. Gestured to the door. Windermere nodded. Leaned over and opened it for him, letting in a sudden rush of cold air. He smiled at her through the open doorway. "Carla," he said. "You here for the game?"

He looked the same as he always had. Unassuming and plain, that same twinkle in his eye. Windermere caught herself staring, looked away. "Guess I missed the game, Stevens," she said. "You want to sit down?"

Stevens slid into the passenger seat. Closed the door and rubbed his hands together in front of the heater. "You on a job or something?"

"Yeah," she said. "Or something."

Stevens smiled at her. "Am I blowing your cover?"

"Not really."

He waited a moment. "You want to talk about it?"

Windermere shook her head. "I'm living it, Stevens. I could use a break." She forced a smile. "What the heck are you doing here, anyway? You have an old-timers' game or something?"

He laughed. "My daughter, Andrea. I'm helping out with her basketball team."

"What, you coach? Those poor kids. Did you win?"

He shook his head. "My first game. It showed."

"So it's your fault."

"Mostly. My partner wasn't exactly on the ball, either."

She looked at him sideways. "Blaming your partner. You haven't changed."

Stevens laughed. "Not a bit." He paused. "I was thinking about you the other day."

"You're still moony. I get it."

"Bull. It's just your picture's in the paper damn near once a week. Then a friend mentioned your name and it got me thinking. I almost called you, in fact."

"A friend, huh?"

"My daughter's basketball coach. My new partner." Stevens sat forward and pointed out the window. "Actually, that's him right there."

Windermere followed his gaze and felt her heart speed up again. Carter Tomlin, walking out the gym doors, his shy, coltish daughter beside him. "Tomlin," she said. "Tomlin mentioned my name."

Stevens frowned. "That's right. Carter Tomlin. You know him?"

Windermere stared out the window at Tomlin in the distance. Watched as he walked his daughter to that big Jaguar of his. Watched him climb in the Jaguar and drive out of the lot. *Tomlin,* she thought. *Carter Tomlin. Kirk Stevens.*

This can't be a coincidence.

50

STEVENS STUDIED Windermere, frowning. One mention of Carter Tomlin and she'd gone stiff as a hunting dog on a scent. Gone was the warmth he'd coaxed out of her earlier; the FBI agent was back in cop mode again. "What the hell is it, Carla?" he said.

Windermere turned and fixed him with that piercing stare of hers. "What did Tomlin say, Stevens? What were his exact words?"

Stevens shifted in his seat. "He asked if we'd stayed in contact," he said. "Said he thought you were cute. No big deal."

Windermere kept her eyes on him. "You've been friends for a while?"

"Just a week or so, maybe. He asked me to help coach."

"And you agreed."

"Work's slow," he said, shrugging. "I could use a hobby. Spend time with my daughter, that kind of thing. I don't get the problem here, Carla."

"You went over to his house and he asked about me."

"Not right away," Stevens said. "We talked about basketball for an hour. He brought up the Pender case. Mentioned you in passing."

Windermere exhaled. Her stare softened. "This case I'm work-ing," she said finally. "The shoot-out in Phillips—"

"I thought you solved that."

"So does my partner. He thinks we killed the ringleader, Jackson. Thing is, Stevens, I make Tomlin."

Stevens started. "No way."

"Listen," she said. "A bank job in Midway, last fall, guy slips a bank teller a note on the back of a parking receipt. Tomlin's parking receipt."

"A coincidence. This guy's an accountant. His house—"

"I've been to his house, Stevens. It's very big. He's got a beautiful family and an expensive car. Doesn't look anything like a bank rob-ber. But I showed him the note, just to see what he'd say."

"And?"

"And he panicked. Fed me some bullshit line about his car get-ting robbed, tried to play off as cool. But he wasn't cool. Stevens. He was scared."

Stevens tried to picture a guy like Carter Tomlin robbing a bank. "I don't see it," he said. "This is my daughter's basketball coach, Carla."

"Yeah? Well, I'm telling you, Stevens, he's guilty."

"An FBI agent comes into his house, starts talking bank robber-ies, of course he gets nervous. Who can blame him?" Stevens smiled. "I get nervous when you start asking me questions."

Windermere didn't smile back. "I saw something, Stevens. I'm not crazy."

"Of course you're not crazy. But come on, Carla."

She glared at him, withering. Then she reached down and turned her key in the ignition. The car rumbled to life. "All right, fine."

"Carla—"

"I get it, Stevens." Her voice came out hard. "I have work to do."

Stevens made to say something else. Stopped when he caught the look on her face. Slowly, he reached for the door handle and climbed out to the cold. No sooner had he stepped out to the pavement than Windermere pulled away, the engine growling and the brake lights glaring as the car disappeared into the night.

Stevens stood alone in the empty lot, staring after Windermere and that big Chevelle. *Carter Tomlin,* he thought. *The guy's a little out of the ordinary, yeah. But a bank robber?* Maybe he'd cheated on his taxes or something. The guy was an accountant, after all.

Stevens walked back through the snowy lot to his Jeep. Drove away from the high school, looking for Windermere at red lights and stop signs, but she was gone again, maybe for good.

He drove home, preoccupied. Thought about Windermere and Carter Tomlin. Thought about Windermere, period. He'd been happy to see her. Too happy, maybe. And now that she was gone, he could almost feel her absence. He felt like he'd betrayed her somehow.

Stevens pulled into his driveway. Turned off the Jeep's engine and reached for the door handle. Then he realized he'd blanked on Andrea's McDonald's.

"Shit," he said, starting the Jeep again. "Damn it, Carla."

51

TOMLIN CALLED RYDIN on Monday. "I'll take the damn job," he said. "I can't pass it up."

Rydin laughed. "Jesus, pal. Don't sound so enthused."

"I'm saying yes, aren't I?"

"All right. When can you start?"

Tomlin leaned back in his chair. "A week, maybe two. I need some time to close up around here."

"Two weeks from Monday," Rydin said. "I'll send over the paperwork."

Tomlin hung up the phone and looked up to find Tricia standing in the doorway. She leaned against the frame, watching him. "Who was that?"

"A friend of mine," Tomlin said. "A job offer. I'm closing the office."

Tricia didn't react. "When?"

"Friday next. We're going to close out our contracts and turn out the lights." He studied her face. "Sorry for the short notice."

She shrugged. Said nothing.

"I'll pay you a nice severance. And I'm happy to write you a reference letter."

"What about the bank jobs?" she said.

He looked at her. "The bank jobs are over," he said finally. "The FBI thinks someone else did it. We keep quiet, and we'll get away clean."

She said nothing for a beat. Then she nodded. "Next Friday, then."

Tomlin watched her walk out of the office. He waited to hear her start typing again, but she wasn't moving out there. *Christ,* he thought. *You can't please everyone.* He turned to his computer and began to review the outstanding accounts. There weren't many. A quick bookkeeping job with the diner down the street, a couple of personal clients to deal with. He could be wrapped up by Wednesday if he tried.

Tricia appeared in the doorway. Looked him straight in the eye. "I have a job for us." She held up her hand. "Wait. It's not a bank, boss. It's bigger money, less risk. No police. We clear a hundred grand, easy. Maybe more."

"Big money, no risk." Tomlin forced a laugh. "Sounds too good to be true."

"It's for real." She took a couple steps into the room. "It's a private score. I'm telling you, no risk at all. No way the cops make a connection."

"A hundred grand. We just walk in and take it."

"We bring guns. We surprise them. A hundred grand, boss, I promise."

Tomlin looked at her. She was wearing a white blouse, and the light from the lobby silhouetted her body beneath the thin material. She was staring at him, waiting for an answer, any hint of boredom gone from her eyes, and he felt a sick thrill run through him and knew he couldn't walk away yet. "I'm listening," he told her. "Keep talking. If it's good like you say, I'll think about it."

Tricia walked into the room and perched on the edge of the desk. "It's good." She gave him that ingénue smile. "It's the best fucking score of your life."

52

WINDERMERE SAT ALONE in her spotless kitchen, staring out through the living room at the city lights beyond. She felt lonely tonight, even more so than normal, and she knew it was Kirk Stevens's fault.

She'd hoped the BCA agent would see something in her Tomlin theory. She'd worked with the guy long enough that she figured she knew a thing or two about how he thought. Instead, he'd shot her down, too.

Easy, she thought. *Your suspect coaches his daughter's basketball team. He's a successful accountant. And he's Stevens's goddamn friend.* Anyone would be skeptical.

Windermere opened a beer and walked through the kitchen to the living room's big picture window. Stared down and out at the city, the cars on the streets and the twinkling skyscraper lights beyond. If she stepped back a ways, she could see her own reflection, and as she stared at it, she realized she didn't like what she saw.

She looked damn exhausted. Pretty much a disaster. Her hair hung bedraggled. Not that she really cared, but she was starting to look old. Goddamned Carter Tomlin would rob her of her youth.

Carter Tomlin. Stevens said he'd made contact a week or so back.

Around the same time Windermere had come to his door, maybe a few days after. And his first meeting with Stevens, he'd mentioned her name. Why?

Easiest answer: he'd cozied up to Stevens to keep an eye on her. And why would Tomlin want to track her if he wasn't guilty of something?

Except that wasn't right. Maybe the guy was just freaked. He'd done something else wrong, a hit-and-run accident. He looked like the kind of guy who'd lose sleep over a speeding ticket. Now the FBI was on his ass, talking about bank robberies. Why wouldn't he be scared?

What about the break-in story? The auto-body receipt? She'd dropped by the place, a little shack with a gasoline smell and a rusty old Mercury in the mechanic's bay. A funny place to take a brand-new Jaguar, she'd thought, but the guy behind the desk punched something into his computer, came out with the service record. Swore he'd done the job. The whole thing stunk pretty bad, but really, there wasn't much she could do.

A guilty man would have asked for his lawyer when the FBI showed up at his door. He would have seen the cops coming. Tomlin didn't ask for his lawyer. Instead, he reached out to Kirk Stevens. It was a weird move, but was it guilty-weird? Not necessarily.

Windermere turned away from the window and walked back into the kitchen. Drained her beer bottle and set it down on the counter. Maybe Tomlin was the red herring, after all. The bank robberies had stopped after the shoot-out with Jackson. Either his partners were real and in hiding or they didn't exist and the real robbers were gone.

So what? she thought. *Risk my career on Tomlin, or go back to CID and kiss Doughty's ass enough times that Harris doesn't fire me?* She could work the Jackson leads until his friends, or Tomlin, or whoever, stepped out of line again, and this time take them down for real.

Windermere stared at her empty beer bottle for a couple of minutes. Then she straightened, grabbed her coat off the chair, rode the elevator down to street level, and walked the three blocks to her gym. She changed in the empty locker room, ran the treadmill for an hour, and then spent forty-five solid minutes kicking the shit out of some poor punching bag. Then she quit and walked home, exhausted and sore, still nowhere near any kind of resolution.

53

DRAGAN PARKED the Camry in front of an industrial park north of Saint Paul, and Tomlin squinted through the windshield out into the darkness. "This is it?"

Tricia poked her head between the two seats. "That one on the end," she said, pointing. "With the security camera."

Tomlin stared across at the building, a low windowless box among boxes. There was a roll-up garage door at the front, and a smaller door beside it, overtop of which a camera was mounted.

"Underground poker," Tricia had told him. "Ten grand minimum buy-in. Totally illegal. My ex used to play."

Tomlin nodded. The police sometimes busted high-stakes poker games, he knew, in suburban houses or anonymous office parks. "How many players?"

"Five or six. And they re-buy all night." She looked at him. "A hundred grand, easy. I'm not lying."

A hundred grand. That meant forty grand each, after Dragan's share. And no police, either. A bunch of illegal poker players weren't going to report a robbery. If Tricia was right, this was damn easy money.

Tomlin admired the girl's profile in the dim glow from the streetlight. She looked like Becca a little, but younger. Wilder. Tricia smiled. "What?"

He shook his head and turned around again. Watched through the windshield as the first car pulled up. Two men climbed out and unlocked the front door. "You've been in there before?" he asked Tricia.

She nodded. "A couple of times."

"What's the layout?" He could feel his nerves starting to tense, the adrenaline ramping up. "How many people? What do we expect when we go inside?"

"There's a front room and a back room. A couple of poker tables in the front and a kitchen in the back."

"Where's the money?"

"At the bar, in the back of the first room. That's where they buy in."

"How many people?"

"Five or six at the tables." She paused, thinking. "A guard at the door, the bartender, the dealer. Tommy—he runs the game—and the waitress. So maybe ten people."

"Armed?"

She nodded. "The guard, definitely. Tommy, too."

"The players?"

"No way. Tommy makes them check their guns behind the bar."

Outside, more cars were arriving. Lexuses and blinged-out Hummers. Young men in flat-brimmed baseball caps and leather jackets. Tomlin watched them stand at the front door and look up at the security camera. After a moment or two each time, the door swung open and the men disappeared inside.

"You can get us in there?" he asked Tricia.

"The boys know me." She winked at him. "They all want in my pants."

Tomlin looked at her again, those big eyes, that ingénue smile. *She can get us in there*, he thought. *She can get in anywhere.* He turned to Dragan. "Keep the engine running."

Tricia frowned. "You want to do it tonight, boss? I thought we were just scoping it out. Getting a feel for the game."

"This is your game," Tomlin said. "You're not ready to take it?"

"I'm ready," she told him. "I'm worried about you, is all. We've been here twenty minutes and you're ready to run in there like a cowboy."

He looked at her. "So you're scared."

"Fuck you," she said. "You want to do this, let's do it. If we're smart we sit on it a week, though. That's all I'm saying. The money's not going anywhere."

The money's here, Tomlin thought. *The money's here, now. Why wait?* "I have a fucking assault rifle," he said, reaching into the backseat for the guns. "What the hell do I care about smart?"

54

STEVENS SAT AT home in his living room, watching the Timberwolves fold to the Chicago Bulls. A waste of a basketball game, he thought, though in truth, he was hardly watching. He was thinking about Carla Windermere instead.

Stevens half wanted to call her, make sure she was okay. Apologize for the other night, outside the gymnasium, though he wasn't sure he'd done anything wrong. She'd shut down so fast on him, like she was hiding her hurt, and he realized his former partner had staked more than she'd shown on her Carter Tomlin theory.

I let her down, he thought. *She opened up to me, figured she had an ally. I pretty much laughed in her face.*

But come on. Bank robbery?

Nancy poked her head in from the kitchen, where she'd barricaded herself behind another stack of paperwork. "You want to talk about it, Agent Stevens?"

Stevens blinked. "What, the game?"

"I bet you couldn't even tell me the score," she said, rolling her eyes. "What's the matter?"

Stevens glanced at the TV, found the score. Realized she was right and shook his head, sheepish. "Bumped into Agent Windermere the other day," he said.

Nancy frowned, just for a second. "She rejected your advances. Poor boy."

"Well, there's that. And she's got a case going sour."

"A sour case and unrequited love." Nancy sighed. "These are the days of our lives."

Stevens pushed himself out of his chair. Crossed the room to her and took her in his arms. "You're catty tonight."

She smiled up at him. "I'm not sorry."

"You will be." He slid his hands under her shirt and leaned down to kiss her. "You ready?"

"Don't you dare," she said, tensing.

"Too late." He ran his hands up her sides, tickling her stomach, holding her tight as she shrieked and struggled against him. Finally, she wrenched free and stepped back, gasping. "Bastard."

"You deserved it."

She brushed her hair from her eyes. "You're next."

"Not ticklish."

"Doesn't matter." She gave him a sideways smile. "I have my own ways."

He followed her into the kitchen and kissed her again. Slid his hands back under her shirt and laughed as she tensed. He ran his hands across her smooth back and felt her relax into him as she returned his kiss, her eyes closed.

"She thinks Carter Tomlin's a bank robber," Stevens said, when he'd pulled his mouth from hers. "Like he does it as a hobby or something."

Nancy frowned. "Heather's dad."

"The same guy. I thought it was crazy, at first."

"But you don't anymore."

"I don't know." Without taking his hands from her skin, he turned her around, his hands on her stomach now. "He has a thing for Agent Windermere, anyway."

"Who doesn't?" she said. "How does he know her?"

"She came by his house," he said, kissing her neck. "Apparently she connects him to a bank heist in Midway."

Nancy sighed as he brought his hand up to her breast. "This is some weird foreplay, Agent Stevens." She spun in his arms, kissed him hard again, pressing her body to his. "Enough talking," she said, between kisses. "You got me riled up, now you deal with the consequences."

SHE DRAGGED HIM upstairs and shoved him down on the bed. They undressed each other, clumsy and urgent, and then she lowered her body to his, and they kissed again and made love, hard and fast.

Afterward, they lay side by side, staring up at the ceiling, gasping and sweaty. Nancy cast one arch eye at him. "Let's see your Agent Windermere do that."

He rolled over and kissed her flushed cheek. "Why bother?"

She let him kiss her. "Damn right."

He watched from the bed as she stood and dressed again, fixing her hair in the mirror. "This was fun," she said, catching his eye. "But now I have work to do."

"I feel so used."

"As you should." She blew him a kiss from the doorway. "This is why I keep you around, Agent Stevens."

Stevens listened to her walk down the stairs. He felt sleepy, closed his eyes, let his mind wander. Found himself thinking about Tomlin again. It was a little weird that he kept bringing up Windermere. It said something. What, though, Stevens wasn't sure. He reached for the telephone on the nightstand. *Speaking of being used*, he thought, picking up the phone and dialing Tomlin's number. *If he wants to keep tabs on Windermere, maybe I want to keep tabs on him.*

The phone rang a couple of times, and then Becca Tomlin picked up. "I'm sorry, Kirk," she said. "Carter's out tonight. I'll tell him you called."

Alert the local bank branches, Stevens thought. "That's all right," he told Becca Tomlin. "I'll try again later."

"Okay," she said. "Have a good night." She paused, then came back. "Oh, Kirk—are you there?"

"Still here."

"We're throwing a little get-together this weekend, just a few of our friends for dinner," she said. "It's kind of a celebration for Carter's new job. Do you have plans Saturday night?"

A dinner party with an alleged bank robber, Stevens thought. *Interesting.* "I'll have to check with Nancy," he said, "but it sounds good to me."

"Perfect. Carter would love to see you."

Stevens thanked her and told her good night. Then he dressed and walked back downstairs. Found Nancy at the kitchen table, poring over a stack of briefs. "We're partying with the bank robbers Saturday night," he told her. "Consider yourself warned."

55

DRAGAN BACKED the car up alongside the warehouse, pulling to a stop beside a Mercedes convertible. "This is good," Tomlin told him. He glanced back at Tricia. "You ready?"

"Always." Tricia picked up a pistol and chambered a round. "You're sure you want to do this tonight?"

"Positive. Get us inside."

Tricia glanced at him again, then out at the warehouse. She leaned forward and squeezed Dragan's shoulder. Stuffed the pistol in her coat and stepped out of the Camry.

Tomlin twisted in his seat to watch her as she walked to the door. There was an intercom button about halfway up the wall, and he watched Tricia press the button and smile up at the camera, just an innocent girl looking for some fun.

Tomlin hid his own pistol in his pocket and picked up a duffel bag and the assault rifle. Then he stepped out of the car and crept alongside the building until he was pressed up against the garage door underneath the camera.

"I just want to party," Tricia was saying. "Play some poker. You guys are too good for me, or what?"

There was a long pause. Tricia kept her smile pasted at the camera.

Finally, the door buzzed, and Tricia pushed it open. Tomlin gripped his rifle tighter, pulled on his ski mask, and followed her into the building.

The place was just as Tricia had described. A main room about thirty feet deep, soft lighting, dark walls. A door to the back room, the light brighter: the kitchen. A bar with a few racks of alcohol and a guy in a suit behind it. Two poker tables, one empty. Six men at the other. And Tricia just inside the door, holding her pistol to the bouncer's wide chest.

Tomlin walked into the room, holding the AR-15 like a Marine clearing city blocks. "This is a robbery," he said. "Move and we kill you."

Silence. The men at the poker table stared at him, then at Tricia, who was backing the guard deeper into the room. Then the guy in the suit spoke up from the bar. "So all right," he said, slowly. "What do you want us to do?"

"Come around from the bar," Tomlin told him. "Call everyone out from the back."

The man nodded and poked his head through the doorway. Said something, and a woman came out, a waitress in a short skirt. She saw Tomlin and Tricia and gasped. "Good," Tomlin said. "Now, who has a weapon?"

The guard glanced at him, then away. Tomlin walked to him and patted him down. Pulled a nickel-plated pistol from his waistband.

"Stupid." Tomlin lifted the butt of his rifle and brought it down, hard, across the bouncer's face. The bouncer fell to the floor. Tomlin looked around the room. "Anyone else?"

The man in the suit reached into his pocket and came out holding a revolver by the barrel. He kept his eyes on Tomlin and put the gun on the floor, slowly. Then he kicked it away. "Cool?"

"Smart," Tomlin said. "Now everyone down on the floor."

The men at the table didn't move, and Tomlin fired a burst into the air. Within seconds every gambler was facedown on the carpet.

Tomlin inhaled the gunpowder smoke, his whole body shaking now. "Cover these guys," he told Tricia. He walked to the man in the suit and knelt down beside him. Put the gun in his face. "You're Tommy?"

A pause. "Yeah."

"Where's the money, Tommy?"

Tommy pursed his lips. Nodded. "Over here, man. Whatever you say."

Tommy led Tomlin around the bar and knelt in front of a medium-size safe. He began to fumble with the combination. "Sorry," he said, wiping his hands on his pant leg. "One second."

Tomlin glanced at Tricia where she paced between the men on the floor. She caught Tomlin's eye and gave him a quick smile, brushing her bangs from her eyes. "Tell them empty their pockets," Tomlin told her. "Wallets, jewelry, watches. Everything out and off."

Tricia stopped in front of the men. "You heard him."

Tommy had the safe open. He remained on his knees, looking up at Tomlin. "Go back and lie down," Tomlin told him. "We'll be out of here soon."

Tomlin waited until the man was settled on the floor again. Then he knelt in front of the safe and peered in. Stacks of hundred-dollar bills, piled high to the back of the safe, each stack worth ten thousand dollars. Tomlin counted at least twenty.

Jackpot.

He set the duffel bag on the floor and started sliding piles of money out of the safe. "Is there money back there?" Tricia called out.

"Oh, there's money," he said.

"I knew it. Didn't I fucking tell you?"

Tomlin emptied the safe. There was a lockbox on the bar, beside a bowl of cut limes, and he emptied it, too. He surveyed the bar and, satisfied, circled back around to the table and knelt beside the waitress on the floor. She was very young, around twenty. She was shaking, crying, naked with fear. Tomlin smiled through the ski mask. "Are you scared?"

The girl swallowed. "Yes."

Tomlin touched her hair, and she flinched. *If I had but world enough, and time,* he thought. He forced himself to stand, and started back to Tricia. Midway there, he watched her eyes go wide. She looked past him. "Boss."

Tomlin caught her look and spun around. Saw a young guy in the kitchen doorway, a scrawny kid with a pistol. "No fucking way," the kid said. "You chose the wrong game, motherfuckers."

56

THE KID HELD his gun sideways, like in the movies. Aimed it square at Tomlin's chest. Tomlin held his rifle steady. "Just be easy," he said.

"You be easy." The kid's face was screwed up with rage or false courage. "This is my house."

Tomlin stared down the barrel of the kid's gun and felt strangely calm. "You shoot me, my friend shoots you. Put the gun down and you live."

The kid spat. "I ain't putting shit down."

"Fine." Tomlin swung the rifle around and fired at the kid, quick. The kid squeezed off three shots, missed with each one, and then Tomlin got him. Four or five shots to the chest, rapid-fire. The impact threw the kid hard into the doorframe, and he hit it and slumped down to the floor.

The waitress screamed, and Tricia screamed, too. Tomlin advanced with the rifle, putting holes in the kid until the kid dropped his gun. Tomlin kicked the gun into the kitchen. The kid was slumped over now, his head down, his chest bloody. Tomlin stood above him, his adrenaline surging. He looked back at Tricia. "You okay?"

She was staring at the dead kid, but she nodded. Tomlin shouldered the duffel bag and walked back to Tricia. He stuffed the wallets and the watches and the rest of the guns into the bag, and then he surveyed the room, the men lying facedown on the floor, the trembling waitress, the dead kid in the back. "Try anything slick and we'll kill you, too," he told them. "Be happy you're alive."

He walked to the doorway and stood there until he was sure the whole room had seen him. Then he emptied the rifle into the ceiling, just to watch the poor bastards squirm.

57

TOMLIN THREW the duffel bag and the guns in the backseat of the Camry and slid in the passenger side. "Let's go," he told Dragan. "Get us out of here."

Dragan glanced at him and pressed hard on the gas. "We make it?"

Tomlin looked back at the warehouse door as the Camry sped off. No sign of life yet. The place still looked abandoned. "We made it."

"Big money?"

"Fucking right." Tomlin rolled down the window and listened, the cold air and the adrenaline making him shiver in his seat. He didn't hear any sirens. He rolled the window up again and looked back at Tricia.

She was staring out the window, breathing heavy. "Holy shit," she was saying. She'd been saying it since they left the warehouse.

Dragan made the main road and turned south, toward Saint Paul. He drove quickly, but with little urgency, blending in to traffic. Tomlin watched the city approach in the distance. Then he glanced back at Tricia again. *All fun and games until someone loses a life.*

He'd imagined he would feel horrified, the first time he killed.

He'd imagined he would feel sick with remorse. Instead of remorse, though, he felt numb. Detached. Hell, if anything, he felt good.

Tomlin turned away from Tricia and stared out the window again. Felt an electric rush course through his body. He watched the night blur past and listened to Tricia hyperventilate in the backseat, and he thought about the survivors and wished he'd killed them all.

DRAGAN DROVE BACK to the garage, parked, and shut off the engine. For a moment, nobody moved. Then Tricia opened her door and climbed out of the car. Dragan followed, and Tomlin watched as Tricia walked to him, wrapped her arms around him, pulled him close. Listened as she sobbed into his shirt. Tomlin waited, tapping a rhythm with his feet on the concrete. "We'll divide up the money tomorrow," he told them. "My office."

Tricia nodded, her eyes swollen and bloodshot. She held tight to Dragan's shirt and didn't say anything. Tomlin watched as she climbed into Dragan's Civic. Waited as the Civic drove off. Then he emptied the Camry, stuffed the guns and the money inside the Jaguar and drove out of the garage. Found a hard-rock station and played the music loud, speeding as fast as he dared back toward Saint Paul.

THE HOUSE WAS DARK when he pulled into the driveway. Becca was already asleep. Tomlin lay down beside her, wide awake, the adrenaline still pumping through his body. He leaned over and nudged her, and she groaned and smiled, sleepy. "Hi, honey."

He kissed her on the mouth, hard. Becca's eyes opened wide. He brought a hand to her chest, and she stiffened. Tried to protest, but he kissed her again, reaching for the drawstring to her pajama pants. She struggled beneath him. "*Carter.*"

"Go with it." He kissed her again. "Let's have fun."

She stayed rigid as he kissed her neck, cupped her ass. Groaned as he pulled her pajama pants off. "I'm too tired, Carter."

"Just relax," he said. "It's all right."

He kissed her again. This time, after a moment, she kissed him back, soft, and he knew he had won. He grabbed her by her shoulders and flipped her onto her stomach and entered her from behind. She cried out beneath him, struggled, and he knew he was hurting her, but he didn't stop. He pictured the dead kid at the game, the terrified waitress, heard the roar of the machine gun in his hands, imagined Tricia in his arms, naked and willing and scared.

He came within minutes, and collapsed on top of her, panting for breath. After a long minute, Becca shifted beneath him. Shrugged him away. Tomlin rolled to his side and lay beside her, listening to the blood pounding in his ears. He stared at his wife's back, and realized she was sobbing.

58

WINDERMERE CAME TO CID early. She'd slept well after her workout, woke up at dawn with a clear mind and a positive vibe. *I'm solving this case*, she thought. *Doughty and Tomlin and Jackson be damned.*

Mathers was lingering around her desk. Caught her eye as she walked down the aisle. "Hey, Supercop."

Damn right, she thought. "Shouldn't you be hungover somewhere?"

Mathers grimaced. "Night shift. You and Doughty are looking at Camrys, right?"

"I'm looking at Camrys. Doughty's eating my prodigious dust."

"My bad." Mathers held up his hands. "You heard about that shoot-out in Saint Paul?"

She shook her head. "Tell me."

"Some kind of poker game," he said. "Underground, in a warehouse. Check the wire. Someone put a Camry at the scene."

"A shoot-out."

"Assault rifles and everything. One dead." Mathers shrugged. "Something's going on up there, anyway."

"Hot damn." Windermere reached for her phone. "That's the power of positive thinking, my friend."

TEN MINUTES LATER, she was peeling out of the FBI garage in the Chevelle again, her foot hard on the gas, the tires squealing and her mind doing smash cuts as she raced for the highway.

An underground poker game. Saint Paul PD hadn't given her much, just an address and the name of the homicide cop on scene. A gold Camry and an assault rifle, though, sounded pretty damn good.

Windermere raced east on I-94, took I-35E north and out of the city. Followed the cop's directions to an industrial district, a train yard. Cruised around until she saw flashing police lights in the distance.

It was a crummy little industrial complex, drab and anonymous. Windermere parked the Chevelle behind a Saint Paul PD cruiser, ducked under the police tape, and glanced up at the security camera above the front door. Then she walked in.

Inside, the warehouse looked like someone's private club. Dark wood-paneled walls, carpet, solid poker tables. A bar at the back, all the liquor top-shelf. The room was crowded with cops—the medical examiner and a forensic technician and plain, nosy cops—all of them clustered around a body in back. A uniform stood guard just inside. "FBI," Windermere told him. "Where's Detective Parent?"

A tired-looking plainclothesman looked up from the huddle. "I'm Parent," he said, walking over. "Who are you?"

Windermere showed him her badge. "What happened here?"

Parent glanced back at the body. Shrugged. "These guys run an underground game," he said. "High stakes. Higher than usual, last night."

"Who's the body?"

"Local kid, nobody special. We found a gun in the back—there's a kitchen back there—figure he tried to make a stand."

"Leads on the murder weapon?"

Parent nodded. "Shells are .223s, and there's a shitload of them. An assault rifle, and the shooter went nuts."

Windermere looked around the place. Pockmarks in the walls. Poker chips still on the table. Cards, too. Some poor bastard had pocket aces. She turned back to the detective. "Witnesses?"

Parent snorted. "Anonymous call. Time we got here, the place was deserted."

"Saw a security camera by the door."

He shook his head. "Wiped."

"Shit."

"Guess they value their privacy." Parent studied her face. "What's the FBI care, anyway?"

"Bank robberies," she told him. "We're chasing a crew, shoots .223 Remingtons and drives a Toyota Camry. Heard there was a Camry involved."

Parent nodded again. "Security camera across the street caught the car parked outside. Can just barely tell it's a Camry."

"Plates?"

He shook his head. "Like I said, pretty blurry."

Windermere circled the poker tables. Parent followed. "You have any leads whatsoever?" she asked him.

"Just pretty much what you got," he said. "The Camry and the rifle."

"So not much," she said. "Shit."

She walked over to the body. A skinny teenager in baggy jeans and an oversized T-shirt, five or six bloody holes in his chest. *Shit*. Parent cleared his throat. "These games, they're kind of a secret. Nobody advertises, you know?"

Windermere looked at him. "Our killers knew this place existed."

Parent nodded. "And someone had to recognize them outside. That door's reinforced steel. These guys walked right in. Means someone unlocked the door."

"They had a partner inside."

"Or someone thought they were friendly."

"Either way, they had an inside connection."

The crew's first murder, thought Windermere. *First a note, then a gun, then a team, then a body. These guys are getting bolder and bolder.*

So who are they? Where are they hiding? And where was Carter Tomlin when this whole thing went down?

59

TRICIA HADN'T ARRIVED when Tomlin got to work the next
morning. He sat in his office with the duffel bag on his desk,
resisting the urge to count the money without her.

He thought about Becca as he waited for his computer to boot up.
She'd spent a long time in the shower in the morning, had emerged
with swollen, exhausted eyes and a tight line to her lips, and had said
very little to him before he'd left for work.

Tomlin thought about her and felt a little ashamed. He'd been
rougher with his wife than he'd ever imagined he could be. He felt
even worse when he thought about the kid he'd murdered. He
felt nauseated.

Tricia came in just before nine. He heard her unlock the door
and walk in, pretended to check his e-mail as she sorted herself out
in the lobby. Then she poked her head into his office. "Hey," she said.

She was beautiful. Radiant. She'd spiked her hair up, and her
eyes seemed bigger than normal. She wore a tight-fitting blouse that
hugged the curves of her body, and a black pencil skirt that ended
just above the knee. She caught his look and grinned at him. "I almost look legit, huh?"

He couldn't help smiling. "Almost." He paused. "You okay?"

She looked from his face to the bag and back again. "I'm sorry I freaked out," she said, sighing. "I talked it over with Dragan." She shrugged. "It was self-defense, right? You couldn't help it."

Tomlin nodded. "He was going to kill us."

"Exactly. Self-defense."

They looked at each other for a moment, and Tomlin wondered if she really believed what she was saying. If she wasn't addicted to the same thrills, deep down.

Tricia unzipped the bag and tipped it onto the desk, spilling cash everywhere. Laughed, giddy, as the cash tumbled out. "Should we dance in it?"

Tomlin grinned at her. At the money. Reached into the pile and came out with a watch. Tricia's eyes went wide. "Rolex," she said. "Holy diamonds." He took her hand, slid the watch up her delicate wrist as she watched him. It was a man's watch, too big for her, slid up almost to her shoulder. Precocious, like she was a little girl playing dress-up. She picked up another watch. "You like Cartier?"

"Why not?" He held out his hand, and she took it in hers, strapped the leather band to his wrist. For a moment her touch lingered, something electric. Then she turned back to the money, and Tomlin watched her as she tallied the stacks, that ridiculous gold watch sliding up and down her sleeve.

There was something irresistible about her, about the grin on her face and the flush on her cheeks. He imagined taking her as he'd taken Becca last night, and he felt a thrill. Tricia looked like the kind who wouldn't mind playing rough.

Tricia dropped the last stack of cash on the desk. "Two hundred twenty thousand, plus the wallets." She laughed, sharp and sudden. "Didn't I tell you?"

"You told me," he said. "I admit. You did good."

She put a hand on her hip. "That's it?"

"Great. You did great."

She held the pose. Winked at him. "I know," she said. Then she turned back to the money and began to parcel out the cash. Tomlin watched her count out Dragan's share, then her own, admiring her body through her tight blouse.

"What are you doing with your share?" he asked her.

Tricia cocked her head. "Maybe buy a car. A convertible. Go on a vacation somewhere. What about you?"

Mortgage, Tomlin thought. *Kids' college funds.* He started to answer. Then he shook his head. "I haven't decided yet," he said. "Something badass."

60

NANCY STEVENS STARED up at Tomlin's house through the Cherokee's passenger window. "Wow," she said. "What a mansion."

Stevens parked at the curb, killed the engine. "Don't get any ideas," he said. "The guy's probably swimming in debt."

"And you think he's a bank robber?"

"I don't," Stevens said, climbing out of the car. "Windermere does, and she might have a point. You'd need to rob banks to pay the heat in the winter."

"All the same," Nancy said, as they started up the walk to the house. "It's a beautiful home. Very romantic."

"Our house isn't romantic?"

She shot him a smile. "Our house is fine, Agent Stevens. If we had a house like this, though, you might get lucky more often."

Stevens rang the doorbell. "Fat chance," he said. "We'd be too busy robbing banks."

The front door swung open, Carter Tomlin behind it. He saw Stevens and hesitated. Then he smiled. "Kirk," he said, stepping back to usher them inside. "And Nancy. Glad you could make it."

Nancy shook Tomlin's hand. "We were just admiring your house."

Tomlin's smile widened. "It's too big," he said, "but we like it. Everyone gets their space. Come on in."

They followed Tomlin through the front hall. Stevens nudged Nancy as they walked. "Told you. It's a handful. He said it himself."

Nancy elbowed him back. "Someone's feeling inadequate."

"Or maybe someone else is compensating."

She laughed, shushed him with her hand, and then they were in the vast living room. Four or five other couples milled about, drinking wine, chatting, playing with Snickers. They were all well dressed and about Tomlin's age. Tomlin introduced Stevens and Nancy to the room, then excused himself, promising to come back with something to drink.

Almost immediately, Becca Tomlin found Nancy and brought her into a cluster of wives by the fireplace, leaving Stevens alone at the door. He looked around the room, then walked to the picture window and stared out over the dark lawn.

"You're the guy who solved Terry Harper's fiasco." Stevens looked right, and found a lanky, fair-haired man beside him. The man held out his hand. "Dan Rydin."

"Kirk Stevens." Stevens shook Rydin's hand. "You know Harper?"

"Work with him at North Star." Rydin smiled. "And with Carter, too, now that the whole neighborhood accountant experiment is over."

"Neighborhood accountant." Stevens frowned. "I thought he was corporate."

Rydin laughed and leaned closer. "Laid off in the summer. He's been doing your grandmother's taxes ever since."

"Huh." Stevens gestured around the room. "Guess he did okay on his own."

Rydin shook his head. "Guess again."

"Yeah?"

"This is all leverage, man," Rydin said. "We're talking copious debt. I'm amazed he kept his family intact."

Stevens looked at Rydin. Rydin grinned back through watery eyes. There was scotch on his breath already. "Usually, these cases, the wife is the first thing to go," Rydin continued. "Divorce, then bankruptcy. Wasn't for me, he'd be sunk."

Stevens smiled. "You're the big hero, huh?"

"Got him his job, didn't I? Saved his life."

Stevens made to reply. Looked up and caught Tomlin's reflection in the window. The accountant stood alone on the other side of the room, holding two tumblers and staring at Stevens and Rydin. He met Stevens's eyes and smiled and came over. "So you've met my new boss." He handed Stevens a glass. "Everything all right?"

Rydin winked at Stevens. "Everything's fine, Carter. Relax."

"Not while you're around, partner." Tomlin smiled at Stevens. "Invite an accountant to a party and you know you're getting robbed, one way or the other."

He looked around the room. "One way or the other," he said again. Then he smiled again. "I'll just check on the caterers. Excuse me."

Rydin watched Tomlin go. Then he nudged Stevens. "Living on the edge," he said. "Told you. I'm a hero."

He laughed and emptied his glass. Stevens watched him. *A hero,* he thought. *Maybe. Maybe not.*

61

TOMLIN WATCHED STEVENS and his pretty wife throughout dinner. Watched them share jokes, laugh together, flirt when they thought nobody was watching. They looked so easy together, so comfortable.

Becca caught his eye from across the dinner table. She smiled at him. He forced himself to smile back. Raised his wineglass and winked at her. She smiled again wider, and Tomlin studied her face and was struck, suddenly and guiltily, by how she'd aged since he'd married her. She'd been a girl, fresh-faced and stunning. She was a mother now. A housewife.

Then Rydin's wife touched Becca's hand and asked her something about the kitchen cabinets, and Becca smiled at him one more time, then looked away. Tomlin snuck another glance at Kirk and Nancy Stevens.

They look perfect, he thought. *Like everyone else at this table. Like they've never struggled to make a mortgage payment. Like they never fight, even. They're in love, and they're happy, and he's barely a policeman. Probably didn't even go to college.*

And she's some kind of Legal Aid lawyer. Older than Becca, but barely looks thirty-five. Miles out of her husband's league, and she looks at him like she'd never had the thought. Laughing and smiling, and they're probably piss-poor.

Her whole life is a waste. What the hell is she happy about?

THEY ATE A WONDERFUL dinner in the Tomlins' stately dining room, four courses, fully catered. The price of the meal, Stevens figured, would have fed his own family for a month. But then, he decided, he might willingly starve for another helping of tonight's prime rib.

After dinner, the partiers migrated back into the Tomlins' living room. Stevens talked to Rydin some more, and some of Rydin's friends, all of them bankers and businessmen. Then, when the conversation turned to best accounting practices, Stevens excused himself and asked Becca Tomlin to point him to the bathroom.

"Around the corner and by the back stairs," she told him, smiling. "Are you having a good time?"

"A great time," he told her. "Dinner was spectacular."

She blushed. "A little over-the-top, but Carter wanted to show off. It's his night."

"Might as well do it right," Stevens said, and Becca smiled and touched his arm and pointed him down the hall to the bathroom.

After he'd finished, Stevens stepped out into the hallway again and found himself alone. Voices carried from the living room, and light, but the hall itself was deserted. Stevens stood in the darkness, thinking about Rydin's commentary before dinner. About Tomlin, laid off. A desperate man in an oversized house. Bank robbery almost made sense.

Stevens shook his head and started back down the hall toward the party. Then he stopped. *Here's your chance*, he thought. *They won't miss you.*

Someone laughed in the living room, loud. Glasses clinked together. Stevens turned and walked down the hall. Found himself in a bright, modern kitchen. The caterers looked up as he stuck his head through the doorway.

"Looking for the little boys' room," he said, backing out. To his right was a little stairway, five or six steps, then a door to the driveway. Another stairway headed down from the landing. *If I were a bank robber*, Stevens thought, *where would I hide my tools?*

Stevens looked back into the kitchen again. The caterers had forgotten him, were scrubbing dishes and scraping plates, chatting with one another. Stevens turned back to the stairway. Paused on the top step. *You don't even have a warrant. Nothing you find is admissible.*

Calm down. It's not even your case. You find something, you let Windermere worry about procedure.

There was a long, low hallway at the bottom of the stairs. A dim yellow light and a bare concrete floor. Stevens peered into the first room, saw a new washer and dryer set, a sink, clothes hanging above. Laundry room. He backed out. Heard the sounds of the party above him, nothing else. They would start to miss him soon. *Hurry up.* Stevens crossed the hall to the next room. Felt around for a light switch and flicked it on. Then he stood in the doorway and stared.

It wasn't going to put Tomlin in jail, anyway. Wasn't evidence of any wrongdoing at all. Still, it was breathtaking. Stevens took a couple steps into the room, the party and Tomlin momentarily forgotten.

It was a huge toy train setup. It filled the whole room. Cities and vast mountain ranges, factories and apartment buildings and marshaling yards. Thousands of tiny trees, and hordes of detailed little people, in corner stores and waiting in the stations, living out their lives. Stevens stared at it, awed. *It must have taken Tomlin months to put this thing together*, he thought. *Almost belongs in a museum.*

He walked deeper into the room, toward the control system at the center of the table. A panel of dials and levers and LED lights, complicated beyond Stevens's comprehension. A little Amtrak train waited in front of the controls.

Stevens found the power switch on the panel. Looked at the train.

Just once around the loop, he thought. *Then back to the party.* He reached for the power switch. Tomlin's voice stopped him. "What the hell are you doing?"

Stevens spun. Found his host staring in at him through the doorway, his face a mask of barely contained anger.

62

TOMLIN STARED IN at Stevens, struggling to keep his breathing steady. The BCA agent stood poised by the control panel, a few feet away from where Tony Schultz's sawed-off shotgun lay hidden in its cradle.

"What the hell are you doing?" Tomlin said again. "How did you get down here?"

Stevens took a step back. Held up his hands. "Carter, I'm sorry."

"You shouldn't be down here." Tomlin felt his heart pounding, and he glanced at the mountain that housed the assault rifle. "You shouldn't be down here. Why are you here?"

Stevens didn't reply. *He knows,* Tomlin thought. He felt his heart start to pound as he realized he would have to kill the BCA agent. Schultz's Sig Sauer waited in a box below the train table, hidden under a pile of spare parts. Stevens didn't look armed. *If I can get to that gun,* Tomlin thought, *I can kill him.*

STEVENS STUDIED TOMLIN. Tomlin stared back like a dog in a fight, his body tensed, his eyes unsteady. *There's something going on here,* Stevens thought. *This is more than a guest wandering off at a party.*

The floorboards creaked above. Laughter filtered down through the ceiling. *Sooner or later, someone's going to notice we're gone.* Stevens looked at Tomlin again and wished he'd brought his sidearm.

"I'm sorry, Carter," he said, raising his hands. "Your wife said you had a train setup down here. I guess I wanted to see it."

Tomlin looked past him again, to the trains. Said nothing. Stevens gestured to the setup, smiling sheepishly. "It's really something, anyway. The detail. Amazing."

Tomlin looked at him, hard.

"Must have taken you months." Stevens smiled and tried to look friendly. Inside, his whole body was tensed, waiting for Tomlin to spring at him or pull a weapon, or whatever he was thinking about doing. *There's something here,* Stevens thought. *A couple minutes more and you might have found it. Instead, you might have to fight your way out.*

63

TOMLIN KNEW the BCA agent was bullshitting. He could see it in the way Stevens's muscles stayed tense, even as he cast Tomlin that same friendly smile across the train room. *You blew it,* Tomlin thought. *Now he knows you're hiding something.*

What now?

The rifle was behind the mountain. The shotgun under the table. The pistol in the box below the benchwork. But if he made a move for any weapon, did anything sudden, the BCA agent would tackle him.

Anyway, none of the weapons were loaded. Tomlin made sure to empty them every time he returned to the house. Safer for Heather and Madeleine. The ammunition was close, but Tomlin knew there was no way he could grab a weapon and load it before Stevens was on him.

Stevens had his hands up, still waiting. Still smiling. *He wants to get out of here as much as you do,* Tomlin thought. *He's prepared to bullshit his way out. That means he doesn't have enough to take you.*

If you show him a weapon, your life is over. Right now, Stevens has nothing. No evidence whatsoever, and no warrant. You keep calm, and you're safe. Really, what were the other options? Try and fight Stevens, overpower him, kill him. And then—what? Go back to the party? Start running?

No. Stevens was ready to bullshit. Tomlin was ready to bullshit, too. He matched Stevens's smile. "Becca thinks I'm crazy."

Stevens nodded. "Yeah?"

"Women never get it," Tomlin said. He shrugged. "Come on back upstairs, huh? Let's have another drink."

Stevens didn't answer for a moment. Then he nodded again. "Sure," he said. "A drink sounds good about now."

Tomlin stepped back and let Stevens lead him out of the room. Glanced around the train room one more time. Then he switched off the light and followed Stevens upstairs, his whole body still tense, his heart pounding.

64

YOU'RE QUIET," Nancy said, as Stevens started the Cherokee and pulled away down Summit Avenue. "Did you have fun?"

Stevens looked back at Tomlin's house in his mirror, lit up and dramatic like a Christmas postcard. He nodded. "Sure."

Tomlin had disappeared after the incident in the train room. He came back twenty minutes later and started subtly moving people to the door. Hadn't looked at Stevens. Hadn't said much. It was only as Stevens and Nancy crossed the threshold, bundled up, and headed back to the car that he'd stepped out onto the porch, hand outstretched and eyes meeting Stevens's. "Glad you could make it," he said.

Stevens hesitated before shaking Tomlin's hand. "Thanks for having us."

Tomlin's hand was damp, but his grip was tight. "Basketball Tuesday."

"Tuesday." Stevens took back his hand and turned toward the front steps. "See you there."

Now Nancy looked at Stevens sideways as he piloted the Cherokee back toward Lexington. "You're too quiet," she said. "What's the matter?"

Stevens drove in silence for a few blocks. He stared out at the road, thinking, his tensed muscles only now starting to relax. *A couple minutes more in that train room*, he thought, *you'd have found it. Whatever Tomlin didn't want you to find.*

A couple minutes more. Instead, you have nothing.

Nancy touched his arm. "Kirk?" Stevens glanced at her. Shook his head. Nancy caught his expression and frowned. "What the hell happened?"

Stevens stared ahead and didn't answer. Then he sighed. "I'm not sure."

"Are you sick? This is scary."

"I'm not sick." He kept driving. "I just have this funny feeling Windermere might be right."

65

TOMLIN STOOD AT the front door, watching the last of the guests drive away. He locked the door and walked back to the dining room, where Becca was helping the caterers clear up the last of the dishes. She smiled at him as he entered. "I'm exhausted," she said, starting into the kitchen with a load of dishes. "Playing hostess is hard work."

"You invited the Stevenses," he said, following her. "You didn't tell me."

Becca put the plates in the sink. Then she looked at him. "I thought he was your friend."

No, Tomlin thought, *Stevens isn't my friend. He's a BCA agent, and you invited him into my home. If I hadn't caught him in the train room, he could have ruined everything.* He forced a smile at Becca. "I'm just worried they were out of their league here."

"I don't think so. Nancy Stevens is one smart lady. She sounds like a hell of a lawyer."

A lawyer and a cop. Roaming around my house. Talk about living on the edge.

"You're not mad, are you?" Becca asked him.

Tomlin thought about Stevens again. Saw some humor in it now.

The dumb cop would kill himself if he knew the shot he'd just blown. Tomlin couldn't keep from smiling. "No," he said, walking to her and wrapping his arms around her. "I'm not mad."

She stiffened. "Carter, the caterers—"

"Forget about the caterers."

Becca remained tense. Everywhere he touched felt like stone. "No," she said. "Not tonight, honey. Okay?"

He kissed her. "Why not?"

She found his reflection in the window. Met his eyes. "Last time, it scared me. What you did."

"Come on. We were just having fun."

He kissed down her neck, brought his hand to her breast. She squirmed around in his grip. "Carter," she said. "I said no."

The last caterer walked into the kitchen, looked at them both, paused at the doorway. Tomlin ignored her. He stared at Becca's reflection in the window, her tired eyes. He closed his eyes and imagined holding Tricia. Becca squirmed again. "Carter."

Tomlin opened his eyes. Met her gaze in the window and thought again about Tricia. "Fine," he said. "Suit yourself."

He left her there. Walked out of the kitchen and back down to the basement, where he checked on his guns and then spent the next two hours fiddling with his trains, creating spectacular, fiery collisions and imagining Kirk Stevens trapped in the flames.

66

DOUGHTY DROPPED a note on Windermere's desk. "Message from Saint Paul homicide," he said. "The detective from that poker game."

Windermere picked up the note. Read it and reached for her phone. "Parent," she said. "I'll see what he wants."

"Already done." Doughty leaned over and held down the receiver. "He found us a witness."

She looked at him. "You talked to him?"

"Set up a meeting, in fact. I also took the liberty of updating the good detective's contact information, since he seemed to think this is your case."

The big cop looked at Windermere like he was waiting for her to react. She didn't. Doughty had been bitchy since she'd returned from the poker game, either pissed off or jealous, or both. So far, she'd ignored him and focused on chasing down leads, but now she struggled to stay cool, wanting nothing more than to wipe the self-satisfied smirk from her partner's face.

Doughty held the moment a beat too long. Then he turned and

started for the elevator. "Grab your coat, Agent Windermere," he called over his shoulder. "Maybe you want to tag along."

DOUGHTY DROVE SLOWLY, too slowly, in his department Crown Vic. Windermere sat on her hands in the passenger seat, thinking about the Chevelle and how fast it could take her.

You have to be a team player, she thought. *You want to be a real FBI agent, you have to learn how to put up with the bullshit.*

Doughty took I-94 into Saint Paul and parked downtown. He led Windermere into a Starbucks beneath a couple of big office towers. Ordered a coffee and let Windermere fend for herself. "He's late," Doughty said, checking his watch.

Windermere waved off the barista. "Who is he?"

"Guess we'll find out."

The front door opened, bells rang, and Windermere looked over as a nervous twentysomething walked in, dolled up in a flashy suit and designer shades. He took off the sunglasses, found Doughty and Windermere, and walked over, looking like a freshman who'd somehow wandered into the prom. "You guys the cops?" he said, his voice low.

"We're better," said Doughty. "FBI."

"Jason Bernstein." The kid looked at Doughty. "I guess I talked to you on the phone." Then he looked at Windermere. "You his partner?"

Windermere nodded. "You want a coffee or something?"

Bernstein shook his head. "I just want to get this done."

Doughty brought his coffee to a sofa and a couple of easy chairs in the back, away from the counter and the few mid-morning customers. Windermere followed Bernstein. The kid looked around, twice, before sitting down. He leaned forward, his elbows bouncing on his knees, jittery.

Windermere sat opposite the kid. Looked at Doughty, who was preoccupied, stirring sugar into his coffee. She looked at Bernstein again. "So what's your story?" she said. "You saw this go down, or what?"

Bernstein looked at Doughty. "I don't want my name on it," he said. "And I want immunity."

Doughty frowned. "What did you do?"

Bernstein looked at Windermere. Didn't say anything. "The poker's not our concern," Windermere told him. "If you were just playing cards, you'll be fine."

Bernstein searched her eyes. "I don't want my name on it."

"No names."

Bernstein swallowed. Then he launched into the play-by-play. The Friday-night game, around midnight. A bunch of the regulars there. "We'd been into it for an hour or so," he said. "Someone buzzed the door, wanted in. Wouldn't leave."

"Game has a security guard, right?"

"Yeah," Bernstein said, "but this was a chick outside. Said she wanted to party. The guard talked with Tom—with the organizer. He told her no for a while. Then he gave up."

"Let her in," said Windermere.

Bernstein nodded. "She came in with a dude, a guy in a ski mask. Had a big fucking gun, an M-16 or something. They emptied the safe, took our wallets, our watches, everything."

"And killed the cook in the back."

"Yeah." Bernstein nodded, slow. "The guy with the rifle was saying something to—to the waitress. Toying with her. Then the guy comes out of the back with a pistol, tries to make a stand. The guy with the rifle lit him up."

Doughty sat forward. "Nobody else has come forward from this thing. No witnesses, nothing. So why you?"

Bernstein looked at Windermere. "The kid's dead, right? Someone should catch heat for it."

"Probably won't get your money back," Doughty said. "If that's what you're after."

"Fuck the money. I can't sleep without seeing that kid's face."

Windermere nodded. "Okay, so what else? The guy was toying with the waitress, you said."

"You said the guy wore a ski mask," said Doughty. "What about the woman?"

Bernstein glanced at Windermere. "He was, like, playing with her or something. He asked her if she was scared."

Bingo. "And the ski mask?"

"The girl didn't wear one." He frowned again. "Thing is, she'd been there before. She dyed her hair since, but it was definitely her."

"She's a player," said Doughty.

"No." Bernstein laughed, hollow. "She was awful at cards. She came with Pete Schneider. Sometimes he let her play with his money. Not a lot, though. She was pretty damn bad."

Windermere smiled at him. "Pete Schneider."

"Pete Schneider," said Doughty.

Bernstein looked at each of them, one at a time. Then he sighed. "I guess you guys want to know where to find him."

67

CHRIS RUSSELL SAT at her desk in the Hastings Police Department, staring at her computer screen, paging through Tony Schultz's hard drive. She'd managed to convince the big dope to hand over his computer. Told him it was probably the only way they'd catch Roger Brill.

"Bullshit," Schultz had replied. "I got personal shit on there."

"I don't care about your porno, Tony," Russell said, and sighed. "Only way to track this guy Brill is to trace his e-mail backward."

"What about his car?"

"His truck?" She laughed. "Tony, you told me Brill drove a dark SUV. You know how many Brills there are in the state driver database?"

Schultz had glared at her. "Said he was from Minneapolis."

"And there's sixty-five Brills in the Twin Cities phone book. None of them is your guy." She put her hand on her hip. "You want those guns back, you gotta give me your hard drive."

He'd glared at her some more. Then he swore, spat, slumped his shoulders, and helped her cart his yellowed computer tower out to her cruiser.

It wasn't like she'd been lying to Schultz. Roger Brill was a god-

damned wild-goose chase. Probably just an alias attached to a free
Hotmail account. If she could trace Brill's IP address, she might have
a lead. And if she could pick up some intel about Schultz while she
tried, hell, everybody wins.

Schultz's hard drive wasn't going to be much help, however. It
was mostly just porn and lame e-mail forwards, a few family pictures.
Russell recognized Scotty Montgomery from a couple of shots.
Scotty Mo was a Hastings patrol officer; he'd married Schultz's little
sister. They had a couple of cute kids, little boys.

So the computer was pretty much a waste of time. Russell had
been hoping for something drug-related, a saved e-mail or something, maybe a spreadsheet. But from the looks of it, Tony Schultz
couldn't even spell *spreadsheet*, much less figure out how to use one.

So, okay, Roger Brill. Russell loaded up Schultz's e-mail page.
Clicked on Roger Brill's message, snooped around. A couple key-
strokes later, she had an IP address copied and pasted. *Cross your
fingers*, she thought, opening up a trace program on her own office
computer. She entered Brill's IP address and waited for the results to
load. Then the page loaded, and Russell shook her head. "Shit."

TC Wireless, the page said. An Internet service provider in Minneapolis and Saint Paul. The trace program had come back with the
ISP's address, instead of Roger Brill's.

It's never easy, Russell thought, as she picked up the phone.
Maybe they're nice people, and I won't need a warrant. She dialed the
Twin Cities phone number and a woman picked up. "TC Wireless.
Claudia speaking."

Russell introduced herself, explained the situation, the e-mail. "I
was thinking if I gave you the IP address, you could get me a bricks-
and-mortar on my suspect," she told the woman.

Claudia sucked her teeth. "One second." Disappeared. Russell
waited through half a song's worth of instrumental soft rock. Then
Claudia came back. "You have a warrant?"

Russell sighed. "Not yet."

"We can't give out information about our clients without a warrant," the woman told her. "It's a privacy thing, you understand?"

"Privacy," Russell said. "Yeah, I understand."

She hung up the phone. Swore again. *TC Wireless*, she thought. *So we've narrowed Roger Brill down to about three million people.* She stared at her computer for a minute or two. Then she reached for her phone again to see about that warrant.

68

KIRK STEVENS SAT in his living room, watching as a fat man on the television marinated a big chunk of rattlesnake. The Timberwolves weren't playing, nor the Bucks nor the Bulls, and Stevens had been channel-surfing for more than an hour, trying to find something to distract him from Carter Tomlin.

It had been a couple of days since Tomlin's party, and Stevens couldn't chase the showdown in the train room from his mind. Couldn't forget Tomlin's face—anger verging on panic—or shake the haunting feeling that he'd blown his best shot at uncovering the man's secrets.

He was hiding something, Stevens kept thinking. *I let him walk out of that basement without giving it up.*

On-screen, the fat man was grilling the rattlesnake on a barbecue the size of an oil tanker truck. Stevens sighed and turned to his wife. "You want to watch a movie or something?"

Nancy looked up from her makeshift bed on the couch, where she'd covered herself in equal parts paperwork, blanket, and dog. She yawned. "I have to make it through this crap before I fall asleep."

Stevens looked at the dog, an eighty-pound German shepherd

his son had insisted they name Triceratops. "What about you, dog? What do you want to watch?"

Triceratops studied him with concerned eyes, then lay his head down and sighed, long and expressive. "Yeah," said Stevens. "My sentiments exactly."

He'd toyed with the idea of calling Windermere. Had argued with himself for two long days, and had decided against it. What good would it do her to know that his instincts matched hers? What proof could he offer?

If I had something concrete, Stevens thought, *I could call her. Right now, all I have is a guy who's maybe a little protective of his model trains. A hunch, nothing more.*

Still, the feeling was agonizing.

Stevens picked up the remote again and changed the channel. Found an action movie. A couple of cops were holed up in a warehouse somewhere while things exploded around them. Nancy looked up again. "Anything but this," she said. "Kirk, please."

Stevens sighed again and turned off the TV. "Where's Andrea?"

"Science project at Megan's."

"JJ?"

Nancy gestured toward the front stairs. "Xbox."

Stevens stood, stretching, and walked out to the front hall and upstairs to JJ's room, where his nine-year-old son sat on his carpet, killing zombies. Stevens mussed his son's hair. "Whatcha doing?"

"*Resident Evil*," his son replied. On his TV screen, a young patrol cop and a woman in a torn evening gown were blasting away at an army of the undead. "Raccoon City is under attack."

"Sounds serious," said Stevens. "You want some help?"

Without looking up, his son passed him a controller. "You shoot with the trigger button."

Stevens picked up the controller and pressed start. Within seconds, the zombie horde was upon him. Within minutes, he was dead. JJ frowned at him. "*Dad.*"

"Sorry."

"You're wasting my lives. I gotta beat the boss at the end of this level."

"Sorry, kiddo." Stevens stood up again. "I'm cramping your style." He walked out of his son's room and stood in the dark hall, feeling bored and restless and indecisive. He wanted to know more about Tomlin, he realized. And not just for Windermere now.

Downstairs, the phone started to ring. Nancy groaned. "I'll get it," he called.

"Too late," she replied. "It's for you, Agent Stevens."

He walked down the stairs and into the living room. Cocked his head at his wife. She shrugged. "A woman."

"Windermere?"

"I don't know." She handed him the phone. "Maybe. Or another of your many admirers."

Stevens took the phone. "This is Agent Stevens."

"Agent Stevens." A woman's voice. Not Windermere. "It's Paula Franklin."

Stevens frowned. "Who?"

"BCA forensics," she said. "In the lab in Bemidji. Got the DNA results for your bodies in the woods."

"Oh." Stevens walked out to the front hall. "Right. Good."

"Ran a hurry-up drill on them, too," Franklin said. "Usually these tests take a hell of a lot longer."

Stevens stared out the window and didn't say anything. The Danzer case seemed years behind him already. After a moment, Franklin continued. "Anyway, no surprises in the results. Sylvia Danzer in the backseat and David Samson in the front."

"Sure," Stevens said. "Just like we figured."

"We had a look at the remains, too," Franklin told him. "Samson's rib cage bore nicks and gouges consistent with a stabbing. Again, no real surprise, given the knife in his chest. Danzer, though, is kind of interesting."

"How so?"

Franklin exhaled. "Well, her arm was broken, for starters. A couple of ribs. And her hands, Agent Stevens—her fingers were pretty torn up."

Stevens frowned. "Cut, you mean."

"And often. The palms of her hands, too. Classic defense wounds, and it looks like the same knife as what stabbed David Samson." Franklin paused. "There was a hell of a fight up there, from the looks of it."

"I'd say so." Stevens glanced back in at Nancy. "I can drive up tomorrow, have a look at the remains."

"No need. I'll send the relevant stuff to your office." She paused again. "Probably enough in the report to close the case, Agent. Congratulations."

Stevens said nothing.

"Agent Stevens?"

"Yeah," he said. "Great. Thanks for this. Your hard work."

"Our pleasure. Let me know if you need anything else."

"Will do." Stevens thanked Franklin again and ended the call. *Case closed*, he thought. *As closed as it ever will be.*

He stood in the hallway, picturing Sylvia Danzer and David Samson, alone in the woods, fighting and dying. He stood there a long time, and when he turned back to the living room, where Nancy and the dog both lay on the couch, fast asleep, he felt empty inside, not accomplished. *At least I'm not worrying about Tomlin,* he thought. *That's something.*

As far as victories went, though, it was minor, and short-lived.

69

THEY FOUND Pete Schneider half asleep in his swank Saint Paul condo. Arrived at his door just as a pretty redheaded girl slipped out, blushing, last night's dress hanging wrinkled from her shoulders. She smiled briefly at Windermere, then ducked past, her eyes low. Doughty watched her walk to the elevator while Windermere stuck a foot between Schneider's door and the frame. She knocked loudly, and called out his name.

Schneider came padding down the hall in flannel pajama pants, no shirt, his shaggy hair mussed. He looked at Windermere through bleary eyes. "Yeah?"

Windermere showed him her badge. "Shit," he said. He opened the door wider and led them down the hall.

SCHNEIDER'S APARTMENT was bachelor-pad chic. Leather and chrome couches, a flat-screen TV. Floor-to-ceiling windows and a kitchen piled high with take-out containers. Schneider sat on the couch and motioned to a couple of easy chairs. Doughty eased himself down. Windermere stood.

"So, what's up?" Schneider said. Windermere wondered if the guy had to work at sounding bored, or if it came natural. "What can I do for the Federal Bureau of Investigation this morning?"

"It's mid-afternoon," said Doughty. "We're here about a girl."

"A girl." Schneider smiled sideways at Windermere. "Which one?"

"How about this?" said Windermere. "You play poker in a warehouse in the North End. Used to bring a friend with you. That's the girl."

Schneider's smile faded. "I should call a lawyer."

"You guilty of something?"

Schneider stared at her and didn't say anything.

"We don't give a damn about the card game," she said. "It's your girlfriend we're after. You tell us about her and you won't need a lawyer."

Schneider sighed. "Fine," he said. "What do you want to know?"

"That poker game of yours, in the warehouse," said Windermere. "There was a robbery. The cook—what's his name, Robinson? He got shot."

Schneider stared at her. "And what, you think she did it?"

"We don't think anything yet," said Doughty.

"Tell us about the girl," said Windermere. "Maybe tell us where you were on Friday night."

"I wasn't there." Schneider didn't sound nearly so bored now. "I haven't been to that game in over a month."

"You lose all your money?"

He looked away. "I went on a cold streak. Been working a lot, trying to rebuild my bankroll."

"Working," said Windermere. "Where?"

"Dooly's," he said. "It's a bar. I was bartending every night this week. Call and check. Everybody in the place knows me."

Windermere studied his face but said nothing. Doughty, mercifully, followed her lead. After a moment, Schneider continued. "Look, as far as Tricia is concerned, I don't know what to tell you. We broke up a couple months back."

"Tricia," said Windermere. "Okay. What about a last name?"

Schneider sighed again, like it was the toughest thing in the world. "Henderson," he said. "Tricia Henderson."

"And that's all you know."

He nodded. "That's it."

"What about where she's living now?"

"She was living here," he said, shrugging, "until we broke up. Then she moved to I don't know where. So, no, I don't know where she is right now."

Windermere glanced at Doughty. Schneider stared at them. "Is that all?"

"Good enough for me," said Windermere.

Doughty stood. Glared at Schneider. "Don't make us come back."

Schneider rolled his eyes. "Wouldn't dare," he said, sounding dead bored again. Windermere shook her head and turned for the door. *Tricia Henderson*, she thought. *Honey, you're next.*

70

INSTEAD OF Tuesday's usual afternoon practice, Andrea's basketball team played an away game in East Saint Paul that night. Stevens drove his daughter across town, barely aware of the pop music she blared from the Jeep's radio. He was thinking about Tomlin some more.

The man was definitely hiding something. He'd looked just as guilty as Windermere had described when he'd found Stevens in the basement. He looked panicked. Hell, he looked half a minute away from murder.

Stevens parked the car and walked with Andrea into the gymnasium. Dropped Andrea at the locker room and leaned against the wall to wait. Pulled out his coaching clipboard. Stared at it, couldn't focus. Looked up and saw Carter Tomlin walking into the gym with his daughter. He, too, looked preoccupied. Gone was the man's preternatural confidence. Gone was his poise. His eyes were shiftier. His posture was bad. He looked like a man shrunk inside of himself.

Stevens watched him approach. Put away his clipboard and held out his hand. "Coach."

Tomlin looked up sharply. Hesitated briefly before he shook Stevens's hand. "Agent Stevens."

Heather Tomlin glanced at Stevens. Blushed bright red when he met her eye. She smiled at him and disappeared into the locker room. Stevens turned back to Tomlin. "Wanted to thank you for having us over the other night," he said. "Finest meal I've had in a long while."

Tomlin avoided his eyes. "Sure," he said. "It's no problem."

"Hope I didn't step out of bounds, wandering off on my own."

Tomlin's blue eyes were hard. His mouth was drawn tight. "Of course not."

Keep him talking, Stevens thought. "How's that new job of yours working out? Must be kind of a relief to be back in the big-business world."

Tomlin hesitated. Then he shook his head. "I don't start for two weeks."

"Gotta tie up your loose ends, I guess."

Tomlin nodded.

"Say, listen." Stevens forced a smile. "Had a bit of a tax situation spring up. Nothing serious. An issue with overtime hours. You got any time this week I could pop by the office? Maybe give me a hand?"

Tomlin stiffened. "I'm busy all week."

"Just take a few minutes. I'd happily pay you."

"Can't do it, Kirk. Sorry." Tomlin shifted his weight. "How'd that case of yours turn out? The Danzers. Any luck?"

Stevens looked at Tomlin. "Yeah," he said, nodding, "I might have a lead. Some hitchhiker, maybe. Just random bad luck."

Tomlin stared across the gym floor, thinking hard about something. "So they picked someone up," he said finally. "And he killed them."

"One more reason to steer clear of strangers, right?"

Tomlin thought a little more. Then he met Stevens's eyes. "Sounds like Elliott," he said. "At least from what I knew."

"Yeah?"

"Almost too nice, that guy," said Tomlin. "Naive. Kind of guy who'd empty his wallet for any sad sack with a story. You got the sense he'd have drowned without his wife."

"Sylvia kept him grounded, huh?"

Tomlin nodded. "Loved him, that was obvious. She just saw through the scams. Elliott never did."

"She was a realist."

"She got the bills paid on time." Tomlin paused. "How did he do it? The hitchhiker."

"Do what?" Stevens frowned. "Kill them?"

Tomlin nodded again. "Just bad luck," he said, his eyes brighter now. "That's what you said, right? They just stopped and picked him up and he killed them."

"Something like that," said Stevens. "We're still putting the pieces together."

Tomlin looked primed to say something else, but just then the locker room door opened and Heather Tomlin peered out. She looked at Tomlin and Stevens and blushed again. "Coach Stevens?" she said. "Are you going to come talk to us? It's almost game time."

Stevens glanced at Tomlin. The man had an eerie look in his eye. Like the talk of the Danzers had sparked something in him. *Carla's right,* he thought. *There's something definitely wrong here.*

"Coach Stevens?"

Stevens straightened. "Yeah," he said, turning away from Tomlin. "Here we go."

71

STEVENS KNEW SOMETHING. That much was obvious.

Tomlin replayed his conversation with the BCA agent in his head. Stevens knew something. He'd picked up on Tomlin's unease in the train room. Maybe he had talked to Windermere, after all. Either way, he was on the scent.

What to do?

At least he had time to consider the problem. With the BCA agent courtside, Tomlin had been reduced to a glorified water boy. The girls seemed more cohesive; they played better as a team. They scored more. They were winning more games. Even Heather looked happier with Stevens on the sidelines. *Coach or cop,* Tomlin thought. *The big dummy's a hero.*

What to do?

The BCA agent hadn't said anything threatening. He'd mentioned the party. Faked a cute apology for searching the basement. Asked, ever so innocently, about dropping by the office. Nothing overt. Nothing threatening. His tone, though. His tone gave him away. He was digging.

So what? Tomlin thought. *Let him dig. He has nothing.*

The smartest thing, Tomlin knew, would be to take the new job at North Star and forget about pulling bank robbery scores. Ease into a new life again. A new, boring life.

The final buzzer sounded. A big win for Kennedy. Tomlin watched the girls crowd Coach Stevens, their flushed faces bright and happy. Caught sight of Heather in the mix. Watched the way she looked at her coach. Hero worship.

The girls disappeared into the locker room. Tomlin watched the crowd empty the gym. Realized he didn't want to be alone with Stevens any longer. He walked out of the gym and into the school proper. Found the men's washroom and locked himself in a stall. *You're smarter than Stevens*, he thought. *You're better than that dummy. He's not going to outwit you.*

Tomlin thought through his conversation with Stevens again. This time, he skipped over the boring stuff. He didn't want to think about the cop anymore. He wanted to think about Elliott and Sylvia Danzer. He'd felt an electric little thrill when Stevens told him the story. A hitchhiker. Some random killer. The Danzers had stopped for him. Offered him a lift out of kindness. Their bad luck. They'd died for it. Utterly random.

Tomlin pictured the kid at the poker game. Saw his face. Courage and anger. Then fear, and the sudden realization he was dying. Tomlin wondered what the kid had thought about as he died. If he'd cursed his own shitty luck or resigned himself to fate. If he'd hated Tomlin for ending his life.

I killed him, Tomlin thought, and he suddenly knew he could never be good again. Couldn't just jump back into some day job again, some civilian life. Not when he'd tasted the alternative.

Tomlin ducked out of the stall and checked that the bathroom was empty. Then he took out his cell phone and dialed Tricia's number. Waited while the phone rang and felt his breath catch when she answered. "Boss," she said. "Hi?"

"Hey."

"Hey." She paused. "What's up?"

Tomlin felt like he was on a roller coaster climbing that first hill. "Let's do it again," he said. This was it. The first drop. He felt his adrenaline start to race. "Another score. Let's do it. Soon."

72

SCHULTZ WRITHED ON his living room floor. Pulled himself to his knees and spat blood. "I don't have the money," he said. "I don't know what the fuck else to tell you."

Ricky nodded to the driver. The driver kicked him again. A square shot to the stomach. Hard, steel-toed work boots. Knocked Schultz a couple feet backward and flat on the dusty floor again.

"You like to play rough?" Ricky asked him. "You like this kind of treatment?"

Schultz didn't answer. Focused on not throwing up. Felt tears of pain in his eyes, squinted through them. Saw the driver's Timberlands and Ricky's Prada loafers. The Timberlands approached again. Schultz tensed again, groaning. Waited for the next kick.

But the driver didn't kick him. He bent down instead and pulled Schultz to his feet. Gripped his shoulders, rough, and turned him toward Ricky. Held him upright as he swayed, his knees buckling.

Ricky studied him from the window. He was small, maybe five and a half feet. Skinny, too, underfed. A tiny spic with a smart-ass mouth and a big fucking friend to help back up his words.

They'd come in the morning. Broke the window in the front door and let themselves in. Schultz was still in bed, sleeping off a bad drunk. He'd listened to the driver's heavy footsteps as he climbed up the stairs. Pulled the sheet over his eyes and pretended the big thug was part of the hangover.

He heard the driver pause at the door, staring in at the tiny bedroom, the dirty sheets on the bed. Held his breath, waiting. *Maybe he'll just leave*, Schultz thought. *Maybe this is a dream.* Then the guy came for him. Schultz was big, but this guy was bigger. Dragged him out of bed. Dragged him downstairs to where Ricky was waiting. Kicked the shit out of him for an hour or two and then did it some more. Didn't even have the courtesy to let Schultz get dressed.

Now he stood, propped up and half naked in his own living room, bleeding, spitting out his new teeth, probably concussed again. And Ricky watched him, a B-movie gangster, probably thought he was ten kinds of tough. "You don't got a family," he said.

Schultz let the driver hold him up. Didn't reply.

"Got an ex-wife in Minneapolis," Ricky continued. "Julie Peters. Fifteen-forty-two Argyle. What I hear, though, it was a nasty divorce. Am I right?"

Schultz said nothing. The driver shook him. Schultz blinked his eyes into focus. Thought about Julie, the bitch. "Yeah," he said.

"No kids, though. No child-support payments."

"Alimony," said Schultz. "Otherwise I could pay you."

"You'll pay me." Ricky walked away from the window, to the dusty easy chair in the corner. Studied it as though weighing its worth. Then he turned back to Schultz. "You got a sister."

Schultz stiffened. "Fuck you." The driver held him tight.

Ricky smiled at him. "Got a couple of nephews."

The driver held him tighter.

"Robbie Montgomery," said Ricky. "And Kyle. Pretty cute."

"*Fuck you*," said Schultz.

"Normally, we'd start taking fingers." Ricky looked around the living room. Shrugged. "But what the fuck you need fingers for, Tony?"

Schultz struggled harder. Couldn't budge. The driver's fingers dug into his shoulder. Ricky watched him and laughed. "Get my money." He nodded to the driver. The driver dropped Schultz. Schultz lay on the floor and watched Ricky and the driver walk out of the house.

73

OMLIN WOKE UP early. Tossed and turned for an hour, then gave up and went downstairs to his train room and set an Amtrak express on a collision course against a long freight. Oil tanker cars. Diesel fuel and hazardous chemicals. A high-speed crash, devastating. He picked the pieces off the floor, and then he took the guns out from hiding, stuffed them in the duffel bag, and carried them out to the Jaguar.

He hit early-morning traffic on I-94. A thousand other rubes heading to their day jobs. Tomlin grinned to himself in the stop-and-go traffic. Turned the stereo loud. Sang along.

Tricia and Dragan were waiting by the Camry when he pulled into the parking garage. Tricia twisted in Dragan's arms as Tomlin parked, smiled at him as he climbed from the car. "Couldn't resist, huh?"

Tomlin shrugged. "Don't ever get old."

She laughed. "I don't plan to."

"What's the target?" Dragan looked calm as a corpse. A lobotomy patient. "Another bank?"

"Something new," Tomlin said. "Something we've never done."

Tricia smiled. "Mr. Excitement."

"What is it?" said Dragan.

Tomlin shook his head. "I don't know yet." He smiled at Tricia. "Let's improvise."

They climbed inside the Camry, and Dragan pulled out of the lot. Tomlin sat in the passenger seat and drummed on the dashboard. He twisted in his seat to look at Tricia. "You blow all your winnings?"

"Hell, no," she said. "How's that mortgage coming?"

"Still miles to go."

"You're really into that American Dream stuff, huh?" She smiled at him. "Wife, kids, big house, nice car?"

"I thought I was," Tomlin said. "I'm not sure anymore."

Tricia looked out the side window. "I'll never get married. Why tie yourself down?" She leaned forward and wrapped her arms around Dragan's neck, gave him a wet, sloppy kiss on the cheek. "Doesn't mean I don't love you."

Dragan smiled a little, pushed her away. "You're going to crash the car."

Tomlin watched the kid drive. Watched him make a point of wiping her kiss from his cheek, trying to play it cool. Couldn't hide his smile, though. Tomlin looked at him. Appraised him. A runty zit, less personality than a cereal box. "Take us east," Tomlin told him. "Across the river."

Dragan nodded and turned onto Central Avenue, crossed the bridge onto the East Bank. They drove northeast, away from the river and out to where the buildings got older and smaller and dirtier, where the used-car lots lining the street were all surrounded by fences topped by razor wire.

"So what's the job, boss?" Tricia said. "You want to boost a Camaro?"

Tomlin stared out the window. *Grand theft auto*, he thought. *Not a chance.* He shook his head. "I'm still thinking."

"So find us a job," she said, laughing. "Let's get started already."

Tomlin looked at Tricia. Felt a little tremor of excitement. He stared out the window some more and tried to think.

"Armored car." Dragan caught Tomlin's eye and gestured out the front of the Camry at a boxy blue van with tiny pillbox windows. The van pulled up to a stoplight, signaled left. "What do you think?"

"Are you crazy?" Tricia said. "Those guards will kill us."

Could be a million dollars in there, Tomlin thought. *They'd have a couple of guards in the back, maybe three.* He wondered if the assault rifle could pierce the vehicle's slit windows. Probably not. They would have to wait for a drop. He glanced back at Tricia. "They'll have a shitload of money."

"You think? How much?"

"Bigger than the poker game. A few hundred thousand at least."

The guards would put up a fight. They would be armed, and they wouldn't hesitate to start shooting. If something went wrong, Tomlin knew, he could die. All three of them could die. The money, though. A million bucks. And the thrill.

Tomlin stared out at the big armored truck. Imagined the guards waiting inside. They wouldn't know what was coming. And their puny pistols wouldn't go for shit against an assault rifle. Tomlin realized he was shaking. Fear, or adrenaline. A combination of both. It was not an unpleasant sensation.

I'll kill them. I'll kill the guards, and we'll walk away rich.

The light changed to green. The van rumbled left. Dragan tapped on the steering wheel, waiting for Tomlin. Tomlin looked at Tricia again. "A million bucks, maybe."

Tricia exhaled slowly. Then she nodded. Tomlin turned to Dragan. "Let's go."

Dragan signaled left and cut across two lanes of traffic, horns blaring behind them as he stepped on the gas. On the road ahead, the van was turning in to a mini-mall complex. It rumbled through the lot and stopped outside a cash-advance store. "Park close by,"

Tomlin told Dragan. "And make sure you're loaded. These guys will shoot back."

Dragan nodded. Slowed the Camry and turned in to the lot. Tomlin reached for his ski mask, his heart pounding through his chest. *This is it,* he thought. *A fucking armored car heist. Badass.*

74

THE GUARDS FOUGHT BACK.

Tomlin and Tricia waited until the armored car parked. Watched from the Camry as a big guard let himself down from the passenger door, walked around to the back of the truck, and opened the rear compartment. Another guard waited in the back with a shotgun. "Shit," Tricia said. "You sure about this?"

Tomlin stared out at the truck. *This is madness,* a part of him screamed. *This is above and beyond anything you've ever done. And you're going in blind. Unprepared.*

Tomlin gripped the assault rifle. Relished its weight, the cold steel in his hands. He could feel the rush. There was no way he was backing down now. He pulled on his ski mask. "Don't sweat the shotgun," he told Tricia. "Just get us the money, okay?"

Tricia stared out at the truck, her mouth tight. Outside, the guard with the shotgun slid a duffel bag to the rear of the truck. His partner shouldered the bag and turned toward the sidewalk.

Tomlin watched Tricia, waiting, until finally she nodded. Tomlin reached for the door handle. "Go time."

THE PARKING LOT was half full. A couple cars parked and a few more pulled out. Tomlin lifted the rifle to his shoulder, drew a bead on the shotgun guard. The guard was watching his partner with the money. He didn't notice Tomlin.

Tricia crossed behind Tomlin, headed for the cash. Tomlin steadied his breathing and found the guard in his sights. Felt his heart pounding as his finger tensed on the trigger. Someone screamed behind him and the guard tensed. Spun around and saw Tomlin. Tomlin pulled hard on the trigger and fired a burst into the rear of the van. The guard staggered backward, fell down.

More screaming now. Tomlin advanced on the van. Heard the *BOOM* as Tricia unloaded the shotgun. Heard plate glass shatter. Glanced over and saw the second guard drop the cash bag. Tricia shouted something, and the guard fell to his knees as she wrenched the bag away.

The van shifted into gear and jolted forward, its big engine roaring. Collided hard with a hatchback, bounced off, and kept going. Tomlin fired another burst and ran after the van, jumped into the rear compartment as it crashed through the lot.

"Stop the fucking van."

The driver ignored him, safe in his bulletproof compartment. Tomlin looked out the rear of the van, saw Dragan helping Tricia with the first duffel bag. He steadied himself against the sidewall and examined the van's contents as the driver accelerated.

Three more duffel bags, each identical to the first. Tomlin grabbed them and threw each one down to the pavement. Looked around the rest of the compartment and saw nothing he wanted. The driver was at the end of the parking lot now, barreling toward the road. Tomlin staggered to the rear of the van. Hesitated, looking down at the blurry pavement below. Then he jumped. Hit the pavement hard, fell to his knees and rolled, feeling grit on his hands, on his knees. He picked himself up and shouldered the rifle. The armored truck sped away.

People weren't screaming anymore. Tomlin looked around and saw bystanders cowering behind parked cars. Heard the sirens in the distance. He brushed off his pants and started back to the first bag of cash where he'd thrown it.

Dragan drove the Camry to him, braked hard, the tires squealing. Tomlin threw the duffel bag into the trunk. Ran to the second, then the third bag, and threw them both in behind. Was about to climb in the car himself when he noticed Tricia's guard in front of the cash-advance store. He paused. *"Get in!"* Tricia shouted. *"We have to go!"*

The guard looked dazed, unsteady. He locked eyes with Tomlin. Tomlin raised the assault rifle. Tricia shouted something else. The sirens got closer. Tomlin could feel the blood pounding in his ears. Then it all seemed to mute. He could almost hear the guard breathing.

The guard didn't run. He stood, waiting, his eyes locked on Tomlin's. *Your life is over,* Tomlin thought. *Are you scared?*

He pulled the trigger, and the guard went down.

75

DOUGHTY PULLED the Crown Vic into the apartment complex and parked in front of the first of three high-rise buildings. Windermere surveyed the parking lot for gold Camrys. A long shot, or maybe not; Tricia Henderson hadn't registered any Toyota with the DMV, but Windermere wasn't about to assume that her little armed robber did anything legal.

If Henderson parked the car here, though, she wasn't leaving it in the open. Everything in sight was a rust-bucket American job, a Japanese SUV, or some anonymous heap buried under the snow. Doughty killed the engine, and Windermere reached for the door handle. "Wait," Doughty said. Windermere waited. Looked at him. "Let's play this my way," he said.

Windermere frowned. "Sure. Okay."

"You jumped all over Bernstein and Schneider. This time, you follow. Understand?"

Windermere stared at him. Then she shrugged and climbed out of the car. "Fine, Bob. Whatever you say."

They walked to the front door, and Doughty buzzed the building manager. The man came to the front door in fuzzy bunny slippers, scratching his head. "FBI," Doughty told him. "We're looking for Tricia Henderson."

The guy stared at him. "Tricia Henderson," Doughty said again.

"Unit 612," said Windermere. She felt Doughty's eyes on her, ignored him. Focused on the manager.

The guy nodded. "The pretty girl."

"Pink hair?"

"The pretty girl. I remember." He led them to a graffiti-stained, grinding elevator, and they rode up six long stories. "Six-twelve," the manager said. "Down the hall."

They walked down the hall to Henderson's door. Windermere knocked, called out the girl's name. Someone down the hall peered out from her own doorway, met Windermere's eyes, and disappeared, quickly. Windermere glanced at Doughty. "Show him the warrant."

Doughty looked at her sideways. "Yeah," he said. "Thanks."

First thing in the morning, Windermere had set to work convincing Agent Harris that Tricia Henderson was a person of interest. Harris hadn't taken much convincing. He'd dug up a judge, who'd faxed in a search-and-seizure warrant, and now Windermere watched as the manager read the thing through, disgust written plain on his face. When he'd finished, he sighed and pulled out a key ring. "Whatever."

Windermere drew her sidearm as the manager unlocked the door and stepped back. She glanced at Doughty, who gestured "go ahead."

Thought you wanted to lead, she thought, gripping her pistol tighter and pushing open the door. The whole place was dark, and Windermere hesitated before reaching in and feeling for the light switch. Flipped the switch and peered in at a messy studio suite, a kitchenette, and an unmade futon bed. The apartment was empty. Tricia Henderson wasn't home.

AN HOUR OR SO LATER, they were standing beside the Crown Vic again, having found little more than Tricia Henderson's dirty laundry upstairs. If the girl was involved, she kept the evidence hidden.

Windermere glanced at Doughty over the roof of the sedan. "You think the building manager will tip her off we were here?"

Doughty stared back at the apartment. "Probably."

"Maybe he thinks aiding and abetting will get him in her pants."

"Yeah," he said. "Maybe."

Windermere sighed and opened her passenger door. "You want to stick around? Wait till she comes back?"

"No," Doughty said.

She looked at him again. "You're sulking," she said. "I didn't let you lead?"

He shook his head. "It's fine."

"I don't get it. What's your beef?"

"No beef." Doughty slid into the driver's seat. "Guess we're staking her out."

Windermere climbed in beside him and was about to say something else when the radio crackled in between them. Minneapolis police dispatch on the scanner, 211 in progress, an armed robbery. An armored car under fire in the northeast, near Central and Broadway. Windermere glanced at Doughty. "Could be our guys."

Doughty shook his head. "We don't know that."

"Shots fired," the dispatcher reported. "Multiple victims."

"That's them," said Windermere. "Swear to God. I can feel it."

"Could be anyone, Agent Windermere. We're not leaving this stakeout."

The radio crackled again. "Witnesses report automatic weaponry and a gold late-model Toyota Camry seen fleeing the scene."

Windermere spun at Doughty. "Late-model gold Camry. What the fuck did I tell you?"

"*God damn it.*" Doughty slammed his hand on the steering wheel. Peeled out of the parking lot and hauled ass, siren blaring, down I-94. He said nothing more to Windermere, kept his dark eyes focused on the road and his mouth a thin line the whole ride into Minneapolis.

76

DRAGAN DROVE FAST, away from the mall. "Take the Interstate," Tomlin told him. Dragan nodded, wrenched the wheel. Pointed the Camry at the highway.

Tricia grabbed Tomlin's arm. "What the hell are you doing?"

Tomlin shook her off, the adrenaline humming. Looked outside his window for police cruisers, any sign of trouble. "*Shit*," Tricia said.

They made the Interstate on-ramp, headed south to I-94. Circled downtown Minneapolis to the Washington Avenue exit and drove, slower now, into the Warehouse District. Tomlin turned the radio to the AM news station. The first reports were starting to come in. "A daring armored car heist in northeast Minneapolis leaves at least two dead," the reporter said, breathless. "Witnesses report three masked gunmen in a gold Toyota Camry."

Dragan swore. "We're made."

Tomlin shook his head. "The car's made. We can ditch it."

They pulled into the lot. Dragan parked between his Civic and Tomlin's Jaguar. Tricia dragged two of the duffel bags to the pavement. Unzipped one of them. "Holy shit," she said.

Tomlin peered in. Saw bricks of cash, solid, a pile of them. *Four bags just like this*, he thought. *Hundreds of thousands of dollars*. He looked at the money. Saw the guard staggering back from the gun-shot. His heart was a jackhammer inside his chest.

Beside him, Tricia squealed. Held up two bricks of cash and wrapped her arms around Dragan. Kissed him, sloppy. Dragan grinned at her, at the money. Kissed her neck and cupped her ass in his hands. Tomlin caught Dragan's eye. "Take two bags," he said. "I'll take the other two. We'll drive back to Saint Paul and divvy it up there."

Dragan kissed Tricia again. "What about the police?"

"What about them?"

"We killed people back there," said Dragan. "They'll be looking for us."

"We'll hole up somewhere," Tomlin told him. "The Timberline Motel in Frogtown. You know it?"

Tricia looked up. "I know it."

Tomlin looked around the parking lot, looked down at the rifle in his hands, the cash. Felt suddenly and absolutely invincible. *Let Stevens and Windermere come and get me*, he thought. *I'm not scared.*

"Be there in an hour," he told Dragan and Tricia. "The police find us there, I'll kill them all, too."

77

WINDERMERE HIT the pavement as soon as Doughty parked at the crime scene. *Let him sulk,* she thought, wading through the crowd. *This is bigger than his little grudge.*

The heist had gone down at a crumbling mini-mall, and the parking lot was a sideshow—the place crawling with cops, news reporters, hangers-on. Windermere pushed through to the police barricade, ducked under, and made her way to the first body on the pavement.

A guard. A heavyset guy in a blue company jacket, three or four bloody holes through it. He hadn't drawn his sidearm.

"Witness says this guy was in back of the truck with a shotgun." Windermere looked up, saw a rookie uniform smiling at her, face flushed with excitement. "Your boy walked up with an assault rifle, put a burst through him. The body dropped out when the driver drove off."

Windermere looked around the parking lot. Automobile carnage everywhere. She could trace a path through the lot to the exit, a trail of crushed bumpers and smashed taillights: the panicked armored truck driver's wake. She looked back at the rookie. "Where's the truck now?"

The cop gestured out of the lot. "Down the road a ways," he said. "Guy drove for a bit, realized he was safe. Pulled over and hid, but we found him."

"He okay?"

"Shaken up, but he's fine." The cop smiled again. "Guess the guy with the rifle jumped in back with him, tried to kill him. Probably could have, if he'd tried hard enough. That bulletproof glass isn't exactly tough shit against assault rifles."

Windermere looked across the lot to the second body, this guy younger, another guard. This guy had managed to pull his piece from his holster, at least. The cop followed her eyes. "Second bad guy had a shotgun. Fired a warning shot, scared that guard into dropping the money."

"You sure it was a guy?"

The cop shrugged. "Doesn't exactly seem like women's work."

"You'd be surprised. How'd this guy get it?"

"What I hear, it was the guy with the assault rifle again. He emptied the armored truck"—the cop pointed—"over there. Then he ran back, helped his friends throw the cash in the little Toyota, and before he left, he took a moment to kill the second guard."

Windermere followed the cop's gaze. "Guy was making a move or something?"

"Not from what I heard." The cop shrugged again. "Sounded like it was straight murder. Kind of a dick move."

A dick move. One way to put it. An impulse kill. Windermere thanked the cop and walked across the lot to where Doughty stood, talking to a plainclothes city cop. "It's our guys again," she told them. "Getting worse."

Doughty scowled. "No sign of the Camry."

"Of course not."

"This truck makes the rounds to all the check-cashing places, paycheck-advance stores in the Northeast," Doughty said. "Guy in the store thinks there could have been a million bucks in the back, easy."

"Shit," said Windermere. "They could disappear with that money."

Doughty nodded. "If they're not already gone."

"I'll send a car to Henderson's apartment. She shows up, we'll nab them."

Doughty scowled again. "I'll do it," he said, walking back to the Crown Vic. Windermere watched him go. *I hope it's that easy,* she thought. *These guys have a knack for pulling vanishing acts.*

78

ON WEDNESDAY MORNING, Stevens pushed Carter Tomlin from his mind long enough to bring the Danzer case to Tim Lesley, the SAC of Investigations in Saint Paul. Lesley read Stevens's report, then Paula Franklin's. When he was finished, he looked at Stevens over his wire-rimmed glasses. "Some kind of kidnapping gone wrong, you're saying."

Stevens nodded. "There's no evidence Sylvia Danzer had ever met David Samson before in her life, let alone that she had any reason to conspire with him to kill her husband."

"Guy murders the husband and takes the wife on a joyride." Lesley frowned. "God knows what he did to the poor woman before the grand finale."

"Or how she managed to get the knife from him."

"Or how long he had her before he got himself stuck in the woods. Christ." Lesley shook his head and looked down at the reports one more time. Then he closed them, firm, and looked at Stevens again. "This is enough for me, Agent Stevens. Good work."

Stevens called Paula Franklin to fill her in. "Case is closed," he told her. "Thanks for everything."

"Pleasure's mine," Franklin replied. "You talk to the families yet?"

"Next on my list."

"Go for it," she said. "Was good working with you."

Stevens called Sylvia Danzer's sister next. She sounded like she'd been waiting by the phone. "She didn't kill him," she said, after Stevens gave her the rundown.

Stevens paused. "Samson?"

"Elliott. Her husband. Those goddamn tabloids made up a pack of lies."

"Sure," Stevens said.

"You talk to the papers, you make sure they get the real story, will you?"

Stevens told her he would. Asked if there was anyone else he could call. "I'm all that's left," the woman said, sighing. "They didn't have any children, and Dad died last year."

"I'm sorry," Stevens told her.

"He swore this would happen, sooner or later. Wish he could have been around to see it."

"Me too," Stevens said. "It's a hell of a thing."

"Make sure those newspapers print a correction, you understand?"

"I will." Stevens hung up the phone. He looked around his cubicle and out at the BCA office. Then he turned to his computer and started to search for Elliott Danzer's next of kin.

BY MID-MORNING, Stevens was exhausted. Elliott Danzer's mother had cried. His father had thanked Stevens, gruff and gravel-throated. Stevens accepted the man's thanks, and promised to pass along any more news. Then he hung up the phone and stared at his screensaver and wondered why he wasn't more excited.

These were the phone calls, Stevens knew, that made cold casework worthwhile. The dusty puzzle came together and the picture panned out, revealing the human element on the margins, the people left behind. This was the reward, and Stevens—proud of the closure as he was—wasn't quite feeling the same thrill. Mostly, he figured, it was Tomlin's fault.

The man was hiding something major. The cocky, world-beating, master-of-the-universe type whom Stevens had befriended was gone. In his place was the hollow man who'd shown up at the basketball game last night. Hard-edged and brittle, suspicious and unresponsive, shifty-eyed. He was guilty of something, and it was probably bank robbery. But Stevens didn't have any proof. Hell, he didn't even have jurisdiction. Could do nothing but sit on his hands like some useless desk jockey and read about the case in the papers.

Or watch it on the news, as things turned out. Stevens had just ended a quickie interview with the crime reporter at the *Star Tribune*—Tim Lesley's idea—when the Minneapolis police dispatcher reported a 211, an armored car robbery in the Northeast. A gold Camry. He hurried into the break room, switched on the old TV set, and watched as the first action news reporter arrived at the scene.

He watched the news report, an audacious armed robbery that left two guards dead, and he felt another shock when Windermere showed up in the background. She looked pumped up now, more like the tough cop he'd known, walking onto the crime scene like she owned it. He watched her for a few minutes, and then the camera panned away, and he walked back to his desk, feeling like the kid who stayed home from the dance.

STEVENS HEARD VOICES by the stairs. Hung up the phone as Special Agent Nick Singer walked into BCA, talking to a woman Stevens had never seen before. A cop, he decided, watching Singer usher her to his desk. A plainclothes cop, her sidearm in a shoulder holster, the outline just visible beneath her jacket.

"No, I know," she was saying. "These guys are just being stingy with the warrant. Real pricks. I was hoping one of you BCA guys could lean on them a little."

Singer pulled an extra chair over for her. "What's the warrant for, anyway?"

"Some shitty robbery." The woman shrugged. "Guy got his guns took, an AR-15, a shotgun, and two pistols. He's been badgering me about it for months."

Singer nodded. "Uh-huh."

Stevens snuck another glance at the woman. *An AR-15*, he thought. *Same weapon as Windermere's suspect used.*

"Guy come down from the Twin Cities, told my victim he wanted to buy a handgun. Victim asked to see a permit and got his head nearly caved." She looked at Singer. "You think you can help me? Only take a few minutes."

Stevens stood and crossed the office to Singer's desk. "You said this guy came down from the Twin Cities?" he asked the woman. "What's he driving?"

Singer looked up and frowned. "Stevens, hey."

The woman shook her head. "Too dark to tell. Some kind of truck, an SUV. Dark-colored."

"Dark-colored." Becca Tomlin drove a blue Lincoln Navigator. "Navy blue, maybe?"

She shrugged. "'Dark-colored,' the guy said. It was night."

An AR-15. A dark SUV down from the Twin Cities. Could be relevant. Could be he was grasping at straws. "Your guy describe the assailant?"

"Tall, I guess. Thin. Probably in his mid-forties. Brown hair."

"Eyes?"

"Two of 'em. Blue." The cop thought of something and laughed. "My guy didn't want to tell me he'd noticed. Thought I'd figure he was a fairy."

Singer cleared his throat. "Stevens, this is Investigator Russell with Hastings PD. You two got something in common?"

"Armored truck got robbed in Minneapolis this morning," Stevens said. "Two guards shot with an AR-15."

Russell frowned. "Lots of those guns around."

"Same weapon was used in a bank robbery in southern Minneapolis a couple weeks back. Suspect was tall, wore a ski mask. Blue eyes."

"Same guy," said Russell. "Both times."

"Exactly," said Stevens. "Robbery in Prospect Park, a couple months back. Suspect matches your description. Brought a pistol. Before Christmas, he was robbing banks unarmed. You said you got an e-mail from your suspect?"

"An alias. Roger Brill."

"Came from the Twin Cities."

She shrugged. "So he said. I'm trying to swing a warrant for this guy's street address. Internet company's being assholes, and so is the judge." Russell looked at him again. "Look, what's your big interest here? I just want an address on that e-mail and get out of here."

"No big interest," said Stevens. "I'm just playing a hunch. Let's see if we can get you that warrant."

79

TOMLIN MET DRAGAN and Tricia at the motel, a shitty no-tell affair surrounded by fast-food restaurants and low-lying warehouses. The desk clerk barely looked up from his TV as he checked Tomlin into a room in the back of the building.

The TV was set to the news. The news showed continuous coverage of the armored car robbery. As Tomlin paid the clerk, he caught a glimpse of Carla Windermere in the background, snooping around the parking lot. The reporter showed a picture of the two guards he'd killed. Then they showed a grainy picture of Tricia with blond hair. "Tricia Henderson," the caption read. "Person of interest."

Shit. Obviously, the Minneapolis lowlife, Jackson, was no longer a factor. Somehow, Windermere had Tricia. And if she had Tricia, she would have Tomlin soon enough.

Tomlin took the key from the clerk and drove around to the back of the motel. He watched Tricia climb from the Civic, laughing about something with Dragan, and he wondered how she'd react when she found out she'd been made. *Not my problem,* he decided. He picked up his cell phone and called Becca at home. "What's up, honey?" She sounded surprised. "Everything okay?"

So the police hadn't come to her yet. "Everything's fine," Tomlin said. "Just thinking about you. Everything okay at home base?"

"Snickers got loose," she said. "The neighbor chased him down for me. Found him in the Hargreaveses' backyard."

"That damned dog."

"Madeleine has dance class," she said. "After school. Can you pick her up on your way home?"

Tomlin looked out at Tricia again. She caught his eye, looked away. "Dance class," he said. *We'll be fugitives by then.*

"She's done at six, and honey, it would make my life so much easier. Heather has some Spirit Club thing, and I don't know how I'll juggle both."

Windermere would be following up on Tricia right now. It wouldn't take long before she made the connection. It was time to skip town. "Let's go somewhere," he said. "A vacation. Right now."

Becca laughed. "What, like tomorrow?"

"Like tonight," he said. "Maddy can skip dance class. We'll just hop a plane, anywhere you want. Pick the girls up and we'll go."

"And go where?" She laughed again. "Carter—"

"I don't start work for a week and a half," he said. "The timing's perfect. Why not?"

"This is crazy, Carter."

"Spontaneous."

"Spontaneous." She laughed again. "Okay. A vacation. Let's just do it."

"Great. I'll see you soon." Tomlin ended the call and stepped out of the Jaguar. Pushed open the motel door. Inside was a sketchy little room with pockmarked balsa-wood furniture and two rumpled double beds. Tomlin turned to Tricia. "You want to turn on the news."

Tricia frowned. "Why?"

Tomlin found the remote for the TV, and flipped to a news channel. "Your picture is all over it," he told her. "Your name, too. Give it a couple of hours and we'll all three be made."

80

STEVENS DUCKED a phone interview with the local CBS affiliate and called in a favor with a judge at the county courthouse. Drank bad BCA coffee and watched coverage of the Minneapolis armed robbery until mid-afternoon, when the judge faxed over Russell's warrant.

Could be nothing, Stevens thought, following Russell out to her Hastings PD cruiser. *Could be a coincidence. Could be I'm so eager to see Windermere again that I'll jump on anything that sounds remotely similar. Nancy would tell you you're pathetic. A lovesick teenager.*

But what if there's a connection here? Stevens thought, climbing in beside Russell. *What if this is the break?* He studied the warrant as Russell drove into Saint Paul, trying unsuccessfully to quell his excitement.

THEY FOUND the Internet provider's office in a nondescript little building on University Avenue, a half mile or so west of the state capitol. Russell parked in front, and Stevens followed her to the entrance, where they cornered a short, middle-aged woman as she locked the front door.

"BCA." Stevens showed the woman the warrant. "And Hastings Police. We need something from you."

The woman looked at the warrant and then at Stevens, then Russell. She sighed. "I'm on break."

"Only take a minute," Stevens said. "Let's go back inside."

The woman sighed again, but she unlocked the door and led them into the building. They walked through a small reception area and into an office, where the woman dropped into her chair and switched on her computer and looked up at Stevens expectantly. Stevens glanced at Russell. "Got an IP address for you to run," Russell told her. "One of your clients."

The woman squinted at Russell. "We talked on the phone."

"Claudia." Russell nodded. "You shut me down."

Claudia shrugged. "You didn't have a warrant. This was a robbery, right?"

"That's right."

"Who got robbed?"

"Can't tell you." Russell smiled. "Privacy issues. You understand."

Claudia frowned and turned back to her computer. Stevens handed her the IP address, and Claudia typed it in. She reached for a pen. "It's a residential account," she said. She wrote down an address and handed it to Russell. Russell looked at the paper, shrugged and handed it to Stevens, who read it and grinned. The Summit Avenue address. Carter Tomlin. Russell looked at him. "Good?"

"Makes my day." Stevens pulled out his cell phone. Dialed Windermere's number, his heart pounding. She picked up, and he heard wind in the background, traffic. "Windermere," he said. "Stevens."

"Caller ID, Stevens. What do you need?"

He paused. "You're working that armored car thing, right?"

"Right."

"Any leads?"

Windermere sighed. "One lead. A woman, one of the robbers.

Headed back to Saint Paul to stake out her apartment. Except her face is all over the news, so she's probably gone. Why?"

Stevens looked back at Russell and Claudia. "Swing by my office on your way." He couldn't keep the smile from his voice. "I have something you don't want to miss."

81

WINDERMERE STARED at her phone. *Damn you, Stevens,* she thought. *I don't have time to play games right now.*

Doughty watched her over the top of the Crown Vic, with one eyebrow raised. "What's the story?"

Windermere didn't answer. Stevens hadn't given her much. Had been downright coy, even. But he'd promised he had something to show her. Of anyone, he wouldn't screw her around.

"Drop me at headquarters," she told Doughty. "I gotta chase a lead."

Doughty frowned. "What about Henderson?"

"I'll catch up. I have to do something real quick first."

Doughty looked like he was about to say something. Then he sighed and shook his head. Opened the car door and disappeared inside.

This had better be worth it, Windermere thought. *Stevens drags me all the way over there to show me his daughter's finger paintings, I'll shoot him.*

DOUGHTY DROPPED Windermere outside the FBI office and drove off without a word. Windermere watched the big Ford disappear into traffic. Then she rode the elevator down to the garage and climbed into her Chevelle and drove it across to the BCA headquarters northeast of downtown Saint Paul.

Stevens was waiting in the doorway when she pulled up. He had a woman with him, a heavy brunette. Windermere stopped the car in front of the doors and leaned across the seat to roll down the passenger window. Stevens came over. "Carla," he said. "Hey."

It was good to see him again. It would be better if he had something decent. "What's the deal, Stevens?"

Stevens glanced back at his brown-haired friend. "This is Investigator Russell," he said. "Hastings PD. She's got a line on a stolen AR-15."

Windermere stared at him. "I'm in the middle of a robbery–double murder, Stevens. No time for goose chases."

Stevens smiled. "Just listen to her story."

Russell told her story. A robbery in Hastings before Christmas. Guns. An AR-15 assault rifle. A middle-aged assailant out of the Twin Cities. An e-mail and an alias.

"Russell traced the e-mail," said Stevens. "Copied down the IPO—"

"IP," Russell said. "IP address."

"—and traced it to an Internet provider. We got ourselves a warrant and harassed them for a while, and they gave us this." Stevens held out a scrap piece of paper. "Take a look."

Windermere glanced at Stevens. Then she took the paper. Read it. Tomlin's address, Summit Avenue. She looked back at Stevens. "Shit," she said. "This is it, Stevens. This is my case."

Stevens grinned. "Figured you could use it."

"Oh, I'll use it. I'll take his ass down." She leaned over and pushed open the passenger door. "You coming with me or what?"

82

THEY LEFT RUSSELL at her car. The Hastings cop begged off the big takedown. "Long drive back," she said. "Mayor wants me working these damn downtown break-ins in the morning."

Stevens promised he'd keep her posted. Then he climbed into the Chevelle, and he and Windermere drove though Saint Paul toward Summit Hill. Stevens watched Windermere as she drove. "Hell of a car," he said. "Must be rough in the winter, no?"

She nodded. "I try to keep it locked up."

"But not this time."

"Needed a pick-me-up," she said. "Driving this bad boy gets me going." She pulled to a stop sign and paused. Then she slammed down on the gas. The tires squealed and the rear end fishtailed, wild, back and forth. Windermere grinned at him. "Better than sex, Stevens."

Stevens peeled himself from the seat. "I'll take your word for it."

She glanced over. Laughed at him. "I missed you."

TOMLIN'S JAGUAR WAS gone, but his wife's Navigator remained, looking like a lost toy on Tomlin's vast driveway. Stevens followed

Windermere across the street to the sidewalk. "A bank robber's palace," Windermere said, staring up at the house. "Imagine."

"After we're done with Tomlin, maybe we start knocking on neighbors' doors. See how everyone else pays the mortgage." He glanced at her. "You were right about Tomlin."

"Of course I was right, Stevens," she said. "You think I make this crap up?"

He shrugged. "I kind of thought you were crazy."

"You and everybody else." An unmarked Crown Victoria pulled up behind them, and two BCA agents climbed out. Windermere straightened. "Here comes the cavalry."

The agents joined them on the sidewalk. "Nick Singer and Greg Rotundi," Stevens said, "meet Carla Windermere." The agents nodded at Windermere and then followed her gaze to the house. "Doesn't look like our suspect's at home," Stevens told them, "but we're going to execute the search warrant and wait for his return."

"Maybe park the unmarked around the block," said Windermere. "Make it so he doesn't see it and bolt."

Rotundi nodded and went back to the car as Stevens led Windermere and Singer to the house. Windermere knocked on the front door. Singer held up the warrant. After a minute, Becca Tomlin appeared through the window. She smiled wide when she saw Stevens, and swung open the door.

"Kirk," she said. Then she saw Windermere, and her smile faded.

"Afternoon, Becca," said Stevens. "Is Carter around?"

"He's still at work." Becca studied Singer, then Windermere. "What's the problem?"

"It's serious, Becca. What time do you expect him?"

"A couple hours, I guess," she said. "I don't know. He just called. Told me he wanted to take the girls on a vacation."

Stevens swapped a glance with Windermere. "Vacation," said Windermere. "Where?"

Becca shrugged. "Anywhere we want, he said. Like a celebration."

Windermere arched an eyebrow at Stevens. Behind them, Rotundi climbed up to the house. "Head down to Tomlin's office," Stevens told him. "Wait for him there. Call us if you see him."

Rotundi nodded, and Stevens turned to Singer, who handed Becca the warrant. "Carter's in some trouble," Stevens told her. "I'm sorry, but we've gotta take a look through the house."

83

THE HAUL FROM the armored truck totaled more than nine hundred thousand dollars. It was enough to make Tricia forget, eventually, about her face on the news. It was more money than Tomlin had ever seen in his life.

It wasn't going to be enough.

Nine hundred grand divided between the three of them meant over three hundred fifty thousand for Tomlin. Added to the poker-game score, and the remains of the bank jobs he'd pulled, and Tomlin figured he had close to half a million dollars in ready cash.

A half a million dollars wouldn't make for much of a retirement. Not for a family of four. *Hell,* Tomlin thought, *by the time we make it out of the country and set ourselves up with a home, we'll be back in the same old situation, working to stay alive.*

I need more, he decided. *I just need a little more money.*

Tricia giggled from the opposite bed. Tomlin stole a glance at her. She had Dragan on top of her, her legs locked behind his back, her arms around his neck. She let him kiss her for a while. Then she pushed him away. "Where are we going to go?" she said.

Dragan thought it over. "Mexico?"

"When?"

"Tomorrow. We leave early and drive to Chicago. Hop a plane."

"What about the money?"

"We'll hide it," Dragan told her. "Wrap it up in our clothes. In a couple of days, you'll be another rich bitch on the beach."

Tricia laughed again, reached and pulled him down to her. Tomlin watched in disgust as they made out, a couple of horny teenagers after the prom.

Mexico, Tomlin thought. *If I was young and carefree and single, half a million dollars would almost be enough. If I didn't have a family to worry about.*

He stood from his bed and walked to the window. Glanced outside, and then back at the kids again. He cleared his throat and they stopped fooling around, smiled at him, sheepish. Tricia sat up, fixing her hair. "What's up?"

Tomlin looked at her, at Dragan. "One more score," he said. "In the morning. Before we all scatter."

Dragan glanced at Tricia. "I don't think so. What's the point?"

"We have enough money," said Tricia.

"I don't," Tomlin told her. "Not enough for my family. Not to get us out safe."

"Your family," said Dragan. "What the hell do we care?"

"You care," Tomlin told him. "You'd better fucking care. I got you this gig in the first place."

Dragan cocked his head. "Maybe. But if you didn't kill those guards, we wouldn't be running. Evens out, doesn't it?"

"I made you a shitload of money. I'm asking one favor. For my daughters."

Tricia and Dragan shared a look. Neither said anything. Tomlin waited. He was still waiting when his cell phone began to ring. *Becca.* "Carter? Where are you?"

"Still at the office, honey," he said. "I'll be home soon. You all packed?"

A pause. "Where are you really?"

He walked to the window and peeled back the curtain. "I told you, the office."

"I just called the office, Carter."

Tomlin stared out the window. Outside, the parking lot was deserted. A train rumbled by, slowly, on the spur line beyond. "Carter?"

There was something in her voice. Tomlin didn't answer. He turned around and saw Dragan kiss Tricia, slide his hand under her shirt. *Half a million dollars would be plenty,* Tomlin thought, *if I had a pretty girl with me on a warm sandy beach. A million dollars would be even better.*

Becca made a strangled noise. "Carter?"

Tomlin eyed Dragan. *And what if we were two and not three?* He looked at Tricia again. Imagined spending the rest of his life with her on some lawless beach. That perky young body. That dirty mind. No mortgage to worry about. Sex all the time.

"Carter, where are you?"

Tomlin ended the call. Switched his phone off and turned back to the lovers. "One more score," he said. "Then you can go."

Tricia pushed Dragan away. Looked at Tomlin hard. "In the morning," she said finally. "Quick. For your family."

Tomlin nodded. "For my family." He lay back on the bed and stared up at the dingy ceiling. Turned up the volume on the TV as Tricia began to make out with Dragan again. *Enjoy your time with her, asshole,* he thought, listening to the rustle of their clothes over the news anchor's monologue. *As of tomorrow, she's mine.*

84

WINDERMERE HUNG UP the cordless extension. "Shit," she said, looking at Stevens. "Lost him."

On the living room couch, Becca Tomlin shook her head. "I don't know what happened," she said. "He just went away."

Windermere swapped a look with Stevens. Then she took out her cell phone and disappeared into the front hall, and Stevens heard her issuing rapid-fire directions to some hapless colleague. He stood at the living room window and looked out over the front lawn. The sun was setting outside now; the shadows had encroached almost to the edge of the house, and the living room was all dark corners and dim light. Stevens looked at Becca's reflection in the glass, her eyes red and her cheeks tracked with tears. They'd asked her to call Carter. He'd lied to his wife; Rotundi had found the office deserted. He was searching the place now.

And meanwhile, Becca Tomlin sat at home and watched her world fall apart. "Bank robbery," she said, her eyes meeting Stevens's. "I just don't understand."

He watched her eyes fill with tears again, and he passed her a box of tissues. "I'm sorry," he told her. He sat on the edge of the couch and put his arm around her, and she leaned into him and began to sob.

Singer came into the living room. "Nothing upstairs. I'll check the basement."

"The model train room," said Stevens. "If he's hiding something, it's there."

"Train room. Got it." Singer walked out again, the Tomlins' yellow Lab trailing after him, tail wagging, oblivious.

THE FRONT DOOR opened, and Heather Tomlin came in, her nose in her cell phone, giggling about something. "Damn," Becca said, standing. "I just need a minute."

"Sure." Stevens waited while she called Madeleine downstairs and herded both girls to the kitchen. Stevens heard muffled conversation, and a few seconds later, Heather came stomping back through the living room and into the front hall, narrowly missing Windermere as the FBI agent came back into the room. In the kitchen, Madeleine Tomlin started to cry.

Windermere raised an eyebrow at Stevens. "Nothing at Henderson's apartment," she said. "My people are talking to the phone company. Hoping we can pinpoint Tomlin's cell."

"Assuming he doesn't ditch the thing," Stevens said.

"Which he probably does."

"Maybe not. He's no Pender. Maybe he forgets the phone."

Windermere shook her head. "If he watches action movies, he'll ditch the phone," she said. "But we'll try anyway."

Stevens nodded. "Fingers crossed."

Becca Tomlin came back into the living room and sat down heavily on the couch. She smiled at Stevens and shook her head. "I thought he was having an affair," she said. "I guess I was thinking too small."

85

SHOULD HAVE suspected something," Becca said. "I wondered how he could still have money, after the layoff, but he never let me look at the bank statements. I just assumed business was good at his new job."

Stevens sat forward on the couch. "Did you ever see anything that looked suspicious? Guns, maybe?"

"He wouldn't bring a gun in this house, not with the children around." She smiled sadly at Stevens. "I guess I just didn't see it. Carter could have an apartment in Minneapolis for all I know. A whole other life."

"There's no shed in your backyard?" said Windermere. "No cottage or second property?"

She shrugged. "You would know better than me at this point."

Singer walked in from the kitchen. "Basement's clean," he told Stevens. "There's a pile of old sports junk, a couple boxes of clothes. Nothing in the train room but trains."

Stevens stared at him. "You're sure?"

"Positive."

"He moved it, then. Shit."

Becca turned to look at him. "What did he move, Kirk?"

"Whatever he was hiding." Stevens looked at Windermere. "He had something down there last week. He didn't want me to see it."

Becca frowned. "How do you know?"

"I went down there," he said. "The party. Carter found me. I thought he would kill me, he looked so mad."

Becca stared at him. "You were snooping around our house, Kirk?"

Windermere stared, too. "You went to a party here, Stevens?"

Stevens looked at Windermere first, then at Becca Tomlin. Both women held his gaze, waiting for answers. Mercifully, he felt his cell phone begin to ring. Checked it: Rotundi. "Sorry." Stevens stood and walked into the hall. "Great timing," he told Rotundi. "Now tell me you found something."

"A little something. Twenty thousand in cash in his bottom desk drawer."

"Weapons?"

"None." Rotundi laughed. "Get this, though: The chick that's on the news today, the punk rocker, Henderson? She's Tomlin's secretary. At least she was. They're closing the office this week."

"No kidding." Stevens thanked Rotundi and hung up the phone. Turned around to find Windermere standing in the living room doorway.

"Anything?" she said.

"Twenty thousand in cash," Stevens told her. "And the Tricia Henderson connection. She's his secretary."

Windermere pumped her fist. "Knew it. So where are they? Where are his guns?"

"Probably getting ready to run," Stevens said. "He knows the heat's on him. He's not coming back."

Windermere stared out the window and thought for a moment. "I don't think he just runs," she said. "Not this guy."

Stevens frowned. "You think he sticks around? Why?"

"Just a hunch, I guess. Instincts. This guy's a thrill-seeker." She shook her head, grim. "I've followed him this far down the spiral, Stevens. I bet he doesn't leave until he's sure he's reached bottom."

86

TONY SCHULTZ PACKED a suitcase and threw a couple pictures of his nephews on top. He dragged the suitcase out to his battered old Ford, chucked it onto the passenger seat, and stood back to survey his house. The Mexicans would be back, he knew, and soon. They wouldn't leave him alive this time.

He slammed the truck door closed and walked back to the house. The money was gone, wherever it was. The money and the drugs both. By now, Brill had spent every penny.

Schultz walked into the house and looked around the front landing. He would drive south, out of state. Somewhere he could be anonymous, start over. Forget about the Mexicans and the drugs. Do something different. Maybe he would get a real job again. Something outdoors. Build houses, or paint houses, or something. Something challenging, something honest. He stood in the landing for a while and wondered what the Mexicans would do when they figured out he was gone. Wondered if Ricky would really come for the kids.

Forget that, Schultz thought. *Scotty's a good cop. Tough. No way he lets anything happen to those boys.*

Maybe it was a bad idea to drive south. The farther south you went, the closer you got to Mexico proper. Hordes of those spic bastards trying to kill you. What about north, northwest? Montana. Hide out on the great lawless plains for a while.

The phone started to ring in the kitchen.

Schultz pictured himself in Montana. A homestead like this one. A real job. A woman. No more drug dealing. No more mistakes. The phone rang again. Schultz walked to the kitchen and answered. "Yeah."

"Carter Tomlin." Scotty's voice. "He's your guy. Some geek accountant up in Saint Paul."

Schultz stared at his reflection in the black kitchen window. Scratched his head. "The hell would an accountant want with my guns?"

"Damned if I know. But the BCA's sure. FBI's in it, too."

BCA. FBI. "You kidding me?"

"Guy used your guns on about five or six bank jobs. An armored truck, too. Killed a couple guards with that AR-15."

"Shit," Schultz said.

"Figured you'd want to know, anyway."

"I guess I did." Schultz spat into the sink. "Was about to hit the road, Scotty. Shit."

"FBI probably gets him. No sense joining in."

Schultz scratched his head again. "No," he said. "Probably not." He paused. "Keep an eye on those boys of yours, would you? A good eye."

Scotty laughed. "Two good eyes ain't enough, brother. Not those two. Be safe."

Schultz told him good-bye and hung up the phone. Carter Tomlin. An accountant. A bank robber. He stared at his tired reflection in the window some more.

A fool's errand, that's what they'd call it. Better for everyone if he just headed west. Skipped the bullshit. Fine, except what about those two goddamn kids? No way he could live with himself if Ricky came back.

Schultz replaced the phone in its cradle and walked back to the laundry room and the ruined, shot-up cabinet where he'd stashed his old guns. He dug around in his closet for the TEC-9 and a couple extra clips, stuffed the clips into his jacket pocket, and laced up his boots. Then he looked around the house one more time, locked the door, and walked out to his truck and fired up the engine. Backed out to the highway and pointed the truck north to Saint Paul.

87

TOMLIN WOKE UP Thursday morning with a splitting head-
ache. Between Dragan's semitruck snoring and his own racing
thoughts, he'd barely been able to keep his eyes closed all night.

He stood, picking his way around the duffel bags on the floor and
fumbling into the bathroom. He turned on the light and pissed, rubbing his eyes with his free hand. *Today's the day,* he thought.

The idea didn't haunt him as much as he'd feared. Today, he
would abandon his family in favor of a sexy little punk rocker and a
beach in the middle of nowhere. It should have made him feel rotten. After all, he'd robbed all those banks for his family, hadn't he?

Hadn't he?

*We could have declared bankruptcy. We could have sold the house
for whatever we could get, ditched the cars, moved somewhere cheaper.*
Becca could have looked for a full-time teaching job. He could have
gone back to school, become a carpenter, done something produc-
tive. There were millions of honest, hardworking men out of work in
America. Very few of them turned to bank robberies to survive.

It wasn't about the money, though, was it? It was about something
else. Power, and control, and proving to Carver and Lawson and

Rydin that he wasn't some dumb neutered fuck, that he wasn't a failure. That even if the firm didn't want him, he could still provide for his wife and children, like they did, like every man should. He'd proved he could do it. His family had survived. Now he would take his reward.

Tomlin flushed the toilet and splashed his face with cold water. Then he walked out of the bathroom and to the motel window, where he lifted the blackout curtain and surveyed the empty parking lot. After a moment, he flung the curtains open. Tricia groaned behind him, and Tomlin turned to watch her disentangle from Dragan, tousled and beautiful, pulling the sheet to her chest. "Rise and shine," he told her. "Time to go."

Dragan rolled over, rubbed his eyes. "I can't believe we're doing this."

"You can sleep for the rest of your life," Tomlin told him. "Today's your big day. Up and at 'em."

"Shit," Dragan said.

"We'll never have to work again, baby." Tricia winked at Tomlin. Then she leaned over and pulled the sheet off of Dragan, exposing his pale skinny frame. "Tomorrow we work on your tan."

Dragan shared a long look with Tricia. Then he groaned again. "*Fine.*"

THEY DRESSED IN silence and walked out and stood on the crumbling sidewalk, shivering in the cold. "We drive back to Minneapolis," Tomlin told them. "Find another truck."

"Why a truck?" Dragan asked.

"Money." Tricia looked at Tomlin. "Right?"

"Exactly," said Tomlin. *And the guards will be armed.* "We take Dragan's Civic. Hit the truck and you can bring me back here. We split the money and bolt, understood?"

Dragan glanced at Tricia. She nodded. He nodded. "Okay, then," said Tomlin. "Let's go."

They took the Interstate westbound toward Minneapolis. Got off on Hiawatha, just across the river, and cruised into Ventura Village, where they stopped at a McDonald's down the street from a couple of check-cashing joints. They ate a greasy breakfast in the rear of the parking lot, watching the procession of cars on the street beyond.

When they were finished eating, Tomlin walked the garbage to a bin and jogged back to the Civic, trying to stay limber. He slid into the passenger seat and fiddled with the radio. Watched the cars pull in and out of the lot and tried to calm his nerves.

Hurry up and wait, he thought. *Where in the hell are the trucks?*

It took nearly an hour. They sat in the Civic, all three of them silent, surveying the road. Tomlin played with the radio. Couldn't decide on a station. Finally, he gave up and turned the damn thing off. Sat back in his seat and tried to welcome the silence. Then Tricia pointed through the windshield. *"There."*

Tomlin followed her gaze and saw the truck lumber by. A van like the last one, big and heavy and blue. *Bingo.* Tomlin glanced at Dragan. "You see it?"

Dragan was already shifting into gear. "I'm on it."

TRAFFIC WAS LIGHT, and the big truck was slow. Within minutes they'd pulled up behind it.

"Follow them," Tomlin said, reaching back for the assault rifle and a pistol. "They'll make a drop, and we'll take them like last time."

Dragan stayed stuck to the rear of the truck. Tricia pulled on a ski mask. She stared at Tomlin through the eyeholes. "No killing," she said. "Not this time, okay?"

"Only self-defense," Tomlin said.

"Boss." She looked into his eyes. "Only if it's us or them. Promise."

Us or them. Tomlin held her gaze. "I promise."

They followed the armored truck. Dragan tapped fast on the steering wheel. Tomlin watched him, his own adrenaline pumping. The truck turned in to another dingy mini-mall. Dragan turned in behind. Tomlin pulled down his ski mask and tightened his grip on the rifle. *Accidents happen,* he thought. *Promise or no promise.*

88

STEVENS WOKE, stiff-necked, in Windermere's Chevelle. He sat up, rubbed his eyes, and stared out the window, half-forgetting where he was. Saw Carter Tomlin's house and remembered. The bank robber had never come home.

Windermere gave him a smirk from the driver's seat. "I was wondering how long you were thinking you'd sleep."

He rubbed his eyes again, blinking in the sunlight. "Sorry. You get any rest?"

"Someone had to watch the house, Stevens," she said, shaking her head. "You should have let me take you home."

"Damn," he said. "What did I miss?"

Windermere shrugged. "Tomlin's wife turned out the lights around one. You were awake for that part, I think. Since then, it's been talk radio and your heavy breathing. No movement outside."

"How the hell'd you stay awake?"

"Stakeout routine." She held up a grocery bag. "Your boy Singer did a 7-Eleven run for me. Red Bull and Mountain Dew, all night long."

"Jesus."

"Part of the job. Except right now, I really have to pee."

Stevens stretched, twisting in his seat, trying to loosen up. "You want to find a gas station bathroom or something? I can hang around here."

Windermere shook her head and reached for the door handle. "Now that you're back in the land of the lucid, why don't we check on Becca Tomlin again?"

Stevens stepped out onto the pavement and stretched some more, rolled his neck around, tried to get to feeling like a human being again. When he turned around, Windermere was halfway to the house, her cell phone to her ear. She ended the call as he caught up alongside her. "Doughty," she said. "My FBI partner. He's not happy this morning."

Stevens frowned. "What's the problem?"

"Had him stake out Tricia Henderson's place all night," she said. "Guess he missed his daughter's dance recital or something. And you can guess how the stakeout went."

"She didn't come home."

"Or she came home and Doughty missed it," she said. "Even odds, one way or the other. She's not there now, anyway."

"Maybe they're gone," Stevens said. "Like, hopped-a-plane gone."

Windermere nodded. "I had my office put a hold on Tomlin's credit cards while you were sleeping. If there's any action, we'll hear about it."

"Except he's swimming in cash."

"FAA's on him, too," she said. "And I doubt this guy's as resourceful as Pender and company when it comes to finding fake IDs. But he could escape on the ground pretty easy."

They stopped at the front door. "If he drove all night, he could be past Chicago by now," Stevens said. "Hell, he could be anywhere."

"I put an APB on his Jag, and his picture's on the news. Maybe we get lucky."

"I hope so," said Stevens. "Luck's pretty much all we have."

Windermere knocked on the door. Inside the house, Snickers

began to bark. Then the door unlatched and swung open, and Madeleine Tomlin stared up at them, still in her pajamas at nine in the morning on a school day. "My mom's sleeping," she said.

"Mind if we come in?" Stevens asked her.

The dog barked louder from somewhere in the kitchen. The little girl studied them for a moment before stepping aside. Stevens and Windermere followed her in, and Windermere looked around the front foyer, frowning. "A little help, Stevens?"

Stevens laughed. "Down the hall to your right." Then he turned back to Madeleine. "How're you doing?"

Madeleine Tomlin's brow furrowed. "Where's my dad?"

"We're working on that," he said. "I'm going to check on your mother, okay?" He kicked off his shoes and climbed the stairs. Reached the second floor and looked around. A long hallway ran the length of the house. There was a closed doorway at the end. The whole house was darker up here, tense and expectant. Like it was marking time before the big climax. Stevens walked to the closed door and knocked. No one answered.

He knocked again and pushed the door open. The master bedroom, half lit through thin curtains. Becca Tomlin lay amid tangled sheets on the bed. Stevens knocked again and called her name. Becca groaned and sat up, fumbling for a light on the nightstand. "What time is it?"

"Just after nine," Stevens told her. "Carter didn't come home."

Becca sighed and sank back into her pillow. She was wearing the remains of yesterday's makeup, and Stevens could see a pile of spent tissues beside the bed. "Can I do anything for you?" he asked her. "Take your daughters to school?"

"Christ." She stared up at the ceiling. "What the hell does it matter?"

Stevens watched her and tried to think of an answer. *She's something like a widow right now,* he thought. *Her husband's long gone.* His mind flashed to Nancy, about the arguments they'd had after the

Pender case, her fear that he'd get himself killed. He shivered, thinking of his wife and the kids all alone, picturing Nancy in Becca Tomlin's state. Had just pushed the thought from his mind when Windermere came up behind him, holding her cell phone. "We need to go," she said, breathless.

Stevens turned around. "What's up?"

"Doughty just called. Tomlin's hitting another bank truck."

He stared at her. "What, *now*?"

"Told you we'd get lucky." She turned for the door. "Now, hurry up, Stevens. Let's go make it stick."

89

THEY PLAYED IT AS BEFORE.

Tricia took the first guard as he walked from the van to the cash-advance storefront. Fired a warning blast with her shotgun and froze the scene.

Tomlin fired a burst at the guard in the back of the truck. Advanced and kept firing as the man ducked for cover, begging for his life. Tomlin laughed in his face. Shot him dead.

Tomlin climbed inside the truck and threw the guard's body to the pavement. Then he searched the compartment. Found three big bags of cash and chucked them out the doors. The rest of the cargo was paperwork. Waste of time. Tomlin jumped out of the truck, lifted the money bags and hurried back to the Civic. He was almost at the trunk when someone fired behind him.

The first bullet smashed a windshield about three feet away. Tomlin felt it whiz by. Heard the glass shatter. He ducked and spun around with the rifle, saw the third guard, the driver, crouched along the side of his vehicle, pistol aimed square in his direction.

Tomlin squeezed off another burst with the rifle. The guy ducked back and hugged the pavement. Stayed covered. Then Tricia came back to the Civic, started hefting bags of money into the trunk.

Tomlin steadied his breathing. Focused on the guard by the truck and fired again. Missed high and wide. More windshields shattered. More screaming. The guard disappeared behind the truck again, safe.

Then Tricia made a noise behind Tomlin. He turned and saw the first guard tackle her to the ground. The shotgun clattered away. Tomlin stayed in a crouch and ran over. Grabbed for the guard as the asshole by the truck started firing again.

Tomlin turned and returned fire. Missed again. The guy ducked back, though, as Dragan started out of the Civic, his pistol drawn. "Don't worry about her," Tomlin told him. "Get back in the car."

Dragan hesitated. Then he moved again for Tricia. Tomlin reached for his own pistol. "Have it your way," he said. "I guess now's as good as ever."

Pow.

Dragan staggered back, his eyes wide, brought his hand to his chest. Tomlin shot him again. Dragan fumbled for his gun. Dropped it. A split second later, he dropped to the pavement.

Pow, Tomlin thought. *You like that?*

The guard at the truck was making another move. Tomlin fired again with the rifle. Heard the click as the magazine emptied. He had extra mags in the Civic, but no time. *The money's already loaded,* he realized. *I could climb behind the wheel and take off, leave Tricia to the law and take every penny for myself.*

He glanced back at Tricia. *Or I could have her, too.* He ducked and hurried back to the fight. Grabbed the guard and threw him away. Drew his pistol again and shot him. The guard writhed on the pavement as Tomlin turned back to find Tricia was gone.

She'd run over to Dragan, oblivious to the third guard and his gun. Tomlin fired at the armored truck and slammed the Civic's trunk closed. Ran to Tricia and dragged her, screaming and fighting, to the passenger door. He wrenched the door open and threw her inside, then hurried back to the driver's side and pulled Dragan's body away from the door. Slid behind the wheel and stepped on the gas.

90

DOUGHTY WAS ALREADY on scene when Windermere pulled up in the Chevelle with Stevens. She parked beside her partner's Crown Vic and climbed out and surveyed the chaos.

Just like yesterday: a sketchy mini-mall, a check-cashing joint, a blue armored truck, and a gaggle of police officers, news reporters, bystanders. A light snow starting to fall, the clouds cold and gray overhead, a storm threatening. A medical examiner's van pushed through the crowd, horn blaring, and Windermere watched its slow progress. *More bodies,* she thought. *This guy's on a rampage.*

Doughty climbed out of his Crown Vic and looked across the Chevelle at Stevens. "Who's this?" he asked Windermere.

"Stevens. He's BCA." She kept her eyes on the scene. Saw a guy walking around in an armored guard's uniform, which probably meant Tomlin hadn't killed everybody. Small miracles.

Doughty made a face like he'd bit into a lemon. "What's he doing here?"

"Stevens gave me Tomlin, Bob," Windermere told him. "He broke this thing open."

Doughty studied Stevens. Stevens held his gaze. *Good for you*

both, Windermere thought. *Let's turn this into a big pissing contest.*
She walked away from the men and toward the cluster of city cops
and forensic technicians. Counted two bodies, plus a crowd at the
ambulance. *Shit*, she thought. *Worse than yesterday?*

She nudged her way through the cops standing ringside. Made
the middle of the mob and looked down at the first body: not a guard.
A young acne-scarred kid in an Adidas soccer jacket. Two shots to the
chest and one to the stomach. Windermere caught the eye of the
nearest cop. "This guy a bystander?"

The cop shrugged. "They say he's a perp."

She looked at the body again. Heard footsteps and turned to find
Doughty and Stevens coming at her. "He's one of them," she said.
"Maybe. One of Tomlin's crew."

Stevens looked past her. He nodded. "Not so easy the second time
around."

"Guess not." She spotted another guard in the crowd. "Hey," she
said. "What happened?"

The guard gave her a thousand-yard stare. "You a reporter?"

She showed him her badge, and he glanced at it and looked off
again. "Ambush," he said. "Three of them. Just like yesterday."

"Who's the dead kid?"

The guard looked past her at the crowd of cops. He shrugged.
"Dunno," he said. "I was too busy not getting shot."

Windermere waited, but the guard wasn't talking. She walked
back through the crowd, looking for his companions. Stevens called
her name. "Over here." She found him by the ambulance, where
a couple of harried paramedics were treating a second guard for a
gunshot wound to the stomach. "Tell her what you told me," said
Stevens.

The guard had the eyes of a battle-weary soldier. Probably in
shock. Another young kid, barely in his twenties. "Just tell me what
happened," Windermere told him. "Take your time."

The guard glanced at Stevens again, exhaled. "We stopped out front here," he said. "I went to bring in the money, and they came in behind us."

"You get a look at their car?"

The guard thought about it. "Civic."

"Maybe a Camry?"

He shook his head. "Civic. Silver, kitted out. Blue racing stripes."

Windermere swapped a glance with Stevens. "So they ambushed you," she said. "How'd it play?"

"They started shooting," the kid said. "I figured they aimed to kill everyone, like they did yesterday. I couldn't stand for it. I made a run at the girl."

Henderson. "Then what?"

"This is what you need to hear," Stevens told her.

"That young kid was driving the Civic." The guard gestured toward the body. "He come out of the car when I jumped the girl. The other guy with the rifle said something to him and then he took out a pistol and capped him."

Windermere looked at Stevens again. Stevens shrugged. "You're saying the one bad guy shot the other bad guy," Windermere said.

"Point-blank. Then he came for me."

"Couldn't have been your partner shot him?"

The guard shook his head. "I saw the guy do it. Corner of my eye. I had the girl pinned, and I looked back and *bang*."

"*Bang*." Windermere looked at Stevens. "Doesn't make any sense."

"He shot Howie, too," said the guard. "Back of the truck. Would have shot me dead, but Carl laid down, covering fire. Saved my ass."

Windermere thanked the guard. Nodded to the paramedics, who lifted Dragon's stretcher and slid it into the back of the ambulance. Slammed the doors closed, and the ambulance drifted off through the chaos. Windermere watched it go. Then she turned back to Stevens. "Two dead," she said. "One guard and one bad guy."

"Both killed by Tomlin," said Stevens.

"Why the hell does he shoot his own guy?"

Stevens shook his head. "Disagreement or something? I can't make it work."

She surveyed the parking lot, her eyes dark and troubled. "He's losing control," she said finally. "That downward spiral I mentioned. And whatever his endgame is, Stevens, it's coming, and fast."

91

TRICIA RAN FOR the bathroom as soon as Tomlin unlocked the door. He watched her disappear. Heard the door slam. Listened to her sob through the motel room's thin wall. He tried the door handle. Locked. He stood outside the door for a minute and then walked back out to the Civic and popped the trunk open. Took the money out and started to move the bags to the Jaguar.

Three bags today. All filled with cash. About six hundred grand. Added to yesterday's score and that was a million five. More than enough to retire on.

Tomlin emptied the Civic of all but a half-used roll of duct tape and the duffel bag with the guns, nearly buried amid a pile of fast-food wrappers. He brought yesterday's bags from the motel room and packed them into the Jaguar as well. Ran out of room in the trunk halfway through and shoved the last couple bags in the backseat. A snow started to fall as he worked, the sky gray and foreboding. The AM newscaster had promised a blizzard.

Tomlin slammed closed the Jag's door and walked back to the room. Tried the bathroom door again. Still locked. No sounds from within. Tomlin knocked. "Tricia?"

Something rustled inside. "Go away."

"We made a shitload of money today," he said. "Maybe six hundred grand. We're rich, both of us."

She made a strangled sound. "I don't care."

He walked back to the beds and sat down and turned on the news. The anchor was talking about the blizzard outside. Said it would cripple the Twin Cities all weekend. Then he switched stories, and Tomlin saw his own face on the screen. The picture was cropped from a family shot, the four of them at Dave and Buster's. Heather's birthday, last year. He had a forced smile on his face. He'd been annoyed, he remembered; the video-game machines were too loud, and their waitress too chipper. The girls, though, had loved it, and he had studied their happy faces in the rearview mirror on the ride home and decided it was probably worth it.

"Carter Tomlin," read the tagline beneath the picture. "Armed and dangerous."

Tomlin shook his head and turned up the volume. "Tomlin, a Saint Paul accountant, is suspected of killing two armored truck guards yesterday in Minneapolis in a daring heist worth a reported one million dollars."

Nine hundred thousand, but who's counting?

"Tomlin is also suspected of having murdered another armored guard, as well as an unidentified accomplice, in a similar raid this morning. The two surviving suspects are driving a silver Honda Civic with street-racer accessories, and are armed with high-powered assault weapons. Authorities are urging citizens to exercise extreme caution when dealing with these two dangerous criminals."

We'll have to get to another city, Tomlin thought. *Chicago's the best bet. Maybe too close, though. Detroit, or Saint Louis. New York, even. Find someone to change our cash into overseas funds. Buy new identities somewhere, get plane tickets, and go. Then Mexico. A quiet beach. Palm trees. Piña coladas and tanning oil.* Tomlin pictured Tricia in some skimpy bikini. *She'll come around,* he decided. *She'll forget her little boyfriend soon enough.*

The newscaster switched back to the blizzard again, and Tomlin stood and walked to the window. Peeled back the curtain and looked out at the desolate lot, at the snow. *We need to get out of here. Before this goddamn blizzard shuts down the whole state.* He walked to the bathroom door again. "Tricia."

"Leave me alone," she said. "Please."

Tomlin leaned against the door. "We need to get moving. Dragan's car is on the news. My face, and yours. They know us. We need to get out before this storm really hits."

Silence. He heard rustling again. Then the door clicked and swung open and Tricia stared out at him, her cheeks flushed, her eyes puffy and red. She stared at Tomlin, depleted, her whole body limp. "What the hell am I going to do?"

Tomlin looked at her, admiring the curves of her body through the tight shirt she wore, the tap pants that clung to her hips. He wanted her, badly. He would have her. "We're getting out of here," he told her. "You and me. Together."

92

SCHULTZ STOPPED AT a Denny's by the highway and tore a page out of the phone book chained to the pay phone outside. He ate a chicken sandwich inside and studied the rumpled paper, a long, greasy list of Twin Cities Tomlins, and then set out again in search of his target.

There were five entries for "Tomlin, C," in the Saint Paul Yellow Pages, their addresses scattered across the four points of the compass. Schultz worked from the outskirts in, worked all day, knocked on four different doors with his gun in his waistband and got nothing but blank stares and headshakes for his time.

The sun was halfway through setting when he turned the truck toward the last name on the list, a Summit Avenue address downtown. Schultz flipped on the news as he drove, sat up straight when he heard Tomlin's name. The fucker was still on the loose: He'd taken down an armored truck yesterday and another one this morning. Two dead in yesterday's heist. Two more today.

He was still at large—that was the main thing—and flush with ready cash. The trouble now would be making the connection. Finding the bastard and taking his money.

Darkness had fallen by the time Schultz pulled into downtown Saint Paul. He parked under a streetlight on a side road, spread a map of the city on his dashboard, and compared it with the page he'd torn from the phone book. Summit Avenue. Not too far away now.

Schultz wondered how Tomlin would act on his own turf. Truth be told, his memory of their first meeting was a little hazy. The concussion had knocked a lot of shit out of him, and anyway, he'd been pretty buzzed beforehand. He remembered the guy's face and how nervous he'd seemed. How surprised he'd been when the geek reared back and hit him.

Schultz piloted the truck through a maze of dark streets, the houses growing in size as he drove deeper into the neighborhood. It was snowing now, heavy, and the truck scrabbled for traction when he pressed on the gas, fishtailed as he pulled away from stop signs.

He found Summit Avenue. The houses were huge now, the lawns vast, and he had to squint through the shadows for house numbers in the flying snow. Then he found the place. As big as any on the block, with an enormous expanse of lawn spread out before it. The lights were on everywhere; it looked like a cruise ship on an empty sea. Schultz pulled the truck over. *Bingo,* he thought. *Bet the bastard has a shit ton of cash hidden in there.*

Schultz picked up the TEC-9 from the seat beside him and reached for his door handle. Then he stopped. Something was wrong, though he couldn't quite place it. There was a big Lincoln Navigator in Tomlin's driveway: probably the same truck he drove down to Hastings. No problem there. Schultz looked up through the big picture window, watched shadows play on the walls as someone moved inside.

Schultz stuffed the gun in his waistband and climbed out of the truck. He started along the sidewalk toward the front walk, creeping slowly, surveying the street as he walked. Halfway down the block, he saw the sedan. A flat-drab Crown Vic, unmarked, a light bar in the rear window.

Fucking cops, Schultz thought, climbing back in the truck. *I could smell them.* He drove away from the house and off through the snow. *I'll find a bar for a while,* he thought. *Have a drink or two, calm the nerves. I'll wait until it's darker and everybody's asleep. Then I'll come back and rob the joint.*

93

TRICIA SAT ON a corner of the bed she'd shared with Dragan. Tomlin watched her. She'd been sitting there for a long time, hadn't moved much. "We should go," Tomlin told her. "There's a blizzard coming."

Tricia blew her nose into some bathroom tissue. She dropped the tissue to the floor. "What happened to him?" she said.

"We need to go," Tomlin said.

She looked at him, her eyes dulled. "Just tell me."

He paced a couple of steps. "They shot him."

"Who did? How?"

He walked to the bed and sat down beside her. "The third guard," he said. "Came out of the truck with a pistol."

"Dragan was inside the car."

"He came out." He touched her shoulder. "I'm sorry."

She exhaled slowly, shaky. Let him pull her close to him, lay her head on his shoulder. He rubbed her back and her shoulders, feeling the straps of her bra through her thin T-shirt, her smooth skin underneath. She was so close to him now.

Tomlin found their reflection in the cracked mirror opposite the bed. She was a mess, her face blotchy and flushed, her hair tangled.

He still wanted her, badly. "We were going to Mexico," she said, her voice wavering. "What am I supposed to do now?"

"Mexico," he said. "We have plenty of money."

She shook her head. "Alone? I don't even speak Spanish."

He looked at her again in the mirror. "You don't have to go alone." Tricia didn't say anything. Tomlin pulled her closer to him, leaned down and kissed her, his mouth on her soft lips. "I'll come with you."

Tricia stiffened in his arms and tried to pull away. Tomlin held her tighter. She fought him. Broke free and slapped him, hard. "What the hell are you doing?"

Tomlin pushed her backward on the bed, and fell down on top of her, pinning her underneath him. She squirmed a little, and he kissed her hard on the mouth like he'd wanted to for weeks. "Don't fight it," he told her. "It's better this way."

"Fuck you." She punched at him. "*Let me go.*"

He parted her legs with his own, pawed at her breasts. Felt her struggle beneath him, his tongue in her mouth, his hard-on bursting from his pants. *It's almost better that she doesn't want it*, he thought. *She's hotter when she's scared.* He kissed her again. Wrenched at her shirt. "You could learn to love me," he said. Then he felt something cold at his temple.

Tomlin blinked and looked down. Tricia stared up at him, her eyes cold. She was achingly beautiful. She was holding Tony Schultz's Ruger to his forehead. "Get off me," she said, pressing the gun tight to his skin. "Stand up, nice and slow."

94

THURSDAY NIGHT WAS game night, as usual. Stevens begged off the stakeout for a couple of hours. Windermere looked at him funny, and he shrugged. "Those girls need a coach. Tomlin isn't going to do it."

"Unless maybe he is," she said. "He shows up at the school and you take him down there."

He looked at her. "I don't think so."

"Me neither, Stevens." She smiled at him. "Go coach. I'll get us an ID on this morning's dead bad guy."

"Singer's on watch at Tomlin's house. Rotundi's got Tricia Henderson's," Stevens told her. "Assuming they're still in the region."

"Even if they are, Stevens, we're in tough. Too many places to hide, and the damn blizzard won't help." Windermere stopped the Chevelle outside Stevens's house. "Break a leg."

"Thanks." He watched her peel off, the big muscle car starting to slide in the snow, and then he walked up to the house.

THE DOG THUMPED his tail when Stevens walked in. Nancy turned up her nose from the couch. "*Phew,*" she said. "You stink, Agent Stevens."

"Long night in a '69 Chevelle," he said, bending down to kiss her. She squirmed away. "Not in the backseat, I hope."

"Not quite," he told her. "I don't exactly have an eighteen-year-old's contortionist physique anymore."

"Nor his stamina." She frowned. "You're working another case."

Stevens nodded. "Carter Tomlin."

"Windermere's case."

He nodded. Nancy looked at him for a long time. "It's going to get dangerous again," she said. "Like the last time."

"I don't know yet." He sighed. "Probably."

She looked at him some more. Then she turned back to her paperwork. "If you get yourself killed, I'm marrying a pool boy."

He looked at her. "It just kind of happened. I'm sorry."

Nancy didn't look up. "Don't be sorry," she said. "Just don't do anything stupid. Okay?"

Stevens thought about Becca Tomlin, alone and devastated. "I'll be careful," he said, feeling his cell phone start to vibrate. "I'll let the other guys get a shot at the hero stuff this time." He pulled the phone from his pocket and looked at it. Tim Lesley.

"Agent Stevens." Lesley didn't bother with preamble. "You booked OT for Singer and Rotundi tonight."

Stevens looked at Nancy again. She still hadn't looked up. "Yes, sir," he said, walking out to the hallway. "They're staking out Carter Tomlin."

"The bank robber," said Lesley. "That's an FBI case, Agent Stevens."

Stevens shook his head. "We're working a separate case, sir. Hastings police requested our assistance with a robbery investigation."

"A robbery investigation." Lesley sucked his teeth. "That's a damned weak reason to pay three agents overtime."

Shit. "I'm sorry, sir."

"Sounds like you want another reason to hang out with your FBI girlfriend again. This is her case, is it not?"

"Yes, sir," Stevens said. "It is."

Lesley was silent, and Stevens braced himself for the shit-kicking. "Well, shit, Agent Stevens," his boss said at last, "I'd like nothing more than to tear you a new asshole, but it seems the FBI wants our help."

Stevens blinked. "Sir?"

"Drew Harris doesn't feel his team can solve this thing on their own. Too many resources tied up with Homeland Security." He paused. "So Merry Christmas, Stevens. The Feds are paying your overtime until Tomlin and his girlfriend are apprehended."

"Shit," Stevens said. "Wow."

"'Shit, wow' is right. Solve this damned case for them, Stevens. Then get back to the office so I can ream your ass out."

"Will do, sir." Stevens hung up the phone. Stared at his reflection in the front door for a moment, and then rustled up Andrea and piled her into the Cherokee and drove off to the game.

95

SHOULD JUST kill you," Tricia told him. "Put a bullet in your head and leave you for the maid."

Tomlin stared at her. At her gun. She'd backed him up and away from the bed. Straightened her clothing and leveled the gun square at his forehead, her eyes deadly cold, her mouth a thin line. Tomlin said nothing. He stood there and waited. Finally, Tricia shook her head. "I'm not like you," she said. "I'm no killer."

Tomlin laughed at her. "You're exactly like me."

Tricia cocked back the hammer. "You think so?" She watched his smile fade, and nodded. "That's what I thought." She backed away from the bed and toward the door, keeping the gun trained on him. "I saw the look on your face when you were killing those guards. The kid at the poker game. You got off on that shit. I know you did."

Tomlin didn't reply.

She reached the edge of the second bed, and the chair. He studied her face as she felt for her coat. Looked from her eyes to the gun. "You're a sick bastard, you know that?" she said. "I figured it was the money that kept you going. I knew you weren't making shit at that crummy office. I figured you just had to survive."

"I did," he said.

"Bullshit." She laughed. "You wanted it, bad. Calling me up nights, begging for another job. You really needed this shit."

Tomlin wanted to beat the smile off her face. Hold her down and do awful things to her, teach her to laugh at him. He took a step forward. She flashed him a smile. "Do it," she said. "Maybe I'll develop a taste for this stuff."

He looked at the gun. Then he looked in her eyes. She would do it, too. She wasn't lying. After a moment, she laughed again. Grim. Shook her head. "So, what, I was just supposed to fall in love with you? We were going to run off together?"

Tomlin didn't answer.

"I guess I should be flattered." She arched an eyebrow at him. "I'm your midlife crisis, huh?" She turned away from him and walked to the door. Didn't bother to cover him with the gun. Tomlin wanted to rush her. He didn't. Tricia turned back to him, one hand on the doorknob. She smiled at him again. "We were good as a team, boss. But this is as far as it goes." Her smile disappeared. "Your keys."

Tomlin frowned. "What?"

"Your car keys." She snapped her fingers at him. "Hurry. There's no time."

Tomlin didn't move. Tricia raised the gun again. "Want to test me?"

He reached in his pocket and took out his keys, the shining Jaguar logo on a leather keychain. He tossed them across the room to her, and she caught them, slick. "The money," she said.

"In my car," he said. "Half of it's mine."

She laughed at him again. "Wrong," she said. "All of it's mine. Be happy you're still alive." She turned the door handle and opened the door. Snow swirled in, and harsh wind. The distant rush of cars in the distance. Tricia backed through the doorway, keeping the pistol aimed squarely at Tomlin. He followed her out to the snowy lot, watched her unlock the Jaguar and climb behind the wheel. A moment later, he heard the big supercharged engine fire up.

He watched the Jag back away. Then it stopped. Tricia's window rolled down, and she leaned her head out. "I see you again, I *will* kill you." She threw something at him. It landed in the snow at his feet. "Good luck, boss."

Then she stepped on the gas, the big Jag sliding sideways as she pulled away. Tomlin watched her drive to the end of the lot, watched the brake lights flash as she paused before turning toward the street. He looked down to the snow in front of him, picked up what she'd thrown. A slim stack of bills in an orange paper band. Ten thousand dollars. Ten thousand dollars out of a million five. Tomlin looked at the money. Then he looked up again. The big Jag had disappeared into the blizzard. Tricia was gone.

96

TOMLIN DIDN'T SHOW at the basketball game. Neither did his daughter. The game was a disaster, anyway. Stevens spent the entire forty-eight minutes thinking about Windermere and Carter Tomlin, unable to focus on strategy, substitutions, or anything else. "It's only a game," he told the girls in the locker room. "We'll get them next time."

He hustled Andrea from the locker room and out through the snow to his Cherokee, where he checked his phone messages as he drove out of the lot. One missed call from Windermere. Stevens called her back.

"They found the Camry," she told him. "A parking lot in Minneapolis. Attendant said some guy, Roger Brill, paid a year's lease in cash."

"Of course he did," Stevens replied. "Anything worthwhile inside?"

"Some fingerprints," she said. "Got my ID for Tomlin's dead partner. A kid named Dragan Medic, lives in Saint Paul. Doughty and I are headed to his apartment right now. You guys win?"

"What?" He blinked. "Hell, no. Blowout."

"Shit."

"Yeah." Stevens paused. Let the silence grow. Knew he should tell her what he'd told Nancy. Knew he should make sure she knew he was done with the cowboy stuff. That he wasn't onboard with another Pender situation. Instead, he coughed and said, "I hear your boss is picking up our overtime."

"Yeah." He could hear the smile in her voice. "Wonder how that happened."

"Couldn't let me get away again, huh?"

"Something like that," she said. "Meet me at Dragan Medic's. I'll call with directions."

This was the moment. This was the moment to tell Windermere he was going home to sit with Nancy and supervise Singer and Rotundi by phone. Stevens let it pass. "Sure," he said. "Good."

She paused. "Something wrong?"

He shook his head. "Nothing. I'll talk to you soon."

Stevens ended the call and drove back toward home. It was really snowing now, piling up on the road, cars slipping and sliding all over the place. Stevens switched the Cherokee into four-wheel drive and kept going, pitying Windermere in her Chevelle tonight. Andrea watched him from the passenger seat. "Who was that?"

Stevens glanced at her. "A colleague," he said. "Agent Windermere, from the FBI. We worked the case in Detroit together."

"It sounds like you're friends," she said, frowning.

"We are friends." He looked at her again. "What do you mean?"

Andrea shook her head. "Nothing." She took her cell phone from her pocket. Checked the screen. "Can you drop me at Heather's house?"

Stevens forced himself not to slam on the brakes. "It's a school night."

"She's home alone, Dad. We're going to go cheer her up."

"You most certainly are not." He looked at her. "Her father's a wanted criminal. You're not going anywhere near that house."

She sat forward. "Everyone else is going. Why can't I?"

"See above." Stevens pulled out his cell phone. "Her dad is a felon. As far as your friends are concerned, you've got another thing coming if you think Heather's hosting a party tonight." He dialed Singer's cell number. "Nick," he said. "Kirk. How's the house looking?"

Singer yawned. "All quiet," he said. "Snowy."

"Yeah." Stevens glanced at his daughter. "Listen, some of my daughter's friends have decided they're going to head over there and cheer up Heather Tomlin. Keep a lookout for them, would you? Shoo them away."

"Teenagers?" Singer laughed. "Yeah, all right. They're not getting far in this weather, though, Kirk."

"Just keep your eyes peeled, would you?"

"Yeah." Singer yawned again. "Roger."

Stevens ended the call. He kept driving. In the passenger seat, Andrea sighed, heavy and dramatic. She crossed her arms. "This is bullshit."

Now he did stop the car. "Pardon me?"

"Well, Dad? It is."

He stared at her for a long moment. She stared straight ahead, her jaw set. "Sorry," he said, "but there it is. And for swearing, Andrea, you're grounded."

She spun at him, her eyes on fire. Stevens held her gaze. Finally, she sighed again and flung herself back in her seat. "This sucks."

Stevens pulled back onto the road. "I know it does, kiddo," he said. "I know."

97

D RAGAN MEDIC HAD lived in Payne-Phalen, northeast of downtown Saint Paul and close to the BCA headquarters. Windermere left her Chevelle parked in the FBI garage in Minneapolis and rode with Doughty across town.

Doughty picked his way through the blizzard, cursing every time the big Ford's ass slid out. Ducked behind a plow for a part of the way, the windshield pelted with ice chips and salt. *Good night to leave the Chevelle home,* Windermere thought. *Baby wouldn't make it a mile in this weather.*

Medic's place was a shitty two-story brick building on Payne, across the street from an abandoned supermarket and kitty-corner to a thriving liquor store. Doughty parked the Crown Vic under a streetlight and turned off the engine. Then he stared out through the windshield and sighed like he had something to say. Windermere watched the snow accumulate on the windshield and melt quickly on the warm hood of the car. She waited.

Doughty sighed again. He spoke in a monotone, like he was too tired for inflection. "This is my case," he said. "I'm the senior agent."

Windermere rolled her eyes. "Sure, Bob," she said. "Whatever you want. Can we check out this apartment?"

"I put up with a lot of your bullshit. A lot of your disrespect."

"We solve this case and it's over. You never have to talk to me again."

Doughty shook his head. "You asked Harris for BCA backup. Without my knowledge or consent."

She looked at him. "We needed manpower. Who else was going to watch Tomlin's house, or Tricia Henderson's? You?"

"You brought the BCA on board because you want to work with Kirk Stevens," said Doughty. "Don't pretend this is a manpower issue."

Windermere looked out the window. Watched a wino struggle past, shoving a broken-down shopping cart through the snow. "I'm just trying to solve this case, Bob," she said. "I'm not trying to step on your toes."

"That's my point, Agent Windermere." Doughty finally looked at her. "It's not your case to solve, and it sure as hell isn't your BCA boyfriend's. I'm senior agent. This is my case."

She sat silently until she couldn't help herself. "All due respect, Bob, but Kirk Stevens has done a hell of a lot more in one week than you've accomplished in a very long month."

He spun at her. "The hell does that mean?"

"Put it together," she told him. "It wasn't for me and Stevens, you'd still be chasing down Nolan Jackson's grandparents. Probably shooting them, too."

"Fuck you," he told her.

"Forget it," she said. "Let's just end this thing." She reached down and opened her door. Stepped out onto the sidewalk and leaned back into the car. Doughty hadn't moved. "You coming?"

Doughty said nothing. Gripped the steering wheel tight. Windermere squinted in at him, the wind buffeting her from every angle with heavy gusts of snow. Then she straightened. "Guess not." She turned away from the unmarked car and walked down the block toward Medic's apartment. Nearly collided with Stevens coming out of an alley. "Whoa," she said. "Where'd you come from?"

He gestured. "Parked back there." He looked past her to Doughty in the Crown Vic. "That your partner?"

She glanced back. Doughty still hadn't moved. "I'm not sure anymore," she said. "You want to check out this building?"

Stevens looked at Doughty again. Then he nodded. "Let's do it."

98

ANDREA STEVENS LAY on her bed, wondering why her dad had to be such a jerk. Heather was all alone, and her dad was on the run. She could use some distraction. And besides, everybody on the team was supposed to be going. Probably a lot of other kids, too. Andrea stared at the ceiling and sighed, picturing Megan and Aaron and everybody else, all of them having a good time while here she was, sitting at home like a nerd.

Her cell phone vibrated beside her. A text message from Megan. "Headed to Heather's," it read. "You coming?"

Andrea sighed again. "Can't," she typed. "My dad's being an asshole."

A minute later, Megan responded. "Sneak out. We all did." Andrea read the message and glanced at her bedroom window, where the snow swirled outside in the streetlight. She'd never snuck out on her parents before. But they'd never really grounded her, either.

Another message from Megan: "Aaron's going to be there ;-)"

That did it. Andrea picked up her cell phone again and called Megan. Megan picked up after the fourth or fifth ring, and Andrea could hear laughter in the background. *I have to be there*, she thought.

"My dad called the cops," she told Megan. "They're going to shut everything down."

"Relax. We just got here." Megan laughed. "The cop's parked out front so we snuck in the back. Heather's mom is like catatonic, anyway. She doesn't care."

"What if her dad comes back?"

"Andrea, it's Coach Tomlin. What's he going to do?"

Andrea stretched out on the bed. "What's he in trouble for, anyway?"

"Who cares? He's, like, a wanted man. He's not dumb enough to come back to the one place people know where to find him."

"Isn't Heather worried?"

"Of course she's worried," Megan said. "That's why we have to be here. No one should have to go through this alone."

Megan said something Andrea didn't catch, and then she came back. "Aaron's here," she said, giggling. "He keeps asking about you."

"Shut up." Andrea stood. "I'm sneaking out."

Megan giggled again. "See you soon."

Andrea put down her phone. *Dad's gone with Agent Windermere,* she thought. *Anyway, it's like Megan said. If Heather's dad is really in trouble, he's not coming home.* She climbed off the bed and walked to her bedroom door. Opened it slowly and peered out. The upstairs was quiet, the only sounds a few muffled gunshots as JJ killed zombies in his room.

Andrea hesitated, her heart starting to pound, and then hurriedly changed into her new skinny jeans and her favorite black top. She checked the mirror and scraped her hair back into a ponytail. *It'll have to do.* Shoving her phone into her back pocket, she crept into the hall and closed the door behind her. She dodged the creaky floorboards as she walked down the stairs. The kitchen light was on, and Andrea could hear her mom on the telephone.

"I'm telling you, David, they're going to lock this guy up for no reason," she was saying. "We need to get to him first."

Andrea paused at the doorway. Stuck her head in the kitchen and saw her mom pacing by the table, the cordless telephone in her hand. She was looking away, pacing fast, gesturing with her hands, urgent. *Perfect.* Andrea snuck around the kitchen to the side door, slipped on her coat, and grabbed her spare house key. Then she snuck out and pulled the door closed behind her.

It was snowing harder now, definitely a blizzard. *I should have worn boots,* she thought, feeling her shoes fill with snow as she walked down the driveway. She stopped and looked back at the house. *Too late now.*

Andrea put her head down and trudged through the blizzard toward Heather's house. The Tomlins lived barely more than a mile away, but in the storm the walk seemed to take forever. An hour had passed by the time she arrived at Heather's block.

Andrea clutched her coat tighter around her and tried to stick to the shadows as she searched for her dad's cop friend. She saw the car about halfway down, parked by the end of Heather's driveway, a big green car with no markings, like the one her dad sometimes drove. It was facing in her direction.

Andrea cut through the neighbors' yard, away from the police car and onto the Tomlins' property. The snow was ankle-deep, and her socks were soaked through by the time she reached Heather's driveway, but the cop still hadn't moved from the police car. It was worth it. Andrea pulled out her cell phone and called Megan. "Let me in," she told her. "I'm freaking cold. And I really need socks."

99

MEDIC'S APARTMENT TOOK up half of the top floor of his apartment building. Two bedrooms, a kitchen, a bathroom, and a common area with a giant flat-screen TV. Stevens examined the TV. "That thing's probably worth more than the building."

Windermere shook her head. "Boys and their toys."

The place was littered with car magazines and dirty clothing. The first bedroom was a disaster area; Medic had stacked cardboard boxes almost to the ceiling, all of them filled with movies and old clothes and video-game systems. Windermere looked in and grimaced. "Tell me we'll find something in the other bedroom," she said. "I don't want to have to search through this mess."

The second bedroom had a queen-size mattress pushed against the wall, the covers in a jumble on top. Clothes everywhere, empty glasses, a box of condoms. Stevens picked his way through the rubble. Moved a stained yellow blanket from beside the bed and unearthed a duffel bag. He glanced back at Windermere.

"Check it out," she told him. "It's probably not contagious."

Stevens grimaced. Bent down and, with two fingers, slid the zipper open. Peeled back the flap and peered in. Then he smiled. Windermere cocked her head. "Jackpot?"

He tilted the bag toward her. Inside, she saw only cash. "Jackpot," he said.

Windermere walked into the room and peered into the closet. Clothes hung haphazardly on wire hangers. More clothes strewn about the floor. Another duffel bag. It looked full. Windermere toed a pink bra on the floor. "As much women's clothing here as men's," she said, looking around. "Unless our friend Mr. Medic really liked to feel pretty, I'd say he had a roommate."

"Yeah," Stevens said. "So where is she?"

Windermere looked down at the duffel bag by her feet. Something wedged underneath. A picture, a familiar face. Tricia Henderson and Dragan Medic on a roller coaster somewhere. Those pictures they take in the middle of the ride. Tricia was laughing, clutching onto Medic, who looked like he was trying real hard not to smile himself. She passed the picture to Stevens. "So there's the connection with Tricia."

"Young love," said Stevens. "And this is where they stashed the money."

Windermere bent down to the duffel bag. "Still haven't got a clue where Tomlin and the girl are hiding, though."

"None whatsoever. So what do we do?"

Windermere walked out of the room and back into the hallway. *The whole place looks like a frat house*, she thought. *Or a little boy's messy bedroom.* She turned back to Stevens. "I guess we tackle this mess."

Stevens stared into the disaster-zone bedroom. "You're thinking there's some kind of lead buried in here?"

Windermere shrugged. "They left the money here, Stevens. Maybe Tricia comes back with Tomlin." She tugged his arm and led him into the chaos. "Let's tear this place apart while we wait."

100

SCHULTZ SPENT THE evening in a shitty bar by the highway, drinking Milwaukee's Best and hitting on the waitress, a lifer with big tits and fire-engine-red lipstick. She was a good sport, had a sense of humor, and didn't seem to mind when he swatted her ass when she brought him his beer. The way she hung around his table, Schultz figured he might have a shot.

"Really snowing outside," she said, as she dropped off his round. "Hope you don't have somewhere to be."

"Just right here with you, darling," he told her, and he watched her put a swing in her hips as she walked back to the bar. She glanced at him over her shoulder, winked when she saw he was watching. *Yup*, he thought. *Definitely got a shot.*

Schultz checked his watch. Nearly eleven o'clock now. He drank his beer slowly and wondered if he might as well just stay put. Drink until close and get cozy with the waitress, set out for Montana in the morning. The waitress sidled up again. Smiled at him. "I'm off at midnight," she said.

Schultz smiled back, weighing the pros and cons. She looked like she'd be a half-decent lay, anyway. Probably knew her share of tricks. Still, those damn Mexicans. Tomlin. And Scotty's goddamned sons.

Guy breaks into your home, beats you with a piece of lumber, steals your guns and your money, Schultz thought. *You just can't let that stand. Sure as hell can't let two kids take the fall.* He reached around and pulled the waitress close. She laughed but let him handle her, didn't protest. "I'm sorry, sweetheart," he told her, his hands on her waist. "I'm late for an appointment somewhere."

She frowned. "You're sure, honey?"

"Wish I wasn't."

"Well, too bad," she said, pulling away. "You get done soon enough, you make sure you come back. I could use the company."

"I'll do that." He paid his tab and left her a decent tip, and she blew a kiss at him as he made for the door. He flashed her a smile and stepped out into the cold, the snow enveloping him almost instantly, and he walked to his truck and climbed in. *Cost me a lay, Tomlin,* he thought, as he fired up the engine. *I'll be damn glad to be through with your bullshit.*

101

FIFTEEN MINUTES LATER, Schultz pulled to a stop at the end of Tomlin's block. The snow was everywhere now, swirling beneath the streetlights and piled up on the cars parked at the curb. The unmarked sedan was still waiting outside Tomlin's house. The cop sitting inside was trying to blend in with the rest of the block, but his engine was idling, and the hood of his Crown Vic was warm enough to melt the falling snow. Schultz cruised past him, slowly, and kept driving.

Tomlin's house was darker now. There was a light or two on in the back, and another in a second-floor window, but the place looked asleep. The only vehicle in the driveway was that same Lincoln truck. It was time to have a look inside.

Schultz drove to the end of the block and turned at the corner. Behind Tomlin's house, the land sloped south, down a ravine toward the Interstate and the Mississippi River, and Schultz followed the road down to a laneway running parallel to Summit Avenue. He shifted the truck into four-wheel drive and set off through the snow. A couple hundred feet down, he came to a pullout with a couple of snow-covered cars. He parked beside them and hid the TEC-9 under his coat as he stepped out of the truck and into the blizzard.

The snow was deep in the laneway, and it was a tough slog, the wind whipping his face and the slush soaking through his shoes. Midway down the alley, Schultz stopped and surveyed the hillside and the rooftops above. He walked to where he figured Tomlin's house should be, and then he dug his hands and feet into the snow and scrabbled up the incline.

When he reached the top of the hill, muddy and winded, Schultz looked around at the monster backyards and saw what must be Tomlin's house a couple yards down, lit up from the back and enormous. There was a gate leading onto Tomlin's property, and Schultz let himself in and walked across the backyard to the rear deck, where a sliding glass door led into a kitchen solarium. Schultz climbed the deck carefully and tried the door. Locked.

A dog started to bark inside, and a moment later, Schultz saw the little mongrel. A yellow Lab, young and exuberant, barking its fool head off with its nose pressed to the window. Schultz stepped back from the door, but the dog wouldn't shut up, even as he retreated into the backyard again. He walked around the side of the house to the driveway, out of the dog's sight line, leaned against the wall, and waited for the dog to calm. He heard a door open about ten feet away, and he ducked into the shadows and forced himself to stay still. *So much for surprising the bastard*, he thought. *Shit*.

Someone poked his head out. A teenager, a boy, about sixteen or so. He wore only a T-shirt and jeans, and he shivered as he squinted into the snow. "Hello?" he said. "Josh? Heather says come around to the side door."

The kid waited there, looking around. Schultz took out the TEC-9 and walked into the light, leveling the gun at his face. "Evening."

The kid scrambled back, his eyes wide. "Who are you?"

Schultz kept the gun steady. "Friend of the family." He glanced down the driveway at the police car out front, the cop still inside, oblivious. "Be a pal and invite me inside."

102

STEVENS STOOD UP from a box of football jerseys and walked to the window. "Jesus," he said. "It's another ice age out there."

Windermere watched him from the floor. They'd torn apart Dragan Medic's second bedroom over the last hour or so, and found nothing. Moreover, Tomlin and Tricia Henderson hadn't returned for the money, and Windermere had watched the minutes tick away, feeling empty and anxious and increasingly desperate. She stood and walked to the window and peered out at the blizzard, the gusting snow like so many mosquitoes beneath the yellow light from the streetlamps. "My partner still out there?"

Stevens shook his head. "What the hell happened, anyway?"

"The usual, Stevens," she said, sighing. "Man stuff. Had to be in control."

Stevens laughed. "He picked the wrong partner."

"Yeah, well. His loss." She stared out into the blizzard. "Except we might need the manpower if we're going to find Tomlin."

She'd sent license plate info and a description of Tomlin's Jaguar to every police outfit in the state. In this weather, though, every car looked the same, and license plates were all hidden by snow. Tomlin's cell phone, meanwhile, was an older model, untraceable by GPS.

Mathers was harassing T-Mobile into triangulating his calls, but the process would take time. Tomlin would be gone long before the locations came through.

Stevens walked away from the window and stood in the middle of the room. He sighed and looked at her. "I need to say something."

She cocked her head at him. "You asking permission?"

"Nah," he said. He couldn't meet her eyes. "It's like this, Carla," he said at last. "I swore I'd never do something like this again. After last time. I'm risking my marriage just being here."

She felt a brief, guilty thrill. "What, with me?"

"Yes," he said. "No. This whole case." He looked around and sighed. "I promised my wife I wouldn't do it. This cowboy stuff."

Windermere looked at him. "Come on."

Stevens stared out the dark window. "Pender could have killed us. You and me both. We're headed down the same road with Tomlin."

"So what?" she said. "Pender didn't kill us. We beat him. We'll beat Tomlin the same."

Stevens shook his head. "I have a family, Carla."

"And, what, I don't?" Windermere tore through the tape on another cardboard box and peered inside: a stack of old *Maxim* magazines. "It's not like I asked you to be here," she said. "Far as I can tell, you were pretty damn eager to get yourself involved." She looked at him. "I don't get it, Stevens. You came here by yourself. You *wanted* to be here."

"I missed working with you. That hasn't changed."

"So work with me. Let's take this guy down."

Stevens exhaled. "I made a promise to Nancy," he said. "This isn't my game anymore."

Windermere turned back to the box. Riffled through the stack of magazines and set it aside. Picked up another box, this one filled with die-cast model cars, Japanese, mostly. No American muscle. She shook her head. "Fine."

"What?"

She turned to him. "If it's too dangerous for you, Stevens, then be with your family. Let me handle Tomlin. Go home."

He stared at her. "I'm not leaving you here alone, Carla."

"Don't sweat it. I'll get Doughty to help here, or someone else on my team. Someone who doesn't need to be home with his wife."

Stevens said nothing. Windermere shook her head. "Go, Stevens," she said. "Just go home."

Stevens didn't move for a minute or two. Just looked at her. "Shit," he said. "Shit." Then he walked out the door.

103

SCHULTZ PUSHED THE kid through the doorway. The Tomlins' dog padded out from the kitchen, locked eyes with him, and started barking again. "You shut that mutt up," Schultz told the kid, "or I'll kill you both."

The kid was pale, shaky. He turned to the dog and held out his hand. "Come on, Snickers," he said. "Come on, be quiet."

Someone called up from the basement, a girl. "Aaron?" she said. "Is Josh here?"

The kid looked at Schultz, terrified. Schultz put his finger to his lips and motioned down the stairs. The kid swallowed and started down, Schultz behind hm. The dog kept barking up above. Schultz turned around and leveled the gun at the little mutt, was about to pull the trigger when the girl called out again. "Snickers," she said. "Shut *up*."

The dog perked up at the sound of her voice, and raced down past Schultz to the bottom of the stairs. Schultz prodded the kid with the gun. "Keep going."

The kid, Aaron, led him into the basement, past a couple of dark rooms and into the back, a rec room with carpet and couches and a big-screen TV. Schultz stopped in the doorway. There were teenagers on the couches, on the floor, cuddled up in the corners. Maybe ten kids in total, all focused on the TV and the dog and one another. Schultz stepped into the room, his gun raised. Someone gasped, and then everybody was looking his way.

Schultz walked to the middle of the room as Aaron booked it to the couch and hid among his friends. "I'm looking for Carter Tomlin," he said. The kids looked at one another. Nobody answered. Schultz pointed the TEC-9 at the closest kid, a scrawny runt wearing camouflage pants. "One more time," he said. "Carter Tomlin."

"He's not here," said a girl, a pretty blonde. Schultz turned away from the runt and looked at her. "He's gone," she said.

"Where the hell did he go?" Schultz asked her.

"He's just gone." The girl glanced at another blond girl, who shied back and buried her face in the dog's fur. "Nobody knows where he is."

Schultz studied the second girl. "How many of you shitstains live in this pile?"

Nobody said anything. Their eyes all seemed to gravitate to the shy blonde with the mutt. Schultz looked at her. "You?"

The girl was crying. "Please don't hurt me."

"She doesn't know anything," the other blonde said. "She doesn't know where her dad is. Don't hurt her."

"Stand up," Schultz told the shy one. The girl cried harder, but she pushed the dog away and stood on shaky, skinny legs. "Come here."

She walked through the mess of kids to where he stood. Stared down at the carpet. "What's your name?" he asked her.

The girl swallowed. "Heather."

"Heather Tomlin?"

She nodded, her eyes screwed closed, tight, her whole body shaking. "I don't want to hurt you," he told her. "I just want my money." Heather nodded slowly. "Your dad robbed me. Seventy grand. That's what I'm after."

Heather shook her head. "I don't know anything. Honest."

"And your dad's gone." Schultz waited until the girl nodded again. "Where's your mom?" Her eyes shot open. Schultz held her gaze and looked at her mean, watching her nearly piss herself out of fear and already feeling like a first-class shitheel.

Christ, he thought. *I just want my damn money.*

"Where's your mom?" he asked her again. This time, the girl swallowed. Looked instinctively to the ceiling. "Upstairs?"

She nodded again, wordless. Schultz turned to the runty kid in the camouflage. "Get her," he said. "Don't try anything stupid. Don't make me be the bad guy."

The kid's eyes went wide. He didn't move. "Hurry, Brian," someone said. Brian jolted like he'd touched a live wire, and hurried out of the room.

Schultz looked back at the gaggle of teens. He examined the braver blond girl, who stood, staring at him, by the couch. "Who are you?" he asked her.

The girl flushed and looked away. Not so ballsy now. "Andrea," she said.

"You live in this house?"

She shook her head. "No."

"Then sit down and keep your mouth shut," he told her. "Mind your business." He waved the gun at her, and she paled and retreated to the couch as someone gasped from the door behind him. Schultz turned to see the little runt, Brian, returning with two people behind him.

A woman, middle-aged. She looked exhausted but beautiful, a peek into her daughters' futures. The girl behind her was younger than her sister, still a child. Mom saw the gun and went rigid. "What do you want?"

"You're Tomlin's wife," he said, and she nodded. "I'm here for my money."

Her eyes were red and swollen, her hair unkempt. She looked like she'd been crying nonstop for a week, but she didn't look at him scared, and she didn't look anymore at the gun. "I don't know anything about your money," she said. "Carter's gone."

"Seventy grand. Then I'll go."

She didn't blink. "We don't have it."

"Your husband's a bank robber, lady. You have it."

"He took the money." She looked at him, grim. "We never saw it. We don't have it."

"In this whole fucking house." Schultz stared at her. She stared back, miserable but defiant. Schultz felt his frustration mounting. Could have punched through the wall. "Find him."

"How?"

"I don't care. Find him, or I start killing these kids." Schultz motioned to a side table, where a cordless phone sat amid empty chip bags and soda cans. "There's your lifeline," he told her. "Use it."

104

TOMLIN LAY ON the bed in the dark motel room, staring up at the ceiling and listening to the blizzard rage outside. He wondered how far Tricia would get in the Jaguar. Wondered if she would really escape.

The ten-thousand stack she'd thrown lay on the flowered bedspread beside him, the soggy bills a bad joke at his expense. Ten thousand dollars out of a million five. Odds were better he'd die in this motel room than spend that cash.

"I see you again, I *will* kill you," she'd said. Tomlin traced the mottled stains on the ceiling with his eyes and wondered if she'd ever get the chance. Cursed himself for being stupid. For letting her get away. He wondered how long it would take before the police found him. Someone, surely, would notice Dragan's Civic parked outside. The desk clerk would remember his face. Sooner or later, the police would arrive. Tomlin figured he'd be waiting when they did.

Tricia had taken the money, but she'd left the guns. The big AR-15 waited inside Dragan's Civic, a pile of ammunition along with it. The shotgun, too, and a couple of pistols. Enough firepower to put a dent in the Saint Paul police force before he finally went down. He cursed Tricia again. The cocktease. The whore. *You should have killed her,* he thought. *You should have watched her die, then taken off with the money. Instead, you let her beat you.*

That was the really bad part. The money was a setback, sure, probably fatal. What really hurt, though, was the soggy stack of bills on the bed beside him, the memory of Tricia's face as she'd driven away.

She'd won. She'd taken the money and the Jaguar and driven off into the sunset. She'd stood at the door with her pistol aimed squarely at Tomlin and laughed at him and dared him to come at her. And he hadn't done it. He'd stood there and watched as she'd driven away. And then he'd walked back into the motel room and locked the door and lay down and stared up at the ceiling and waited for the police to find him.

He'd kept Dragan's keys. Could feel them in his pants pocket. But he didn't drive away, didn't bother to run. Because he was a chump, after all.

The blizzard raged outside. Tomlin listened to the wind howling and stared up at the stains on the ceiling, thinking about Tricia and feeling plain fucking sick with envy. Then he heard his phone ringing. It had been ringing for a while, he realized. He'd been so lost in his thoughts, he'd ignored it. Now he listened to the tinny ringtone, the police probably, setting a trap. The phone rang a little longer, then stopped. A moment later, it started again.

Tomlin sat up. *Let them trap me,* he thought. *It's bound to happen soon enough, anyway.* He stood up and fished the phone from his coat. Looked at the display. His home number. He waited until the phone was silent again. Then he paged through the call log. Five missed calls. All from home. The phone rang again. The same number.

Here we go. Tomlin flipped open the phone and held it to his ear. Expected to hear Carla Windermere, or Kirk Stevens, or some other cop. Or maybe Becca, selling him out, pretending nothing was wrong. Instead, he got someone different. Someone worse than the cops. "Tony Schultz." The man's voice was harsh and triumphant. "You remember me, Brill?"

Suddenly, Tomlin felt even sicker. "What do you want?"

"I want what you took, Tomlin. Can't make you give me my teeth back, but I do want my money."

"Your money." Tomlin laughed, cold. "I don't have it."

Schultz snarled. "Bullshit."

"My partner just robbed me. Took every cent. Sorry."

"Sorry don't cut it, brother." A pause. "You got a nice place here, Tomlin. A nice family. Your baby girl's got a nice bunch of friends."

"You don't understand. I don't have your money."

"I understand fine," Schultz replied. "Maybe you don't understand. Come home and talk to me, or I make a pile of bodies in your basement. We clear?"

Schultz hung up before he could answer. Tomlin put the phone back in his coat pocket. Then he sat on the bed and looked around the motel room some more.

105

T ONY SCHULTZ PACED Tomlin's rec room, his boots leaving a muddy trail on the carpet. *Show the fuck up, Tomlin*, he thought. *Show up, so I can get my goddamn money.*

He'd trashed the house looking for the stash. Dragged Tomlin's daughter—the older one—with him, and told her mother if she tried anything funny, he'd shoot the girl in her head. He'd searched every room in the house. Tore open mattresses and pulled clothes from the closets. Far as he could tell, Tomlin wasn't lying. The whole house was clean. Unbelievable.

Schultz dragged the girl into the train room at the end. Stared in at the huge setup, examined it closely. Then he ripped the train table to pieces, ruined it, put holes in the mountains, and destroyed the cities. Trashed the whole room as Tomlin's daughter wept beside him. He found nothing. Stalked back to the rec room and collared Tomlin's wife. *"Where is it?"*

She stared at him and said nothing. He drew back his hand to slap her. She didn't flinch. "I don't fucking know." She spat the curse like she'd been saving it for months. "I don't fucking know anything."

He held her before him, his open hand raised. Then he released her. "*Shit*," he said. Tomlin's wife glared at him as she retreated. She didn't say anything more.

SCHULTZ COULD FEEL time wasting. He studied the collage of terrified faces around him and wondered if he could kill any one of them. He'd been asking himself that same question all night.

Carter Tomlin he could kill. The cop outside, maybe. But these damned teenagers, Tomlin's daughters, his wife? Schultz had hoped Tomlin would jump when he heard his kids were in danger. Prayed the bastard wouldn't try to test him. But the clock was ticking now, and Tomlin still hadn't showed. Schultz's TEC-9 was slick in his hand. He kept pacing.

The blond girl, Andrea, was staring at him. She held his gaze when he looked at her. Still ballsy. Schultz tried to wait the girl out, but damned if she wouldn't blink. Finally, he rubbed his eyes and looked away. Swore under his breath and paced the room some more, waiting for Tomlin to show.

106

TOMLIN PEERED UP at the lights of his house through the windshield. He looked down the block at the buried cars, the snow in the streetlights. Then he looked at the house again.

Be realistic, he thought. *Schultz isn't going to kill anyone. Not a couple of kids, not over fifty grand and some drugs. He's waiting for you to turn up, and if you don't, he'll get scared and run. Call in a tip. Let the police do their jobs.*

He sat in the car and stared out at the house, looming out of the snow like a ghost in the fog. He looked at it and realized he was scared. He was afraid to see Becca again. Afraid to look at his daughters, now that they knew who their father really was. He was scared, most of all, that he would walk into that dream home and find them all dead.

He was scared, all right. Terrified. But he couldn't walk away from his family, not after all that he'd done. He put his foot on the gas pedal and drove toward home.

SPECIAL AGENT Nick Singer sat up in the driver's seat of the un-marked Crown Vic. He'd been snoozing a little, waiting out the blizzard, and now he rubbed his eyes and stared out at the brake lights in the distance.

Damn it, he thought, *but that kind of looked like a Civic.* The car made the end of the block and turned left, away from the Tomlin house. Singer stared out the window and wondered if he should follow.

You're dreaming, he thought. *Too goddamned bored. Tomlin would be a fool to show up around here in that Civic tonight. He's probably in Bermuda already.*

Singer looked out at the street, but the Civic didn't return. The snow kept falling. Nothing else moved outside. He shifted in his seat, slid down a little. Turned up the radio and tried to get comfortable.

TOMLIN DROVE the Civic down to Irvine, the long, narrow laneway that passed beneath the backyards of the Summit Hill mansions. *Stupid to park the Civic in the driveway,* he thought, *what with every cop in the state looking for it.*

The snow had piled up in the alley, and the Honda struggled to find traction in the drifts, but Tomlin wrestled the car along anyway. He parked below his backyard and looked up through the driver's-side window. Found the narrow concrete stairs the previous owners had cut into the hillside, and above them, the top of the house. One light in Madeleine's bedroom. Otherwise, darkness. Tomlin took the assault rifle with him, and a spare magazine. Stuffed a pistol in his pocket and stepped out of the Civic and climbed up the stairs to the yard.

Someone else had been there, and recently. His big footprints were just starting to fill up with snow. *Schultz.* Tomlin crept through the backyard and stopped in the shadows. He looked out at the street and saw no movement, and he gripped his rifle tighter and steadied his breathing. Then he reached for the door handle and twisted it open.

107

WINDERMERE STOOD amid the mountains of cardboard boxes in Medic's spare room, listening to the wind howl outside. *What the hell am I doing?* she thought. *What the hell did I do?*

Stevens was gone. She'd chased him away. He'd lingered in the hallway, then out by the door, and she'd listened to him and wanted to walk out and say something, apologize, but she didn't. She stood in Medic's disaster-zone room until Stevens had walked out of the apartment and into the blizzard. And now she stood alone, cursing Stevens and cursing herself. Cursing Carter Tomlin for good measure.

You idiot, she thought. *Making Stevens the bad guy because he doesn't want to spend his whole life on a stakeout with you. Because he has a family.*

Except plenty of good cops have families. And Stevens is damn good. He'd proved it with Pender. He was proving it with Tomlin, until he'd walked off the job. So she was a little overeager. So she took Stevens personally. She'd been partnered with Bob Doughty for a month. Who could blame her?

You smothered him. And when he didn't want to play, you shut down and chased him away. There's your problem.

Still.

She wanted to smack Stevens. Grab him by the ears and yell into his face until he understood her point of view. Until he made the connection. The man was wasting his talents at the BCA. And, worst of all, Stevens *knew* it. He'd liked chasing Pender, and he'd liked chasing Tomlin. But for whatever reason, he couldn't get his head in the game. Couldn't accept the risks.

Become a librarian, she wanted to tell him, if you don't like the risks. You're the same cop your wife married. Suck it up, grow a pair, and come back to work. But of course she'd said none of this to Stevens. She'd told him to leave, and he'd left. And now she was here, in this messy shitbox room, sifting through soft-core porn and old gym socks and waiting for her big break. And meanwhile, Stevens was gone, and Tomlin probably was, too.

108

TOMLIN PUSHED the side door open, stepped back, and leveled the assault rifle at the doorway. Then he waited. Nothing moved inside the house. The building was silent. It felt empty.

He killed them already, Tomlin thought. He stepped through the open door and onto the landing. Heard nothing, still. Then something moved, suddenly, at the base of the staircase. Tomlin swung the rifle around, his finger tense on the trigger. Then he relaxed.

Snickers. The dog came bounding up the stairs, tail swinging like a whip. He reached the landing and leapt up at Tomlin, his big tongue searching for Tomlin's free hand. Tomlin let the dog lick his hand as he thought things through. The dog didn't like the basement. Went downstairs only grudgingly, and only when the girls were watching TV.

There was a light on downstairs. *Shit,* Tomlin thought. He waited some. Listened. The dog nipped at his fingers. Nothing else moved in the basement. *Only one way to do this.* Tomlin raised the assault rifle and started down the stairs, slow and deliberate, avoiding the creaky spots. The dog lingered on the landing, whining a little, pawing at the door.

Tomlin reached the midpoint of the stairway and crouched, his rifle at the ready. Saw nobody lurking in the narrow hallway below. A light on, in the back, toward the rec room. He pressed against the wall and slunk forward and down, ready to shoot at anything that moved.

He reached the bottom and paused again. Heard muffled noises from down the hall. Hushed voices. The whisper of socks on the carpet. The rec room. Tomlin started for it, slowly, keeping tight to the wall and tense on the trigger. Midway down the hall, he glanced in his train room and stopped. Stared. The whole layout was ruined. Schultz had destroyed everything, crushed his vast mountains and upended his cities.

Tomlin forced himself to keep moving. Left his shattered layout behind and walked to the next doorway, the dark laundry room. He flipped on the light and swung in with the rifle, but nobody sprung out to surprise him. Tomlin flipped off the light and crept toward the rec room. Paused at the doorway, then peered in the room. Ducked out again quickly. *Where the hell did all those damn kids come from?*

The room was filled with teenagers. About ten of them, boys and girls. Heather's friends. Schultz's hostages now. *Good Christ.* Tomlin looked in the room again. This time, Schultz himself grinned back.

He was still a big bastard. Tomlin could see the faint scar where he'd hit the man with the scrap two-by-four, saw the glint of recognition in the man's dark eyes. Schultz was holding a gun, some kind of automatic, and he waved it at Tomlin. Tomlin ducked out of the doorway and waited for the bullets. Instead, he heard Schultz laugh from inside, a harsh, gravel-truck laugh. "Come on in, Tomlin," he said. "Don't be a stranger."

109

NICK SINGER STARED up from the unmarked Crown Vic toward Tomlin's house, thinking about that Civic some more. The driver had hit the end of the block and turned left. Not much to look at, unless he was taking a short cut to Ramsey Street, down toward the Interstate and the river. Not much back there, otherwise.

Singer stared up at the house. A light on in the back and upstairs, nothing moving. Everything calm. He rolled down his window and listened but heard nothing. The snow billowed around him, but the whole night was muted, the only sound the occasional crackle from the radio inside his car. *Hell of a shortcut on a night like tonight,* Singer thought. *In a little front-wheel drive car like that, too.*

Singer stretched in his seat and checked the time. Nearly one in the morning, and still lights on inside. Pretty late to stay up, a mother and a couple of youngsters. Though who could blame them, a situation like this? Dad's off robbing banks, killing people, Mom's nowhere the wiser. Stevens said something about the guy coaching his own daughter's basketball team.

Crazy.

Only thing down that side street besides a shortcut to Ramsey was a laneway running roughly parallel to Summit Avenue. Down about thirty feet, a little fifteen-mile-an-hour access road. Be a tough slog through the snow back there. And Christ, but that Civic had looked a lot like the one they were talking about.

Singer studied the house a bit longer. Every light that had been on when he'd started his watch had stayed on. No new lights had come on in the meantime. *Shit*, he thought. *They're probably just watching a movie. Hanging out in the kitchen or something.*

Still, better go up and have a look around, just to keep Stevens and Lesley happy. Singer stifled a yawn and turned off the ignition. Climbed out of the Crown Vic and trudged up to the house.

SCHULTZ WATCHED Tomlin's dog's ears perk up, watched the mutt bolt from the room, and he knew that Tomlin had arrived. He waited. Heard Tomlin creep into the basement. Saw it in his daughter's wide eyes when her dad poked his head in the doorway. The doorway was empty by the time Schultz turned around, but he could hear Tomlin moving outside. A moment later, the bastard reappeared, and this time, Schultz was waiting for him. "Come on in, Tomlin," he said, as Tomlin ducked away. "Don't be a stranger."

Tomlin stayed silent a beat. Then: "Let the kids go."

Schultz glanced back at the teenagers, all of them silent and unmoving, huddled together as if, packed so tight, they could stop bullets. He shook his head. "Come on inside," he said. "Join your family. We can talk this thing over like a couple human beings."

"Let my family go," Tomlin called. "Then we talk."

"Give me what you stole, and they walk."

A long pause. Then: "It's upstairs."

"Bullshit."

"Secret room," Tomlin said. "This place was built by rumrunners. Lots of hidden compartments. I'll show you."

Schultz felt his frustration mounting, his bullshit meter going haywire. He'd searched the whole goddamn house already. Hadn't found any secret compartments. Son of a bitch. He looked at the teenagers again. They stared back at him, waiting. Schultz shifted his weight. "You're feeding me a line."

"You want your money or not?"

Schultz stared at the empty doorway. "God damn it." He reached for Heather Tomlin, wrenched her from her mother. "If this is some kind of goose chase, I'll start with your daughter."

"No goose chase," said Tomlin. "I'll get your money."

Schultz pulled Heather Tomlin closer to him. The girl stifled a scream. Screwed her eyes closed tight again. Schultz gritted his teeth. "Upstairs," he told her, raising the TEC-9 to her throat. "Let's hope your daddy's not lying."

110

TOMLIN HAD BEEN at a party once, in a neighbor's house a few blocks away. The host had taken a few of the men on a kind of grand tour. He'd showed off the dining room and the drawing room, and a little sewing room tucked into one corner. Then he'd stopped in a long hallway and slid back a wall panel, revealing a tiny alcove filled with shoe boxes and books.

"Secret compartments," he'd said, grinning. "Useful for stashing booze. They say Capone himself spent a night in our guest room."

The next day, Tomlin had tested every wall panel in his home for his own secret room. Eventually, he'd given up, disappointed and envious. Schultz, though, wouldn't know that. Schultz would have to believe him.

Tomlin watched as the big man maneuvered his daughter into the hallway, his machine pistol pressed tight to Heather's neck. Heather stared at him like he was a life raft on an empty sea. She looked like a child in the big homesteader's arms.

Schultz followed his gaze. "You just get me my money," he said. "Your daughter will be fine."

Tomlin kept his eyes on Heather. Forced a wry smile, like, *What have we gotten ourselves into now?* She gave him a forced little smile back. It made his heart ache to see it.

Schultz tightened his grip on her shoulder. "Drop the rifle."

Tomlin looked at Schultz again. There was no way he could kill the big man without risking Heather's life. Not here. Upstairs, maybe. He could separate the man from his daughter and beat him like he'd beaten him before. Anyway, he still had his pistol.

Tomlin bent down, slowly, and placed the rifle on the floor. Then he backed down the hall, his eyes on Schultz. Schultz followed, pushing Heather ahead of him. He picked up Tomlin's rifle and held it in one hand, the machine pistol in the other, Heather tight in the crook of his arm. "Careful," Tomlin told him. "You shoot me and you'll never find your money."

Schultz grunted. "Keep moving."

Tomlin glanced at his daughter one more time. Then he turned and started up the stairs, hoping like hell he could bullshit his way out.

111

SCHULTZ GRIPPED the girl tight and prodded Tomlin with the gun. "Hurry up," he said. "Time's wasting."

Tomlin glanced back and nodded. Seemed to climb the stairs even slower. *God damn it*, Schultz thought. *I don't have time for this shit.*

Sooner or later, the whole situation was going to unravel. The cop outside would decide to check on the house. The FBI would trace Tomlin back to his home. Something, eventually, would go wrong. Schultz didn't want to be here when it did. "I didn't find any secret compartments," he told Tomlin. "This better not be some kind of game."

"You didn't know where to look." Tomlin's voice was flat calm. "They say Al Capone spent the night here, back in the day."

Tomlin made the landing, turned, and walked up another short flight of stairs and into the kitchen, every light in the room burning bright. He turned back to Schultz with a smile on his face. Calm. Friendly. Everything easygoing. "Of course, nowadays, we just use the rooms for storage."

I don't care, Schultz thought. *I just want my money.*

He could still sense the bullshit. Tomlin was trying to buy time.

There weren't any compartments. There probably wasn't any money. And that was bad news for everyone. Especially Schultz. It meant he would have to start killing people. He glanced down at Tomlin's terrified daughter and still wasn't sure he could shoot her. Tomlin led them out toward the front hall. "Upstairs," he said, glancing at Schultz again. "I'll show you."

SINGER DUCKED AWAY from the front door when he saw Tomlin appear down the hall. *Shit*, he thought. *The bastard came home, after all.*

Singer stayed crouched low, out of sight. Drew his sidearm and peered back through the window again. What he saw made him duck even lower. Tomlin's daughter. And a monster of a man with two big machine guns. Tomlin was leading him right for the door.

What the hell is going on?

Singer pressed himself against the wall of the house, stayed as low as he could, and waited for Tomlin to open the front door. *The big guy's the first target,* he thought. *Neutralize those machine guns, then worry about the bank robber. Just make sure you don't hit the girl.*

He waited, every muscle in his body tensed, ready to spring out the second Tomlin opened that door. Waited, and kept waiting.

Tomlin didn't open the door.

Singer snuck another look through the window. Tomlin wasn't there. He craned his neck higher and saw the big guy's big ass disappear up the front stairs.

Shit.

Singer glanced at the Crown Vic across the front lawn. Knew he should dash back and call Stevens for support. He looked back in the window again. The big guy was almost gone. And no telling what he planned to do with the girl.

Singer looked at the Crown Vic again. Then he stood and shoved open the front door. *"Freeze,"* he yelled. *"Police."*

SCHULTZ STOPPED ON the stairs. *Shit*, he thought. *Game over.*

"*Drop your weapons,*" the cop yelled. "*Drop or I'll shoot.*"

Tomlin stared down at him from the landing above. Stared past Schultz, at the cop. His daughter broke free and dashed up the stairs. Disappeared down the hallway. A door slammed.

Schultz caught Tomlin's eye. He gripped the TEC-9 and thought about killing the bastard. Paying him back for that cheap shot with the lumber, and all of the bullshit besides. Then he shook the thought away.

I move wrong and that cop pulls his trigger. This piece of shit's not worth dying over. "I'm dropping my weapons," he called down to the cop. "I surrender."

112

TOMLIN WATCHED AS Schultz's whole body seemed to deflate. The big man sighed. "I surrender."

He bent down and put the assault rifle on the stairs, then the machine pistol beside it. Straightened again, and held his hands high. Turned around slow to face the cop at the bottom. Tomlin looked past the big man to the front hall, where the cop stood, a young guy, his service weapon drawn. There were no other cops. Just the one. *The night watchman*, Tomlin thought. *Probably called for backup already. Time's wasting.*

Schultz walked down the stairs, slow and deliberate. Tomlin started down after, just as slow. Hoped the cop hadn't noticed him yet. As he walked down the stairs, he pulled the pistol from his waistband, very slowly.

SINGER WATCHED THE big man descend the stairs. The guy had a look on his face like a death-row inmate, like he'd always known it would end this way. Singer kept his gun on him. "Easy," he told the guy. "Take it easy."

"I'm not going to do nothing," the guy said. "It's Tomlin you have to worry about."

Singer reached for his handcuffs. *Police instincts,* he thought. *I knew something was up.* He pictured Tim Lesley's face when he came into HQ with the two of these assholes. Wondered what Stevens would say.

The big guy was nearly at the bottom of the stairs. Singer backed up a step. Readied his handcuffs. *Deal with this guy first,* he thought. *Then worry about Tomlin.* He looked past the guy as he went to apply the cuffs. Just for a brief second, but that's all it took. He realized he'd made a terrible mistake.

Tomlin stood on the stairs, halfway up. He was holding a polished black pistol. He was aiming it straight down at Singer.

Singer swore. Then the shooting started.

SCHULTZ WAS NEARLY at the bottom of the stairs, wrists out and ready for the cuffs, when he saw the cop's eyes go wide.

"Shit." The cop fumbled with his pistol. Dropped the handcuffs to the floor. Then the whole world exploded as Tomlin started shooting.

Schultz pitched down to the hardwood. Ducked his head, his ears ringing, half deaf. When he looked up again, the explosions had stopped, and the room smelled of cordite and blood. The young cop lay on the floor a few feet from Schultz, his eyes open, not moving.

Schultz rolled onto his back. Looked up the stairs at Tomlin and his pistol, the same pistol Schultz had tried to sell him a week before Christmas. Tomlin descended the stairs, slow now, his eyes moving from Schultz to the dead cop and back again. Schultz stared up at Tomlin. At the pistol. A .45 Sig Sauer P250. An online classified ad. A goddamn concussion and a mouth full of broken teeth. And now this.

Tomlin's blue eyes were icy cold and malevolent. "Guess I should have done this the first time around," he said. Then he pulled the trigger.

113

STEVENS'S CELL PHONE began to vibrate. He took the phone from his pocket and glanced at it. Rotundi. "You on the radio, Kirk?" Rotundi's voice was urgent. "You following this?"

"No," Stevens said, straightening in his seat. "What's up?"

"Saint Paul police dispatch just put out a call for available Summit Hill units. Shots fired. Summit Avenue."

Stevens felt his stomach flip. "That's Tomlin. Where's Singer?"

"Tried him on the radio," said Rotundi. "His phone, too. Can't reach him."

"Let me try him," said Stevens. "I'll call you back." He ended the call, and dialed Singer's number. Waited as the phone rang, then a click, and Singer's voice mail. *"Shit."*

Stevens was sitting in his Cherokee in a Payne-Phalen alley, a block or so down from Dragan Medic's apartment. He'd been trying to decide whether or not to go home. Whether he should go back into Medic's apartment and apologize to Windermere. Whether an apology was what she was after.

Shots fired on Summit Avenue. Singer's unreachable. Whatever Carla's after, it's going to have to wait. He turned the Jeep's engine over and pulled out of the alley. Drove onto Payne and parked in front of Medic's building. Called Windermere. "Something's going down at Tomlin's house," he said. "We need to get over there."

A long pause. Then: "I'm coming."

Two minutes later, Windermere opened the passenger door and climbed inside the Cherokee. Stevens hit the gas and pulled away from the curb. Drove as fast as he dared through the snow.

Windermere watched him. "What's the situation?"

"Shots fired," Stevens said. "Singer's AWOL."

Windermere looked at him some more. Then she shook her head and sat back in her seat. "Shit," she said. "Connect the dots."

114

TOMLIN HELD HIS daughter close. "It's over, honey," he told her, guiding her around the bodies in the hall. "You're safe now."

It was no use. Heather buried her face in his shirt and sobbed. Tomlin rubbed her back and guided her downstairs to the basement, where Becca and Maddy and the rest of the kids were still huddled together in the rec room. They shrunk back when Tomlin walked in. "It's okay," he told them. "It's all over."

Nobody said anything. Nobody met his eyes. Slowly, warily, they picked themselves off the couches and carpet. Kept their distance as they drifted out of the room. Tomlin crossed to Becca. "Everyone's okay." He reached out to pull her to him. "Everyone's fine."

Becca stiffened when he touched her. She said nothing. "The police will be here any minute," he told her. "We have to go."

She shrugged out of his grasp. "I'm not going anywhere."

"Honey." Tomlin could hear sirens in the distance. "It's time to go."

"Don't call me honey." She spun at him, shoved him backward. "I'm not your fucking honey, you liar. You fucking *murderer*."

He ducked back. "I did this for us," he said. "For you and the kids, believe me."

"Bullshit. Bull*shit*." She was crying now. "You killed those people for us? Those armored truck guards? You did that for us?" She shoved him backward again, harder. "Bullshit, Carter. Bullshit."

The sirens were definitely out there, getting louder. Tomlin felt like he was drowning. "Becca," he said. "We all had to eat."

"Fuck you," she said. "You could have found a real job."

"I tried."

"You tried," she said. "You're a failure. You're a weak little man."

The sirens were everywhere. "Becca—"

"That's why you robbed those banks," she said. "Why you killed all those people. You had to pretend to rape me just to get hard, you—"

He slapped her. Fucking bitch. Becca staggered back, her eyes wide. "Yeah, hit me," she said, sneering. "You're a big fucking man. Hit me again, you son of a bitch."

Maddy burst into fresh tears in the corner. A couple of Heather's friends lingered nearby, staring at him, shocked. The whole room suddenly felt foreign. Even Becca looked like a stranger. Tomlin heard her sink to the floor, sobbing, as he turned away. He walked out of the rec room and glanced in at his ruined model trains one more time, and then he flicked off the light and climbed the stairs to where Snickers still sat at the door, whining. Tomlin opened the door and the dog hesitated. Glanced back at him once and then dashed off, disappearing into the blizzard.

Tomlin walked up to the kitchen and into the front hall, looked through the window and saw blue and red lights reflected on the snowy lawn. *Shit*, he thought. *Out of time.* He stepped over Schultz's body, and the young cop's, and climbed up the stairs to where Schultz had dropped the machine guns. *At least we're going out shooting.*

He shoved Schultz's automatic in his waistband, opposite his own pistol, and shouldered the assault rifle. Then he stepped back over Schultz's body and walked into the kitchen, and there was Andrea Stevens standing by the landing, looking at him. "Coach Tomlin?"

She stood there, young and pretty and blond, a lot like his own daughter but confident, self-assured. She stared at him like she'd never been scared by anything in her whole life. Tomlin studied her, an idea forming in his head. *How much is a little girl worth?* he wondered. *How much would Stevens pay to get her back?*

He'd mortgage his house. He would empty his bank accounts. Pay every last penny he owned. Anyone would, for a girl like this.

Tomlin grabbed her. "Come on." The girl screamed and struggled, but Tomlin held her tight, squeezed her so hard he thought he would break her in half, and he opened the door and dragged her into the night.

115

TOMLIN DRAGGED Andrea Stevens, screaming for her life, through the backyard and down the snow-covered ravine to Dragan's street-racer Civic. The snow had blanketed the windshield by now, and the tracks out of the laneway were filled. Tomlin opened the rear door and shoved the girl in the back, put the assault rifle on the roof, and trained the pistol on her. "Don't even move."

He kept the pistol on the girl and looked around the car. Felt around the floor and came out with the half-roll of duct tape. "Turn over," he told the girl. "Cross your arms." He taped her arms behind her back, tight, and then taped her mouth shut to keep the little bitch quiet. Threw the assault rifle onto the front passenger seat. Then he climbed in the front seat, turned the key in the ignition, and stood on the gas. The goddamn car wouldn't move.

The wheels spun, the engine howled, but the car stayed put. Tomlin shifted into reverse and tried to rock the car out. Didn't work. The front wheels spun and the car rocked a little, and the air outside turned acrid with the smell of burnt rubber, but the car wouldn't move. Snowed in.

"God damn it." Tomlin pounded on the steering wheel and looked in the rearview mirror at the girl, struggling, wild-eyed, in the backseat. He forced himself to calm down. Think. "We need a new ride," he said.

Becca's Navigator. Tomlin looked up the ravine toward the house. Gauged the distance. *Fuck it*, he thought. *I have an assault rifle and a hostage. Let those bastards try and take me.* He climbed out of the car and pulled Andrea out of the backseat. She struggled. He smacked her. She only fought harder. Tomlin grabbed her by her duct-taped wrists and dragged her to the ground beside the car. Lifted her to her feet and shoved her back up the stairs toward the house.

The girl didn't go easy. Tomlin fought her up every step to the backyard. Across every inch to the driveway. Somewhere out front, more sirens sounded. Cops yelled. Tomlin could see them moving around inside the house, but they hadn't come into the back yet. Soon, though, they would.

Tomlin dragged the girl to the house. Pushed open the side door and grabbed Becca's key from the shelf on the landing. He ducked out again, pointed the fob at the snow-covered Navigator, and pressed the button once. The lights flashed as the doors unlocked, and he pressed the button again. Held it until the engine rumbled to life.

He hurried to the truck and pulled open the liftgate. Shoved the girl inside, slammed the gate closed, and made for the driver's-side door.

Someone yelled something from the end of the driveway. Tomlin looked up and saw a couple police cars, a few indistinct figures. He lifted the rifle and sprayed a burst down the driveway. Glass shattered. People shouted. The shots echoed like fireworks as he climbed behind the wheel. He turned the wipers on high, cleared the snow from the windshield, then wrenched the gearshift into drive and stepped on the gas, and the big truck lurched forward, picking up speed as it descended the driveway.

Someone started shooting from the road, fast firecracker pops. Tomlin gritted his teeth and sped toward the police cars. A Saint

Paul patrol car was blocking the driveway, and he spun the wheel hard, sending the Navigator careening over the snowy lawn.

Another shot. This one put a hole in the windshield. Tomlin gunned the engine and the truck rocked down the slope, bounced off an unmarked sedan, and jostled out to the snowy street as the police emptied their guns behind him.

He was driving too fast. More shots came at him, wild. Tomlin prayed they didn't puncture the fuel tank. He stood on the brake pedal as the truck hit the road. It slid across the icy pavement and put a big dent into somebody's Buick, ricocheted off the car, metal grinding on metal. Tomlin hit the gas again, heard the tires struggle for traction, and then the rubber found purchase and he was speeding off down the block, the police still shooting nonstop behind him.

He blew the stop sign and sped down the next block, glanced in the rearview and saw blue-and-reds approaching from the rear. He turned at the next intersection, kept going, kept turning. The SUV's four-wheel drive held the truck to the road, and Tomlin knew the cops' rear-drive sedans wouldn't have a prayer so long as he kept the truck moving.

Andrea Stevens squirmed around in the back, yelling something through her gag. So she was still alive. The police hadn't shot her. She was going to make a hell of a bargaining chip.

Tomlin blew stop signs until he came to the main road. Then he looked in the mirror. No cops. *They'll be looking for this truck*, he thought. *You need to swap the plates and go hide somewhere. Then you can figure out what the hell happens next.*

He felt very tired, though, and as he turned onto Seventh Street and drove away from Summit Hill, Tomlin realized two things: The first was that Becca's cheesy workout dance music had been blaring out of the truck's speakers since he'd climbed behind the wheel. The second was that he'd been shot.

116

STEVENS WRESTLED the Cherokee through the blizzard toward Summit Avenue. Windermere watched him from the passenger seat. *He stuck around*, she thought. *That has to mean something.*

They drove across Saint Paul in silence, Stevens's brow furrowed as he focused on the snowy road. Then he pulled to a desolate red light and glanced at her and saw her eyes on him. He looked away, out over the windshield, and he sighed. She waited.

The light turned green, and he pressed on the gas. The Jeep slid a little, and then the wheels caught. Stevens glanced over at her again. He shook his head. "I'm sorry, Carla."

Windermere looked out the window, the whole city a snowbound apocalypse. "It's fine."

"What I said—" He followed John Ireland Boulevard into Summit Hill. "It didn't come out how I wanted. I made a promise to Nancy. That was my point."

"I got your point." She didn't look at him. "I thought I told you to go home."

He drove another half block without saying anything. Then he looked at her again. "I had to at least stay until your backup arrived. Couldn't just abandon you."

"I'm FBI, Stevens," she said. "I don't need you holding my hand."

He drew back as though she had hit him, and she regretted her words immediately. The Jeep suddenly felt claustrophobic. Windermere reached for the door handle and wanted to scream. Instead, she sat straight in her seat and stared out the front windshield. "Just drop me at Tomlin's," she said, hating how hard she sounded. "I can solve this damn thing on my own."

Stevens shook his head. "I'm staying, Carla."

"Bullshit. Go back to your family."

"I have a BCA agent gone AWOL," he said, and his eyes were hard now, his jaw set. "Like it or not, this is my case now, too."

Windermere said nothing.

"Let's just get this thing dealt with," Stevens said. "Move on with our lives."

He sounded so run-down that Windermere nearly cracked. She might have, had she not looked out the window at that instant and seen the blue-and-red light show in front of Carter Tomlin's house.

Stevens slowed the Cherokee. Both agents gaped at the carnage. "Holy," said Stevens. "Holy—"

"Shit," said Windermere. Stevens released the brake, and the Jeep idled into the mix.

117

WINDERMERE STARED OUT the passenger window. A Saint Paul police cruiser sat angled halfway into the middle of the road ahead of them, its side panels dented and mangled. Windermere glanced at Stevens. "You see that?"

Stevens nodded. "This guy's Buick took a hell of a beating itself."

Tomlin's front lawn looked like it had just hosted a monster-truck rally. A mess of tire tracks led from the empty driveway to the road— directly through the mangled cruiser. There were people everywhere: city cops running around blind, neighborhood looky-loos, and kids— teenagers—all over the place. Total chaos.

"Becca Tomlin's Navigator is gone," said Windermere.

Stevens followed her gaze and nodded, grim-faced. They climbed from the Jeep and started up toward the house. The teenagers were everywhere. They milled about in little clusters of kids and parents, five or six little groups spread across the grounds. Tears and hugs all around. Windermere looked at them. "What the hell happened?"

"A party." Stevens surveyed the lawn. "A pity party for Heather Tomlin. I told Singer to make sure he got rid of the kids."

Windermere frowned. "Guess he didn't."

"Andrea wanted to come tonight." Stevens shook his head. "Had to ground her to keep her inside."

Windermere looked at him. Then she looked at the clusters of kids and parents again. "A party," she said. "Jesus."

A big Saint Paul city cop came barreling at them from the driveway. "Who are you?" he said, his hand on his holster.

"FBI." Windermere showed him her badge. "What happened?"

The cop studied the badge and stepped back and looked sheepish. "Guy made a run for it," he said. "Ruined my cruiser."

Shit. "Someone chasing him?"

"Three units. Tough night for a chase, though."

Windermere looked at the empty driveway again. "He took the truck, huh?"

"That's right." The cop nodded. "Broke through the line and sped off. Crushed my cruiser like it was a Hot Wheels toy."

"Where's the BCA agent?" said Stevens.

The cop looked at him, looked at Windermere. Then he looked up at the home. "Maybe you want to see it for yourself."

They followed the cop through the clustered families toward the mansion, every light in the place blazing. To a one, every kid they passed had the facial expression of a plane-crash survivor, and as she approached the house, Windermere felt a sense of foreboding, like whatever these kids had lived through, it was awful, and evil, and waiting inside.

The cop led them up the front steps and stopped by the door. "It's messy." He looked briefly at Stevens and then back at Windermere.

Stevens frowned. "Let's just see it."

The cop shrugged and pushed open the door. Another city cop stood inside, and the first cop nodded to him. "FBI."

The second cop stepped aside, and Windermere saw the bodies.

118

THERE WERE TWO BODIES. A big guy at the base of the stairs. A beard and red flannel and a shot at close range through the forehead. The other body was Singer. Stevens swore. "Son of a bitch."

The BCA agent lay flat on his back in the hallway, his blood pooling red-black around him. There were at least three shots in his torso, and his service pistol lay on the hardwood a few feet away. Stevens crouched beside the body. Swore again.

Windermere looked at the cop by the door. "So what the hell happened?"

The cop shifted his weight and avoided her eyes. Saint Paul police had arrived to check out the report of shots fired, he said. Screwed the pooch a little bit before someone spied Singer's abandoned sedan and clued in to the Tomlin factor. "We called for backup," he said, shaking his head, "but the guy moved too fast."

He'd taken his wife's Navigator. Sprayed the uniforms with machine-gun fire and then drove the truck straight at the line of patrol cars, swerved at the last minute and cut across the lawn, played bumper cars at the curb, and hightailed it down the street.

"That truck handles a lot better than our Impalas, I'll tell you," the cop told her. "Hell of a blizzard out there."

Windermere looked him over. Then she pulled out her cell phone and called the FBI office. Reached Mathers, working the night shift. "Supercop," he said. "You in on this mess in Saint Paul?"

"I need to update our APB on Carter Tomlin," she said. "He's in his wife's Lincoln Navigator SUV—"

"We shot it to shit," the cop interrupted. "He won't get far."

"His wife's SUV," Windermere told Mathers. "Look out for body damage, gunshots and the like. This guy just killed a BCA agent, and he's on the move again. Talk to the state patrols in Wisconsin, the Dakotas, and Iowa. The Canadians, too, at the border crossings. Tell them to keep an eye out for this guy and his truck."

"Gotcha," said Mathers. "What about Henderson?"

"Good point." Windermere turned to the city cop again. "The woman, Tricia Henderson. She was here, too?"

The cop shook his head. "All the kids say the guy came alone."

Windermere relayed it to Mathers. "Henderson's somewhere else," she said. "They split up. Keep looking for her, but Tomlin's job one."

"I'll get the word out," said Mathers. "You talk to Doughty?"

"No," she said. "Was I supposed to?"

"Last I heard he was pissed. I thought you guys patched up your differences."

"We're all pissed, Agent Mathers," she told him. "There's a psychopath on the loose. Keep me posted."

Stevens still hadn't moved beside Singer's body. Windermere walked to him and put her hand on his shoulder. He was rigid beneath her touch.

"Mr. Stevens?"

Tomlin's eldest daughter stood in the doorway, looking at Stevens across the bodies. Windermere straightened and hurried across to her. "Come on, honey," she said. "You don't need to see this."

The girl ignored her. Stared at Stevens. "Did you talk to Andrea yet?"

Windermere stopped. She turned back to Stevens, who was looking at the girl with a forced plastic smile. "I'll call home in a bit, check on her," he said. "I'll tell her everything's over and that you're fine, okay?"

"No," the girl said. "That's not what I mean."

Something about the look on her face made Windermere go cold inside. "What is it?" Windermere asked her. "What do you know?"

Heather had the spotlight now, and she shied away from it. Gathered herself and looked at Stevens again. "She was here, Mr. Stevens. She snuck in with everybody else."

The smile dropped from Stevens's face. "God damn it. Where is she now?"

"She's gone, Mr. Stevens." The girl started to cry. "Nobody knows where she went. She's just gone."

119

ANDREA STEVENS LAY in the back of Coach Tomlin's SUV, struggling with the duct tape that bound her wrists together. She felt the truck slow but couldn't see anything except streetlights and snow, wedged as she was in the cargo compartment.

She'd heard Coach Tomlin throw his guns into the backseat. If she could just get her hands free, she could take one of the guns and shoot him. Then she could escape, and maybe someone would tell her what the hell was going on.

The big man who'd taken everyone hostage said Heather's dad was a murderer and a drug dealer and a bank robber. Andrea had figured the guy was a whack job at first, some weirdo with a gun and a grudge, but then Coach Tomlin had come home with that rifle and he'd basically copped to everything. Then he'd killed the big man, and the police officer, too.

So he's a murderer, Andrea thought. *What does that mean for you?*

Don't think about that. Focus on getting free. Tomlin had taped her up tight, but she'd managed to work her wrists looser. Not completely free, not even close, but just loose enough to give a little hope.

She felt the truck pulling over, and then it came to a stop. Tomlin groaned from the front seat. "Jesus, fuck," it sounded like. *Maybe he got shot*, Andrea thought. She had put her head down and tried to pray when she'd heard people shooting, but she was being jostled around too much to focus on God. So she'd tried to make herself small and—miracle—it had worked. Nobody had shot her.

But maybe Tomlin was shot. He could be dying right now. The police would find the truck and his body and then they'd find her in the back. Her dad would be furious, but she would be safe, so he would have to get over it, sooner or later.

Tomlin coughed, a wet, phlegmy sound that made Andrea want to puke, and then the truck started moving again. *Crap*, she thought. *Not dead yet.* She wedged herself in against the floor and the backseat, and worked again to free her hands.

I wonder what he's going to do with me. She remembered the way the coach had been looking at her just before he'd grabbed her, and she felt her insides go cold. At fifteen, Andrea was already used to the sidelong looks from men double and triple her age. The way Coach Tomlin had looked at her, though, was nothing like those other men. Those other men wanted her for their own perverted reasons. In Tomlin's eyes, she'd seen only hatred.

Andrea could feel the panic starting to rise again, and she forced herself to breathe slowly. *Dad's saved hostages before*, she told herself. *You're going to get free.* She worked on the duct tape on her wrists. *Come on, damn it.* Felt the truck start to speed up and imagined how Tomlin would react when she pointed the gun at him. She wondered if she really could kill him.

Then the truck shifted, and Andrea was thrown across the rear compartment. By the time she could regain her position, the truck was slowing again. Then it stopped. She listened to Tomlin breathing heavily in the front seat, and then he turned off the engine, and she heard him walk around to the back. He opened the liftgate and looked in at her.

He was bleeding. He'd been shot in the stomach, off to one side, and his coat was matted with thick red-black blood. His hand, too, was bloody, and he pressed it to the hole in his coat and winced as he looked down at her, his eyes duller now but still filled with hate.

Andrea stared up at him. He wasn't holding a gun. *Just get out and start running*, she screamed at herself. *He's shot. He won't catch you.*

Too late. Tomlin reached in and grabbed her. "Come on." She swore at him through the gag as he wrenched her to her feet. They were in a parking lot, she saw, outside a motel. Shady, low-lying buildings and fast-food restaurants in the distance, empty lots and dark warehouses closer. The parking lot was nearly empty, and the snow swirled around her.

Tomlin dragged her to a motel room and shoved her through the door. He walked her to an unmade bed and pushed her down onto it. *Here it comes*, she thought, squeezing her eyes closed. But her coach left her there, and she squirmed onto her side when she heard him moving around the room. He locked all three locks on the door, and then he staggered to the other bed and collapsed down onto it. He stared up at the ceiling, breathing hard, his bloody hand pressing down onto his wound.

He's hurt bad, Andrea thought. *He's got to die soon.* She struggled with the duct tape but couldn't get it to give any more. She couldn't struggle too much, anyway, or else he'd figure out what she was doing.

The tape wasn't giving. *Crap.* Andrea felt the panic rise again, and she screwed her eyes tight and forced herself not to cry. *You're stronger than this jerk*, she told herself. *You have to survive.*

120

STEVENS WOKE UP Nancy. She groaned into the phone. "What time is it?"

"Where's Andrea?" he said. "Is she in her room?"

"What?" The tension in his voice seemed to jolt her. She was wide awake now. "What are you talking about, Kirk?"

"Check her room." He was in Tomlin's kitchen, though he had no idea how he'd arrived there. The whole room was blurry white light. "Hurry, Nancy. Please."

"I'm going," she said, fear creeping into her voice. "What's going on, Kirk?"

"She snuck out to Heather's," he said. "After I left. Tomlin came home, and there was a shoot-out. No one's seen Andrea since."

Nancy gasped. "Oh my God."

"She's probably in her room. She snuck back in while you were sleeping, and she's pretending she never left. It's fine."

Of course it's fine, Stevens told himself. *What the hell would Tomlin want with a fifteen-year-old girl?* He heard Nancy call out Andrea's name. Heard her knock on her bedroom door. He waited, his whole body tense. Then Nancy started to cry. "She's not here, Kirk."

Stevens steadied himself on the granite counter beside him.

"Must have tried to walk home," he said. "I'll search the neighborhood. Pick her up on the way."

Nancy sobbed into the phone.

"You keep an eye out for her. In case she beats me. Okay?"

He waited. She sniffed. "Okay."

Stevens ended the call and stood in the blurry kitchen. Someone said his name. He blinked and found Windermere beside him. "I talked to the kids outside," she said. "One girl—Megan something—said she called Andrea, told her to sneak in. Nobody can remember her leaving."

Stevens clenched his fists tight. "Son of a bitch."

Windermere touched his arm. "That doesn't mean she's with Tomlin, Kirk. None of the city cops saw her in Tomlin's truck, either."

"She just disappeared," he said.

"She's on her way home," said Windermere. "Let's drive the route."

121

STEVENS TRIED ANDREA'S cell phone again. Got her voicemail message, so chipper and upbeat it took his breath away. He swallowed and left her a message—"I'm not mad. *Please* call."—and then put his phone down and concentrated on the road.

They drove slowly, peering out at the houses and the beached, snowbound cars. The blizzard had subsided a little, and visibility was better, but they saw nobody on the sidewalks as they worked a grid pattern between Summit Hill and Lexington.

After an hour or so of slow searching, Stevens pulled up outside his house. Light shone from almost every window, as though Nancy Stevens had tried to make her home a beacon for her missing daughter. Stevens parked and climbed out of the car, Windermere behind him, and together they walked to the house.

Nancy was pacing the living room. He knew as soon as he saw her that Andrea hadn't shown. She stopped pacing and looked at him, caught his expression, and swayed on her feet. Stevens rushed to catch her, and she held him tight, her fingers tearing at his sleeves. "Where is she, Kirk?"

"We'll find her," he said, helping her down to the couch. "I promise, we'll find her."

Windermere caught Stevens's eye. "I'll keep looking."

"I'll come with you," he said.

She shook her head. "Stay with your wife."

Stevens stared at her. The thought of sitting at home, helpless, while his daughter was gone seemed perverse, but Nancy gripped his arms tighter, and he realized he couldn't leave her behind. "God damn it." Stevens hesitated. Then he tossed his keys to Windermere. "Take the Jeep at least."

Windermere caught the keys. She looked back at him briefly, and then she walked out the door.

122

WINDERMERE DROVE the Cherokee back toward Summit Hill, searching at every streetlight and intersection for Stevens's pretty blond daughter. *One plus side to being alone,* she thought. *Nobody else to worry about.*

All the same, Windermere knew she was worried for Andrea Stevens. More than worried. She was scared. The girl wasn't at Tomlin's house with the rest of the kids. She wasn't at Stevens's house with her parents. Where the hell could she be?

The simple answer was the scariest. Windermere pushed it away.

Maybe she'd panicked and run off somewhere. Maybe she was hiding in the hedges around Tomlin's house, or down in the ravine or something. Maybe she got hungry and went to McDonald's.

Or maybe she was hurt. She caught a stray bullet and crawled someplace secret. She'd have left a trail, though, blood or footprints. And someone would have seen her and tried to help.

Carter Tomlin was missing. Andrea Stevens was missing. The simplest answer was the worst answer. Tomlin could have shoved her in the back of the truck. It was dark outside, and the truck was moving fast. Maybe she had her head down. Plenty of reasons the uniforms might have missed her. The notion made Windermere sick.

The cops riddled that truck with bullets, Windermere thought. She had a sudden vision of an abandoned SUV somewhere, Stevens's daughter dead in the backseat, Tomlin, once again, nowhere to be found.

Knock it off. Be positive. You're going to find this girl.

She drove until she'd looped through the neighborhood three or four times, and then she drove back to Tomlin's mansion. A cop—the same cop who'd given her the bum's rush the first time—spotted the Jeep and came hauling ass to the middle of the road. Windermere showed him her badge again, and he waved her through, then chased after her. Windermere slowed and rolled down her window.

"Windermere, right?" the cop said, panting. "Been looking for you. Something out back you might want to see."

Windermere followed the cop up the driveway into Tomlin's backyard, where the cop gestured into the snow. "Down the ravine," he said. "Follow the trail. Maybe you make something of it."

Windermere started to reply, but the cop was already turning back to the road. She set out quickly into the snow, stepping deep into the drifts, the snow falling into her boots and soaking her feet. There was a weird kind of trail parallel to her own—several trails, actually. Big footprints, bigger footprints, and then a kind of Morse code track: long dashes and short dots, two tracks side by side. Windermere examined them, didn't get it. She skirted the footprints, and followed them to a narrow concrete stairway headed down a dark slope.

She descended the stairs and came out at a narrow laneway. A car parked nearby, Dragan Medic's silver Honda Civic. It looked snowbound in the deep drifts of the alley, though the patch under the front tires was rubbed through and bare to the pavement. The driver's-side doors were wide open.

Windermere circled the car. She looked down at the front tires again, the black pavement beneath. *He got stuck,* she realized. *Tried to drive off in this thing and couldn't do it.*

She bent into the open driver's door and peered inside the cabin, half expecting to find Andrea Stevens curled up and hiding. No luck. Windermere stepped back from the Civic and let her eyes wander. Then she saw it. It was a small footprint, much smaller than any she'd tracked through the yard. A girl's footprint, or a child's. Windermere stared at it for a second before everything came together.

Tomlin had dragged the girl back to the Civic. Stuffed her in the car, but got stuck in the snow. So he dragged her up to the SUV. Must have thrown her in the back before he drove off. Windermere stared at the car, her mind racing, the hole in her stomach growing larger. *Tomlin's got her,* she thought. *How in the hell am I going to tell Stevens?*

123

THE NIGHT CLERK at the Timberline Motel yawned and stared through the empty lobby at the snowy night beyond. It had been a quiet night, quieter than most, even for this time of year. Only four or five rooms filled; really, no need for a night clerk at all.

The clerk put down his paperback, yawned again, and glanced at the TV in the corner. The news kept running the same story: some psychopath killing people down in Summit Hill. The guy in the picture actually looked kind of familiar. He was a tall guy, about middle age, with dark brown hair. An anonymous-looking dude. White-collar. Not the kind of guy you'd figure would kill a bunch of people in the good part of town.

Unit 42. That was it. The clerk had seen the guy earlier when he'd taken out the trash, a high-class-looking guy with a smoking-hot chick in tow, the girl's hair neon pink and spiky, her face breathless and flushed like she couldn't wait to get back to the bedroom.

Christ, she was a hottie. He'd watched her as he made his way out to the dumpster and back, more than a little jealous. The chick looked younger than he was, for God's sake.

The TV was showing something new, a shot of a pretty teenager, a high school picture or something. "Fifteen-year-old Andrea Stevens," the tagline read. Then they showed a picture of the older guy again. A killer and a kidnapper. Probably a fucking pedophile, too.

The clerk turned up the volume. The reporter was saying the man had disappeared with the girl after the Summit Hill shoot-out. He was driving a beat-up Lincoln Navigator and was heavily armed. Appealing for leads, blah, blah, blah. But they kept the picture of the guy on-screen, and the resemblance was fucking uncanny.

The clerk stood from his seat, stretching, and pulled out the logbook from under the counter. It was a three-ring binder with forms for every guest, first name, last name, credit card information. The clerk paged through to unit 42. Checked the registry. The guy's name was Brill, Roger Brill. He'd paid cash. Listed his vehicle as a Jaguar XJR, black.

On the TV, they were saying something about a guy named Tomlin. Tomlin, not Brill. Could have been an alias, though. The guy did pay cash. He'd been here for a few days. Why would a guy rent a shitty motel room when he had a Summit Hill mansion nearby?

The clerk looked out the window, and then back at the TV. The anchor had switched stories by now and was talking about last night's hockey game, the Wild losing again. Outside the lobby, the night looked damn cold. The clerk figured he could go out and check the lot for that Navigator, but he'd more than likely find himself staring at a black Jaguar, some out-of-towner on a little bedroom vacation with his secretary or something. Why bother?

With a sigh, he sat down again and reached for the TV remote. Switched off the news and found a decent B movie that promised explosions and tits. He sat back in his chair and watched the opening credits roll, wondering what the guy in 42 was doing with that punk chick right now.

TOMLIN LAY ON his back on the motel room bed, his hands pressed against his bullet wound, his breathing shallow and his mind numb.

On the bed beside him, Andrea Stevens shifted position and whimpered through her gag. Tomlin watched her for a moment.

A few hours ago, he'd stood in this room with Tricia and a million five, cash, a fast car parked outside, a ticket to an easy getaway. Now here he was, broke and back in the same shitty motel room, with a fifteen-year-old hostage and a bad bullet wound. A giant step backward. Devastating.

You need to do something, his mind screamed. *You need to get your wound treated, and you need to ditch that Navigator and get moving to someplace where the whole state isn't seeing your face on the ten-o'clock news. And you need to figure out what to do with the girl.*

Tomlin looked over at Stevens's daughter again. The police would have figured out he'd stolen her by now. Kirk Stevens would know. The dumb cop would be emptying his 401(k) trying to work up a ransom. Tomlin could swap the girl for the money and a plane ticket somewhere warm. Maybe chase down Tricia while he was at it, make the little bitch even up.

All good. Except he was dying. He could feel it. The bullet wound burned his insides like a hot poker, and he'd bled, black and viscous, all over his coat and the truck. No doctor would save him, even if he could. Not without calling the police.

There's no way to fix this. You'll be dead by tomorrow.

He watched Andrea Stevens, asleep on the opposite bed, and felt hate well up inside him, envy for her perfect life. He thought about the wreckage of his home, pictured Heather's terrified, traumatized face. *She'll never recover from this,* he knew. *She'll never trust anyone again.*

Tomlin ached for his daughter, a sudden, heartsick pain. He imagined her growing up without him, silent and afraid, and he felt a terrible guilt, and regret. On the opposite bed, Stevens's daughter groaned and rolled onto her side. Tomlin studied her, her perfect features creased with worry and discomfort. *She'll walk out of here tomorrow,* he thought. *I'll die in this motel room and the police will find her eventually, and a couple of months down the road, she'll have forgotten about her scary night with crazy Coach Tomlin. She'll live a long, happy life, and I'll be just a speed bump.*

It didn't seem fair. Tomlin wanted Andrea to suffer as Heather had to suffer. He wanted Stevens to grieve as he grieved. He wanted to share his own misery with the BCA agent.

The girl could be a statement. One last terrible score. The thought gave him comfort as he lay there, blood-soaked and waiting for the dawn. *I'll kill her,* he thought. *And I'll make Stevens watch.*

124

WINDERMERE STOOD ON the sidewalk outside Stevens's house, staring back through the living room windows to where the BCA agent and his wife had camped out. *Man*, she thought. *I could use a cigarette right now.*

She'd smoked for only a year or so, her first year at Stetson Law, when the pressures both external and inside her head had threatened to overwhelm her. She hadn't liked smoking; it felt dirty, and weak, but it sure as hell helped with the nerves, and now, pacing the sidewalk in front of Stevens's home, Windermere felt more nervous than she had in years.

You think you're scared. Imagine how Stevens feels.

She'd delivered the news about Andrea herself. Called Mathers to kick-start an AMBER Alert, updated the Saint Paul city cops hanging around Tomlin's mansion, and then forced herself to drive across to Lexington in Stevens's Jeep, trying to figure out how exactly to tell him.

"You want to come outside for this one," she'd told him, when he met her at the front door, his eyes an open question. Stevens had glanced back at his wife and stepped onto the porch, and she'd drawn a deep breath and just told him. He hadn't said anything at first. He'd inhaled sharply, and then kind of nodded, off-balance.

"You're sure."

"The whole city's looking for her." She put her hand on his shoulder again, and squeezed. "We'll find her."

She doubted Stevens heard. He'd stared out at the street and muttered something to himself, and then he'd gone back inside. A few seconds later, Windermere heard Nancy burst into fresh tears in the living room.

Now Stevens's little house was filled with police from every force in the region. BCA, FBI, Saint Paul and Minneapolis PD, a couple of sheriff's deputies from the counties, all had converged in the pre-dawn hours to try and hammer out a strategy. Right now, Windermere knew, police were combing the Twin Cities for Tomlin's Lincoln Navigator, but there were only so many officers and so much ground to cover. Windermere paced, wearing a path through the snow, feeling powerless and jumpy and scared.

A black Chevy Tahoe appeared at the end of the block. It cruised up to Stevens's house and pulled to a stop at the curb. Windermere watched as Drew Harris climbed out of the driver's seat. The Special Agent in Charge looked impeccable, even at so ungodly an hour, the picture of an FBI senior officer. He greeted Windermere with a nod. "Your BCA agent's inside?"

She nodded back. "With his wife."

Harris looked past her and up to the house. "Fill me in, Agent Windermere." She gave him the abridged version. Harris listened. Then he nodded again. "What do you need?"

"Manpower. More people looking." She gestured up to the sky. "And we need daylight, and less snow."

"Snow's supposed to let up. In a couple of hours, you'll have daylight. People will wake up, see the news. They'll start looking."

Windermere looked out at the street. *It's the hours in between I'm worried about,* she thought.

"I've got a helicopter on standby as well," Harris said. "Won't do you much good now, but when the sun comes up, maybe."

"Yes, sir."

"You talk to Mathers about the HRT guys?"

"Saint Paul PD's got a tactical team ready," she said. "If it comes to that."

"Let's hope it doesn't." Harris took out a package of Marlboros. He tapped out a cigarette and then offered the package to Windermere. She reached for a smoke. Then she shook her head. Harris shrugged and replaced the package. Lit up and glanced at her again. "You did good," he said. "Made no friend of Bob Doughty, but you tracked this guy down. You were right."

"Being right doesn't get this girl back any quicker."

"No," said Harris. "It doesn't."

Harris studied her as he smoked. "Can you handle this?" he said. "Your friend's little girl is abducted. There's a fair chance she comes back to us dead. Are you prepared?"

Windermere felt her insides turn over, but she met his eyes. "Yes, sir."

"I can give this case back to Doughty," said Harris. "Or another agent. If you feel you're too invested in this thing to make the correct decisions—"

"I want this case, sir." Windermere held the SAC's gaze. "I can handle it."

Harris nodded. "Good." He flicked his butt away and turned up the path toward Stevens's front door. Windermere watched him walk to the house and disappear inside, watched him reappear in the bright living room window to shake Stevens's hand and say something to Nancy, the FBI officially announcing its presence. Then she turned back to the road and resumed pacing, alone, running scenarios in her mind and waiting for sunrise.

125

TOMLIN LAY AWAKE through the night, listening to Andrea Stevens as she slept. Occasionally, the girl would moan something, or whimper through her gag, and once she sat straight up in the bed, straining at her bonds and looking wildly around the room, before sinking back onto the sheets.

He lay awake until sunrise, feeling his wound throbbing, listening to the girl breathe. He pictured the look on her face when he finally broke her, when he'd destroyed that confidence, that improbable courage. Better yet, he pictured the look on her father's face when he realized he was too late to save her.

The dawn finally broke, and Tomlin found his way to the bathroom by the dim edges of cold winter sunlight seeping around the curtains. He pissed and then splashed cold water on his face before studying himself in the mirror.

He'd aged at least a decade since the layoff. No longer did he look boyish and charming and handsome. He looked worn-out and beaten, and when he tried to smile at the mirror, he couldn't conjure playful and confident anymore. Only scary. Grotesque. He looked like a mug shot. Or a corpse.

Soon enough. Tomlin dried his face and walked out into the room, his wound sending spikes of pain through his body. He walked to Andrea's bed and shook her awake. "Up and at 'em, princess," he told her, savoring the way her eyes widened when she looked at his face. "You've got a big day ahead of you."

THE NIGHT CLERK woke with a start. He looked around the motel lobby, wiping the drool from his chin, and saw that he'd fallen asleep on top of his book. In the corner, the TV was blaring some spastic infomercial, and the clerk dug out the remote and turned the thing off. Blinking, he surveyed the lobby. Checked the time. Nearly nine in the morning.

He stood to make himself a fresh pot of coffee. Glanced out the window and saw a big SUV waiting to turn from the parking lot into the road. Must have come from one of the units, he realized. It had woken him up as it passed the lobby.

The clerk rubbed his eyes and stared out at the truck. It was a big blue hulk with some serious body damage. Like it had been chewed up by a giant puppy. The clerk looked closer and shook his head. *Holy shit*, he thought. *Those are bullet holes.*

The Summit Hill guy was supposed to be driving a shot-up Lincoln Navigator, a blue one, he remembered. That was a big blue Lincoln Navigator out there. And those were definitely bullet holes.

The clerk watched the truck pull out onto the street, headed southwest, and then he hurried back to the front desk, where he picked up the phone and called 911. "Yeah," he said, when the dispatcher answered. "I think I just found that Summit Hill psycho."

126

STEVENS SAT ON his living room couch with Nancy asleep on his shoulder. He watched the cops clustered around the house, making coffee in the kitchen and talking in hushed voices out in the front hall.

Triceratops, the big German shepherd, came padding through the living room. He paused in front of Stevens and regarded him briefly with big, concerned eyes, before ambling off to insinuate himself among the Saint Paul city cops in the hallway. *Let the dog play host*, Stevens thought. *I don't have the energy.*

He hadn't slept, not at all. Couldn't do it. Every time he closed his eyes, he saw Andrea's face. Nancy's. She hadn't accused him of anything, but the way she'd looked at him last night, she didn't have to.

I could have prevented this. Tomlin wasn't even my case.

He'd spent the night wide awake and sick with worry, Nancy's face pressed to his shirtsleeve. He'd passed the time talking to the cops who'd drifted through the room, and when that got old, he sat back and simply stared at the walls, the telephone, feeling damned helpless and imagining the worst. What if Andrea tried to stand up to Tomlin? What if she tried to escape? What if Tomlin was some kind of pervert, some sicko with a thing for teenage girls?

Tim Lesley had stopped in overnight. He'd left just after dawn to wake up Singer's young wife and deliver the bad news. He'd hugged an exhausted Nancy and then regarded Stevens, his normally severe features now creased with compassion. "We'll find her," he said.

We'll find her. The night's rallying cry. Stevens, though, was finding it tough to believe the hype. Carter Tomlin was a psychopath. He killed like he enjoyed the act, unlike Arthur Pender, who'd killed out of necessity, a survival mechanism. Negotiating with Pender in Detroit, Stevens had felt like he'd at least known the rules of the game. He'd known Pender wouldn't kill his hostage unless his own survival was in jeopardy. Tomlin was unpredictable. Evil.

Stevens heard the front door open and looked up to see Windermere walk in, carrying a tray of coffee and a paper McDonald's bag. She handed Stevens the bag and studied his face. "You get any sleep?"

He shook his head. "Couldn't."

"Shit." She gestured to Nancy. "How's she doing?"

"She's sleeping, at least."

"And your son?"

"Upstairs. He's asleep, too." And thank God. JJ had stayed in his room the whole night, unaware of the fiasco playing out downstairs.

"We're going to find this guy, Stevens."

He sighed. "So they tell me."

She started to say something else. Then she stopped. "Yeah," she said finally. "Must be a lot of people blowing smoke up your ass."

"Even if we find this guy, Carla . . ."

"Yeah. I know."

Stevens reached into the fast-food bag and unwrapped a breakfast sandwich. He looked at it and realized he wasn't hungry. "I should be doing something," he said. "Instead of just sitting here."

"You are doing something," said Windermere. "You're taking care of Nancy."

At the sound of her name, Nancy shifted on Stevens's shoulder. Then she sat up, groaning. She looked at him. "Time is it?"

"About nine," he told her.

"Anything happen?"

Stevens shook his head. Nancy looked around the room, blinking sleep away. Then she sat forward and put her head in her hands. "Oh my God."

Stevens rubbed her back. "Agent Windermere brought breakfast."

Nancy looked up and saw Windermere for the first time. "You're Agent Windermere."

Windermere nodded. "I'm sorry we had to meet like this."

"Me too." Nancy took the bag from Stevens and peered inside. Then she shoved it away. "I'm not hungry, Kirk."

Stevens set the bag on the floor as Nancy buried her face in his shoulder again. Windermere stood. "I'll let you two be," she said, starting toward the front door.

Stevens felt his cell phone vibrate in his pocket. "Hold up," he told Windermere, shifting Nancy off him and digging for his phone. He pulled it out and looked at it. Felt his heart shift gears. "It's Andrea." He flipped open the phone as Nancy sat up straight beside him. "Andrea?"

Nothing. Stevens stared at the phone. The silence was pregnant, malevolent. Stevens held the phone to his ear again. "Hello?"

He could hear breathing, labored. Cops filled the living room, watching Stevens. "Carter," he said. "Where are you? Where's Andrea?"

Another long silence. Then: "I guess your life isn't so perfect after all."

Carter Tomlin. His voice was raspy, strained. He sounded more like a cancer patient than a killer. "Carter," said Stevens. "What do you want?"

Tomlin laughed. Couldn't hold it. Coughed instead, a terrible racking cough. Stevens wanted to reach through the phone and tear the words from his throat. Windermere was making eyes at him. Mouthed a question: *Where is he?* Stevens shook his head. "Talk to me, Carter. *What do you want?*"

Tomlin coughed again. Swore. "We're going shopping, Agent Stevens," he said, his voice high, singsongy. This time he laughed, and it stuck. "Hurry up and come find us before we get bored."

"Shopping," said Stevens. "Where—"

Tomlin hung up. Stevens tried calling back. Got no answer. Tried again and still no one picked up. He stared at his blank handset, his pulse pounding in his ears, and tried calling again, feeling his world disintegrating around him.

127

ANDREA STEVENS LAY in the back of Coach Tomlin's SUV, fighting with the duct tape and wishing for a drink of water. She felt awful this morning, worse than the time she and Megan stole some of her dad's vodka and tried out getting drunk. Her mouth tasted like a garbage can, her head hurt, she was thirsty, and she needed to pee. Tomlin had woken her up and bundled her into the back of his truck before she was fully awake, and as she tried to find a comfortable position in the cargo compartment, Andrea cursed herself for not running when she could have.

Tomlin was really hurting now, she could tell. She'd listened to his shallow breathing all night, waiting for him to die or pass out so that she could escape.

No such luck. He'd survived, and now they were driving again, someplace far. She'd been in the back of the truck for a while, struggling with the duct tape and trying desperately not to pee herself.

"Kidnapped Girl Wets Herself, Dies." Andrea wondered how her friends could take her death seriously if it came out in the news that she'd soaked her pants before the big climax.

Calm down, she told herself. *You're not going to die. You're going to get out of here, and if you wet your pants along the way, at least you'll be alive, damn it.*

First things first: she had to get out of the duct tape. Andrea shifted in the back of the truck, searching for a better angle. Then she found something. A jagged piece of metal, about halfway up the door. Andrea turned her back to it and felt around with her hands. It felt like a bullet hole. Probably from when the police were shooting at the truck.

It just barely missed me, she thought. *Holy crap.* She considered her luck for a moment. Then she shook her head and focused on getting free. The rim of the hole was a ring of torn metal jutting out just a bit from the door. To reach it with her bound wrists, she would have to prop herself up, and she squirmed, digging in with her feet and pressing down into the carpet with her forehead until her skin burned. She rubbed the tape back and forth, trying to score the thick material, but every time Tomlin hit a bump in the road she lost her balance and fell.

It was a long, frustrating process, made even worse by her swelling bladder. Every time she made progress, Tomlin would turn, or swerve, or bounce over something, and she would fall back to the carpet, wanting to scream. But she gritted her teeth and tried again, and eventually she could feel the tape start to give.

Yes, she thought, grinning through her gag. The first layer of duct tape came loose, and as she struggled with it, she was able to work her wrist free. She reached up to remove the gag from her mouth, and that's when she felt the truck start to slow. A moment later, they'd stopped. The engine shut off. Andrea listened to Tomlin wheezing for breath in the front seat. *Crap,* she thought. Then she couldn't hear Tomlin anymore. *Maybe he died,* she thought. *Just like that.*

Andrea sat up and looked around the vehicle. They were in a parking garage somewhere. She glanced at the front of the truck and saw the back of Tomlin's head. He was holding a phone to his ear— her cell phone. He wasn't saying anything.

Then he did speak. It was almost a whisper. It sounded painful and scary. "I guess your life isn't so perfect after all." He said nothing else, and Andrea wondered who he had called, whose life was supposed to be perfect. *Compared to yours*, she thought, *I guess just about any life looks good about now.*

Tomlin coughed like he was dying, and Andrea watched him, bent almost to the steering wheel, his whole body shaking. Then he cleared his throat and sat straighter again. "We're going shopping, Agent Stevens—"

Dad. Andrea stiffened. *Come and get me. Hurry.*

Tomlin's voice was a nursery-rhyme nightmare. "Hurry up and come find us," he said, "before we get bored."

Dad. Shopping. What the hell is he talking about?

Then Tomlin put down the phone. She heard him open the door. *Crap*, she thought, ducking back into the cargo compartment. *Crap, crap, shit.* He was coming around back for her. Andrea fumbled with the duct tape, and managed to re-gag herself. Then she wrapped the tape around her wrists as best she could, hoping Tomlin wouldn't look too close. She wanted to sit up and grab one of Tomlin's guns from the backseat, but there wasn't enough time; he was at the rear of the truck now, opening the back gate, peering in at her like a zombie hungry for brains.

Andrea tried to look innocent as Tomlin stared at her, catching his breath. The garage was crowded behind him, cars everywhere. No bystanders nearby, though. Nobody to help her.

Tomlin was carrying that big army gun, not even bothering to hide it. He looked like he had another couple of guns stuffed in his pants, too, and for the first time, Andrea stopped worrying about herself, and started to wonder just what Heather's dad had planned. He smiled down at her. "How about a little shopping spree, princess?"

Andrea squirmed. Pretended to protest through the gag. Tomlin reached in and grabbed her. "Let's go," he said, dragging her to her feet. "Find you something nice to wear for your daddy."

All of a sudden, Andrea knew where she was. She'd been here at Christmas, with her mom, trying to pick out something nice and inexpensive for her dad. They'd come in the morning, dodged the crowds for hours, and come out after dark, empty-handed. She'd bought him a book about Michael Jordan instead.

Tomlin wrenched her forward, shoving her through the long rows of parked cars. In the distance, Andrea could see the mall entrance. The Mall of America. She stole another glance at Tomlin's big rifle, and felt sick as she wondered just what he was going to do.

128

RIDING IN AN FBI helicopter high above the Twin Cities, Windermere stared down at the Timberline Motel, the police cars parked outside looking like Matchbox toys. Beside her, Stevens gripped his armrest tight. *Poor guy,* she thought. *Bad enough that his daughter's been kidnapped. Now they force him up in this deathtrap machine.*

Saint Paul PD had taken a 911 call earlier in the morning. A city cop named Monaghan relayed the story to Stevens and Windermere. "Energy Park. Some sleazebag motel. Desk clerk said he just saw the guy's truck pulling away."

"Headed where?" Windermere said, her adrenaline kick-starting. "We have eyes on him yet?"

"Patrol cars en route. Clerk said he was headed toward Minneapolis."

"He have a girl with him?"

Monaghan shrugged. "Clerk didn't see. But he checked the guy's room out after he made the call. Phoned back and said there was blood everywhere."

Windermere turned to Stevens just in time to watch the big cop go pale. His wife hid her face beside him. According to the forensics team on-site, though, the blood was type A. Stevens's daughter was type O.

So Andrea hadn't bled all over Tomlin's motel room. Probably Tomlin had. Probably, he was shot. If they were lucky, he was dying somewhere. Stevens had said the guy sounded like a corpse on the phone.

Except he was still in transit. Meaning he was still dangerous.

The radio crackled. Saint Paul city cops, still unable to locate the Navigator. They'd sent units speeding to the motel and then spider-webbing out along the main thoroughfares, had searched I-94 and every road headed toward Minneapolis and still come up blank.

Unbelievable. Tomlin must have had a horseshoe lodged some-where intimate. He'd spent the night at the fleabag motel, easy-peasy, and it was only when he'd decided to leave that anyone sat up and took notice. Shopping, he'd told Stevens. What the hell did that mean?

Both Minneapolis and Saint Paul police departments had cruis-ers headed to every major shopping mall in the region, but the snow was still crippling and the traffic intense. And anyway, there were almost more malls and big-box stores than police cruisers in the Twin Cities. If Tomlin had chosen some out-of-the-way Target, no-body would find him in time.

The pilot looked back at Windermere. "You want me to bring her down?"

Windermere looked out at the motel again. "Not much point," she said, staring out the window. In the distance, she could see the Bank of America in Midway, where Tomlin had started his little spree. Then the First Minnesota branch in Prospect Park, and Darcy Passat's house a few blocks away. *How long ago that was,* Winder-mere thought. Her visit to the bank teller's home felt like years in the past, given all that had transpired since.

And now Tomlin was gone again. Had faded into the backdrop of the city like a cloud of smoke. Windermere stared out over the bleak, snowbound landscape, and prayed she could find him in time.

129

TOMLIN SHOVED Andrea Stevens down the row of parked cars, struggling to keep his breath. Damn it, he hurt.

Forget the pain. He shouldered the rifle and pushed the girl forward. *You'll be dead soon, anyway. Just make it until Stevens arrives.*

The mall was crowded despite last night's blizzard, the parking lot packed full of snow-covered SUVs and salt-encrusted minivans. Tomlin looked around in disgust. The last time he'd been to the Mall of America had been more than a year ago, before the layoff. Heather had dragged him to the Hollister store, and Becca to Williams-Sonoma, where he'd waited for hours while they spent hundreds of his dollars on overpriced crap. He himself had paid six hundred dollars for a pair of shoes that day, and the memory made him want to swallow the barrel of his gun.

Andrea glanced back at him, and he prodded her with the assault rifle. "You like malls, don't you?" he said. "Every girl likes a mall."

The girl said something through her gag. It sounded like a plea. Tomlin smiled at her and nudged her again with the gun. "Keep going."

They walked through another row of parked cars, getting close to the Nordstrom that anchored this end of the mall. Tomlin heard voices to his right, looked and saw a middle-aged couple approaching. They were so lost in conversation that they didn't notice Tomlin and the girl until they'd almost collided. Then they looked up.

"Sorry." The man smiled at Tomlin, sheepish. The woman saw the gun and gasped. The man followed her gaze and looked back at Tomlin, still smiling, like he thought the whole thing was a joke.

Tomlin winked at him. "Don't mention it." He swung the rifle around at the man's stomach. Then he pulled the trigger.

ANDREA SCREAMED through her gag as Tomlin shot the man, rapid-fire. The guy collapsed to the pavement, and Tomlin laughed, high-pitched and crazy, before turning the gun toward the woman.

Crap. Andrea kicked Tomlin in the shin and tore her wrists from the duct tape. Tomlin spun at her and she shoved him backward as hard as she could. Then she turned and ran, zagging between the parked cars, her head down, expecting the maniac to cut her down with that big army gun.

But he didn't shoot at her. She tore at her gag and threw it aside as she ran for the mall. Behind her, Tomlin finally woke up and fired, a harsh staccato burst, deafening in the confined concrete lot. Andrea threw herself to the ground, panting for breath. Somewhere, a car horn sounded. She could hear the woman sobbing behind her and Tomlin's footsteps on the pavement. *Crap,* she thought. *Crap, crap, crap.*

She was about fifteen yards from the sky bridge to Nordstrom. People were already poking their heads out the doors, curious. "Get back," she screamed at them. "This guy has a gun."

Nobody paid attention. Tomlin came closer, laughing again. *He's freaking crazy,* Andrea thought. *He's totally lost it.* She picked herself up and ran for the door, waiting for Tomlin to fire again. He was probably aiming straight at her. She pushed the thought from her mind and kept running, her head down. Kept screaming at the dumb mall people to move.

Tomlin fired another burst. This time, the Nordstrom door shattered. People screamed. Ducked to the ground. Andrea reached the edge of the parked cars and dashed across the bridge to the ruined doors. She threw herself inside the store and crawled out of Tomlin's sight.

More people were coming, attracted by the commotion, concerned looks on their faces. "Call nine-one-one," Andrea yelled to them. "There's a guy with a really big gun." Then she ran again, deeper into the department store, dodging between counters and clothing racks as Tomlin's gun roared again behind her.

130

THE RADIO CRACKLED in the FBI chopper. The pilot looked back at Stevens and Windermere. "Something heavy going down at the Mall of America," he said. "Some guy just walked into Nordstrom with a machine gun."

Stevens felt his heart syncopate. "Tomlin."

Windermere nodded. "Definitely." She looked at the pilot. "Take us there."

The pilot swung the helicopter toward the mall, and Stevens gripped the armrest tighter, willing his stomach to stay settled as the chopper picked up speed. He spoke to the pilot through his headset. "My daughter," he said. "Any information?"

The pilot shook his head. "Nothing."

"Shit." Stevens pictured his daughter. Then he pictured Tomlin, the madman. *Shooting up the Mall of America. What the hell for?*

Windermere caught his expression, reached over and touched his hand. "This is it," she said. "This is where we get him."

Stevens gripped her hand and said nothing. Stared out the window as the Twin Cities passed by below, the vast Mall of America compound looming in the distance. *Hurry,* he wanted to scream. *Hurry. My daughter's down there.*

The chopper sped toward the mall. Stevens shifted in his seat, nearly overwhelmed by the adrenaline rushing through him, desperate to get down to his daughter.

131

TOMLIN'S HEART POUNDED as he chased Andrea Stevens into the department store. She was running ahead, gaining ground, and Tomlin struggled to follow.

Don't fucking lose her, he thought. *Not now.*

It was all happening. The wound in his stomach throbbed, but Tomlin could barely feel it. He could hear people shouting, alarms sounding, the rush as a stampede of shoppers made for the exits, but everything seemed muted and distant, like the sound track to a vivid dream.

A salesclerk poked her head up from behind a cash register. She locked her wide eyes on Tomlin's for a split second, and then he swung the rifle around and let off a burst. The woman dropped out of sight, screaming, and Tomlin fumbled to reload before he finished her off. He was down to his last clip in the AR-15. And then whatever Schultz had in his little machine gun. The pistol he would save for the girl.

Something moved on Tomlin's right and he spun around and saw a security guard making a break for him, trying to play the hero. Tomlin pulled Schultz's gun from his waistband and squeezed off five or six shots before the gun recoiled, wild, and sent a burst to the ceiling as the guard collapsed to the floor.

Tomlin relaxed his finger on the trigger and walked to the guard. The guard stared up at Tomlin like a fox in a trap. "Are you scared?" Tomlin asked him. The guard didn't answer. Tomlin kicked him in the gut, hard, and the guy screamed out something in Spanish.

"Are you scared?"

The guard spat blood. Then he nodded. Tomlin smiled. "Good."

"Please," the guard said. Tomlin shot him again. Then he straightened and surveyed the store. Racks of clothing jostled and shook like trees in the wind all around him, people hiding behind them, whispering, gathering courage. More heroes. Tomlin let off another burst with the machine gun and smiled as the whispers died away. He finished loading the assault rifle and set off through the aisles after Andrea Stevens.

ANDREA RAN THROUGH the department store. She heard people screaming, heard glass shattering around her, the sirens still so far away. *Keep going*, she thought, her chest burning. *Get the hell away from this psycho.*

Ahead of her, people were stampeding for the door, ducking and slipping on the tile floor, hurrying for the relative safety of the crowded mall corridors. They left the store empty behind them; a few stragglers cowered behind counters and cash registers, but mostly the place had cleared out. *You can't lead him out there*, Andrea thought. *He'll mow those people down with that gun.*

The police would be coming soon. If she could hide away from Tomlin for a little while longer, stay alive until they arrived, they would catch him and kill him and everything would be over. She crouched down behind a cosmetics counter. Peered out into the aisle and heard more shooting. More screaming. She couldn't see Tomlin. *He's coming*, she thought. *You need to move.*

Andrea counted to five in her head. Then she ran. Bolted across the aisle to the next counter over. Kept her head down. Kept running. She ran toward the far end of the store. Rounded a corner and nearly tripped over a man lying flat in the aisle. "Are you hurt?" she asked him.

The man shook his head, no. Didn't move. "Run," she told him. "Get out of here. He's coming this way."

The guy still didn't move. Andrea felt her panic rising. *"Run,"* she said. "Do you want to die?"

The guy lay with his head on the floor. Andrea hesitated for a moment and then took off again. She reached the end of the store, the far wall. The fitting rooms and a door to the stockroom. She leaned against the wall, her head down, catching her breath. Listened for Tomlin and still didn't hear him.

Where is he? She surveyed the store, the shattered cosmetics counters, their bright fluorescent lights flickering and dying, the exit to the parking lot with its ruined doors, the empty escalators and the clothing displays shot to tatters. She could see a couple of survivors hiding amid the carnage, but she couldn't see Tomlin anywhere.

He's out there. The thought paralyzed her. *He's out there somewhere, and he's coming for you.*

132

THE PILOT LANDED the helicopter on the roof of the parking garage, and a harried-looking plainclothesman met Stevens and Windermere as they stepped out to the pavement. "Gibbs," he said. "Narcotics, Minneapolis PD."

Stevens frowned. "Narcotics."

"My day off." Gibbs shrugged. "Kids wanted the new *Call of Duty*. Guess they got the real deal instead. You guys running this show?"

Windermere nodded. "FBI," she said. "And BCA."

"My daughter's in there," said Stevens. "With the gunman."

Gibbs looked at him again. "Holy shit," he said. "You're the guy." He studied Stevens, then shook his head and started toward a stairwell. "Come on," he said, looking back. "I'll tell you where we're at."

"GUY CAME IN from the parking garage," Gibbs told them as they descended. "Shot someone on his way inside, a guy up from Milwaukee with his wife. Then he walked into the Nordstrom and laid waste to the place.

"We don't have a casualty count." Gibbs glanced at Stevens. "But that place was packed this morning. Some kind of sale. He's still in there now."

"You have containment?" Stevens asked him.

Gibbs nodded. "Couple guys are working through to the mall-side entrance."

"Our man in there has an assault rifle and a bad disposition," said Windermere. "You're going to need more than a couple of guys."

Gibbs shook his head. "Don't have the manpower yet. Guards inside the mall don't have sidearms, and it's still chaos on the law-enforcement side. We're still talking first responders, patrol cars. Uniforms with their pop guns, no better."

"No FBI support for another twenty minutes," said Windermere. "Traffic's still shitty from the snow."

Stevens frowned. "He'll shoot up the whole mall before we get our act together."

Gibbs led them out of the stairwell and onto another parking garage level. In the distance, Stevens could see the bridge to the department store, unnaturally bright in the shadows of the garage. Another patrol car sat askew by the entrance, and Stevens could hear more sirens whooping up from the level below.

He looked across the bridge and saw a security guard lying on the polished white floor inside, unmoving. *Andrea's in there.* He felt another chill shudder through him.

Gibbs was pointing out the first casualty, a middle-aged man lying in a puddle of blood on the pavement, a woman crouched over him, sobbing. The narcotics officer looked up as Stevens started toward the mall entrance. "Where are you going?" Stevens ignored him. Kept walking.

The store looked deserted as he crossed the pavement toward it. Soft-rock instrumental music drifted out from the shattered doors, and the security guard hadn't moved from the white floor inside. Windermere caught up beside him. She put her hand on his shoulder. "Hold up, Kirk."

Stevens stopped. Cast her a wry smile. "Guess I get to play cowboy after all."

"You don't have to go in there," she said. "We'll have SWAT and HRT here any minute. Let them handle this."

"Bullshit." Stevens shook out of her grip. "There's no time, Carla."

Windermere studied his face. Then she nodded. "You're right," she said, reaching for her sidearm. "Let's go get him."

133

TOMLIN CIRCLED the store, crouching behind the rows of clothing as he stalked the girl. He could hear police sirens, could see the first blue-and-red cherries flashing outside in the parking garage. Soon the cops would come inside, and everything would be over.

Tomlin moved quicker now, as quick as he could, his ammunition low and his time running out. He would find the girl before the police came in, grab her, and hold her until Daddy arrived. Then he'd make Stevens watch as he killed her, and when she was dead, the police could do what they wished. And they would. They would kill him, he knew.

Tomlin welcomed death now. He pictured Becca at home with Heather and Madeleine, probably watching this whole disaster on the news. He pictured Carver and Lawson in their cushy downtown offices, pictured Tricia in his Jaguar, spending his money. He looked out at the parking garage and the flashing police lights, and he realized there was nothing now, nothing in the world he wanted to stay alive for beyond killing that girl.

Tomlin angled his way toward the shot-up cosmetics counters

where he'd seen the little bitch hiding. She was gone. He swung the rifle around, searching. Nobody moved, anywhere. *Shit.*

He looked past the cosmetics counters at the mall doors beyond. Saw a couple of city cops crouched at the exits, and let off a burst in their direction. If she was smart, she'd have run out into the mall and hidden in one of the myriad stores beyond. No way he could shoot his way out of the department store, not before the police took him down. If she'd gone out the doors, she was gone.

"Shit." Tomlin leaned back against a stylized poster of Angelina Jolie and tried to catch his breath. The store was quiet. Everyone who wasn't dead or dying had escaped by now.

Except, there, something moved to his right. Amid the clothing racks in women's wear. *Bingo.*

Tomlin picked up his rifle and started across the store, a guerrilla warrior stalking his enemy. He steadied his breathing. Felt his heart pounding in his chest. Turned a corner and found a man on the floor.

He lay between the aisles, clutching a rack of dresses and hyperventilating into his shirtsleeves. He was about middle age, slightly overweight. Tomlin prodded him with his toe, and the man gasped and turned over. Looked up at Tomlin with undisguised fear. "Where did she go?" Tomlin asked him.

The man stared at him, shaking. Tomlin looked around. Saw nothing. Heard nothing but the man's whispered pleas. He took out Schultz's machine pistol and shot the man in the kneecap, and the man screamed, loud, and kept screaming. Tomlin kicked him. "The girl. Which way?"

The man just kept screaming. Tomlin shot him again. He screamed louder. This was fucking tiresome. Tomlin nudged the guy onto his back and shot him, three times, in the chest. The man gasped and burbled and went silent. Tomlin kicked him again. "Waste of time."

Something moved by the door to the parking garage. Tomlin

looked up in time to see a man running into the store, his head down, and then a black woman behind him. *Windermere. And Kirk Stevens. Right on time.* He fired the machine gun over the clothing displays. Emptied the clip at them and smiled as the cops hit the ground.

Should keep them occupied for a minute. He turned back to the dead man on the floor beside him. Looked up and saw a sign on the wall about fifteen feet away. *Fitting Rooms.* Tomlin smiled wider. He drew his pistol from his waistband and started for the door.

134

ANDREA HEARD TOMLIN shoot the scared man on the floor, and she knew he had followed her. *Great,* she thought. *So what now?*

The entry to the fitting rooms lay on her right, the door to the stockroom on her left. She could hear Tomlin breathing behind her, a few aisles over, gasping for breath and, it sounded like, laughing, the fucking psycho.

He was getting closer. She had to move. She looked around quickly and crossed the aisle to the wall. Pushed open the swinging door to the stockroom, ducked inside. A maze of shelves and hanging gowns, shoes and boxes and mannequins wrapped in plastic. Andrea walked deeper into the room, looking for a place to hide or, barring that, a weapon.

She heard the door swing closed, loud, behind her, and quickly she realized her mistake. Tomlin would see the door swinging. He would follow her in. Andrea hurried through the stacks of boxes and the racks of hanging clothing. At the end of the aisle was a counter, a workbench with cabinets beneath it. It would have to do. She ran for it.

Behind her, the door swung open again, and Tomlin laughed and called out her name. Andrea reached the cabinet and thrust open the drawers. Stared inside. Full of junk. Cleaning solution and paper towels and clothes hangers and about a million other useless things taking up all the space.

She looked around. *Damn it.* She could empty the cabinet, but then he'd see the debris and know where she'd hidden. She looked back at the door. Heard Tomlin coming closer and turned to the cabinet again.

She had an idea. She emptied the cabinet as fast as she could. Scattered clothes hangers all over the bare concrete floor, the cleaning supplies, too. Then she slipped between the rows of creepy, naked mannequins, squeezed in between them, and waited.

There was a bottle of bleach lying a few feet away. Andrea looked around for Tomlin. Couldn't see him. She knelt down and reached for the bleach, came up two inches short.

"*Crap.*" Andrea leaned into the aisle, stretching as far as she could, gripping one mannequin's leg for support. Fingers outstretched, her face contorted into a grimace. She almost had the damn thing. Then Tomlin grabbed her arm.

He bent down and looked at her, smiling his nightmare smile. Wrenched her up and out of the mannequins, sending them toppling down around her. They made a noise like a bowling alley as they fell to the floor.

"Found you." Tomlin's breath was hot and rotten. He smiled at her like the perverts on the street. Pulled her closer.

Andrea kicked him, hard. Struggled out of his grip and scrambled backward on the concrete floor, through the pile of mannequin parts, hands searching for the bleach bottle. She found the bottle and retreated quickly, fumbling with the cap as Tomlin came after her. The cap slipped and failed to catch, and Tomlin was nearly on her again. *Stupid child-safety locks,* she thought. *Open, god damn it.*

She got the cap open just as Tomlin closed on her arm. Swung the bottle toward his face with her free hand. The bleach spilled out at him, leapt out, splashed into his eyes, and Tomlin made a noise like an animal and loosened his grip again. Andrea dropped the bottle and ran.

135

TOMLIN CLAWED AT his face. His eyes burned. Bleach. Had to be. He heard the door nearby swing open and swung around at it, forcing his eyes open through the incredible pain. Saw only blurred colors, but it was enough to see Andrea Stevens escaping.

He held the rifle like a talisman and staggered toward the door. Tripped over a mannequin and fell hard to the floor. Swore and picked himself up, fumbling for the rifle, and kept going. Forced his eyes open and felt around for the doorframe, found it and pushed through and staggered out into blinding light. Instantly, his eyes were on fire. He staggered backward, breathing hard, swearing, squinting at the wash of bright colors and firing at random. Then he saw her.

She was nothing but movement and contrast, a darker color against a light backdrop moving quickly away. Tomlin steadied the rifle and fired at her. She kept moving. He pulled the trigger again and the rifle clicked empty. *Motherfuck.*

Tomlin followed Andrea Stevens down the aisle. Dropped the rifle and pulled the pistol from his waistband. Steadied it in her direction and aimed at her again.

WINDERMERE HAD HIT the floor when Tomlin shot across the store at them. Stevens ducked down beside her. "You okay?"

"Never better," she told him. "Keep going."

They stayed low behind the clothing displays and covered ground quickly. Reached the last spot where they'd seen Tomlin, and Tomlin wasn't there. Windermere raised her head above the displays and surveyed the store. Saw nothing and heard nothing. Tomlin had disappeared.

Then a tremendous crash, close. Stevens pointed to the end of the store, the wall a few aisles away. The fitting rooms and a swinging stockroom door. "In there."

They hurried toward it. More crashing. The door swung open, and Windermere leveled her gun, finger tensed on the trigger. Relaxed as Andrea Stevens came out at full speed. Stevens called out her name, and his daughter zagged for him.

The door swung open again, and Carter Tomlin staggered out, a monster. His clothes were matted in blood, and he clawed at his face with his left hand. With his right hand, he clutched an assault rifle.

Windermere stood and took aim. Tomlin screamed something, anguished, and fired a burst with the rifle. Windermere swore and ducked down behind a bathing suit display. Heard Tomlin shoot again as he moved toward her. Crouched behind the display counter and waited for him to come closer.

STEVENS CALLED OUT to his daughter. His daughter ran for him. Her eyes were wide and terrified, her legs working double time. Stevens looked past her and saw Tomlin in the aisle, unsteady, aiming a pistol at Andrea through tortured eyes.

Tomlin grinned like a Frankenstein monster. "Princess."

Stevens launched himself at his daughter. Tackled her to the ground as the bullets flew past. Heard the air whoosh from Andrea's lungs as she landed on the tile floor, the bullets missing by inches as she scrambled for cover.

Tomlin lumbered closer. Laughing now. Andrea struggled to her feet, broke Stevens's grip, and kept running. Stevens fought to hold her, couldn't do it. He flipped onto his back. Fumbled for his side-arm, couldn't draw it in time. Then the madman was on him.

Tomlin smiled something gruesome, his eyes barely slits, his clothing rank and bloody. He could barely hold the gun steady as he aimed at the girl. Stevens scrambled backward. Tried to keep his body between Andrea and Tomlin's gun. "Don't do it, Carter," Stevens said. "Please."

Tomlin grinned at him. "Kirk," he said. "Glad you could make it." Then he turned his ruined eyes toward Andrea again, his finger tensed on the trigger.

WINDERMERE HEARD TOMLIN pass her. Stood and watched him stagger after Stevens. Watched Andrea break free from her father and run off down the aisle. Tomlin saw this, somehow, through his squint-closed eyes. She watched him take aim at the girl.

Windermere took her own aim, square at Tomlin's back. As Tomlin steadied his trigger finger, she tensed hers. Beat him to the pull by about a half second.

POW.

Tomlin went down. Andrea kept running.

136

TOMLIN PITCHED FORWARD onto the tile. Tried to put out his hands to catch his fall; nothing worked. The ground loomed, a white blur, and then he was down. He lay on the floor and watched Andrea Stevens disappear into the distance.

Windermere walked up beside him. He could feel her kick the pistol away. He forced himself to roll over. Fixed her blur with his slit eyes. "Kill me." He sneered at her. "Kill me, you bitch."

WINDERMERE STARED DOWN at Tomlin. Watched him over the barrel of her pistol. Tomlin smiled skyward, an ugly, evil smile. "Kill me," he said again.

She could pull the trigger right now. Kill him real easy. Nobody would care. "Do it," Tomlin said. "Pull the trigger."

She wanted to do it. Knew it would feel good. She tensed her finger on the trigger. The metal was warm. Tomlin's voice was ragged, desperate. "Do it," he said. "Kill me, you bitch."

He wants it, too, she realized. *He wants to be dead.* She let her finger off the trigger. Tomlin's smile disappeared. He spat. "Fucking bitch."

She shook her head. "I'm not killing you, Tomlin."

Tomlin screamed, incoherent. Writhed on the tile floor, cursing, clawing at his eyes, his face a mask of frustration and hate. *Like a baby without his bottle*, Windermere thought. *Behind that charming façade, an impotent little man.*

She watched Tomlin's tantrum. Felt the pistol in her hand and ached to pull the trigger. *Don't do it*, she thought. *Don't let him off easy. Make him suffer.* She put the gun away. Stood over Tomlin and waited for backup to arrive.

STEVENS FOUND ANDREA hiding in one of the fitting rooms, amid a pile of clothes hangers and discarded designer jeans. She was sitting on the floor, hugging her knees, when he pushed the door open. "Is it over?" she said.

Stevens felt a wave of relief so powerful it forced him backward. "It's over."

Andrea studied his face for a long moment. Then she pulled herself to her feet. "Are you mad?"

Stevens couldn't help himself anymore. He rushed to her and brought her into his arms, wrapped her in a bear hug. "*Daddy*," she said, but she let him hold her.

He lifted her, buried his face in her hair. "I'm not mad," he told her. "As long as you're okay."

"I'm fine, Daddy." She pulled back, her eyes wide. "Except I really, *really* have to pee."

137

TWO WEEKS LATER, with Carter Tomlin recovering from his wounds and preparing to face his litany of charges, Carla Windermere drove her daddy's Chevelle across the Twin Cities toward a greasy diner in downtown Saint Paul.

It was a beautiful day, the first hint of spring after a long, dreary winter. The sky was bright blue and sunny, the snow melting on the ground, and Windermere kept the big muscle car comfortably above the speed limit as she drove down the Interstate toward the city.

She passed Midway, the exit that led to the Bank of America where Tomlin had first tasted crime. Then she passed Summit Hill, and she lifted her foot from the gas pedal, thinking about the million-dollar dream home and the beautiful family, the fantasy life that Tomlin had abandoned.

It was hard not to dwell on the first visit she'd paid to that Summit Avenue home. She'd known he was her man within minutes, had left his house sure that she'd caught him. Instead, she'd flubbed the kick. She'd let herself be distracted, and people had died.

Tomlin's Mall of America spree was a rampage. He'd killed the tourist from Milwaukee in the parking garage and a security guard inside the department store. There was another casualty, too, a man they'd found dead in women's wear, and three or four other victims with serious gunshot wounds. A disaster.

Plus the dead kid from the poker game, and the armored car guards. Nick Singer and Tony Schultz. Dragan Medic, and who knew who else? All of them dead. All of them killed by Tomlin. *You could have stopped him,* Windermere thought. *You could have saved them all.*

STEVENS WAS ALREADY at a table when she walked into the diner. She ordered a coffee and walked to his table, and he smiled at her as she sat. "Fashionably late."

Windermere looked around. The place was an old railroad dining car, a long counter and a couple of cramped booths. It smelled of grease and old coffee. "Just couldn't believe this was the place," she said. "Feels like I'm risking my life."

Stevens laughed. "This place is a landmark," he told her. "Figured you could use a real taste of Saint Paul."

He still likes me, Windermere thought, studying his face, his kind eyes. *Lord knows why.* She shook her head and took a sip of her coffee. "How's your daughter?"

"Andrea? She's fine." He laughed. "She keeps talking about she wants to be a cop."

Windermere looked at him. "Bull."

"An FBI agent, she said. Like you." He winked at her. "I told her one Windermere was more than enough. Said she could be a lawyer, like her mom."

"Law degrees make FBI agents, Stevens," Windermere told him. "Careful what you wish for."

"Duly noted. Guess she'll have to be an astronaut instead."

Windermere cocked her head. "We could use her in Minneapolis. After Carter Tomlin, I'm short a partner."

Stevens frowned. "Doughty?"

"Filed a complaint. Put in for reassignment. As of right now, I'm flying solo."

"Probably for the best, right?" He shrugged. "Thought you hated your partners."

She couldn't help but say it. "All but one."

Stevens sipped his coffee and didn't say anything. Windermere looked around the restaurant, cursing herself out. *Stupid*, she thought. *Don't push him again.*

Stevens stayed quiet for a while. "I guess you're on a new case now," he said finally.

Windermere exhaled. She met Stevens's eyes. "Still tying up ends," she said. "They found Tomlin's Jaguar at Chicago O'Hare. Long-term parking. Tricia Henderson's fingerprints everywhere."

"She bolted."

"With the money, apparently. Probably living easy on some beach somewhere."

"Shit," Stevens said.

She nodded. "Yeah."

They sipped their coffees in silence some more. Windermere stared down at the pockmarked table and suddenly felt very tired. "I could have stopped him," she said, looking up. "Tomlin. Before he started killing."

Stevens shrugged. "Maybe."

"Not maybe, Stevens." She met his eyes. "I knew he was guilty. He knew I knew. I let Doughty pitch that Jackson nonsense, and Tomlin went crazy. He killed ten goddamn people, and I could have stopped him."

Stevens touched her hand. "Nothing you can do now," he said. "It's over."

THEY FINISHED THEIR coffees, and Stevens walked Windermere back to her car. "We should do this again," Stevens said.

She smiled at him sadly. "We said that last time, Stevens."

"For real, this time. We're friends now."

They reached the Chevelle and stood on the sidewalk beside it. Windermere looked at Stevens. "You have your family," she said. "And your BCA job. And I was such a bitch, anyway."

"You saved my daughter's life, Carla. I won't question your methods."

"I'm still sorry, Stevens." She shook her head. "I just thought it would be fun to be partners again."

Stevens frowned and looked away. Was silent a beat. "I'm not FBI material, Carla," he said finally. "I'm a pretty good state policeman with an excellent goddamn partner. We did good work with Pender and even better with Tomlin, but I'm just not cut out for this hero stuff all the time."

Windermere didn't answer. *Yes, you are*, she wanted to say. *Ask Pender and Tomlin just how good you are. You belong in the Bureau and you know it.*

"I'm happy, Carla. I am."

That's bull, she thought. *You'd be happier working with me.* Then she stopped herself. Forced a smile and punched Stevens lightly on the arm. "Probably too much flying for you, anyway, the cases I work."

He grinned back. "Not enough airsickness bags in the world."

She wanted to smack him and kiss him and scream all at once. Instead, she made herself turn away. "Keep in touch, you big dummy," she said. Then she climbed into the Chevelle and settled behind the wheel. Turned the key in the ignition, and the engine howled to life.

Stevens stood on the sidewalk and watched her. Before she could speed off, he walked over and tapped on her window. Windermere rolled it down. Stevens looked in at her, cocked his head. "You have plans for dinner?"

"I don't know," she said. "Why?"

"We're going to try and have a barbecue," he said. "You could come over. Try some famous Kirk Stevens charbroil. Emphasis on the charred."

She hesitated a moment. Then she smiled at him. "I have plans," she said, lying. "Anyway, I doubt Nancy wants to see any more of the woman who's always putting her man's life in danger."

"Andrea's back safe. You're more than welcome."

Windermere shook her head. Wanted to tell him no thanks and step on the gas, peel off back to Minneapolis and her empty apartment, and get drunk, alone. "Andrea would love to see you," said Stevens. "Like I said, you're her hero."

Just one twitch of her right foot and she'd be halfway down the block. Gone. Free to drive off and kill a six-pack and wallow over Tomlin and Stevens and whatever else she could think of. But she didn't really want to go home, she realized. She didn't want to let Stevens go, not this time. Not again. "What do you think?" Stevens asked her. "You feel like a burger or what?"

Windermere looked at Stevens. Felt her heart start to race, and tried to play nonchalant. "Yeah, okay, Stevens," she said. "Maybe I'll stick around for a while."

ACKNOWLEDGMENTS

I remain ever grateful to Stacia Decker, my agent, and Neil Nyren, my editor, for all of their wisdom and encouragement. I'm exceedingly fortunate to have landed with such a Hall of Fame team, and this book owes much to their patience and dedication.

Thanks also to the fine people at Putnam whose hard work would otherwise go unheralded, including (but certainly not limited to) Alexis Welby, Katie Grinch, Lydia Hirt, Margot Stamas, Kate Stark, Chris Nelson, Sara Minnich, Marilyn Ducksworth, and Ivan Held.

Thanks to my home team at Penguin Canada, in particular Steve Myers and Beth Lockley. And a million thanks to the copy editors and proofreaders who've saved me from embarrassments both minor and major altogether too often.

Steve Berry, C. J. Box, Alafair Burke, Lee Child, Jonathan Kellerman, John Lescroart, Thomas Perry, and John Sandford lent their names and kind words to my cause. I'm still pinching myself. Thanks to you all.

Thanks to Ilsa Brink, who built me a stunning website and who works tirelessly to maintain it.

Thanks to Kristi Belcamino, Alex Kent, Mickie Turk, and Officer Lynn Cronquist and Sergeant Michael Young of the Minneapolis

Police Department for dedicating their time and expertise to showing me around the Twin Cities, and for giving me plenty of excuses to come back to Minnesota.

Thanks to the booksellers whose enthusiasm for *The Professionals* inspired me as I wrote this second installment in the Stevens and Windermere saga, and to the readers who tore through *The Professionals* and came back demanding more.

Thanks to my friends, old and new, whose extraordinary love and support continues to overwhelm me. Truly the best part of publishing is sharing my success with you all.

Thanks, especially and always, to my family.